# IN THE DARK

## A JENNY AARON THRILLER

ANDREAS PFLÜGER

TRANSLATED BY
SHAUN WHITESIDE

DOVER PUBLICATIONS, INC.
MINEOLA, NEW YORK

*For Anne. Always*

*Bibliographical Note*

This Dover edition, first published in 2019, is an unabridged republication of the English translation published in 2017 by Head of Zeus Ltd., London, which was originally published in German in 2016 by Suhrkamp Verlag, Berlin, under the title *Endgültig*. The text has been modified for an American audience.

*Library of Congress Cataloging-in-Publication Data*

Names: Pflüger, Andreas, 1957– author. | Whiteside, Shaun, translator.
Title: In the dark : a Jenny Aaron thriller / Andreas Pflüger ; translated by Shaun Whiteside.
Other titles: Endgültig. English
Description: Mineola, New York : Dover Publications, Inc., 2019. | "This Dover edition, first published in 2019, is an unabridged republication of the English translation published in 2017 by Head of Zeus Ltd., London, which was originally published in German in 2016 by Suhrkamp Verlag, Berlin, under the title Endgültig. The text has been modified for an American audience."
Identifiers: LCCN 2018048322 | ISBN 9780486827612 | ISBN 0486827615
Subjects: LCSH: Blind women—Fiction. | Serial murder investigation—Fiction. | Women detectives—Fiction.
Classification: LCC PT2716.F64 E5313 2019 | DDC 833/.92—dc23
LC record available at https://lccn.loc.gov/2018048322

Manufactured in the United States by LSC Communications
82761501    2019
www.doverpublications.com

If there is still time in the end
I don't want to ask myself
why I must die
I want to know
why I have lived

# A Note on
# German Police and Politics

THE *BUNDESKRIMINALAMT* (BKA), is the Federal Criminal Investigation Office. It is based in Wiesbaden in the west of Germany, with a second large base in Berlin. The agency has around 3,000 agents and operates nationwide, focusing on cases of international organized crime and terrorism.

The *Landeskriminalamt* (LKA), is the State Criminal Police Office. Each state in Germany has its own police force, governed by slightly different rules and duties. The BKA provides assistance to the LKA in forensic matters, research and criminal investigations.

The Conference of State Ministers and Senators of the Interior—*Ständige Konferenz der Innenminister und senatoren der Länder*, also known as the *Innenministerkonferenz*—is a regular conference on law enforcement issues attended by the interior ministers of the various German states. In some states, including Berlin, these ministers are called senators, hence the rather unwieldy name.

# THE SAGRADA FAMILIA

NOTHING CALMS her down as much as cleaning her gun. Anyone else would have to check the cartridge chamber to be sure that it's empty. Not her. She knows the exact weight of the magazine that's sliding into her hand, right to the last gram. She knows that there is no ammunition in the barrel of the Browning Hi Power, just as she knows that her eyes are green. And sometimes black.

In four seconds she has depressed the magazine release, moved the slide and lifted the barrel and recoil spring assembly free of the frame. High-class Belgian workmanship.

How often she has been grateful for that.

She first killed at twenty-two, when a drug dealer wanted to take her life and forgot that it takes two to tango.

A year later, when the ransom money was being handed over, she was prepared for the moment when the bag of newspaper cuttings was opened, but not for the 2-inch revolver that the little boy's kidnapper had in a leg holster. For the next few months she had to sleep with the lights on.

He wasn't the last.

There were others, too, and she will remember all of them forever.

The hitman sent by Ilya Ivanovich Nikulin with a special hello found her in Moscow. He played cat and mouse with her in the underground car park of the Hotel Aralsk until she was the cat and he the mouse and she could hear him squeaking. She wasn't bothered about the bullet he took to the belly. But even today she still finds herself being stared at by the young hotel clerk who took a ricochet from her Browning right in the middle of the heart, she sees the eyes of the woman whose hand she held until it was all over.

She carefully brushes the barrel and the breech with gun oil over the basin of the luxurious bathroom, and reflects that there was one occasion when she didn't clean her pistol.

Naples. The alleyway near the Basilica of Santa Chiara, where the *capo* of the Mazzarella clan was waiting, the one with whom they had negotiated the fake purchase of ten million counterfeit Euros. When he had spat the word "*puttana*," revealing that she'd been unmasked, the quickness of her reactions had been of no use.

She pulled the trigger, but the shot didn't go off.

The previous day, she and Niko had had to fly back to Berlin for a few hours. The Secretary of State for the Interior had demanded to be informed in person about how things were going; a human tortoise who would never understand the difference between an action memo and a .357 Magnum. After that she had let off some steam in the shooting simulator, three hundred and fifty cartridges, had hurried to get to the airport, back to Naples, to the meeting with the *capo* where a combination of condensation, combustion gases and powder residues jammed the Browning.

That will always be a lesson for her.

The barrel of his Luger rested on the bridge of her nose. She was surprised to realize that she wasn't scared. She just thought that the gap in the *capo*'s teeth, which he was wolfishly revealing, would be the last thing she ever saw.

But instead he fell at her feet without a sound.

Niko.

A shot to the head with a Colt from a hundred meters.

You can't learn something like that.

She scrubs all the parts of the gun with a children's toothbrush, taking care not to leave any scratches, and sees with satisfaction that the oil is turning deep black; only then is it right. She pushes the toothbrush into the barrel and cleans it from the inside. She's aware of how much she likes touching the steel, indestructible and at the same time soft and warm.

That was what it was like when her father first took her to the old quarry as a twelve-year-old girl. He taught her how to shoot, telling her everything that a policeman can pass on to his daughter.

She got her first gun on her eighteenth birthday. A Starfire 9 mm pistol, used but well-looked-after, which weighed only four hundred grams and fit her hand perfectly. She loved that pistol, a real little jewel.

She rubs the steel with a Kleenex and sniffs at it.

Enjoys the smell. Nutty. Sweet. Clean.

Four seconds to put the Browning back together.

The loud click with which the breech slips back in is the best beta blocker.

But not today.

Jenny Aaron goes into the bedroom of the suite. Niko Kvist is lying on the bed. He's studying the dossier for the third time. Aaron doesn't need to. Her memory is high-performance software; it only takes her five minutes to store everything:

In February 1912 in Paris Marc Chagall painted *The Dream Dancers*; two lovers, entwined on a dizzyingly high tightrope stretched between the towers of Notre Dame. Chagall liked the painting so much that he kept it. When he returned to Russia just before the outbreak of the First World War he gave it to his muse and later wife, Bella.

In the early 1920s they took it to Berlin, where it hung in their bedroom and delighted Bella. But when Chagall confessed to her that he had had an affair, she sold *The Dream Dancers* to a Jewish gallery-owner to punish her husband.

Four years after seizing power, the Nazis confiscated all the works of Chagall that they could get hold of and mocked them as degenerate in the House of Art in Munich. After the exhibition the works were supposed to have been sold on in Lucerne. But the night watchman at the museum, lonely after the early death of his wife, had fallen in love with *The Dream Dancers* and gazed at them in the silence of his long nights. He was not a brave man. But the idea of not being able to look at the picture anymore was so unbearable to him that he made it disappear before it was transported away and successfully pretended he knew nothing about it. He hid the painting in his attic until the end of the war. After that it hung in his sitting room opposite a heavy wooden sideboard.

When he died at a very old age his children had the painting valued. Of course they were unable to keep *The Dream Dancers*. It went to the rich daughter of the gallery-owner who had bought it from Bella Chagall. She knew that the painting had meant more to her grandfather than any other, and wanted to honor his memory; so she gave it to the Nationalgalerie in Berlin on permanent loan.

There it was stolen. Cut from its frame in broad daylight. Cold-blooded. With surgical precision. Without a trace.

Two years: nothing. Early in November Niko was given a tip-off by an informer: a man called Egger had the Chagall. It took Niko three weeks to make contact in Bruges.

His cover story: investment banker, mad about art.

Egger wanted three million pounds sterling. In Barcelona.

That's why they're here. Two secret intermediaries with a bag full of money.

Aaron's cover story: the expert, there to pass her opinion on the painting.

Niko gets to his feet. He puts his arm around Aaron and tenderly strokes her cheek. He smells good. They have been together for a year. No one in the Department must know, or they would be forbidden to work together. They're good at keeping secrets. But they have so little time to themselves. Three times that year Niko has been on assignments that didn't allow him to go back to Berlin. And Aaron twice. Warsaw, Helsinki. During their fortnight's leave in Marrakech they barely left the little riad on the Djemaa El Fna. They were dream dancers in the blistering heat of the days and the cold of the nights. The wind from the Atlas Mountains blew icily down the alleyways. It was an irrelevance to them, like food and drink.

After Naples, Barcelona is only their second mission together. But in Naples they were still creeping around one another like two cats sharing a bowl of milk. She now knows: there's a difference between sleeping with the man you love when you're on holiday and sleeping with him just before a mission. Why is she so tense? She doesn't get it. Barcelona is routine, she's carried out far more difficult missions. And yet last night she couldn't sleep, and couldn't help shaking, while beside her Niko breathed like a child.

In her solitude she tried to find the number to match the shaking.

She has assigned a number between one and ten to every emotion. One for pleasure; two means gratitude; four is perfect control; five says contempt; six, compassion; seven, not being able to wait for something; eight means pride; nine means almost being happy. Ten is adrenalin.

She tries never to think about three.

It's time.

She puts the Browning in the room-safe along with Niko's Colt. Where they're going they can't take guns.

The lift door closes. Three floors down. Aaron shifts her weight from one side to the other and back again, cranes her neck, pushes her shoulder blades together, moves them in a circle, rotates her arms, spreads her toes in her ballet pumps, limbers up to increase the elasticity of her movements.

Without noticing, she touches the scar on her left collarbone. Not her only one. But the important one.

Niko says: "I know a great restaurant at Parc Güell. How about we leave it for a day and celebrate tomorrow?"

"Another time." She doesn't want to stay here a moment longer than she has to.

In the foyer a boy is sitting beside his mother. He has an ancient face, eyes like stones with sea salt drying on them. He is reading a comic. *Daredevil, Blind Justice.* Aaron feels the boy's eyes on her back. She looks around. His mother has got to her feet and is trying to drag him to the lift, but he doesn't move, stays where he is and stares at Aaron.

*

The colleague from the special unit of the Mossos d'Esquadra who is playing the role of her chauffeur holds open the door of the Daimler. Jordi. The other two, Ruben and Josue, are playing bodyguards and follow in a second limousine.

These boys are her life insurance.

Jordi drives fast. Massive rectangles of reinforced concrete thrown up in the 1970s. Aaron likes all things geometrical.

Barcelona is breathing the last of its light. The sky is a fakir walking on glowing coals of cloud.

A ten plus. The adrenalin crashes like a tide against the ventricles of her heart. She knows four kinds. The adrenalin immediately before contact: what awaits me, a handshake or a bullet? The adrenalin in the danger of death. The adrenalin of injury. The adrenalin when you think about a mistake you made.

You always have to reckon with the possibility of a mistake.

Niko says: "Look."

Aaron knows she will see the Sagrada Familia, on the right, Gaudí's temple of madness, triumph of faith, ruin of Catholicism, monument to the greatest victory and the most brutal failure, breathtaking, glorious and at the same time the disturbing absence of any order, boundless and frightening.

She turns her head and looks out of the window.

But there's nothing there. Nothing at all.

The cathedral has been engulfed in a black hole, an abyss whose mass is so huge that the light pours in, a maw that extends like the universe, sucking in Jordi, Niko and Aaron as if they were asteroids on the edge of a galaxy.

Panicking, Aaron tries to feel for Niko, but her hand is alien, cut off from her body, and refuses to obey.

She closes her eyes and opens them again.

They are at the junction with the Carrer de Mallorca. Street lights flicker on. Taxi drivers laugh by their rank. Lovers meet outside a cinema. A dog tugs on a leash. A child cries.

Aaron whispers: "Give me a number between one and ten."

Niko's face is startled, teasing.

"Please."
"Three."

They are a group of three, already waiting outside the warehouse in the harbor. A black Audi. Aaron sees immediately that it has been customized.

Egger is tall, gaunt; lean, even though he must be about forty-five, Aaron guesses. Budapest shoes. His suit is made to measure. He has a white camellia flower in his buttonhole. The hand he holds out to her is manicured and cool and smooth. He has the ease of a man who reads Dostoyevsky in the original Russian. But his strong neck muscles tense like steel cables, even when he tilts his head only slightly and says in a soft, sonorous voice to Aaron: "I would even have waited two minutes for you."

He's arrogant. Presumably because he rarely meets people whose intelligence is a match for his. Aaron doesn't doubt that he knows the precise value of *The Dream Dancers*. Not just the price he has negotiated. No, its *real* value, the truth and clear-sightedness and depth that allowed Chagall to paint the picture in just one day, the power that Aaron herself felt when she looked at a mere reproduction.

How beautiful the original must be. Suddenly she wonders why Egger doesn't want to keep it, why he wants to sell it on.

He makes no attempt to introduce the woman and the man who are with him, and who must be ten years younger than he is. The woman is attractive and confident. She reveals a remarkable sense of balance when she totters around the Audi on six-inch stilettos. If she was holding a water glass, full to the brim, she wouldn't spill a drop.

The younger man has eyes like black plastic tokens, flat and lifeless. If it weren't for the cigarette-stub dangling from the corner of his mouth it would look as if he had no lips. His nose has been broken, then straightened. There is a birthmark on the back of his right hand.

But the similarity with Egger is unmistakable.
*Brothers. Strange.*

They both wear holsters, Egger can't hide his even with his double-breasted Savile Row suit. Aaron bets that Token-Eyes' Glock 33 is his pride and joy. Egger probably doesn't need such a thing. He isn't the kind of person to show off his firearms. And he has style: a gun with a plastic grip wouldn't suit him. More like a Remington 1911 or a Beretta Target.

The holsters are empty, Aaron can tell at a glance.

*A confidence-building measure.*

Niko asks: "Where's the painting?"

"Where's the money?"

In response to Niko's nod Jordi opens the big bag on the passenger seat of the Daimler. In Berlin they had talked about using fake notes. But they would only go into action once the picture had been handed over, and since they couldn't expect Egger to bring it to their rendezvous, they had opted for clean, used banknotes.

Egger looks at them with an expression bordering on mockery. He lifts one cheekbone by a millimeter: a kind of smile. "Just you, the women and me. Your men stay here with him." The brother. "See him as security."

Niko thinks for a moment. "Agreed."

They follow Egger and the woman into the warehouse.

And Aaron knows: that was the first mistake.

She had wanted to go in armed, with a calf holster under her loose trousers, but the decision was up to Niko, who already knew Egger. "He won't even trust someone as beautiful as you. He'll frisk us both."

*He didn't. Why not?*

Aaron glances behind her. The Catalans shake their heads as Token-Eyes holds out a pack of cigarettes to them. Good lads, she'd worked that one out on a shooting training course; she wanted to know who she was entrusting her life to. Afterwards they were all invited to dinner at Ruben's house. Children clambering over the furniture, laughter, paella, brandy from Andorra that brought tears to their eyes.

Later she had gone out on to the terrace to smoke. Trees struck deals with the wind. Windows shone through their branches as if in an advent calendar. What could Aaron expect on the third of December? Party music, nearby. But Aaron was far away. Jordi came and scrounged a cigarette. They smoked like two people who know there isn't a chocolate behind every little window of the advent calendar.

Jordi said: "I've been doing this for too long. I've stopped sleeping. In January I'm getting a desk job."

The warehouse door falls shut behind Aaron. A coffee depot. The smells are so intense that for a moment she gasps for breath. Dandelions, caramelized sugar, damp pipe tobacco, freshly split wood.

On a sack of coffee, a tube. The painting.

Aaron asks: "May I?"

The woman hands her the tube.

Aaron has unusually good hearing. Once at the range Pavlik rolled out some cartridges from the ammunition store.

Aaron knew without looking: five.

Now, when she hears three faint pops, one after the other, she knows that there's no painting in the package.

That Jordi will never get his desk job.

A Remington suddenly appears as if by magic in the hand of the man who calls himself Egger. Aaron leaps over sacks, feels the bullets splitting the air, rolls away and jumps to her feet in a single movement, sees Niko falling to the ground, runs in a zigzag to the hall at the back, and meanwhile a red-hot pincer grabs her arm and she can think nothing but Niko! Niko! Niko!

Two doors, a game of roulette. She stakes everything on red, pulls the right-hand door open and finds herself in a pitch-dark corridor. She stumbles forwards, feeling her way, until she bumps into a wall. Black. Wrong door, blind alley. She presses herself into a niche in the wall. Something hot runs down her arm. No pain. The light goes on. Like a machine, her heart pumps raging fear into her bloodstream. Light footsteps. The woman has taken off her stilettos and is barefoot.

Another five meters. Aaron sees the light switch on the opposite wall. Too far away. She spins the thought like a coin, trying to find an alternative.

Doesn't find one.

Four meters.

Three.

Aaron flies out of the niche. The woman fires. Right hand, graze wound. Aaron hammers her fist against the switch. Darkness. She drops to the floor, fires two shots that miss their target. She performs a quick scissor kick, which cracks against the woman's ankle and knocks her over. Her index and middle fingers jab into the woman's solar plexus and she gasps for air. Aaron notices that the woman is bending her gun arm, she grabs her head, twists it violently around and hears her neck breaking.

She takes the pistol, feels that it's a Walther and removes the magazine. Empty. The machine she has for a heart pumps desperation into her veins. But perhaps there's still a bullet in the barrel.

*Please, please, please.*

Aaron is shaking too hard, she can't gauge the weight. She doesn't dare pull back the slide to see, too loud.

Her heart rate is far too high. It needs to get down to between sixty and seventy, and she's at over two hundred. In this state she couldn't even pull the trigger.

Aaron forces herself to breathe slowly with her diaphragm, enlarges the volume of her lungs, supplies her muscles with oxygen and allows herself half a minute to bring her heart rate down. Enough?

She stands in the dark. Takes one last deep breath, in, out. Her right hand feels the light switch.

*Now.*

Aaron turns on the light. Token-Eyes. Fifty meters away. Her finger twitches against the trigger. She's never heard a better sound than that shot. She hits Token-Eyes in the neck. He turns around and topples over. Sixty drumming footsteps. Token-Eyes stares at the ceiling. His jugular isn't injured, but he can't move. Shock. There are three cartridges missing from his silenced Glock 33. Jordi, Ruben, Josue.

Jump into the hall, stand, aim two-handed, reduce your body surface. No Egger.

*Niko! Niko! Niko!*

He is lying in the foetal position beside the empty tube. His shirt is wet with blood. She can feel his pulse. Aaron wants to shout, she's so glad. Red foam appears on his lips. His voice is like his breathing when he sleeps. "Get out of here."

She tries to pull him up, ninety kilos of muscle, but can't do it. Tries again. Tries and tries.

Where is Egger?

Niko grabs her hand. He pulls Aaron to him, puts his mouth to her ear. She understands the words but doesn't grasp their meaning.

"You've got to," he struggles to say.

Egger appears magically in the warehouse as if suddenly appearing on stage. Aaron throws herself in his direction. They fire at the same time. Five shots that sound like one. He darts away. She doesn't know if she's hit him. No. Aaron hears him putting in a new magazine.

Niko's gaze. An eternity.

She runs off. The Remington fires out a quick sequence of shots. Aaron wedges the Glock between her teeth and catapults herself into the open with a double flip. She takes a hit, her right arm again, and loses her balance. She crashes on to her back, fires two shots over her head through the door and rolls for cover.

She sees the three corpses.

Aaron wants to spring to her feet, but can no longer feel her own body. She prays that the auxiliary power unit will kick in and produce the five per cent reserve that a person still has when he thinks: it's over.

She bends her little finger.

OK.

Two fingers.

OK.

*Move!*

She creeps to the Daimler. Collapses against the wheel.

The key is in the ignition.

The heavy limousine leaps away with a roar. Egger dives out of the hall. Bullets shatter the rear window. A bullet slices the back of Aaron's neck. She swerves into the Via de Circulació. Five hundred meters at full speed. On the left she senses rough cliffs, on the right harbor lights race past like photons in a particle accelerator.

Only now does she feel her bullet wounds. Her right arm seems to be made of ice, her hand a ball of flame. Blood runs down her back.

Aaron looks in the rearview mirror.

And sees the Audi.

She puts her foot on the accelerator and takes the vehicle up to two hundred and fifty. Eggers catches up. His car is half a ton lighter and twice as powerful. Ahead of her a van pulls out to overtake a truck. Aaron looks from the overtaking lane to the hard shoulder. The mirror scrapes a road sign, comes away and whirls into the darkness.

Egger is jammed up against Aaron's back bumper. They plunge into the tunnel in the Plaça de les Drassanes.

Two hundred and sixty.

Despairing, she is forced to admit: *This is the best I can do.*

The Audi pulls up effortlessly beside her.

Eggar and Aaron look at each other.

A moment that outlasts the whole of time.

In front of her she sees a shadow, a car. Her eye twitches to the carriageway, no hard shoulder, she can't avoid it, knows she has only a few blinks of an eye left, as she raises the gun with her injured arm.

Her finger is on the trigger, but Egger is faster.

Something explodes inside Aaron's head. A lightning flash cuts through the world like a sheet of paper. Aaron sees everything in extreme slow motion, in dazzling white as if in a grotesquely over-exposed film: the roof of the car turning until it's underneath her, the banknotes fluttering like dry leaves from the bag of money, her face in the rearview mirror, amorphous landscape, snowy desert, eternal nothingness.

Then the same thing all over again, but a thousand times faster, a single whirlwind, pain, screaming.

And another lightning flash.

In a nanosecond the world has ceased to exist.

Aaron hears steel eating into the concrete and at last everything is still still still. The last thing she will remember will be the smell of coffee, as repellent as cold ashes.

# 1

THE STEWARDESS asks again: "With milk?"

"Black." Aaron reaches out her hand and feels the cup being placed in it. She hears the pilot's voice: "In thirty minutes we will land in Berlin. It has already been snowing all morning. Please keep your safety belts fastened, we are expecting some turbulence."

Aaron forces herself to drink the coffee.

Since she has been working for the BKA, the Federal Office of Criminal Investigation, in Wiesbaden, there have been several opportunities to travel to Berlin for work. The office has a branch in the district of Treptow, where the security group, the anti-terror center and the "special unit" department are based. But Aaron has always been able to avoid it.

She grew up in the Rhineland, but in her early twenties she made Berlin her home, which it still is in some way even today, even though she hasn't been there for five years. She feels that quite clearly, with every kilometer closer to the city. Impatience floods through her, the joyful anticipation of arrival, a tingle. It irritates her, because on this return journey, the twenty-four hours that she will stay, fear is her luggage.

Five years. Aaron didn't even close down her flat in Schöneberg; her father did that for her.

In Berlin she left behind only a few people that she misses. The life she led hardly allowed her to have friendships. Pavlik and his wife Sandra were, in fact, the only ones. When she moved to the nameless Department at the age of twenty-five, he immediately took her under his wing.

13

The only woman among forty men.

It was from Pavlik that she learned that everyone, however long they had been there, had nights when the shivering came.

That came as a great relief to Aaron: being hugged, and also being allowed to console others.

Nonetheless, in the years that have passed since Barcelona she and Pavlik haven't spoken. They talked on the phone occasionally for the first few months. But they were both helpless. Pavlik tried to act as if nothing serious had happened in Spain, and took refuge in coolness because it was the only way he could deal with it. And Aaron could find no words to express what it means for her, she still can't even today. Eventually they only heard each other breathing. And then the calls stopped.

*Will I still recognize his voice?*

"We are now coming in to land at Berlin-Schönefeld. Please fold away your tables and put your seats in the upright position."

"Oh great!"

When Aaron's neighbor furiously throws her coffee cup at her, she realizes that she has left it half full on the table, and must have spilled it over the man's trousers.

"Are you blind?" he snarls.

"Yes."

The ground stewardess leads Aaron into the hall—"I assume someone is coming to collect you?"—and leaves her alone.

As she stands there calmly, with her suitcase beside her, she could be a perfectly normal woman in her mid-thirties, tall and attractive. She doesn't give away the fact that she is quivering inside because she knows who is going to collect her. Until recently she had worn the armband with three black circles on it that identifies blind people in Germany. But sometimes she would be standing on the pavement or in the supermarket, lost in thought, with no particular destination in mind, and all of a sudden she would be grabbed out of nowhere and dragged away because some over-keen assistant thought that she wanted to cross the road or get to the escalator. When she protested, the baffled person would just leave her there, completely over-whelmed, and creep away. And she no longer knew where she was.

Aaron taps her watch. The computerized voice tells her: "Sixth of January. Wednesday. Fourteen minutes and seventeen seconds past eight."

*Perhaps they'd got the wrong flight. What then? A taxi?*

That's a nightmare. You go and stand where the first taxi might be, hear the boot being packed and travel destinations named, next car, doors closing, driving away, and you're left standing there like a Jehovah's Witness. Waving would look ridiculous. Luckily a driver eventually bawls her out: "Hey, are you getting in or not?"

Suddenly Aaron knows that Niko has been standing there looking at her all along.

*Shot to the spleen and the lungs. Lost two liters of blood.*
*Survived.*

At last he touches her shoulder. "Hi." He hugs her as if they'd said goodbye only yesterday.

Aaron smells iodine. Cut himself shaving. She doesn't want to, but her left hand does, reaches under his leather jacket and brushes the grip of the gun. A Makarov Single Action.

He takes her suitcase and they walk to the exit. In the old days Aaron usually wore flat shoes. Now that she's blind, her steel spike heels are her echolocators. Against a hard surface like this one, but only in places that are quieter, in enclosed spaces. Aaron drifts through a cathedral of noise, the whispers, shouts and chatter of many voices, rattling luggage trolleys, ringing mobile phones, squealing babies, a metallic announcement in bad English and another, in German, which interrupts and squabbles with the first. She is forced to take Niko's arm.

Outside the cold hits her in the face. Snowflakes dance on her skin. Niko's light, sinuous gait, which can't deceive her, because she was once a beast of prey like him.

Aaron clicks her fingers hard several times, knows that Niko is surprised, doesn't explain, taking her bearings. Each object reflects sound differently, has a wavelength of its own. But one problem, of course, is the backdrop of sound. When she walks through the city for too long, by evening she's in bits and her head is throbbing.

"Careful, there's a litter bin."

She knew that already. Not least because she can smell bananas and rancid hamburger.

Even better would be clicking her tongue, her sonar with which she produces sounds close to her ear in such a way that they aren't diverted and scattered. The echoes model the world, illuminating them like a stroboscope. Aaron can determine the size and density of objects at a distance of between five and two hundred meters, and receives a pixelated image of them.

Like a bat or a dolphin.

At first she couldn't believe it. In the rehab clinic there was a woman who had been blind for some time and who came every day to stand by the patients during their first desperate weeks. She went walking with Aaron in the clinic's gardens, stopped, clicked her tongue and said: "On the right there are six trees. Beeches, chestnuts or oaks. On the left two, but smaller, maybe plane trees." She thought the woman was pulling her leg. But a doctor who came by was not surprised and confirmed it. "But they aren't planes, they're young birches."

The woman clicked again and tapped Aaron on the arm. "There's a house over there. I would say it's a hundred meters away. And there's a car parked about twenty meters ahead of us."

It was true.

Aaron thought: I've got to be able to do that as *well*.

People who are blinded later in life seldom master this skill as well as people who have been blind since birth and practiced it all their lives. But Aaron has trained as if possessed, which is how she has always faced every challenge.

Her first success was the alleyway between two buildings at the clinic, which she recognized by the draft and heard immediately afterwards. Aaron's clicks bounced off the walls of the buildings, whirred to and fro and back to her, until the sound finally dispersed. She explored the alley and bumped against the container she had located. Victory!

But Aaron only uses the click sonar when she's alone. In Niko's presence it would seem silly. Would he think she was Flipper?

Aaron stops. "First let me have a cigarette." Niko could have no idea how long it took her to practice bringing the match to the cigarette as if it was the most natural thing in the world, and look casual about it.

He asks: "How are things at the BKA?"

"Good. What about you?"

"A lot of paperwork. Boring."

*Of course. That's why you've got that Makarov on your hip. There's a good argument for that little trinket: the extremely light trigger resistance.*

When she's sure he can't hear her, she clicks her tongue, a power click with her lips parted in an O. She locates a street lamp. Or two? Off to the left a pillar. Advertising? Ventilation? On the right is a coach, engine running, a noisy school class, scraps of words, a Scandinavian language.

What Niko calls seeing is only an echo of light. That's why he can see the lamp post, the pillar, the coach, the schoolchildren.

So now she's in Berlin. How does she know that? Because the pilot said: "We will shortly be landing in Schönefeld?" Because someone is shouting through an open car window: "God alive, I can't believe these car parks!?" Wiesbaden is the silent corridors in the BKA where she initially thought: Am I alone here? Frankfurt green sauce in the canteen, children's laughter in the playground behind her house, the rattle of the Nerobergbahn. All the cities she travels to leave her with the textures of the hands she has shaken, the spices in the food, the call of a muezzin, the different noise of police sirens, a gust of wind in a huge square. That's London, Cairo, Paris for her. And Berlin? Warm, breathing fur cuddling up to her, a cry in the night, but also the feeling of having been almost happy.

City freeway northbound. Aaron concentrates on the sound of the windscreen wipers that are wiping away the snow. She tries to synchronize her heartbeat with the constant, even interval.

*I'm grateful to you for a lot of things, but most of all for the fact that you were never alone by my bed in Barcelona. I wouldn't have been able to bear the silence between us. You never uttered a word of reproach. But I will be eternally ashamed, to the depths of my being.*

*Until my dying day.*

No member of the Department ever left a wounded comrade behind.

Only her.

There was only one person she could talk to about it.

Since she's been able to think, her father was the most important person in her life. *Aren't all girls like that?* Later he became her mentor, then her adviser, her confidant. For many years they were both short of time and didn't see each other often. And they didn't need to. They were connected by many things, but they were one in the knowledge of how long a fraction of a second is.

Jörg Aaron. Old hand in GSG 9, the counter-terrorism unit. 18 October 1977, 22:59 hours, barracks of Mogadishu airport. Helmut Schmidt gave the go-ahead for the storming of the "Landshut" aircraft. Colonel Wegener stands in front of the troops and asks: "Who's going in first?"

Ten men take one step forward.

Jörg Aaron takes one more.

He is the one who pushes open the escape hatches in the fuselage and kills the first two terrorists with shots to the head.

For fifteen years he's always been at the front. Later commander of GSG 9. On first name terms with Yitzhak Rabin. Cross of Honor. Legend.

At every stage of her career she saw the glances.

*So that's Jörg Aaron's daughter.*

In the hospital he was the first one who held her hand. Who fed and bathed her and rocked her in his arms when she cried. Who made sure that the third-floor window couldn't be opened.

"I ran away. I just left Niko to his fate."

"You were scared, that's normal."

"How am I supposed to live with that?"

"Stop thinking about it."

"Say it."

"You'll learn to get up and go to sleep again. Eat, drink, breathe. There will be lots of days, good days, when you forget. But you'll never get rid of it."

She asked him: "How do my eyes look?" Because she knew he would tell her the truth, ruthlessly.

"Perfect and gorgeous."

The best sentence of all time.

After a week she had been able to answer questions. Two officers from Internal Affairs flew to Spain and spoke to her by her bed. They were like all the others Aaron had sat opposite over the years. Accountants with no adrenalin in their veins, no fear of death, no pain.

Her father insisted on being present when she was being questioned. It was against the rules, but they didn't dare refuse him.

He was Jörg Aaron.

They read Niko's statement to her. "'I had one bullet in my spleen, one in my lung. Jenny couldn't move me. She was under fire, had to get help. She made the right decision.'"

"Miss Aaron, can you confirm this account?"

The question wasn't a complicated one. She wanted to answer it, too. But she didn't know what to say.

"Miss Aaron?"

"Yes."

How often she has thought about that "yes." Eventually she convinced herself that it meant: "Yes—could you please repeat the question?" and not "Yes, that's what happened." But the "Yes" stayed in the files as an agreement.

"You were up against three adversaries. By now you'd already eliminated two of them. Is that correct?"

"Yes." That was what she'd been told.

"Miss Aaron, you are part of the Department. You were trained in combat shooting and in four martial arts techniques, you are extraordinarily resilient and have distinguished yourself in extreme situations. You couldn't get rid of the third man?"

She should have told the truth: that she doesn't remember. She knows that she glanced back once at Jordi, Ruben and Josue before the hall door closed. And next thing she's lying outside the warehouse, unable to move. Bending her little finger. Somehow getting to the car. The rear window shattering. Flying along the freeway, with next to her, where Niko should be, only a bag of money.

Seeing the Audi in the rearview mirror and knowing: it's over.

A glance, a shot. Over.

"Between the warehouse and the tunnel, according to our calculations, four minutes must have passed. Do you reckon that's correct?"

Her father's voice was a fingernail on a blackboard. "Do you think my daughter looked at a stopwatch?"

"It's about the following, Miss Aaron: if you wanted to call for help, why didn't you? You didn't call the Flying Squad from the Daimler, and you didn't try to make a connection."

Four minutes.

They sped past like seconds and lasted for centuries.

"Miss Aaron?"

"I'd been shot several times," she managed to say helplessly.

Again her father leaped to her support. "Let me tell you something, you clowns. None of you has ever sped along a crowded freeway with a hitman on your tail. From my modest experience I can assure you: it's hard to make a phone call."

Aaron was asked to sign.

The men left. Her father's hand rested on hers. She felt his blood thumping in it. They didn't speak.

She knew that he was ashamed for her.

But he loved her.

He had another one and a half years to go until he retired and left the service that meant everything to him and yet not half as much as his daughter. He found the rehab clinic for her in Siegburg, near

Sankt Augustin, where her parental home stood. Every morning he read to her from the newspaper before he worked with her. He was unforgiving if she failed to do the simplest things. He practiced shopping with her, and telling by the weight of the fork whether she had speared a piece of meat or a potato, helped her learn to do her make-up again, and above all he spurred her on: *Again! Again! Again!*

How often she heard from her mobility trainer: "You're trying to do too much, only people blind from birth achieve perfection."

Every time her father said: "My daughter can do it!"

And he also plagued her into using her hated cane, unfortunately with limited success. Even today Aaron only has a moderate mastery of it, because she is too reluctant to be identified immediately as a blind person.

He swotted up on Braille with her, and was the guinea pig to whom she expectantly served up the first steak that she had fried herself. At that point she didn't yet know how to tell the difference between salt and pepper, that salt makes a sound when you shake it and pepper doesn't. When her father, coughing, croaked, "Delicious!," they both laughed like lunatics.

But above all he taught her the most difficult thing: to receive help, to accept that she will be dependent on others for as long as she lives, and that she must perceive that not as a burden but as a necessity.

On the first day when she dared to leave the rehab clinic on her own, there was only one way to go: to him. She had spent the night anticipating the moment when he would open the door and she would surprise him. Aaron knew that he was at home because a friend wanted to come and see him. She was so proud when she caught the right bus and, after getting out, had taken her bearings from the guidelines she had learned, had been steered as in childhood by smells and sounds, until she knew at last: I'm home.

She felt for the gate and heard murmurs. She was asked to step aside. Men walked past carrying something. She heard the hoarse voice of her father's friend: "It's me, Butz."

He had collapsed after the words: "The Minister of the Interior gave me this whisky when I joined the service." Aaron will never get over the fact that she was unable to say goodbye to him, and tell him she would be dead without him.

The traffic is more sluggish as they approach the Fernsehturm. Aaron can tell by Niko's breath that he is looking at her again and again. She turns her eyes directly towards his. He concentrates on driving. Accelerate, brake, accelerate.

"Sorry about your father."

She just nods.

Niko had served under him. He didn't have to apply, her father had chosen him from among a thousand possible candidates. Eventually he dismissed Niko, keeping the reason to himself. He had never been as disappointed as he had been by Niko, Aaron sensed as much when Niko's name was mentioned. It was a blow to her father when they became a couple. Once she asked him what had happened between them. Her father said only: "He's a ship in search of an iceberg."

A thumping heart brings the memory to a close. Niko has turned off the wipers. He leaves the freeway. "The guys in the Fourth have copied the file in Braille."

Which she can't read. She curses the fact that she burned two of her fingertips on the stove last Friday.

Aaron reads with her left index finger, which she won't be able to use for at least a week.

"You know the facts. Tell me."

Reinhold Boenisch, fifty-nine, life for four murders, in prison for sixteen years. Two days ago the prison psychologist had visited his cell before going home because he had invited her for a cup of tea.

Boenisch killed her, and since then he hadn't uttered a word.

Apart from the sentence: *I'll only talk to Jenny Aaron.*

# 2

IN THE double door system at Tegel Correctional Facility Niko has to hand over his gun. Excessively correct control in spite of their IDs. Papers are meticulously checked. There is whispering.

Ten things that Aaron doesn't like to hear:
    the rattling of heavy keys
    crows
    whispering
    "Are you blind?"
    chalk on a board
    car engines at top speed
    water boiling over
    "I'm just doing my job here."
    traditional German pop songs
    lies

"What is that?" Aaron knows that the officer who takes her handbag is referring to the telescopic walking stick that isn't recognizable as a blind person's cane to the undiscerning eye.

    "What does it look like?"

    A colleague says: "A club. It's staying here."

    Aaron reaches out her hand. "May I?"

    She swiftly extends the stick and hears a murmured, "Sorry."

    As they leave, someone says very quietly, probably too quietly for Niko to hear: "Does she remind you of anyone?"

An officer takes them to the prison Psychology Service. As a case analyst and interrogation specialist, Aaron is involved in large-scale areas of investigation at the BKA, organized crime, terrorism, where the victims are only abstract qualities, shadowy entities. Here it's different. She wants to know who the murdered woman was, to understand what life she was torn from.

The wind drives the snow along ahead of them. Aaron feels the flakes on her wrist, hasty, wet guests which don't want to stay. She's been here often, she imagines the broad, apparently deserted grounds, she knows that all the inmates are working now, or locked in their cells. The Psychology Service is based in the school building, to the back near the sports ground. Her thoughts slip into the past, she hears furious men shouting. "Play the ball! Too dumb to wank!"

This time she hasn't linked arms with Niko, but allows herself to be guided textbook-style, thumb and index finger on his elbow, half a pace back, her hip behind his, but without making contact. Her mobility trainer would be delighted.

But she only does this so as not to be aware of the holster under Niko's jacket and feel like a dry alcoholic in an off-license.

"How old was Dr. Breuer?"

The murder victim's colleague has been crying a lot. Her voice is hoarse, dull, empty. "Thirty-three. Her birthday was in December. She invited all her colleagues to go to the cinema."

"How long had she been working in the correctional facility?"

"Three years. We knew each other from university. Then I started here, for a bit of security. Melly always wanted her own practice. But it didn't work. She waitressed part-time, it wasn't a life. When the job here came up I was on at her until she applied."

Tears start to come, but get stuck in her throat.

"Did she like the job?"

"No. She found everything here oppressive. She started losing her spirit. I said: 'It happens, you'll get used to it.'" The tears work their way up a little further, but still don't reach her eyes.

"Did she have family?"

"A sister in Norway, who's coming today. Both her parents are dead."

"Was she married?"

"She was on her own for a while, because she'd had a few bad experiences. But she'd had a boyfriend recently. Tall, handsome. Melly was really smitten. When she came here in the morning even the wallpaper seemed to brighten."

"What did she look like?"

No reply.

"Do you have a picture you could show my colleague?"

Her voice quivers. "She was tall, about a meter eighty. She had black curly hair, freckles and skin like porcelain. Melly was beautiful, she was special. In spite of her black hair she seemed temperamentally quite cool. But she wasn't, in fact."

Aaron feels dizzy.

"You look very like her."

"How often did Boenisch come here?"

"Every week. He hardly opened his mouth. She wondered why he came at all."

"Was she uneasy when she went to see him?"

"Not at all. She was really glad that he invited her to have a cup of—" She breaks off.

Aaron gives her time.

"She said: 'Hey, maybe he's going to thaw.'"

"I'd like to see Dr. Breuer's notes."

"I'll put them together for you. Half an hour?"

"Fine."

The woman reaches for Aaron's hand. "Thank you."

"What for?"

"No one from the Homicide Unit has asked about Melly at all. They haven't even been here."


On the path leading to Block Six, from which the snow has been cleared, her heels create a rough-grained image. Aaron also clicks her fingers and immediately recognizes the fence that surrounds the building, and even if she didn't know the place she would be able to tell by the clicks that it wasn't a wall.

Four or five meters to the entrance. She stops in front of the door just a second before Niko, which must irritate him. A familiar smell inside. Sweat, disinfectant, bad food.

Ten smells that Aaron doesn't like:
   hospitals
   fish
   the perfume "Femme" by Rochas
   raclette
   coffee
   the air in the underground
   prisons
   chrysanthemums
   cigarette smoke
   fear

A new building. They are passed on to an officer who leads them to the second floor. A mop slaps against the linoleum. Apart from the inmates and the domestic staff who prepare the food, clean, change the laundry, there are no inmates here in the late morning.

"How did Boenisch behave?" she asks the officer.

"He didn't stand out. In a few weeks he would have disappeared into preventive detention. The building's just over there, all smart as anything. Twenty square meters, kitchen, tiled bathroom, big garden. Only a matter of time before they introduce room service."

Another smell. "They smoke dope here," she says to the man.

"And snort, and jack up, and drink. Tell us how to stop it and we'll do it straight away."

Suddenly she feels eyes on her back. Involuntarily she turns around. Always the same stupid reflex.

"Here it is." Aaron hears the man opening the seal with a key from his keyring. "You'll be fine." As he leaves, he mutters: "In Vietnam they eat feet." His footsteps fade away like those of a man counting every day until his retirement.

"I'd like to go in on my own first." Aaron steps into the cell and closes the door. She stands still. The smell is so subliminal that it takes her a minute to be aware of it. Tea. She kneels down and feels around on the linoleum. Just before she reaches the plank bed there's a sticky patch with a thin dry trickle disappearing from it.

She straightens up. She knows what a cell looks like. Ten square meters, plank bed, wash basin, toilet, cupboard, television. Still, she clicks her tongue, very quietly so as not to cause a hubbub of echoes in the small room. Her lips form an "e," which produces a sound with a high resolution. The sound comes dully back from the left-hand wall. She clicks again. Waist-height, above the bed. Aaron kneels on the mattress and feels her way along the bookshelf. Her fingers glide over the greasy, tattered paperbacks. The second-to-last book is bound, the cover intact. She sniffs the paper. Slightly woody, as if freshly printed. When she is about to put the book back she notices that there's a gap in the middle.

There's a DVD or a CD between the pages.

She opens the door. "What kind of books does he have?"

Niko looks at the shelf. "*With You by My Side... Your Breath on My Soul... The Joy of Knowing You... Cherry-Red Summer.* Shall I go on, or do you feel ill already?"

Aaron holds out the book that she's removed from the shelf. "What about this one?"

"*... Because They Are Made for Kissing.* Another piece of schmaltz."

"Read out the blurb, please."

"'The black detective and psychologist Alex Cross faces an almost insoluble task.'" He pauses, then goes on reading. "'On the campus of a university in North Carolina attractive young women are being abducted and raped by a psychopath.'" Niko's breath quickens slightly. "It's about a serial killer."

"Open it up. What's inside?" Aaron asks.

"A DVD. *Mr. Brooks,*" Niko says hesitantly.

"Do you know the film?"

"No."

"I do, though. It's about a serial killer as well. Mr. Brooks is secretly observed at work by a photographer called Smith. But Smith doesn't go to the police. Instead he blackmails Mr. Brooks so that he can accompany him on his night-time trips." Aaron hears Niko's breath slowing. "Is there a DVD player in here?"

"Yes."

"Are the walls decorated? Photographs, posters, postcards?"

His silence is so deep that you could throw a stone into it and never see it again.

When it becomes unbearable, he says: "Just a drawing."

This time Niko's silence presses Aaron against a wall that she has built herself. It is an infinity before she hears his voice again. "It's from a newspaper article, by a court artist. From the trial, back then. You're in the witness stand."

The wall, built over sixteen years, collapses. Aaron is hurled into the chair in Moabit district court. She clings to the armrest for support as she answers the questions of Boenisch's defense lawyer. His strategy is based on diminished responsibility: he wants to ensure that his client is sent to a psychiatric hospital. Boenisch is staring at Aaron the whole time. A fly crawls along his underarm. He doesn't notice. Her eye darts to the courtroom artist. His charcoal scratches on the notepad.

"Jenny?" Niko asks, bringing her back.

"You said he suffocated the woman with a plastic bag. What sort of bag?"

"What do you mean?"

"Transparent or printed?"

She hears him scrolling on his tablet. "Doesn't say."

"Call Forensics."

Niko phones Forensics. "C&A bag. With the logo."

"So she was allowed into the cell unsupervised?" Aaron asks.

"Of course. She had keys to every block."

"Did anyone see her going in downstairs?"

"Hang on." He scrolls down. "There were two jailers in the guard room. She said hello, she was in a good mood. No one noticed that she didn't come out."

"What time was this?"

"Half-past three. It was the beginning of recreation. You know what happens then. Chaos. The jailers are under a lot of stress."

"And she got off work as early as that?"

"She wanted to do some overtime."

"So Boenisch must have killed her between half-past three and a quarter to four. And then?"

"He stayed in his cell, no one was interested. They locked the door at half-past nine. Someone on the late shift looked in on him briefly, but didn't notice anything. Presumably he had hidden the corpse under his bed."

Aaron goes into her inner chamber. Now she's in the loneliest place in the world. She retreats in here when she wants to see everything from a great distance and therefore more clearly. She hears her voice from a long way away: "So that's it until the next morning?"

"Not quite. At half-past one in the morning something happened. Boenisch pressed the emergency button in the cell. A jailer looked in on him. Boenisch complained of a bad headache and was given some aspirin."

*I'm sure he was delighted with that. Knowing what's under his bed while they look after him and pay him respect.*

"They had a regular check at six in the morning. He was lying beside her in the spoons position."

"How many cups were used?"

Niko scrolls. "Two."

"Milk, sugar?"

No scrolling. She was the only one who would ask that question.

"Why is that important?"

"Was she raped?"

"No."

"What injuries did she have?"

"Broken larynx."

"What do the walls look like?"

"Painted white."

"Nothing else?"

Long pause. "Black smears. Opposite the bed."

"How high up?"

"About half a meter."

Aaron leaves the inner chamber. "What do you think?"

"Boenisch broke her larynx so that she couldn't scream, and pulled the bag over her head. She defended herself and her shoes rubbed against the wall."

"Why wasn't Melanie Breuer missed at the exit desk? She would have had to clock out."

"They were having a farewell party."

*Hence the fastidious check.*

"Now they're in serious trouble."

She goes back down to the guard room with Niko. Burnt toast, coffee turning bitter in the pot for hours. "I'd like to talk to the two people who saw Dr. Breuer coming in the day before yesterday."

"Schilling is off sick."

"And the other one?"

"Special training."

Aaron reads between the lines: *You're just trying to pin something on us.*

The prison officer who brought her to Boenisch's cell smells of cigarette smoke and yearning glances at his watch. "Any the wiser?"

"Since when has Boenisch had a DVD player in his cell?"

"No idea. Must have put in an application. As I say: pure luxury here."

"Had he seemed different over the last few days?"

"I never gave him a cuddle."

Niko snaps at the man: "Do you think it's funny that he spent the whole night next to a corpse?"

"I don't think anything's funny around here."

She asks: "Which prisoners was he in close contact with?"

"Bukowski."

Niko would have asked the same questions if he had been on the case. But the Department was only asked for administrative assistance.

*The guys from the Fourth Homicide Unit probably don't want to deal with a blind woman.* "She used to be one of yours. Are you being her nursemaid?"

He yells at the officer: "Can you be more precise? Why's he in, since when, where does he work?"

"Armed robbery. Four years. Car repair workshop."

"Take us there."

Black metal gate on rollers. An angle grinder squeals. A soldering iron does a spot weld, splat-splat-splat, there's a smell of burnt sparklers. Aaron shields the flame of her lighter against the wind. Outside, an announcement at Holzhauser Strasse U-Bahn station comes over the wall. "Stand back from the platform edge!"

Bukowski is brought out. "Hi there. Got a cig?"

The phlegmy rattle in his voice is one big warning to him to stop smoking. But it's also an excellent soundbox. Aaron sees muscles, tattoos, a bull neck. She holds the pack out to him, gives him a light, catches the smell of fresh liquid soap.

*I bet you won't guess that I'm blind.*

Niko asks: "How well do you know Reinhold Boenisch?"

"So so."

The administrative employee smokes too. "Don't talk crap. You're always hanging around together."

"He tried to get too close. I didn't want any of that."

"That's right, you're a good person."

"That's what I always say."

"Did you notice anything unusual about Boenisch lately?" Aaron asks. "Did he keep himself to himself, was he disturbed?"

"He's always disturbed. He says there's a party going on in his head."

"Did you know he was seeing a shrink?"

"We all do. Did you ever see her? Really hot. Sorry. I shouldn't say that to you, should I?"

Aaron knows that he would be grinning all the way to the top of his head if his ears weren't in the way. She stamps out her cigarette.

She's been practicing for a week. "Mr. Bukowski, a man like you wouldn't have someone like Boenisch as a friend. He's a big guy, but he isn't good at defending himself. Men who murder women are pretty far down the pecking order in this place. He needs a fighter to protect him, and you're that guy. In return he gives you some of his wages. Can we agree on that?"

Bukowski snorts.

Niko says: "Your business partnership is over, Boenisch is going to be transferred anyway." His voice is confident, authoritative. Aaron knows that tone, the one he used in Naples the first time they met to declare, quite calmly, 'Ten million isn't a problem.'"

"And?"

"Telly in the evening for as long as you want."

Bukowski thinks.

"Have you got a girlfriend waiting for you outside?" Aaron asks.

"Why?"

"Two hours in the contact room." She already feels the need to smoke again.

"Can I have another cig?"

Aaron gives Bukowski her last one. She sees him rolling the cigarette back and forth between thumb and forefinger, and smugly blowing a smoke ring.

"He comes and talks to me on Sunday. Wants to know can I beat him up. I think he's taking the piss. But he means it. I whacked him a couple of times. He has a screw loose."

# 3

THE CORRIDOR is endless. She notices her footsteps getting slower and slower. Niko stops by the open door.

"You don't need to do that."

"I do."

In the contact room she immediately hears the excited squeak of bedsprings. An officer shouts, "That's enough."

She holds out her hand. Whenever they greet anyone, Aaron is always faster, so that she doesn't need to try to find the other person's hand. She would never touch Boenisch if it wasn't absolutely necessary; the very thought makes her want to throw up. But Aaron wants to read his hand.

He grips her hand with both massive cuffed paws. They are damp and quivering with anticipation.

*What does he look like, sixteen years on?*

His voice has the pleading undertone that she knows and has never forgotten. "I'm so sorry that you're blind. So sorry."

*Here, let me give you an erection.*

"I want to speak to Mr. Boenisch on his own."

Niko snorts: "Out of the question."

She pulls him a little way away. Her heels tell her that there's another meter of air between her and the wall. Aaron whispers: "If it makes you feel any better, chain him to the radiator."

"Forget it."

"He won't say a word if you're here."

Niko reluctantly brushes Aaron's hand away, thinks for a moment and goes.

Shifting chair, metal on metal, footsteps, slamming doors.

The bullet entered the back of her head and passed through both hemispheres of the cerebral cortex. But the optical nerve was undamaged. Aaron sees very clearly. She takes her bearings from breathing and the voice, and has learned to direct her eyes ten degrees above the position of her interlocutor's mouth so that he has the impression of being looked at.

But in interrogations she does something different. The sighted person tells the blind one things that he wouldn't confide in anyone else. Because the blind person can't see you turning red, kneading your hands, staring into the distance, wrestling for words. He thinks. It's like a confession. The sighted person thinks he's safe behind the black curtain that separates the blind person from him, but he's blind too.

Aaron looks past Boenisch. She wants him to feel superior to her.

She sets her phone down on the table and starts the recording. His breathing is quick. He can hardly wait for her to ask the first question.

"Are you happy with the food here?"

He exhales a stream of sour air, so disappointed, so disappointed that it isn't a perfect first sentence.

That's why it's exactly the right one.

"Yes."

"You work in the laundry. Do you get on with your colleagues?"

"I suppose." He could cry, because she's messing everything up.

"Do they treat you well?"

Boenisch groans.

"What is it?"

"One of the guards beat me up. My ribs are black and blue. Do you want to feel?"

"We'll have to report that. Let's do it later."

Aaron continues unmoved for the next five minutes: how often his aunt visits him, whether he would rather watch television in the common room or on his own, when he turns out the light in the evening, how good the reception on his transistor radio is, the quality of his mattress. All subjects that she's absolutely fascinated by.

*The novel is only the packaging. It's about the film.*

Boenisch is about to crack.

She asks: "How do you like *Mr. Brooks*?"

At last. He gasps happily for air, and Aaron is back in that hot August sixteen years ago, when she was studying at police academy on a six-month internship at the Sixth Berlin Homicide Unit and was assigned to the special unit that had been set up a few days before.

Two lawyers from a Charlottenburg chambers with over a hundred partners had disappeared without trace just a week apart. Both had worked until late in the evening; the night porter at the office block was the last one who saw them alive. Of course a connection was drawn with one of the clients of the chambers. But the chambers specialized in boring tax law, and the women had never been involved in the same case.

And they seemed not to have anything to do with each other out of the office.

No ransom demands. There wasn't the slightest trace.

Aaron was given the job of making contact with the families, who were growing more desperate by the day. She could see it on her colleagues' faces; it was hard always coming out with the same phrases: *Don't give up hope. We're doing everything possible. If you like, of course you can have counseling.*

Soon the faces of the husbands and children wouldn't leave her in peace. The files eventually took up two meters on the shelf. About a hundred people from the area were questioned. Friends, relatives, colleagues, neighbors, staff and members of a gym. The possibility was even considered that the women might have had a secret lesbian relationship and gone into hiding.

Aaron read everything until she knew each sentence off by heart.

The night porter had been questioned four times.

*So Dr. Marx took the lift straight to the underground car park at about eleven o'clock?*

*Yes, about eleven. I was about to go upstairs and do my rounds, and she was in the lift when the door opened. I said: "You go on down, Doctor, I've got plenty of time."*

The next time:

*I know it was exactly eleven because I looked at my watch: it must have been something very important if she's been in the office for so long, I thought. She pressed the wrong button and ended up with me in the foyer. I wished her a pleasant evening. She didn't talk to me.*

And then:

*It must have been five to or five past. She wanted to go back up because she'd forgotten something. Probably papers. She was rattled about something.*

*How do you mean?*

*Just a bit strange. Curt.*

The interrogations were carried out by various officers and filed away in different dossiers, which was why no one had noticed the contradictions. What time was it exactly? Did the woman talk to him or not? Had she pressed the wrong floor or did the lift stop in the foyer because the porter had pressed the button? Did she want to go down or up? If the latter, why had he not gone up with her if he was going on his rounds anyway? Had he gone to sleep, and had no idea when the woman had left the building? But in that case why would he have tied himself up in contradictions? He would only have needed to claim that he was somewhere in the building and hadn't a clue when she went home.

That night porter was Reinhold Boenisch.

He tries to lean forwards. Aaron hears the handcuffs jerking along the radiator. She forces herself to do something kind to Boenisch and moves her chair towards him half a meter.

He exhales gratefully. "I'm ashamed that I watched that film. I shouldn't have done. It aroused me a lot." His voice is quivering. "Do you know it?"

"Yes."

His breathing is pure ecstasy.

"How long have you had it—and where did you get it?"

"Not long. Somebody recommended it," he says evasively.

An important sentence. Aaron listens to the echo of its meaning.

"Who was it?"

"Somebody."

"Somebody you like?"

"I don't know."

*Certainly not Bukowski. The idea of choosing a psycho-thriller hiding behind a trashy title as a cover for* Mr. Brooks *so that it didn't stand out among Boenisch's other books and got past the censors is too clever for him.*

"I shouldn't have watched that film."

Again the handcuffs scrape. Aaron allows Boenisch another ten centimeters or so.

"I'm so glad you came that time. So glad. You saved my life. You were my—" He's crying, can't go on talking, his flip-flops slap on the floor and he can't get out the whirl of words that fills his mouth.

It's such an effort to reach out her hand and stroke Boenisch's shoulder that she gets a cramp in her arm. He eagerly stretches his shoulder towards her. "My angel. Thanks for knocking at my door."

Yesterday she was in Paris on a joint investigation between the BKA and the French anti-terror unit RAID. When, between two meetings, she heard Niko's voice on her voicemail for the first time in five years, she couldn't clear her head for several minutes, she was tongue-tied. Over the hours that followed she was dealing with an Al-Qaeda sleeper arrested in Wuppertal who had been caught with plans to carry out attacks in France. She got through it somehow. Then she went outside, smoked a cigarette and heard the hum of the huge, breathing building. *I won't do it. You can't force me to.* But suddenly she found herself thinking about her athletics training at school, how she missed the mat when pole vaulting and broke her elbow. After everything was healed she went to the sports ground.

She knew she would be scared of that bloody crossbar forever if she didn't vault at least one more time. After that it was fine.

So Aaron called Wiesbaden and asked her secretary to inform the Department and book her a flight from Orly. She Googled the Berlin weather report for the third of August sixteen years ago. That's how she knows that it rained in the evening, for the first time in ages.

Boenisch lived in his parents' house in Spandau, up by the forest. The trees on the property would have been dripping with moisture. It must have smelled of soil, leaves, dust.

But she can't remember anything.

Except for ringing the doorbell on the garden gate in the dark.

It was a long time before Boenisch opened the door. More questions? But he's already told them everything… Of course, if he could help. He asked her in and apologized awkwardly for not coming to the door more quickly, because he'd been watching television and always had to turn the sound up so loud because of his bad hearing; he only had one eardrum now, the other had burst when he was little and his father beat him with the belt again.

Suddenly he started shaking and Aaron felt sorry for him. His cat weaved around her legs, but didn't purr. One of its eyes was lined with black, the other with white. Its tail had a kink.

"Ah, I didn't even ask you—would you like a drink?"

"A glass of water would be nice."

He went into the kitchen. The cat miaowed. Aaron ignored it. She put one hand on the television.

Cold.

She saw too late that Boenisch was standing in the kitchen door.

"I don't have any more fizzy water. Is tap water OK?"

His forehead was drenched in sweat.

She said hastily that she had forgotten an important appointment and unfortunately had to go; there was no rush, they could talk another time.

Boenisch looked sad. "Pity." When she tried to get past him he grabbed her like a mouse. He was incredibly strong. He threw Aaron down on the stone floor, knelt on top of her, took her phone from her, pulled her up, dragged her to the basement door, pushed her down the pitch-dark steps and shut the door.

She has forgotten so much. But not that stench. She threw up immediately. She doesn't know how much time passed before she was able to breathe again. Her left collarbone stung. She could feel the bone sticking out. Her whole side was numb.

Retching, Aaron felt her way forwards. Found something furry, an animal, a dog, stiff, as if stuffed, hoped for a second that the stench came from there. And a second later touched the first corpse, the skin of the bare legs doughy, repellently soft.

Aaron screamed and screamed until her body was one terrible great pain, and at the same time she could no longer feel it.

She lay there whimpering for a hundred years, she wanted to dream herself out of this hell into her father's arms and couldn't do it.

Couldn't do it.

Every now and again an airplane whispered over the house. Somewhere out there was the world. People. The cinema where she had planned to see *American Beauty* that evening.

Another hundred years passed before the basement door opened. Boenisch came into the darkness. He had a torch and shone it in her face so that she couldn't see his.

He sobbed: "What am I supposed to do with you?"

She wanted to plead for her life and couldn't get a word out.

He left and locked the door again.

Aaron knew that she would never come out alive from this dungeon if she couldn't find a way of turning off the centrifuge that was tirelessly slinging her heart against her ribs.

Above her head Boenisch put on a record. Roy Orbison: "Pretty Woman." It crackled and droned.

*Dad, what should I do?*

*Where are you? You have to work with what you've got.*

Aaron thought: *I can't do it.* But her hands were starting to feel their way around.

The second corpse. The gaping hole in the throat, tissue that felt like dry cake.

Keep going. Keep going. And then a feeling of happiness swept through her. A nail. Long and rusty. Aaron gripped it with her fist, crept backwards, took her bearings from the first corpse and the dog, found the steps, took off her shoes, crept up the steps.

At last she knelt by the door.

*Dad, I can't see anything.*

*Don't see, know.*

*The nail is too big, I can't get the door open.*

*It isn't fear that paralyzes you. Fear is good, it keeps you alert. But damn it all, you've got to control your breathing! I showed you how!*

Trembling, she pulled off her sweater, rested her right hand on her navel, breathed hard against it and as she breathed out concentrated on making sure that her belly arched all the way to her spinal column.

The drum-beat of her heart quietened.

How incredibly glad she was.

Aaron felt her way along the brickwork. She found a crack between two bricks and pushed the nail in. Stamped on it with her bare foot, bent the nail, ignored the pain.

*Please don't break! Please don't break! Please don't break!*

It didn't.

She guided the nail into the lock. Wiggled it. Registered that it opened.

She pushed the nail back into the wall and bent it straight.

*Please don't break! Please don't break! Please don't break!*

It didn't.

A small chink was enough to see Boenisch. He was striding back and forth, every footstep accompanied by a sob, his back turned towards her. The cat sat on the sofa and stared at Aaron.

She had only this one chance. She pushed the door open completely. Tensed her muscles.

At that moment Boenisch turned off the music.

Her pulse raced to over two hundred.

Boenisch picked up the phone.

Too much adrenalin. She was frozen.

When he had dialed four numbers, he was about to turn around with the phone in his hand. The cat jumped past him on to the windowsill and, hissing, swept a flowerpot to the floor. During the second in which he was distracted, Aaron fought down the adrenalin and threw all her strength into five steps across the stone floor. She rammed the nail into the back of Boenisch's neck and drove it right in almost as far as it would go. He uttered a dull gurgle. His hands flailed in the void. She pulled the nail back out and leaped backwards. Blood sprayed into her face. Boenisch toppled over without a sound. There was a sauce stain on his shirt. His eyes gazed pleadingly. Aaron felt a crazed desire to let him bleed to death like a stuck pig.

She sat down on the sofa and watched Boenisch dying.

The cat paid him no attention. It trotted over to Aaron and jumped into her lap. Purred. Its white eye was shut, and it looked as if it was winking with the black one. Aaron stroked its thin back.

When she turned her head, she saw her father sitting beside her, as he had done on the day she passed her police entrance exam, and they took a rest on a bench after a long walk.

*Where? In the forest? In the park? On the Rhine? Was I excited? Did he show me how proud he was of me? And my mother? Did she pretend to be happy for me?*

She remembered his words: "Before flying to Mogadishu there was something I kept from Wegener, otherwise I wouldn't have been allowed to go on the mission. Jürgen Schumann, the captain of the *Landshut*, had been a star fighter pilot and stationed at Büchel military airport; at the same time when I served there in Airborne Brigade 26. A really good guy, ten years older, he took me under his wing and helped me a lot when I had a problem with my superiors. In Mogadishu the first thing I heard after landing was: 'The bastards have shot the pilot!' At that point I should have said it; you won't get anywhere in this job without emotional detachment. I kept my mouth shut. We neutralized three terrorists, Souhaila Andrawes alone survived. She was lying by the toilet at the back, severely wounded, she'd been kicked aside. The others got the hostages out. I could have done it. Bullet between the eyes. The end. I thought about it. Just for one second. When Andrawes was carried out she made the victory sign for the cameras. It was still the right thing to do, though. Never forget that."

Aaron called for support and an ambulance. While waiting she stroked the cat. They told her she'd been in the basement for eight hours. If they'd said two days or two weeks, she would have believed that too.

The siren ends lunch break in Tegel. "What do you like most about *Mr. Brooks*?" she asks Boenisch.

He doesn't reply.

"Don't worry, you can tell me, we can both keep secrets."

The sound of a plane, right above their heads, beginning to land. The roar of the turbines devours Boenisch's words.

"I didn't hear you."

"The main character," Boenisch says again.

"Mr. Brooks, the respected citizen who goes out night after night, kills people at random and never gets caught?"

"Mr. Brooks isn't the main character."

"What?"

"You know who the main character is!"

"Tell me."

"Smith!"

"The man who blackmails Mr. Brooks so that he can go with him when he commits his murders? Someone who isn't capable of killing people himself? What does he have to do with you? Since when have you just wanted to watch?"

"No, Smith could have done it! Mr. Brooks takes him to the cemetery so that Smith will shoot him. Smith pulls the trigger! He pulls the trigger!"

"Mr. Brooks had made the firing pin unusable."

"But Smith doesn't know that! He pulled the trigger!"

"So? He'd known for ages that Mr. Brooks wouldn't let himself be shot just like that. For Mr. Brooks it was a game. Smith is a pitiful coward."

Boenisch wails. Aaron calls: "Niko?" He comes in. "Mr. Boenisch and I are going to take a little break."

"No! I don't need a break!"

You do, she thinks as she and Niko leave the room. She wants Boenisch to get wound up again.

To become as greedy for her as he was at the start.

Outside Block Six Aaron takes a deep breath. She wishes she hadn't given Bukowski her last cigarette. "Will you get Dr. Breuer's notes from the Psychology Service? I'll wait here."

She feels Niko moving away. She can't hear his footsteps, even though they must be crunching on the snow.

Ten things that Aaron likes to hear:
Janis Joplin
children's laughter
the sea at turning ebb tide
a pencil on paper
rain on a corrugated iron roof
Harley-Davidsons
sparrows in the spring
the click of her Dupont lighter
the page of a book being turned
purring

Unconsciously she turns her face towards Jungfernheide, the nearby forest. She's a long way from a road, she feels springy moss under her shoes, twigs brushing the back of her neck, she hears the rustle of little birds and wonders when she was there last.

When she was carried out of Boenisch's house she asked after his cat. No one had seen it. After she was allowed to leave hospital, Aaron went immediately to Spandau and talked to Boenisch's neighbors, but they didn't know where the cat had ended up either. She stuck pieces of paper with her phone number on lamp posts and trees in the area. No one had seen the cat. No one ever called.

But then, months later, she woke up in her flat, and something was nipping at her big toe.

Marlowe.

Her black, smug, fat cat, who had come dancing into her life overnight, as if he had known he had to step in for someone else.

Aaron can't remember where he suddenly arrived from. Her favorite idea is that he traveled on the roof of the car when she came out of a chocolate shop where she had been buying some *langues de chat*.

She doesn't know how old he was when he arrived, but she does know that they immediately belonged together. He made it quite clear that he had sought her out. When she went to bed he lay in the crook of her arm and purred her to sleep because he knew she was afraid of her dreams. Every morning he nibbled at her big toe at exactly waking-up time, and didn't go to his food bowl until she was having breakfast too. He snuggled with her when she needed him to and left her in peace when she had to concentrate on a thought. He was busy with cat matters and very serious and her best friend.

*Thank you for allowing me that opportunity.*

She never discovered how Marlowe spent his days. But when she got out of her car he was always sitting fat and round on the windowsill waiting for her, although she never had a sense that he had been lonely. Aaron sat down on the sofa, the cat hunkered on the table, and they played that game that you play with your eyes, where you have to shut your eyes and try and guess who's going to look again first.

Later, when she was with the Department, she spent a lot of evenings at Sandra and Pavlik's, and every time Marlowe knew in advance. He liked them, and their children. He sat expectantly by the door or happily on the windowseat, and when he was with the twins he would even pretend for their benefit that he was interested in a ball or a toy car because he knew they liked it.

*But he didn't like Niko. Was he jealous?*

She often had to leave him on his own, sometimes for weeks at a time, and when she did so she gave him to an old lady in the building who was alone and enjoyed Marlowe's company. When Aaron came back, he jumped into her arms, bumped her with his head for a moment to say hello, and wasn't hurt because he knew she must have had good reasons for being away.

One morning she slept in because Marlowe hadn't woken her. He was very weak and breathing quietly. Terrified, she drove him to the vet. It was a tumor. He wouldn't live long, but he wasn't in pain, they told her.

The following day Aaron was supposed to go on a mission that would last a long time. She wanted to take her annual leave. Her boss was sick, and his deputy said it was impossible. Aaron announced that she would quit the service. She got the leave. For many hours she rocked Marlowe in her arms and told him what he meant to her. She knew he understood and felt exactly the same. When she woke up the next morning, he had fallen peacefully asleep in the crook of her arm while watching over her dreams as always. She buried him under a birch tree in the Jungfernheide and went often to his grave and talked to him until she flew to Barcelona.

Could she ask Niko to drive her there afterwards? No, Niko wouldn't understand.

He comes as silently as he had disappeared. She gives a start when he says: "I've got the medical notes."

Two minutes later she is sitting opposite Boenisch again. Aaron senses his impatience. But first she has to go back to the night when she saved his life and his house was swarming with police officers.

# 4

WHY WOULD someone like Boenisch, who had two blood-drained women's corpses in the basement and a third victim, injured, defenseless, still to look forward to, make a phone call?

And who to?

The four numbers on Boenisch's phone had the area code for Kassel. One was a number he had called a few times. It belonged to a man called Helmut Runge. The police dragged him out of bed at dawn. A traveling salesman in bathroom tiles, fifty-two, married, thirteen-year-old daughter, a son about to leave school. A life as interesting as dust on a sideboard. Runge said he had met Boenisch a few years before in a pub in Spandau, when he was in Berlin on a sales trip. They had met now and again, darts, cinema, sometimes for a drink. Boenisch was a poor bastard, he said, he had no one to talk to, he sometimes called up and droned on. But two dead women… Runge drank down a glass of schnapps at six in the morning.

The most remarkable thing that the search of his house brought to light was the collection of Kinder eggs in his den. Runge had alibis for the days when the women had disappeared: on the first he was at a sales reps' seminar in Minden, on the second at a birthday party in Peine where he had stayed until midnight. Thirty witnesses, including his wife.

At that point it was quite clear to the investigators: Boenisch had acted on his own.

Hour after hour Aaron stood behind the two-way mirror and watched the interrogation. Boenisch's eyes were one big waterfall.

Again and again he cracked his head against the tabletop. "I did it! I did it! I did it!"

They showed him photographs of some missing women, unsolved cases from the past few years. Boenisch admitted to murdering two joggers and took the police to the place in Spandau Forest where he had buried the body parts. There was no doubt that he was the perpetrator.

But Aaron couldn't forget the bowl of mouldy leftover food in Boenisch's basement. The women hadn't been killed immediately after their abduction, and in the days that followed Helmut Runge could easily have been in Berlin. He was on a sales tour of Sachsen-Anhalt—"they order tiles like lunatics." That was only a hundred and twenty kilometers away.

No one would listen to her. She was injured, traumatized, they said, she needed to recover and forget. She had to wear a cast for six weeks, during which time she was exempted from her probation period.

Her father came to Berlin. He asked the right questions: was the record scratched? How many steps were there? What sort of nail was it?

With him she could cry at last.

*Is that all I want?*

*Did I ever cry before I woke up in Berlin?*

But he too said: *You've got to forget it.*

Never.

On the website of Runge's employer Aaron found a report on a sales reps' seminar. Runge had the second-highest sales figures in the northern area. He held a trophy aloft. She enlarged the photograph. His fingernails were yellow, untended, almost like claws. Why could no one else see that? Aaron immediately thought about Boenisch shining the torch at her and sobbing: "What am I supposed to do with them?"

Why did he want to call Runge, of all people?

"I needed to talk to someone about something, distract myself so that I didn't kill the one in the basement too quickly."

Aaron bought half a bookshelf of specialist literature. The first sentences came from Charles Manson: "If ever a devil existed on earth, it's me. He took over my head whenever he wanted."

Evil is a moral parameter, not an algorithm. And yet among all serial killers, with the exception of snipers, there are constants as valid as mathematical axioms.

The "butcher" adapts the murders to the situation, improvises, and acts randomly and spontaneously.

Boenisch, on the other hand: "I thought for a long time about which one I would take. And that's exactly when I was given chocolate by Miss Marx for taking her car to the car wash. That's when I knew: she's the one! And that Lamprecht one was always so stuck up, come on, jump to it! She really got on my nerves."

The butcher is incapable of developing feelings for other people, and sees them only as objects. Shifting a chair has the same significance as torturing, killing, dismembering the body and eventually throwing the parts away like rubbish.

Did that apply to Boenisch?

Everyone in the office building said that he never forgot a birthday, kept aspirin and plasters ready in the drawer for emergencies, he visited sick people in hospital. The neighbors said he was always ready to help. At Halloween the children liked to ring on his doorbell because he was so good at pretending to be scared; they got by far the most sweets from him. In hard winters, when he came home at six in the morning after the night shift, he cleared the snow for the whole street and scattered sand on the pavement.

Type two is the "planner," a much rarer species. The nice guy that everyone likes. He has a steady job, a regular life.

Like Boenisch.

The planner carefully chooses the crime scene. Everything has to be perfect; a quiet, safe place.

Like Boenisch's basement.

He never changes his plan, he needs that for maximum satisfaction. The slightest change would destroy everything.

Both times he had waited for the late end of a working day, anaesthetized the women in the underground car park with chloroform, and only after the days of the fattening phase, in which anticipation feeds the imagination until it's as fat as foie gras, cut their throats in the basement.

Did not rape, or at least did not penetrate, either of them. He claimed to have done exactly the same thing with the two girls in the forest. Chloroform, basement, waiting, throats, decomposition.

But had Boenisch taken pictures of the corpses? No. Had he kept a souvenir in the house, a piece of jewelery or clothing that he could play with whenever he liked? No. Had he crept around the houses of the families to catch a glimpse of their suffering and get additionally turned on?

"Ordinarily on the way to work I have to go past Lamprecht's house, so I took a detour."

Too many no's.

Boenisch doubtless had murderous fantasies and necrophiliac obsessions. But Aaron thought he only wanted to murder—and couldn't. He had carefully sought out the women and locked them in his basement, a highly arousing piece of foreplay. Someone else had killed them, someone with whom he had engaged in a kind of symbiosis, like a blenny and a moray eel. Reinhold Boenisch was allowed to watch and keep the corpses.

The basement was his paradise.

He even took sexual satisfaction from being arrested. He masturbated while giving his confessions, he thought it was wonderful that he was seen as the perpetrator, and that people saw him as the man that he so wished he was. Compassion would have been an extra kick.

He tried everything, but no one gave it to him.

Only Aaron, now. "I know it's very hard for you. Was the break long enough, or should we wait a little longer?"

He says hastily: "No, that's fine." She hears him energetically rubbing his cuffed wrists. "How blind are you? Can't you see anything?"

"Why Melanie Breuer?"

"She reminded me of someone."

*Now you're hoping I'll ask: who?*

*You'd love to tell me, you really would.*

"How did you feel when you went to her?"

Boenisch's breath scratches disappointedly in his throat. "There was always the pressure in my head. She must have noticed. She was an expert."

"What happened when she came into your cell?"

"She looked at my books. But not that one. I put it away."

"And then?"

"We drank tea. Side by side, there's not much room. She wasn't wearing perfume, but she smelled good. Exactly as I imagined. She touched my arm. My hands were on fire."

"How did she like her tea? With or without sugar?"

Aaron knows that Boenisch doesn't like sugar. He lacks a protein molecule, an anomaly, one in a hundred thousand, a marginal note in his medical file.

"Without."

She tries to irritate him. "I've asked around. Dr. Breuer only ever drank her tea with sugar. Why are you lying?" He tugs so hard on his handcuffs that she pushes her chair half a meter back.

"Perhaps the break wasn't long enough after all."

He pleads. "No, please! I'm sorry!"

In her fourth week off work, Aaron's collarbone had recovered sufficiently that she was able to drive all the way to Kassel. The two murders were fresh, Helmut Runge must still have been in the cooling-off phase. Over the next little while a new victim was unlikely, but perhaps he would make a mistake, take Aaron to the hiding place where he kept his souvenirs.

She prepared to follow him on a sales tour in her rattly Beetle. No need. Runge was on holiday, and spent it with his family on the allotment. Aaron took a room in the bed and breakfast with the fat landlady who always watched her curiously when she went out of the house with her camera. There are no tourists in Kassel.

Once Aaron stared provocatively back, and the woman murmured: "A cat can look at a queen."

Runge made a bird house, grilled pork chops with other allotment-keepers, went canoeing with his son, went on an excursion with his wife and children to Heide Park near Soltau, lay in his hammock, solved crosswords, read war stories.

*What did the bird house look like? He painted it. In what color? Was it a canoe, or was it a dinghy? What was going on in my mind when I lay at last in the forest glade and watched Runge through the telephoto lens? Was I furious because he was behaving so normally? Did I hope I was wrong?*

Her mother called. Her voice was filled with concern. And she knew nothing about Boenisch and his cellar. Her father said it was better that way. Aaron had invented a sporting accident, stupid, but quickly healed.

Her mother asked: "Won't you come to ours? You have friends here, they'll be delighted."

"Oh, Mum, I have to swot so much for college. And in two weeks I've got to carry on with my probation period."

Meanwhile she didn't take her eyes off Runge for a second.

"Take care, sweetie," her mother said sadly.

"Sure." She focused the viewfinder. Runge was having his wife rub his back with sun cream. She put on a little too much and recoiled when he suddenly lashed out at her.

One morning the fat bed-and-breakfast landlady was sitting behind her table crying. At first Aaron tried to pretend she hadn't noticed, thinking the woman wouldn't want a complete stranger poking her nose into her life, but when she was standing in the doorway she heard another sob and asked: "What's wrong?"

They had a coffee together. The woman was glad to have someone to talk to. Her daughter had abandoned her studies, Geography and Physics, at a time when they were taking on teachers. It was her ex-husband's fault. He owned a bar in Hanover, and had persuaded his daughter to start with him as a business manager, telling her she would be able to earn a lot more money. She had always been Daddy's girl, and if he had had an ice-cream stall in Greenland she would probably have gone there too.

Aaron realized how good it felt to listen to someone. That was one of the reasons why she had wanted to become a police officer: listening, with a view to understanding someone's fate, because it's only then that you can act in a just way. She wasn't yet aware that she would become a quite different type of police officer, and follow her father on to the thin ice, beneath which you could see the faces of the dead with every step you took.

Now she was involving herself in the concerns of the woman who no longer knew what to do; she saw her child rushing headlong into disaster, just as she herself had done when she had married that man. She couldn't remember what she had once seen in him. She shook her head and sighed: "It never rains but it pours."

While Aaron struggled to find the right words and recommended that the three of them sit down and discuss the matter, she couldn't help thinking of her own mother. She would talk to her friends in a very similar way, telling them how despondent she was that Aaron wanted to become a police officer because of her father, too young to understand what sort of life it would be and what it meant for her mother. She only had Aaron and her husband. Now she would have to worry about both of them.

The fat landlady gratefully shook her hand. "That was a huge help." When Aaron left, the woman's heart was a little lighter and her own a little heavier.

*As if it was yesterday. I even remember that the stocking on her right leg was laddered.*

A day earlier than Aaron's planned return to Berlin, Runge's daughter fell off her bicycle on to a stony path. She hobbled tearfully to the allotment, her knee covered with blood. Her mother threw her hands over her head and treated the wounds inside the house. Runge didn't budge from his hammock. He set his book down and dozed.

Aaron called the Homicide Unit and asked if she could stay away for another week. Of course. Take as long as you like.

Nothing for the next two days. But in the two after that Runge did something strange. He drove alone to the station in Kassel. There he sat for hours in the station hall. No paper, no book, no one to pick up. He was absorbed in himself and didn't move. Like a salamander on a cold stone.

On the second day Aaron waited until he left the station and then stumbled into him carrying a city map. "I'm sorry, can you help me? I'm looking for the Brothers Grimm Museum."

Runge didn't know her, he had never seen her before. His eyes were tar-stained pebbles, his voice thin and inexpressive. His horny yellow claw ran over the map. "It's not far at all. Straight on, right at the crossroads, second left, then you're walking straight towards it."

"Very kind, thank you. I got lost. That's what it's like when you don't have anyone to walk with you."

*You're the big bad wolf.*

*But believe me, I'm not Little Red Riding Hood.*

If Runge had offered to show her around a bit, perhaps with an outing to Wilhelmshöhe, a little trip that was worth it because you had a wonderful view, she would have got into his car, and once he revealed what he was, shot him without hesitation with the Starfire in her handbag. But he wished her a good day with his salesman's smile.

Aaron went back to the Homicide Unit. The fact that she, a twenty-year-old agent on probation, was the only one to have spotted the contradictions in Boenisch's statements, won her considerable respect. However, there was also much shaking of heads that she could be so reckless as to drive to Spandau on her own. An experienced colleague saw how distracted she was, and was concerned about her. Aaron was on the point of confessing to her.

But she didn't.

Before Christmas she had a week's holiday. She hired a car and followed Runge through the Bremen area. He did his rounds, joked with the customers, watched television in the evening in his cheap hotel, turned the light out early, had a fish sandwich at lunchtime, always taking out the onions, bought Christmas presents for his family. A pearl necklace, nine hundred and eighty marks; Backstreet Boys concert ticket for his daughter, Stadthalle Kassel, forty-three marks; briefcase for his son, who was starting to train as a banker, one hundred and nineteen marks.

On the third evening he drove to a little restaurant in Delmenhorst. But he didn't get out. He sat in the car and looked through the brightly lit window with the sticker saying "Zum krummen Eck," in honor of a nearby mountain resort. Aaron parked on the other side of the road and saw the waitress joking with the customers.

She checked the magazine of the Starfire.

Runge waited until the restaurant closed. The waitress stepped out on to the pavement. She was one of those women whose dreams of a life that they have never lived lie pasted on their faces like a thick layer of make-up. She got into Runge's car. They kissed, and looked as if they knew each other. He gave her a prettily wrapped box. She threw her arms around him and kissed him on the lips. He put the pearl necklace around her neck.

Aaron couldn't move. She followed Runge and the woman to a block of flats in a run-down part of town. When the curtains were drawn on the first floor and the light went out, her heart was beating as hard as it had in Boenisch's basement. What was she supposed to do? Warn the woman? And then? She would hardly believe her, and she would tell Runge everything. She certainly wasn't in immediate danger, or else he wouldn't have bought her the pearl necklace. Would he give a gift like that to a victim? Probably not. He must have known the woman for a long time, and killing her wouldn't have fitted in with his scheme. Those thoughts, which collided like the balls on a Newton's cradle, haunted Aaron's night.

She started from her sleep in the first dirty light of morning.

Aaron hadn't noticed that she had parked in a disabled space. Two bored policemen had stopped their patrol car and knocked on the window. They asked to see her disabled permit. Aaron asked woozily if they didn't have anything better to do. And then she had to get out for a telling off.

The door of the building opposite opened. The waitress, wearing her dressing gown, said goodbye to Runge. She was still wearing the necklace. When he walked to his car, he saw Aaron with the two policemen. He stopped and recognized her.

Runge showed no reaction.

As he got into the car he dropped his key.

She spent Christmas Eve with her parents. The presents had been unwrapped; her mother was making dinner on her own, just because Aaron is absolutely hopeless at cooking.

Her father murmured: "Right, let's take a walk around the block."

A deserted street, New Year's Eve fireworks already going off. Silent, cold, restless night. Aaron knew her father had seen through her, and got everything off her chest. The perpetrator's profile, her "time off from her probation period," the moment when Runge lay peacefully in his hammock. His lover in Delmenhorst. The only things she left out were the Brothers Grimm Museum and the loaded Starfire in her handbag.

"So he's having it off with the waitress. It happens."

"And his reaction to his daughter's injury?"

"Maybe it wasn't his day."

"He was totally relaxed. And the girl was bleeding really badly."

"Maybe his old woman was getting on his nerves."

"He doesn't even see his wife."

"I know a few guys at Sixth Homicide. Good people."

She stopped furiously. "Have you even been listening to me?"

He put a reassuring arm around her and they walked on. "When you were little, a couple lived in that house over there, he was a master electrician, I'm sure you won't remember them. They came to dinner once. There was bad blood between them and I had to keep topping up his schnapps glass. Eventually the women went and chatted in the garden, probably about clothes, and he vented his spleen. They had a poodle."

*What was he talking about?*

"He snapped: 'Bloody awful mutt. Every morning there was a yellow stain on the carpet in my study. My wife was away at a spa for two weeks, and I dumped the brute in the forest. On Friday she came back, I told her the dog had run away. She went nuts and put up signs all over the place. Yesterday the damned thing found its way back, but only just. Since then my wife hasn't said a word to me. This morning it turned out that the stain in my study was from a broken heating pipe. I'm a dead man walking.'"

Again they stopped.

"The obvious thought is sometimes the right one. But sometimes you just can't accept it. You need to lock up Boenisch and Runge forever. If you don't do that, you'll go round the bend."

She knew her father was right.

Boenisch stood trial in February. The unusual gravity of the crime was established. Boenisch was given life followed by preventive detention. When he was sentenced he burst into convulsive tears.

Sixteen years later he's crying again. Aaron hears him forcing out the same thick, eager tears as before.

"Why did you suffocate Dr. Breuer with the plastic bag? You could have throttled her, wouldn't that have been more arousing?"

"She asked if I wanted to change my job," he sniffs in something half-way between a sob and a hiccup. "She talked and talked. I silenced her. It's so lovely when they're quiet. Like in a glider, when you can only hear the wind."

"The plastic bag was opaque. But you love seeing fear in women's faces. What do you get from a fight to the death that you can't even see properly?"

He thinks. Hates the question. Chokes on his tears as if they were an unusually big piece of meat. "The bag was all I had."

"There are plenty of transparent ones in the laundry."

He tries to sound even more afflicted; perhaps then she would change the subject from that bloody bag. "I was so disgusted with myself."

*When she came in in the morning the wallpaper seemed to brighten.*

Aaron puts her phone away and gets to her feet. "No, you weren't. You're a coward who lets someone like Bukowski beat him up so that he can complain, someone who gets an erection when people think he's a murderer. You're not Mr. Brooks. You're Smith. A bedwetter. And you and I are finished now."

Boenisch roars like an animal. "I'll kill you, you whore! I'll finish you off! I'll pull your blind eyes out! Cunt!"

Aaron is scared that the radiator will come away from the wall. The door flies open. Niko. He leads Aaron out of the room.

"I should have stabbed you back then! Drunk your blood!"

Last of all she hears the prison officer: "Shut it, or I'll slap you one."

She can hardly wait to wash her hands.

Snow creaks under his shoes like peanut brittle. Niko asks no questions. He's good at that. Aaron used to be good at that too.

In her first life the questions were different. Which legend you choose. How much manpower you need. Which weapons.

The answers always helped you to concentrate on the facts. The best position. The perfect second. The safest lie. Aaron wishes such answers existed now.

"Hi." The man they pass isn't a prisoner. She registers a trace of clean sweat and sun cream.

Ten smells that Aaron likes:
  freshly tarred roads
  country bonfires
  dubbin
  a forest after rain
  peppermint tea in Marrakech
  her skin

currywurst
sawdust
"Eau d'Issey" by Issey Miyake
hot chestnuts

The prison administration is in Section II. Aaron feels the star-shaped Wilhelmine monster looming in front of her, the "spider" in which Alfred Döblin has Franz Biberkopf locked up in *Berlin Alexanderplatz*, the intimidating mass. Red bricks, bullet holes from the war, behind them the streets of cells, arranged in a star shape, level with the first floor the rusty metal net that is supposed to prevent suicides.

Aaron doesn't know Director Hans-Peter Maske, who took up the position four years ago. "Miss Aaron, Mr. Kvist, please sit down." He speaks quickly, trying to adopt a routine tone, but the tension can be heard in his voice.

He tries to adopt the voice he would use for routine matters, but Aaron notices how tense he is. Niko walks her to the lounge area, and she runs her hand over the back of the armchair.

Aaron runs her fingers along the arm of the chair in the meeting room.

"Can I get you something to drink?"

"No, thanks."

Maske pours himself a cup of coffee. It smells resinous, bitter, almost metallic. Chrysanthemum. When Aaron turns her head to the left, the smell gets stronger.

*Desk job.*

"Celebrating something?"

"A promotion. From March I'm going to be in charge of the office for the Execution of Penal Sentences in the Senate."

"Congratulations."

"Thanks."

She doesn't like his voice. There's something fake about it, like a smile when you've been insulted, or pursed lips concealing bad teeth.

Maske opens a little plastic container of coffee cream. "Of course we're all very upset about Dr. Breuer. Terrible."

"I'm sure you have an idea what happened?" Aaron asks.

Maske's words assume powerful overtones which immediately make him sound aggressive. "It's not rocket science."

"Meaning?"

"Boenisch will be transferred to the closed psychiatric institute. Where, in my modest opinion, he should have been for the last sixteen years."

Aaron is aware that when he gives this answer Maske is facing not her but Niko. She's familiar with that from many conversations. Some people don't see her because Aaron doesn't see them. With others it's thoughtlessness. There have also been some who have sensed that she notices, and do it on purpose, to hurt her.

"Boenisch has a novel about a serial killer and a film on the same subject. I assume that neither of these come from your library. How could such a thing get through the postal check? Didn't any of the screws notice?"

"Would it be asking too much to avoid using that term for our prison officers? It's discriminatory."

"And would it be asking too much to look at me when you're talking to me?"

"I'm sorry." He blows into his cup and takes a sip. She imagines that he licks the rim when he's alone. "We'll try and trace the paper trail."

A rub of coarse fabric. Jeans. Next to Aaron, Niko crosses his legs. "Mr. Maske, could it be that everyone here was thinking: Boenisch is never going to get out of here anyway?" he asks. "So it doesn't matter what he watches or reads?"

"I can't tell you what six hundred and fifty-five prison officers think."

"Officers who have to follow rules. In other areas, the tax office, for example, that mightn't mean much. But here it does. I don't know how they're going to take that at the Senate."

Aaron suppresses a smile. Guys like Maske are a red rag to Niko. It might be fun to see what would happen if the director irritated him a little more.

"Polemics won't get you anywhere with me."

"Yeah? That's not the sense I have."

Maske brings his cup crashing down.

"You spilled a bit," Niko says, topping himself up.

"Is it possible that there was a second man in the cell, who left it unnoticed shortly after recreation began?"

Aaron's question is rhetorical. All prisoners wait for the moment when the block is opened. They do deals, they run to weight training or yard exercise, dash around, let off steam, join the seething mass along with the officers.

Maske's voice gets a touch higher. "Hang on. You're trying to suggest that there was a second perpetrator?"

"No. I'm trying to say that Boenisch isn't the perpetrator at all."

"Please. That's ridiculous."

"Why?"

"Have you got a witness?"

Now Aaron has had enough. "Mr. Maske, when you come home in the evening, and the streets are dry, but in the morning you look out of the window and there is thick snow on the ground, you know that it's been snowing. Do you need a witness for that?"

"At the time in question there were sixty prisoners on that floor. Perhaps you should question them all," Maske replies.

Of course he knows the rules by which power, and its lack, are distributed among the prisoners. Whoever it was who murdered Melanie Breuer, he will be a man to fear. If there is a witness, he's not about to say anything.

Aaron gets to her feet. "I want a list of all the prisoners in Block Six. Reasons for their arrest, group behavior, psychological assessments. By tomorrow, if you would be so kind."

Maske's voice becomes thin and high. "Does Miss Aaron have the authority to make such requests?"

Niko gets to his feet as well. "No. But I'll talk to my colleagues from Fourth Homicide, who are working on the case. They'll give you a call."

"You probably think that because you're from the Department you can just swan in and do anything you like?"

Aaron stops by the door. "I wonder whether the film and the novel had to pass through a check. Boenisch could just as easily have got them from a prison officer. So I would also like the names of anyone who had contact with him. Or even better: their personal files."

It would be really nice to see Maske's face right now. But it's just as nice to imagine what his evening's going to be like.

Aaron carefully feels her way down the stairs, steps slippery with snow brought in from outside, and she's grateful for the banister. They step into the cold sun. She tries to imagine a blue sky and can't remember what blue looks like.

At twenty-one she graduated best in year, and got nine job offers. She opted for the LKA, the State Office of Criminal Investigation in Berlin. Her special abilities were quickly recognized. Only four years later Aaron had to fight for her life with Nikulin's hitman in Moscow.

In that same winter Helmut Runge had a serious car accident. He was revived but died in hospital. In his boot they found the corpse of a woman from Wolfsburg who had been missing for two weeks. Runge was carrying a key to the lockers in Kassel station. In locker number three there was a suitcase containing his mementoes.

Hair. Jewelery. Underwear. Toenails. Teeth.

The pearl necklace, his Christmas present for the waitress from Delmenhorst, was in there too—he had killed her on her fortieth birthday. Thirteen murders in all, the first ten years before, the last three after Boenisch was sentenced. The two joggers, to whose buried body parts Boenisch had brought the police, were also among them. But there were no souvenirs of the women in Boenisch's basement.

It was assumed that the two men had met over the internet, a space that was still outside the law in those days, where one was largely unobserved. There was no proof. Boenisch continued to insist that he had killed the women alone.

# 5

As they drive along the city freeway she doesn't get a single glance from Niko, at least none penetrating enough for her senses. And still not one single question.

*Thanks.*

Headquarters is on Budapester Strasse in the western part of the city. The Department belongs neither to the LKA nor to the BKA, and it doesn't appear on any organization chart.

No one applies to join. You get recruited.

After the arrest of Ilya Nikulin, Aaron's phone rang. It quickly became clear to her that the man who had asked her for a meeting in the Ministry of the Interior was familiar with her career from police academy onwards. Every investigation, every judgement, every distinction.

Her future boss said: "We want you."

"Who's 'we'?"

"It's our task to go where it would be pointless to deploy any other forces."

Witness protection, not even entrusted to the BKA.

Hostage rescue operations for which fully equipped Special Enforcement Commandos—SEK—would be too conspicuous and too slow. Where the body is the weapon.

Handing over the ransom money in kidnapping cases.

High-risk undercover investigations.

Secret operations for Europol.

Anti-terrorism through infiltration.

Precision work.

"Of course we'll give you time to think."

She didn't need it.

There isn't much that Aaron misses. The camaraderie, yes; the solidarity between them, which was so close because no one else understood them. They were there for each other. When a second woman joined them after three years, Aaron spent a lot of time with her, wanting to help her adjust to a life that no one can prepare you for. She talked to the woman for a long time after she had killed for the first time, and knew that there were no words to make it easier.

*She started losing her spirit. You get used to it.*

Her colleague only stayed for a year and then agreed to be transferred. Aaron doesn't miss the adrenalin. Guns, fine. But it's a consolation that she will never again have to take a human life.

*Only the one. You or him.*

Niko comes out on the Kaiserdamm, which is actually a detour. Aaron can tell by the fact that it's uphill. When she collected visitors at Tegel airport she used to go that way too, for the view.

It didn't happen often. Her mother, once a year. What was Aaron supposed to talk to her about, if the life she led was confidential? They loved each other. But within an hour they'd told each other everything. After those few days they always parted reassured. Still, Aaron was left with an aching feeling at the airport.

Every now and again her two remaining schoolfriends came to visit. They thought she worked for the Fraud Squad. But it was good to fish out the old stories. In *The Grass Harp* by Truman Capote there are two sentences that describe Aaron: "I was eleven, then I was sixteen. Though no honors came my way, those were the lovely years."

She was pleased most of all to see Mary-Sue, the daughter, the same age as herself, of the guest family Aaron had stayed with for six months in Arizona, in Cayenne, the only town in a seventy-mile radius. There was only one color there, but it had lots of names: crab-tail red, double-bass red, basketball red, clown's-nose red, rubber-raft red, coral-snake red, tongue red. Dusty, dirty, swirling, magic red.

There was even "inner-pussy red" and "outer-pussy red," and for a seventeen-year-old bumpkin from the Rhineland that was a real shock. Aaron can't help smiling when she remembers.

*Blue is gone, but red is still there.*

Cayenne was where she first fell properly in love, of course with the quarterback of the high school team. Did they make out behind the shed at Mr. Payne's drugstore? Or in his room when his parents were away? Or in the desert, driving off into it in his father's pickup, which always looked as if it was covered with dust? Somewhere. Did she sleep with him, was he the first? Or was that Tim from the parallel class in Sankt Augustin? Were the two boys similar? Of course. Aaron has always liked boys like that, boys who don't boast even though they could. Who are a bit rebellious but still have manners, who work out and who know the novels of Max Frisch.

She drove into the city via Kaiserdamm with Mary-Sue from Cayenne as well; that was particularly good fun because it was the first time Mary-Sue had ever been there. Wow! Speer's "Germania," but the most beautiful axis in Berlin. A wide view across the Tiergarten to the Television Tower, in between the Victory Column with "Golden Elsa" who would be gleaming in the frosty sunlight right now.

*How clearly I can still see it all.*

"Sightseeing tour?" she asks, turning towards him.

"The sky is totally overcast. You can't see anything."

*And for that lie I thank you too.*

Aaron's favorite book by Frisch has always been *Gantenbein*. A man claims to be blind because he thinks that otherwise he won't be able to bear his life. As a blind man he doesn't have to judge anybody, not even himself. That's his liberation. He leaves other people with their secrets, because they were what tormented him, the impossibility of ignoring them. That way he can be happy.

On the other hand they expect her to see what sighted people can't, to sense the truth as she alone can. Listen to the sound of lies. They want her to judge. It isn't a liberation for her, it's a lonely prison. But she has one thing in common with Gantenbein: people who have something to hide are afraid of her when they work out that she isn't blind at all.

Perhaps in the end Gantenbein's last words will come true for her as well. Aaron tries to remember when she last had the feeling: "I like life."

Underground car park, diesel, tire rubber. The building has twenty storeys, but only four are rented by the Department. The others are divided between estate agents, legal offices, insurance agencies. None of their staff, however long they had been employed there, have any idea what happens on those four floors. From the separate area in the underground car park, which has its own entrance and is exclusively at the disposal of the Department, you have to enter a code beside a steel door to access the special lift.

He stops on the second floor. "You go on ahead," she says. "I'll follow you." No questions. She takes two more floors. Feels carpeted floor, her pumps are useless. Aaron clicks her fingers, but the sound is too diffuse. She rattles her stick along the doors, finds the right one and opens it a crack.

All the training halls smell the same.

Ambition. Rage. Frustration. Humiliation.

This one smells of something else: the memory of Boenisch's basement. *Fear is good, it keeps you awake.* She started learning karate at the age of eighteen, but it was only because of Boenisch that she *really* learned it.

Another smell: obsession. Her total will to eliminate any adversary, to be able to control any situation.

Aaron hears quick commands: "*Chinkuchi!*" Stabilization of the limbs. "*Kaishu!*" Hand open. "*Haishu!*" Hand closed. "*Yaze Neko!*" Strike, avoid. "*Chikara!*" Courage.

By the master's severe corrections she can tell that the Kata is part of preparation for the second Dan. She herself has a black belt in *Gōjū-ryū*, the most effective of the four Japanese styles. Aaron has reached the fifth Dan. To get to the next stage will take as many years as the level of each Dan; for the ninth she would have to be as old as her father. No one has the tenth, because it would mean that you can't make any more progress.

Or as her father said: "If someone has reached the tenth Dan, he's either spiritually dead or a total idiot."

Most Olympic fighters have the third Dan. Aaron passed the test for the fifth a year ago, blind.

*Don't see, know.*

Four times a week she trains on the Neroberg in Wiesbaden. None of the guys from the BKA like to fight with her. Admittedly, of all the senses, sight is the most dominant, but the cortex, that high-powered processing machine, has focused on new tasks and updated Aaron's perceptual abilities. Body warmth, breath, draft, vibration of the floor, instinct.

Reliable parameters.

The biggest problem was the lost physical feeling. Even a sighted person can barely stand on one leg for ten seconds with his eyes closed, because the fixed point is missing. For the same reason, many blind people are uncertain in their movements, because they don't know that it's worth training their sense of balance. After countless hours Aaron noticed that her balance, which she had always considered perfect, was on a new level.

She could dance on the tip of one toe.

Punch to the solar plexus. Elbow block. Splits. Hip rotation. Reverse crescent kick. Outer knife hand. Double strike. Crane. Inner knife hand Tiger.

The Bushidō says: everything is preordained and has its rightness. The warrior who recognizes this liberates himself. Even from the desire to live at any price.

The previous evening she bled herself dry on the Neroberg. At ten o'clock she was drinking beer in the men's changing room. She always showers at home anyway, and she doesn't learn anything from watching the boys. Then Boenisch snuggled up to the corpse in the spoons position and was happy.

Aaron is being observed. She feels that it's Niko, before he pulls her to him. She tries to defend herself, but also, even though it's only a hug, to lie to herself.

She can't.

No member of the Department has ever left a wounded comrade behind. She's the only one.

Aaron broke the seventh virtue of the Bushidō: *Chu*. Loyalty.

Now she is a blind Samurai, she has received her punishment.

She pulls away from Niko. "Let's go down."

On the second floor she is overwhelmed by sounds. Telephones, countless footsteps that she can't assign to anyone. Men whispering, a vacuum cleaner. She likes rooms that she can map, the clear definition of all the sounds: the creak of new carpet, the squeaking of a door in the wind, the quivering of water in a glass, the quiet heartbeat of reflection.

But she recognizes Ulf Pavlik. Not by his voice, by his gait. When he was in his early forties, he had a motorbike accident and lost the calf of his left leg. He went on taking his carbon prosthesis to the limit. *Does he still have the Agusta?*

He makes it easier for her and punches her on the arm. "Looking good."

She grins. "You too."

Two voices that ring a bell. Fricke and Wolter?

"Hey Aaron, put on weight?"

"Around the eyes."

Her laughter, which follows the moment of shock, lets Aaron know that Niko hasn't told them exactly what happened. They never got to read the report from Internal Affairs. For these men, Aaron was a machine and Barcelona was just bad luck, kismet.

But she knows.

The sixth virtue: *Meiyo*. Honor.

Lost.

Fricke taps her shoulder. "Got to go, see you tonight?"

"I've got a lot of work on."

"It's Pavlik's birthday."

*Damn it, I forgot.*

"He's turning fifty. We've clubbed together and we're giving him a Zimmer frame."

"Idiots," Pavlik replies. "I don't need a walking aid, I need a wheelchair."

She holds out a hand to him. "Come here, old man."

Aaron hugs him; his *latissimus dorsi* stiff as a trampoline, his upper arms and shoulders tough as iron; you have to be like that as a precision sniper, to absorb the recoil. Not a single gram of fat, peak training. At that moment she knows that he's been thinking about her a lot as well, and whispers: "Love you to bits."

"Afterwards. Roof terrace," he whispers back.

Pavlik goes with the others, and only now does she notice that Niko has gone too. That's one of the things she hates most: that people disappear from one second to the next, as if they'd never been there.

She stands there uncertainly, not knowing what to do, having lost her bearings when she hugged Pavlik, and wonders whether the lift is to her left or her right. She feels for the wall. Runs her hand along it. Touches smooth stone.

The memorial plaque for the men who were killed.

Aaron's fingers slide over the engraved letters, read the names. Seventeen comrades. For a few heartbeats she lingers over four of them. Three have been added, strangers.

As if from nowhere Niko is back. "Jenny—my boss—Inan Demirci."

"Hello, Miss Aaron." The voice is relatively low in her throat, almost free of tension and at the same time very controlled.

Aaron holds out her hand. Demirci's fingers are long, slender, firm. "Nice to meet you."

"I suggest we go to my office."

Niko takes Aaron by the arm, but Demirci says: "Thank you, Mr. Kvist, your presence will not be required."

# 6

THE ROOM is cool.

*She also likes to reflect.*

Aaron is very familiar with the office that her former boss furnished so functionally that all judgements were received quite calmly and matter-of-factly.

*Your decision was correct—self-defense—Internal Affairs exonerates you—your temporary suspension is lifted.*

She knows that Demirci has been in charge of the Department for just a month. She is only forty-seven, very young for such a high-profile position. Previously she was in charge of the Homicide Unit in Dortmund. The first Turkish woman, the first woman full stop, to have made it so far.

*Hence the slight tension in her voice. You have to be better and tougher than everyone else. Particularly here.*

The conference table is in its old spot. But in Aaron's mind it is no longer surrounded by chairs. Now they are *in front* of the table, because she has developed the habit of mentally arranging objects in sequence of contact.

"Would you like a coffee?"

"That would be great, thank you. Black, no sugar. But with a spoon, please."

If Demirci is surprised she doesn't show it. She pours coffee for Aaron and herself. A very good perfume, Aigner No. 2. *I assume she doesn't wear any make-up, or hardly any.* Aaron stirs her coffee and taps the spoon against the cup. A clear ringing sound, everything's just like before. Almost. She taps again, her mind apparently else-where, and receives a second, darker echo from the opposite wall.

Suddenly she thinks: there's someone standing there.

"You will be aware that Fourth Homicide called us in because of you. Do you mind if I record the conversation for my colleagues?"

"Of course not."

"Sixth of January. Killing of Melanie Breuer, psychologist in Tegel Correctional Facility. The accused, Reinhold Boenisch, was questioned by DSI Jenny Aaron. Miss Aaron, did Boenisch tell you anything?"

"Yes."

"Did he confess to the crime?"

"Yes."

"What motive did he give?"

"It doesn't matter. It wasn't him."

A truck drives past down below. The high-frequency hum of the window panes is the only sound for five seconds.

"What brings you to that conclusion?"

"Boenisch's capacity for repression. He isn't capable of murder. He can only do that in his imagination."

"He's serving a life sentence for four homicides."

"I'm sure of it. You read my statement at the trial."

*That's so much junk as far as you're concerned.*

"Miss Aaron, that must have been an incredibly dramatic situa-tion for you, traumatic, even, but I assumed that at a distance of so many years—"

"Can I present you with the facts?"

An irritable sigh. "Please do."

"First: Boenisch had himself beaten up by a fellow prisoner three days ago, to win my sympathy at the interview."

"Did Boenisch admit that to you?"

"No. But the prisoner he paid to carry out the attack did."

"I'd have said the same thing in his position."

"Second: Boenisch has a film in his possession. It's about a serial killer who never gets caught. In his imagination Boenisch assumes the identity of a minor character. He projects qualities of the murderer on to that character, qualities that he doesn't have in the film."

"Do I know this film?"

"*Mr. Brooks.*"

Demirci taps something down on a tablet.

*Ten-finger system, sixty words a minute, probably by touch. Perfectionist.*

"Third: he wouldn't tell me who gave him the film."

"What does that prove?"

"Fourth: Boenisch could hardly wait to talk to me about *Mr. Brooks.* He clearly got a lot of pleasure from the idea that I thought he was the perpetrator."

"A lot of murderers enjoy confessing."

"Fifth: he invited the victim into his cell. According to his attested personality profile he would have done that with the intention of killing. If that was the case, it means he had been in the excitation phase for twenty-four hours and exploded when Melanie came through the door. Except that Boenisch first drank tea with her."

"'*Melanie.*' You lack detachment."

"Are you of the view that we are dealing with cases and not with people?"

"Are you trying to lecture me?"

"Are you?"

A rustle of stiff paper. "He didn't necessarily issue the invitation with a view to committing a homicide. It may be that the situation was too much for him. I have the report from Forensics. My impression is that they've worked very carefully."

*The people from the Homicide Unit didn't even ask about Melly. They haven't even been here.*

"Sixth: the plastic bag he's supposed to have suffocated the woman with doesn't accord with his criminal profile."

"He improvised."

"Seventh: he hates improvising. Eighth: he suffers from Klinefelter Syndrome, a thyroid condition that led to unusual growth levels during puberty. He's two meters tall and unusually physically strong.

Melanie put up strong resistance. But Boenisch immediately saw to it that she couldn't move a millimeter."

"I have a feeling you're working towards a punchline."

"Whoever got hold of *Mr. Brooks* for him is the actual perpetrator. Boenisch was able to choose the victim and witness the killing. A win-win situation."

Aaron takes a sip of coffee.

Is nauseated.

Has another sip.

*Did he look at a photograph of Melanie Breuer? No, she'd come to that.*

Demirci clears her throat. "Of course I've heard of you. You were recruited by the Department at the age of twenty-five. No one before or after you has been as young as that. And you were the first woman. Now you're the only blind criminal profiler and specialist interrogator in Germany. At the request of the BKA president an official exception has been created for you. You have my respect."

"Ninth: Boenisch lost control when I shattered his self-image."

"Loss of control in an impulsive criminal. It's hardly an argument."

"Tenth: he already knew I was blind. How?"

Demirci chooses her words carefully. "Kvist told me you carried out the interrogation all by yourself. However capable you might be—do you really think you can grasp every aspect of a personality?"

*I was waiting for that one. And how elegantly you dodged the word "blind."*

At the BKA they only gave her a chance because of her name. No one could imagine that she would pass the tests. In fact she failed when she was given the minutes of the interrogation in Braille and told to identify the moments when the suspect gave himself away.

She asked to be able to hear the interrogations. She stood three times behind the two-way mirror. This time she got a high score and identified the crucial evidence.

*Feel your way between the words.*

*Guess what has gone unsaid.*

*Listen to the sound of lies.*

Now, when they get stuck on a case they say: *wait till Aaron has seen him.*

She gets to her feet. "I'll stay for as long as necessary. Kvist will find me the material for the rest of the investigation."

Demirci turns off the tape machine. "You've turned your phone off, so the BKA can't find you. They expect you in Wiesbaden as soon as possible."

*Did she make that up? No, it's true. We're under pressure.*

Aaron juts her chin towards the spot on the wall from which she received the dark echo.

"What's that?"

Demirci is speechless for a moment. "A suit of Ottoman armour from the fifteenth century. A present."

"It's good to have armour."

"A metaphor?"

"Personal experience."

Aaron gets into the lift and presses the button for the twentieth floor. The smell of roulades and over-boiled potatoes hangs in the cabin. The door opens, the wind tugs at her coat. Careful footsteps until she reaches the parapet at the edge of the roof terrace.

She knows she's looking westwards, into the sun, she feels greedy for light, even just the idea of it. Aaron imagines the world until it seems completely real to her, a fata morgana, hyper-real as a daydream.

She sees Zoo station, its gray steel merging with a low-hanging cloud that drifts in front of the sun. A bat drops from the roof, sweeps round the mosaic of the Neue Gedächtniskirche, which sparkles gaudily for a moment in a beam that pierces the cloud, darts like an arrow to avoid the light, seeks the cloud, finds it again above the Bikinihaus, dives to the baboon rock in the zoo and makes its way automatically to the cave where it has to wait because it's too early for hunting. The baboons ignore their familiar guest and raise their bright red rumps at a school class taking selfies. Aaron is absolutely sure they are the children who boarded the coach at the airport that morning. Even though it's only half-past three, the chains of Christmas lights that will hang over Tauentzien and Kurfürstendamm until early February are already coming on, glow worms in the frost, noticed by no one but a little girl with black curls, who has never been in such a big city before, pressing a bag of hot chestnuts to her, knows that her father is holding her other hand and is happy.

The evening is like a window blind slamming shut. The Christmas lights harshly stab the blackness that engulfs the girl and the city, become fainter, fainter, until they are just tiny smouldering dots on a radar screen. Then it's pitch black. Headaches eat their way into Aaron's eyes. Somewhere a stuttering starter motor, a flooded engine, a car-horn concerto, a plane.

At home she has a picture by the painter Eşref Armağan. Although he is blind from birth, he paints landscapes in wonderfully beautiful colors. Endless bridges over lonely bays where sailing boats dance. Lighthouses on cliffs, circled by albatrosses. Magical still lifes, bowls of fruit with pears, raspberries, honeydew melons so juicy you want to sink your teeth into them. Armağan was thought to be a charlatan until he was given tests at Harvard Medical School. He sat in a lightless bunker, observed by cameras, painted and silenced all the doubters.

When his visual brain activities were measured, they turned out to be those of a sighted person.

Aaron loves Armağan's painting, always has done. After her father died she bought one. It cost thirty thousand Euros, and she paid for it out of her inheritance. The dealer was surprised that a blind woman was buying a painting by a blind artist, and offered at least to describe to her what the picture showed. But she didn't want that. She touched the canvas, felt the rough relief of the colors under her fingers, because Eşref Armağan had painted this picture with his, and knew: *it's mine.*

It hangs in her bedroom. Aaron often looks at it and sees a woman standing on a dizzyingly high tightrope between the towers of Notre Dame, fearless because nothing can touch her, not even death.

A year after Barcelona the flat of a hoarder in Dresden needed to be cleared. A fire was burning between piles of rubbish and all that remained of *The Dream Dancers* was a charred scrap of sky. It wasn't the only painting he had stolen, but it was the last one he destroyed.

He said: "If I can't see it anymore, no one can."

Footsteps. Pavlik. Aaron turns around. "Have you got a cigarette? I'm out."

Something strikes her right hand, falls in the snow.

"Shit," growls Pavlik. "I bet Büker fifty Euros you'd be able to do it." He picks up the pack of unfiltered cigarettes, puts one in her hand, lights it for her and smokes as well.

"How's the Agusta?" she asks.

"I ride a Hayabusa now. Bright green, your color."

"What cc?"

"Just 200."

"Cool."

Her headache is getting worse. Aaron senses that Pavlik is weighing words and discarding them. What he says to her must be significant, because he's the man who's good at being succinct. In Barcelona he just asked when she was starting again.

She flicks her cigarette butt away. "OK, what is it?"

Pavlik looks past her, breathes shallowly. "Sascha Holm was transferred to Tegel a month ago."

She has heard two really bad sentences in her life.

*It's me, Butz.* And: *There's no point in operating.*

This is the third.

Sascha Holm is Token-Eyes, the brother of the man in Barcelona who called himself Egger. Later, when her father thought he could talk to her about it, Aaron found out that one of the three Catalans, fatally injured, had managed to make an emergency call. Ruben. While she was disappearing endlessly into the tunnel under Plaça de les Drassanes, the MEK—the Mobile Task Force—arrived at the warehouse. They did what Aaron had neglected to do. Niko was resuscitated by a doctor and saved.

Token-Eyes pulled through as well. His DNA was linked to four unsolved murders: a passer-by in a bank robbery in Augsburg, two traffic cops at a road block on the Côte d'Azur and a Portuguese woman whose sole crime was that she wanted to leave Token-Eyes after they'd been going out for a year.

He was sentenced to forty-eight years in prison in Barcelona, and ended up in the notorious La Modelo jail.

Nothing could be pinned on his brother. They only know his name: Ludger Holm. He can't be charged with a series of other crimes if they can't name a single one. They don't even have his prints on anything. But a man who offers an undercover dealer a stolen painting that he never owned, who knows that he is going to run into five elite police officers with an MEK in their wake in Barcelona, must be pretty cold-blooded.

She thinks of the moment when she felt eyes on her back in Tegel. Was it Token-Eyes? Did he like the look of her? Was he waiting for her?

Aaron pulls herself together. "Why?"

"A woman in Berlin started writing to him a year ago. She went to Barcelona twice. Sascha requested a transfer and Tegel agreed."

"Who is this woman?"

"A florist. She has a shop in Rudow."

"I want to talk to her."

"I know."

City freeway, half an hour south-east. Pavlik isn't a great talker. He likes to set out his terms so that he can consider them in peace; he doesn't form his sentences as he utters them, he's already thought them through a long time ago. Now, in the car, he doesn't say a word. He's waiting for the question that scares her. It contains its own answer. But she can't save him from it, or from herself either.

"Does Niko know?"

Pavlik says nothing.

"So that's a yes."

"He didn't want to worry you."

"I'm a grown-up."

"Yes. Except that you were with Boenisch. You should hear the guys. They all think you've got the biggest balls they've ever seen."

"Thanks for that too."

*He just drove with me to Tegel and didn't say a word.*

Her hand brushes the artificial leather of the seat, and immediately joins its fellow in her lap.

Ten things that Aaron doesn't like touching:
  sweaty hands
  coffee beans
  artificial leather
  rusty metal
  records
  tablet boxes
  nylon
  her stick
  cigarette packs
  window handles

She hears a local train on her right. The rattling breaks off. Pavlik turns off the windscreen wipers. They are in a tunnel.

Innsbrucker Platz.

She lived around the corner from here. Everything in the place was hers. She only took a single piece of furniture to Wiesbaden: the old, cracked leather sofa from the flea market by the Mauerpark, which has its quirks, but is what it is.

The little boy from the flat next door liked the sofa as well. His parents fought a lot. When they did that he would climb over the balcony and in through Aaron's window. They read comics together and played Superman and Superwoman, and she often thought how nice it would have been to have a little boy like that. Once she was careless, and was cleaning her Browning when he jumped into the room. He was very shocked. She told him it was for firing blanks, but made him solemnly swear he wouldn't tell anyone. That was her greatest fear: that someone would come out of her real life and do something to someone she was fond of.

Pavlik hasn't said a word for two minutes. Aaron can distinguish between a hundred different kinds of silence.

And she knows this one very well.

"What kind of car? For how long?"

"A blue Phaeton. Since Innsbrucker Platz."

She is aware of Pavlik taking his foot off the accelerator, the standard maneuver: slowing down and forcing the car behind to overtake, seeing if your pursuer falls back to keep his distance.

"And?"

"He's still there."

"Do you want to take a look at him?"

"Yes. Hold on tight."

The car brakes hard. She is pressed into the seatbelt. Aaron can tell that the Phaeton has to swerve to avoid a collision. Pavlik puts his foot down. Now he's chasing the other car.

"Did you get a look at his face?"

"No. Darkened glass. I'll try and see what he's doing." He shows why he's the best driver in the Department. She is slung to the left, to the right, shaken to her bones, grips the strap. So Pavlik's catching up with the car. "Impressive."

"What?"

"He took the Buschkrugallee exit at two hundred, without touching the center line."

"Have you lost him?"

"We've got his number."

Which will be no help to them. She knows, he knows too.

When they enter the little florist's shop in Rudow, her nose starts tickling. She has a lot of pot plants at home. The first time she paid a visit her carer thought uncertainly that Aaron must choose them for their scent, or select plants that were particularly nice to the touch, but

Aaron smiled and said: "No, I just like flowers." White orchids most of all, and they have no scent whatsoever.

She hears a voice. Young, weary. The words a drawl, torn from dark thoughts.

"Hello. Can I help you?"

"Are you Eva Askamp?"

"Yes?"

Aaron knows that Pavlik is showing his ID. "We'd like to talk to you about Sascha Holm."

The woman's voice sticks in her throat. "Why?"

She's probably had to explain herself on a regular basis: to committees, to the prison governor in Tegel, to enforcement officers, friends, her family.

*And yet our visit has thrown her off course.*

"How did you meet Sascha?"

"Through an ad in the prison paper."

"You read Spanish prison papers?"

"It was a local one from here."

"What did he write?" Pavlik asks. "Poetry?"

"He said he wanted to meet someone who would understand him and see that he's not as people think."

"Touching."

Aaron says to Pavlik: "Is Miss Askamp pretty?"

"Yes, very." His phone rings. He goes outside.

"You could have a normal relationship, plans for the future, a love life," Aaron says. "Instead you choose a multiple murderer? Someone who has no feelings for anyone except his brother, who's even worse than he is?"

"He's not like that. He's suffered a lot of injustice." Her voice is slow, the kind familiar to Aaron from depressives or the psychologically unstable. Everything about her voice is passive and weak.

When she started working for the BKA two years ago she began an intensive study of criminal psychology. She knows how horribly similar the biographies of women who fall in love with murderers tend to be. A defenseless mother, a brutal father. Unconsciously they seek out men who are exactly like him, who exploit them and treat them like dirt. Until they see a convicted criminal as their prince charming. He's in jail, they're safe from him. They can control him and flee into a fantasy of love. These women are so desperate to believe that they've found happiness at last that they are happy to swap lies for reality.

Eva Askamp should find a different defense for the man.

"What kind of injustice?" Aaron asks.

"Everything."

No conviction in her voice. She's learned everything by heart.

"Where did Sascha grow up?"

Nothing.

Pavlik comes back. "I'll make it easy for you: what's his brother's name?"

The woman knocks something over. A vase. She bends down to pick up the pieces. A delaying strategy.

Aaron notices a new smell. She moves her head in that direction. Camellia. She sees herself shaking hands with Holm in Barcelona. He bows to her. She smells the flower in his buttonhole. Warm, bland, like face powder.

"There's a camellia somewhere," she says to Pavlik. "Is it white?"

"I have no idea what camellias look like."

"Miss Askamp?"

"Yes, white."

"I'd like to buy it."

"It's already been sold."

A child's quick footsteps. "Mum, when are we going home?"

"In a minute."

The boy goes off sulking to the back of the shop.

Aaron asks: "Have you been married?"

"Yes."

"Separated or widowed?"

"My husband died two years ago."

"You ran the shop together?"

"So?"

Aaron turns to Pavlik: "Is it a good area for something like this?"

"I don't think so. There's a discount store on the corner, they wouldn't be able to compete with that."

"Money problems?" Aaron asks.

She hears that the woman is on the brink of tears. "I don't know what that has to do with you." Bits of china rattle into a bin.

"I'd be willing to bet that you have a framed photograph of your husband on your bedside table."

The voice cracks and loses its last foundation. "Get out of my shop."

Door open, snowy air. Aaron turns around again. "You've made a big mistake. Get your son away from here and don't tell anyone where you are."

# 7

TWO UNFILTERED cigarettes in the car. A snow-plough scratches Morse code signs, two short, two long, two short. Aaron's thoughts skid as if on a slide.

Pavlik breaks the silence: "Ludger Holm."

"Yes. He paid the woman to play the part of his brother's pen-pal in jail. To bring him to Berlin."

"Because of Boenisch."

"Of course."

"How would Holm have found out about you and Boenisch?"

"It was in all the papers."

"You know what that means," Pavlik says in a voice that sounds like road salt under boots.

"Sascha murdered Melanie Breuer in Boenisch's cell. He's the man who got hold of *Mr. Brooks* for him."

"Who?"

"Doesn't matter. Boenisch was a perfect way of luring me here."

*I'll only talk to Miss Aaron.*

"That woman you killed in Barcelona—"

"Nina Deraux."

"—she was Sascha's lover."

"And three months pregnant. But it was his brother who came up with the plan. Sascha isn't clever enough."

Screeching tires at a traffic light. She leans her head against Pavlik's. Senses his calm. How could he leave anything to chance, fail to take everything into account? "Now you should say, 'I'll put you on the next flight.'"

"Yes."

"But you don't want that."

"No."

"How many men have you put in place?"

"Two are keeping an eye on her shop. Opposite side of the street, first floor. Another two are observing her flat."

"How many are going to contact me?"

"Two again. They waited at the airport, followed you and Kvist to Tegel and went from there to the Department."

"And are following us."

"Thirty meters to the left, a Volvo."

"They were the ones who called before."

"They chased the Phaeton for a few minutes, but he shook them off."

Aaron says: "I'm their bait."

"Is that a problem for you?" Pavlik asks.

"No."

"I thought not."

"Is Eva Askamp's phone being tapped?"

Pavlik hesitates for two seconds before murmuring, "Can't do it. We'd need legal authorization."

Aaron holds her breath for a second.

*For authorization you have to go down the official route.*

She says: "Demirci doesn't know."

"No."

"Why?"

"I tried. Couldn't persuade them."

The significance of this makes Aaron shiver. Pavlik does his own thing. The men follow him, always have done. He's risking his job to protect them.

He puts his arm around her. Something unites them at that moment; not least the things they haven't said since they've seen each other again.

*No one will do anything to you as long as I'm there.*
*You and Sandra are the most important people for me.*
*We've both missed you very much.*

"Does Niko know about this?"

"No. If Demirci finds out they'll throw me out. The lads can tell you that I claimed to be working on behalf of Demirci. I'll bring you to the hotel."

"Can't we go to Jungfernheide first? I need to pay a visit."

"Here it is," Pavlik says.

Standing by a grave that you can't see, that you just imagine, is nothing. Aaron could be in the Atacama desert, by the Dead Sea, thinking of Marlowe there, and she would be no closer to him and no further away. As near and far from her father and her mother in the cemetery in Sankt Augustin. After a minute's silence she wants to go back to the car.

On the forest path Pavlik puts an arm around her waist. "When I smoked he gave me such a reproachful look. After that I stopped enjoying the cigarette."

"Hm, that's familiar."

"I was quite pissed off," he recalls. "That thing with the Chechen you know about. You and Marlowe were at our house. I was sitting on the porch swing hating the whole world, myself most of all. He jumped into my lap. No idea why, but I stopped thinking about the Chechen after that."

"Yes, he was like that."

Pavlik stumbles, clings to Aaron.

"What's up, old man?"

"You're one to talk. It's pitch dark here."

"Welcome to the club."

They drive to Leipziger Strasse. Pavlik has booked a room for her at the Hotel Jupiter. The concrete bunker was a hotel even back in the days of the GDR, it was called the Puschkin back then. It was refurbished after the Wall came down and the façade was renovated, but it remained a monument to socialist ugliness. The Department sometimes uses the building as a place to put up crown witnesses for a few days. There's only one lift, which is why the rooms can be easily secured.

When Pavlik is about to get out, she holds him back. "Will you tell me what you look like?" She senses that he's startled, and manages a smile. "I mean, five years on."

"Still a meter eighty-five. A few more gray hairs, going thin on top these days, but I'm not fussed. An Albanian broke my nose last year, I look like a boxer. Sandra goes on about how I should get it fixed, but balls to that, you can't fix an ugly man."

Suddenly Aaron remembers that she once glued photographs of Pavlik and Woody Harrelson up in her locker and scribbled *separated at birth*. The memory suddenly fills her with happiness. She smiles. "So that Harrelson lookalike thing doesn't cut it these days?"

"No, that one still works. Except I can't manage the blue eyes. You know: my eyes are somewhere between stray mutt and mud-wrestler."

They laugh for a moment. Aaron puts the unexpected memory in her pocket like a sweet.

In the hotel lobby Pavlik hands her over to two men from the Department. Aaron doesn't know them, but that's hardly surprising. Very few people can stand it for long. If someone's been here for three years he's considered a veteran. Aaron was part of it for six years. She would probably have been transferred too in due course, because she was finished, burnt out.

An easy lie to tell.

If she's honest, she never wanted anything else. Pavlik is exactly the same. The oldest one in the Department, been there forever. How long can he stay fit enough to keep up with the best of them? And Sandra? She knows the demands that are made of her husband, she faces more and more sleepless nights. One morning, she will tenderly embrace him and whisper: "Enough." What then? Desk job? Pavlik?

He issues terse instructions to the two men in the lobby. They're called Kleff and Rogge. They ask the necessary questions calmly and straightforwardly. Aaron can't imagine faces to match the voices. She did that at first, but in the long run it took up too much of her strength. And she no longer finds it important to do it with people she's just met.

Fourteenth floor. She goes with them to her room. Pavlik made sure that she got the one at the end of the corridor: it's the easiest one to guard. Endless fluffy carpet. She counts her steps, wishes she knew already how many there were, where the corridor turns, changes direction, then she wouldn't have to link arms with the taller of the two men, Rogge.

Her mobility trainer was determined to wean her off step-counting. "Imagine a flight of stairs with a lot of steps which you have to take frequently, for example, at your place of work. Let's say there are seventy. Easy to remember, not a problem. Everything's fine for a while, you feel confident. One day you're on the stairs and your phone rings. Or a colleague speaks to you. Or a thought distracts you. What number had you got to? Thirty-seven? Two steps short of the top? You sure? A moment later you're going to fall. Not convinced? Then let's take your office. Let's say you know that it's exactly twenty steps from there to the toilet. Works perfectly until you find yourself standing in the mop cupboard or the gents' toilet."

Not one of the blind people that Aaron knows counts their steps. Just her. In the Department she had become conditioned to doing several things at the same time, even at high speed, and being completely focused on all of them. Memorizing a dossier while she's mid-conversation; analyzing two problems and controlling her breath at the same time; reading her surroundings, filing away sounds and smells and still concentrating on her body.

She asked her trainer to walk with her through a building that she had already mapped, and give her calculations to do at the same time.

She didn't get a step wrong.

No, knowing the number of steps is a source of happiness. Twelve from her office in the BKA to interrogation room VIa. Nineteen from the door of the canteen to the till. From the bed, five steps to her painting. Thirty steps straight on, fifty-six to the left from the bus stop on Marktplatz in Wiesbaden to the Caligari Cinema, where she goes to the late show to watch films she already knows. Seventeen from the main path in the cemetery to her father's grave. From there, six more to the grave of her mother who left him because he was the reason Aaron joined the police. Light and heavy steps.

The steps of Kleff and Rogge are lithe and springy. But how good are they really? Aaron wants to put it to the test.

She reaches with her free hand for the clicker that she always carries with her. Like a tin frog, it produces a loud clicking noise. Her echo location in places where the sounds are muffled, such as a snowy landscape. Now, in her handbag, it sounds like a shot fired with a silencer.

Rogge swiftly swings his hip to the right and grabs Aaron by the waist. He whirls her around a hundred and eighty degrees until she's right in front of him and falls on top of her. The "Kaperski man-euever." In the half-second that it takes him to perform it, she hears the rasping noise as Kleff pulls his gun from its holster, spinning, kneeling down and holding it at the ready.

Aaron can hardly breathe because she's got a hundred kilos on top of her. "OK. Sorry," she manages to say.

Rogge helps her up. "Never do that again."

Kleff opens the door with his card. They go in.

"Hello, Kvist."

"Hello, Kleff. Hello, Rogge."

*He doesn't sound surprised. In Schönefeld it took him no more than five minutes to spot the people shadowing her.*

The two men leave her alone with Niko.

"What are you doing here?"

"Your suitcase was still in the car."

He comes up to her. Aaron can't avoid him. She should push Niko aside but doesn't know what furniture is in the way and she doesn't want to stumble around in front of him like a blind woman.

"I thought for a long time about whether I should tell you. But it must be a coincidence. There's no connection between Boenisch and Sascha Holm."

"Both in Block Six! Just a coincidence?" she exclaims.

"All the long-term prisoners are in Five or Six."

"But they don't have invented pen-pals!"

He holds her by the arms. "Jenny, you're imagining things."

She pushes him away and shouts: "What gives you the right to treat me like a child?"

"Think about it. It's insane." He touches her again.

"Clear off, and stay out of my sight!"

And knows: it was the other way around. *She* cleared off. And him staying out of her sight is *her* punishment.

His voice leaves her with the pain she deserves. "If it makes it easier for you."

The door closes. Her heart thumps as if it isn't in her chest but somewhere a long way away, a speeding metronome that she wants to throw out of the window to make everything quiet again.

*It's what he's been thinking for five years.*

*That I cast him aside like a bag of rubbish.*

She struggles to the bathroom and stands under the ice-cold shower until her skin is so numb that she no longer feels the water.

The fifth virtue: *Shin.* Truth and truthfulness.

Telling Niko that she loves him.

Too late.

Wet, her teeth chattering, she sits down on the bed. She plugs her headphones into her mobile phone and chooses the app that she uses for her diary. The computer voice reads:

"*23 April. What happened to me during the second when I opened my eyes in hospital?*"

Skip.

"*26 June. Which dress did Niko like me to wear?*"

Skip.

"*11 July. Did I hold that woman's hand in the Hotel Aralsk in Moscow? Was it cold? Did she say anything? Did she have parents, siblings, a husband, children?*"

Skip.

"*13 July. Why was I sent to Moscow? I was tailing Ilya Nikulin. But why me? I was only twenty-five, I wasn't even in the Department yet. Why was I given that mission?*"

"*1 August. Where was my cat's favorite place? The sofa? No, Marlowe wasn't my cat. He looked after me. Did he sleep curled up in my right arm or my left? Did he like liverwurst?*"

Skip.

"*15 September. Did my mother cry when she left? Did I?*"

Skip.

"*8 October. Did it rain the day my father died? What did his favorite shirt smell like when I buried my face in it? Did I even do that, or was it just a dream?*"

Skip.

"*9 October. My first car was blue.*"

Skip.

"*3 November. What color was my first car?*"

Skip.

"*2 December. Back to Barcelona. The most important questions: how long did I spend in the warehouse? What happened during that time? What state was Niko in? Did he touch me? Did I touch him? Did we speak? What did we say? Why didn't I try to eliminate Holm? Why did I flee, leaving Niko behind? Why didn't I call the MEK, why didn't I call an ambulance?*"

Aaron turns the radio up full, the television, ignores the hammering on the wall, wants to numb herself, erase her own presence.

Exhaustion hits her like a blow to the face. Her eyes miss the rhythm of day and night. Some blind people don't care, but she constantly feels jetlagged. At first she was awake for seventy hours at a stretch and then slept for twenty.

Last night: not a second.

She rummages in her handbag, and doesn't immediately find the tube of stimulants that she hates, she panics, finds it, loses it, trembling, creeps around on the carpet, reaches for the pills, feels two, tries to swallow them, her mouth is dry.

# 8

HE STANDS in the dark looking across the street to the hotel room. He is naked to the waist, every muscle tattooed, and every tattoo a memory of a pain. He spent a year or two in Sofia and carried out three or four murders for the Bozhkov clan, without any fuss. The money was nice, enough for him to spend a few years in the Antilles, in the house by the sea, which meant nothing to him, just as nothing that he doesn't carry under his skin means anything to him. He came back to Europe when he thought his brother had spent long enough atoning for his error. When Aaron's time in the first circle of hell was coming to an end. During his life he's killed forty or fifty or sixty people, including the man and woman who are lying by the door because he wanted to see Aaron this evening. If she had another hotel room on another floor, it would have been another flat. She has drawn the curtains, but the night-view goggles receive her thermal profile. She sits on the bed with her face buried in her hands and thinks she knows what loss is. He could kill her now, just as he could have killed her at any time. In Wiesbaden he followed her every step for three months. In the cinema he sat next to her at the night-time screening, would only have needed to reach out his hand. She was watching *Taxi Driver*. Of course. Travis Bickle comes back from Vietnam, and the sleeplessness and loneliness hammer like drills in his head. What would have happened if Bickle had never found the little prostitute? Would he have become a one-man slaughterhouse? How romantic. He wasn't concerned with saving the girl. She was interchangeable. He was just looking for an excuse to kill, he would have found other targets. But then he wouldn't have been celebrated as a hero. Is that what fascinates Aaron, the ridiculous happy ending? No, it's the theme of a man running amok. The Samurai knew: only someone in a hopeless, desperate state, far beyond reason, can do great things. The real meaning of people running amok is scattered among the piles of corpses in Blacksburg, Littleton, Erfurt, Utøya. In fact it means that an extremely determined warrior is trying to turn a lost battle around with a single death-defying deed. That would have been worthy of a Samurai, and would have brought healing for Aaron. That is what she longs for. To give meaning to her shattered life by sacrificing herself. She certainly tells her father about that, at his grave in Sankt Augustin. Would he understand? Hardly. Jörg Aaron always coldly calculated the risk: he was a mathematician of killing. He lacked a motivation like Boenisch's basement, and that was what distinguished him from his daughter. What would he think about the fact that she goes into every training session as if it were a requiem mass? Aaron trains for him, the man who would only need to reach out his hand. She knows it, he knows it. It was surprising that she managed to escape in Barcelona. In the tunnel he had the advantage; she is left-handed, but she had to fire with her right hand, her injured side, which was why she could never be as fast as him. And yet a blink of an eye had been crucial. She had her chance, now she's no longer an adversary. For five years he left room for the last tattoo. He feels it over his heart. Aaron will feel it too. He will accept her sacrifice.

# 9

AT ABOUT eight o'clock Kleff and Rogge take her to the shooting range where Pavlik is celebrating his birthday. On the way the two men exchange only a few words, but Aaron can hear how glad they are that she's decided to go.

*Boys' nights out are the best thing.*

"How's he getting on with Demirci?" she asks.

Rogge laughs. "She's stiffer than a two-day-old corpse. But Pavlik will crack her."

"He recently brought in a goldfish bowl and put it casually on the conference table," Kleff says. "There was a crab in it. Great brute of a thing; he wanted to see how Demirci would react. She just kept going and didn't say a word."

"But the look on her face!" Rogge giggles. "Pavlik says he's going to put a stuffed fox on the table next time."

Aaron laughs too. Typical Pavlik.

She understands the men. They want to know who they're risking everything for. Anyone who wants to lead them has to be a part of it. Like her old boss. Irish pub, barbecues at his house, the whole troop, full to the rafters. He went up to everyone and clapped them on the shoulder. *Without you it would all be a load of crap—Nice girlfriend you've got, how's that working out for you?—Take a few days off—Aaron, you need to eat more. And get some sleep.*

He was informal with them, as they were with him. Before he took over the Department, he had been a commander with the SEK, the special unit, and before that he was an undercover agent with the BKA. There was no situation that he hadn't experienced himself. He never demanded the impossible of them.

Only the *almost* impossible.

If one of them took a bullet, her boss went to the members and talked to them for a long time. He didn't just share in their grief, he grieved himself. He let them cry and he cried along with them. In the Department he summoned them all together, apart from the ones who were on missions, and told them he was shutting up shop for a week. One of their comrades was dead. They had to take a break. And if during that week the minister responsible wanted to use the Department, he could kiss his fat arse.

He held the fort himself and didn't waste a word on the subject.

In Barcelona he sat by her bedside twice. On the first day and then again a week later, after he had read the report from Internal Affairs. He had some schnapps with her, which they drank from tooth mugs, and he growled that he'd thrown the useless papers in the bin. He was like her father in many respects.

By way of goodbye he kissed her on the forehead. "You know what I've always admired most about you? That you know the difference between right and wrong. You're a policewoman, you've never been anything else and you never will be."

She couldn't accept that at the time, although she came to accept it later.

He's now enjoying his retirement in Sweden and finally had time for his hobby, deep-sea fishing. When Aaron first started with the BKA he sent her a letter. In Braille. She read it five times. Inan Demirci has a lot to learn.

There's music at the shooting range, a crowd of people. Hanging in the air is the best smell in the world, which Aaron can't bear anymore, shots fired from guns freshly cleaned with Ballistol.

Here they have drunk, partied, grieved.

Pavlik hugs her.

"I haven't got you a present," she says, embarrassed.

"Yes you have. And in such a pretty package. You're my guest of honor." He whispers: "That was some stunt you pulled off at the hotel."

"He broke two of my ribs."

"Serves you right." Pavlik is dragged away, calls, "Got to go, see you in a bit!"

"Come and sit with me." Demirci. "I'll do this." She is speaking to Kleff and Rogge. Aaron feels as if she's been ambushed, she doesn't feel like seeing Demirci.

The fourth virtue of Bushidō: *Rei*. Politeness.

Demirci guides Aaron to a table in a tolerably quiet corner. "Would you like something to eat?"

"What is there?"

"Pasta salad and bratwurst, pasta salad and meatballs, pasta salad and steak."

"Bratwurst. And a beer."

Aaron hears the laugh that she would recognize among a million others. Warm, a belly laugh, relaxed. He's nearby.

She shovels the food hungrily down. Blind people love eating, everything tastes more intense. But the food has to be either delicious or dreadful, nothing in between. She asks Demirci for seconds. The pasta salad was made by Sandra, it tastes of chopped onion, music from the boom box in the kitchen, white wine spritzer, a bit of a chat, eBay shopping, a giggle.

She eats the bratwursts with her fingers.

Ten things that Aaron likes to touch:
  snow
  pine cones
  ice-cold beer bottles
  damp potting compost
  warm fur
  bratwursts

small hands
mother-of-pearl buttons
guns
her painting

She pushes her plate away, slips a Marlboro from the pack, snaps
open her Dupont and notices Pavlik's boss moving her chair.

"It's no smoking in here," Demirci says.

"When did you give up?"

"Is it that obvious?"

"Otherwise you'd have moved your chair away rather than closer."

"Can I have one?"

When Demirci takes her first drag Aaron knows what she is feeling. The pure happiness with which she fills her lungs, the disappointment at having done it, the greed of smoking the cigarette all
the way down to the filter.

Every few minutes someone comes and pats Aaron, strokes
her arm. *It's me, Dobeck—Hi, Krupp here—Krampe—Nowak—
Fricke—Great that you're here! I've missed you! You're looking great!
Terrific dress!*

Butz stays a bit longer. He stands next to her with his hand resting
gently on her shoulder, so that she knows he's there. Their connection needs no words. Before he goes, he kisses her on the forehead.

No one speaks to Demirci.

The third virtue: *Omoiyari*. Empathy.

"You're wondering why Pavlik invited you. If you think it's because
you're his boss, you're wrong."

"Are you sure you're blind?"

"He's worried. It's time for you to get on with the lads. Soon we'll
be joined by one of them, because Pavlik has seen that I'm the only
one talking to you. Don't talk about work. Say something nice.
Perhaps: 'I bet twenty Euros that you're in the top five in the shooting competition.' And don't call them 'Mr.' Their surname's enough."

"Why?"

"Because that's what they need."

Silence for five drags. Then Demirci says: "I met your father once."

"Really?"

"I come from a small town, Babenhausen, you won't know it. My father was a tailor, he spent everything he earned on my training. When he got German citizenship that was very important for him. Jürgen Schumann, the pilot of the *Landshut*, that plane that was hijacked in Mogadishu, lived a street away and was one of my father's customers. My father always puts flowers on his grave on the anniversary of his death. He says: 'Mr. Schumann was a hero.' I went with him once. Your father was standing there. At police academy I wrote a paper about him. They met quite often by the grave. My father introduced yours as an 'old flying colleague' of Schumann's. He didn't know who Jörg Aaron was, what he had done in Mogadishu. Your father didn't mind. But he talked to my father as if talking to a friend. I was very struck by that."

All of a sudden Aaron is glad that she's sitting with Demirci.

A chair is pulled up. Fricke. "So, is Aaron bothering you?"

Of course Pavlik had to send *him*. Fricke is the joker of the squad. Eventually he will laugh about his own death. For five minutes Aaron hears Demirci trying to relax, making a real effort and not doing too badly.

Fricke nudges her. "I've got one for you: if a blind guy and a paralyzed guy are playing football, the paralysed guy always wins. Why's that?"

"He shouts, 'Goal!'" she grins.

"Hi, Jenny."

Over the years she has wondered so often what it would be like to meet up again with Sandra, her best girlfriend. Aaron was worried that she would tell her off for not getting in touch, for leaving her behind without a word, just the letter that bore only two words: *please understand.*

But now everything's very simple.

She leans her head against Sandra's, remembers the evenings she spent with her and Pavlik, her family, the things she was able to take for granted, the twins she used to play hide and seek with, even though she didn't need to hide because she was perfectly at home.

Most of the men in the Department are married. That's how they want it, they seek out people with a settled lifestyle: guys who are self-contained and can soberly calculate a risk. Aaron has barely seen their wives, let alone got to know them. They were kept away, they weren't supposed to know exactly what their husbands did, and they didn't want to either. It was better for everyone that way.

Sandra is different. When she and Pavlik fell in love she was nineteen, he was twenty-three and still a paratrooper. She was the reason he joined the police; she didn't want to spend the rest of her life catching the odd weekend with a soldier. From the very first she made it clear that she would share everything with him, otherwise they could call it a day there and then. She was right for him and he was right for her. She didn't have the twins until she was thirty—before then her job as a goldsmith was important to her. Later she said to Aaron: "You've got to live your life before you do anything else." Whatever her husband brought home, she took it from him and locked it away.

They were always a team.

After Pavlik's motorcycle accident his boss didn't think for a moment about transferring him. He was too important. But Sandra knew she wouldn't have a minute's peace until she was sure that his body was working perfectly. She gave him six months, then she wanted him to fight with Aaron.

He was in the garden of their terraced house in Lichterfelde, where the hedges were too high for the neighbors to peer in. Sandra had waited until the twins were off on a school trip. She made Aaron promise not to go easy on her husband. Pavlik and she made no concessions to each other; they acted like enemies. He was as quick as ever. His lower-leg prosthesis worried Aaron, particularly when he had to propel himself with his feet, and she was aware of how painful it was for him to jump. They were off the same assembly line. At the end they knelt in front of each other for several minutes and couldn't speak. Even Aaron's hair hurt. Sandra threw them raw lamb cutlets. They drank schnapps and played Scrabble.

In the shooting range they're a match for each other. "Your pasta salad is the best," Aaron says and wipes the tears away. Sandra sobs as well. "And no one tucks in like you do! Oh yeah, did Ulf tell you?"

"What?"

"We had another girl. Last February."

"No way!"

"No, really. Amazing. At forty-five."

"What did you call her?"

"Guess."

Aaron takes a minute to think. Tears fill her eyes again; she hugs Sandra, who is blubbing too. "I'll be damned!" It's all she can say.

"What sissies we are!" Sandra manages to say.

They laugh and cry, inseparable.

Once they argued. When Aaron confided in Sandra that she was with Niko. Sandra was outraged. Aaron was making a mistake, she told her.

Why?

Niko wasn't good for her, that was why! "He's not even your type!"

At that point Aaron got furious too. A little time before that she had told her father about herself and Niko. His reaction had been similar, but less violent. Why did everyone think they knew what was good for her and what wasn't? Sandra replied that Niko lived in the overtaking lane, always with his foot to the floor. How long was that going to work out?

Pavlik only had two friends in the Department, André and Niko. Aaron had been surprised that Sandra never invited Niko over, and didn't want the children to meet him.

It was only when Sandra said, "Every time he's on duty with Ulf, I sit by the phone and pray that it won't ring," that Aaron understood what it was. Niko had no family, it didn't occur to him that his colleague would leave a wife and children behind.

*A ship looking for its iceberg.*

"And? Is anyone waiting for me at home?" Aaron said and knew at that moment that she had wounded her friend. Because they were her family. And if anything happened to her, it would be as bad for Sandra as if she had lost her children or her husband.

Aaron threw her arms around Sandra and noticed that she was trembling; she was trembling herself and left that evening without really having become reconciled. Two days of radio silence, Aaron was hurt. Then one morning by the coffee machine Pavlik said: "Sandra asks if you'd like to come for dinner with Kvist. Say seven?"

Aaron brought a bottle of limoncello. Niko had even bought a bunch of flowers. They talked a lot of nonsense and laughed as a storm brewed, and it was as if they had sat like that many times before.

The men were still playing Scalextric with the twins. After the warm summer rain Sandra and Aaron sat together on the porch swing in the garden, listened to the raindrops on the leaves of the trees and sipped limoncello. The wet grass tickled their bare feet; they said nothing, but they were together.

Sandra said: "Let's do this more often."

The shooting competition begins. Fricke joins the others. Demirci bends down to Aaron. "Thank you."

"Make sure you join the lads. They're expecting you to shoot as well. You'll come last, with a depressing result. Pretend to be seriously upset."

For the next three quarters of an hour Aaron and Sandra are the only ones not at the shooting stand. Sandra holds her hand in silence, keeping her thoughts to herself.

For a confident marksman, fifty meters would be the maximum competition distance shooting with a pistol. Here they're firing at eighty. Ten shots with their strong hand, ten with their weak one.

Aaron can identify the members of the old squad by their frequency. Butz: a clockwork mechanism, accurate to the millisecond, sober. Dobeck: a quick shot, followed by a more hesitant one, undecided as always. Fricke: nine easy shots in a row. Both times he pauses before the last one. He wants to get the bullet into the hole made by the first one: that's his grand finale. After his second sequence a whisper runs around the room. He's done it, with his left hand. Pavlik: relaxed, controlled, a precision marksman.

Demirci: cramped, unrhythmic. "Damn it all!"

Laughter. Niko: ten, quick as a sewing machine.

*Of course he'll win.*

Pavlik bends down to Aaron. "Your turn."

"Are you drunk?" Sandra growls.

"Only one. I want my fifty Euros back."

Aaron gets to her feet. "All fine."

Pavlik leads her to the stand.

She says quietly: "Number six."

Everything falls suddenly silent. Aaron feels all eyes on her. In the sixth lane she stands in firing position at the shooting stall. Her fingers find the notch precisely in the middle, the notch where André had rested the grip of his Heckler & Koch because his life was slipping away from him like sand; sad, lovely, lost André, who was undercover for so long that in the end he didn't know which world he belonged to, and no one could save him, not even Aaron.

Pavlik lays her left hand on the pistol.

*My Browning.*

He whispers: "I picked it up for you."

The grip is warm and soft, and has been waiting for her. She feels the weight. Only one bullet, in the barrel. She knows this lane like the back of her hand. She stamps twice with her heel, listens to the echo, corrects her stance by moving five centimeters to the left. She stands facing the target head-on, her feet a shoulder-width apart, her right foot set slightly back. She straightens the arm holding the pistol and bends her other elbow slightly to minimize the kick.

She breathes half in, half out.

Eighty meters.

*Don't see, know.*

When her finger touches the trigger, Aaron knows that she's going to hit the bull's eye. But in the fraction of a second between that idea and reaching the pressure point, light flashes in front of her. She is standing, half breathing in, half breathing out, in an endless corridor in Barcelona, and wondering whether she will hear a shot or just an empty click. Aaron is so caught up in that sudden, hyper-intense memory that she falters. A dull roar rolls in, as distant as if through a soundproofed window, until the window flies open and there she is right in the midst of the yelling, whistling, trampling of the men around her. Again she is catapulted into the corridor. She is holding Nina Deraux's Walther, she sees Token-Eyes and pulls the trigger. Token-Eyes bends his knees, turns around, drops the Glock. Red mist issues from his mouth.

*And then? What did I do then?*

Aaron hopes, her heart thumping, that the pictures will continue and guide her to the hall where Niko is fighting for his life, but that door stays shut.

Pavlik takes her in his arms. "Perfect."

*No. Just off. A nine, scraped the ten.*

She murmurs: "Anyone can lie to me. Anyone but you."

The music begins again. Aaron can't breathe.

"Have a Little Faith in Me" by John Hiatt.

Niko takes her hand. "Come on."

She allows herself to be led away, she belongs here, nowhere else, she kicks open the door to her inner room, chucks the truth inside, shuts the door and dances with him.

Aaron loves Niko's movements, his hands, his skin, his constant certainty. Niko's father was Finnish. He taught him the meaning of *sisu*, an untranslatable word that contains many others: strength of will, perseverance, resolution, boldness, a fighting spirit even in hopeless situations.

Someone had to stop André. Only the people from Internal Affairs learned what had happened in Prague, where Niko had tracked down and killed his friend.

His statement ended up in the safe. No one ever asked Niko or mentioned André's name again.

Only once, when he was drunk and desperate, did he whisper: "Ruthlessness is *sisu* as well."

But he's not like that.

He breathes into her hair. "Since you've been gone, I've been blind."

# 10

THEY DRIVE to the Hotel Jupiter. Niko follows Kleff and Rogge. Aaron knows that he is keeping a distance of only two meters so that other cars can't push in. They don't speak. She concentrates on the windscreen wipers. Every time they stop at the lights she hears the faint scrape of Niko's shirt collar as he looks backwards because he doesn't trust the mirrors and wants to check if they're being followed.

He takes her to her room and comes in with her.

He kicks the door shut with his heel and tries to kiss her. But she can't allow that, because then she would be lost.

"I need to ask you something."

His disappointment draws him away from her like a wave.

"What exactly happened in Barcelona?"

"What do you mean?"

"In the warehouse. I can't remember." She has been afraid of this for so long. But she needs to know once and for all.

He says nothing.

"Please tell me."

"My body wasn't responding. You tried to pull me up. It didn't work. Holm fired. We were sitting ducks. Blood ran down your arm. I thought that was it for me. I wanted you to let go of me."

"Why didn't I fight Holm?"

"He was a machine."

"So was I."

Aaron can't make sense of Niko's words, they dash around madly in her head. *I wanted live that you I give you when don't believe if I had been your place in the tunnel.*

The floor shakes. Niko catches her.

The door to the library of her perfect memory was always open to her. Pictures, moments, thoughts, feelings, everything in its place. Aaron has spent many hours there. Sometimes she was almost happy, often sad. But it was her life and she was able to look at it.

One morning she woke up, and a fire had broken out in the library. Since then she has had to watch as it gradually devoured all the images, all the memories of the time before she was blinded, every sensation that she had ever had, every precious moment, leaving only the facts as if in a police record. When her mother died, and her father. What school she went to. How many people she has killed.

Soon she couldn't imagine any colors but red, and numbers turned into pure arithmetic. A double-barreled revolver in a calf holster, two weeks in Marrakech, two rooms in Schöneberg. Four seconds to disassemble the Browning. Five years between the basement and the underground car park in Moscow, five since her eyes opened. Her lane, number six. Seven means not being able to wait for something. But she had forgotten what numbers look like, tried to draw a two in the air, a four, five, six, seven. Couldn't do it.

She went to a neurologist, her initial fear was that she suffered from dementia. He gave her an appointment at a clinic. They tested her powers of concentration, her receptiveness, her sense of orientation. The doctor said: "I wish I had a bit of what you've got." They considered a thyroid function problem, made a magnetic resonance image of her brain, examined her cerebrospinal fluid. All perfect. She was dismissed with the words: "Maybe what you need is a course of psychoanalysis."

To talk about what? Cowardice? Shame? Dishonor?

For days and nights Aaron desperately wrote down everything that she could still remember and didn't want to lose. She filled page after page in Braille; she's still working on that chronicle even today. But the entries became further apart and shorter and gradually came to seem more and more pointless. Because as soon as a memory exists only as a copy and the original has been destroyed in the library, it becomes the narrative of a total stranger. As if Aaron hadn't experienced what is there, and only this strangeness.

And how was she supposed to describe ice flowers, hoarfrost on meadows? The light from the gas lamps in Chamissoplatz, the flickering sky over Chella, the view across the sea in the morning? The wonderful scenes of her childhood and the place in the forest where she had her first kiss, vanished along with the sound of the voices of her mother and father, the tune of the  toy clock that lay under the Christmas tree when she was a child, the faces of the people she had loved, her own face, which exists now only in a single photograph, until everything is destroyed and burned and only cold ash remains, to be blown into the void by the wind.

There are things that the flames have spared. The red of cayenne pepper, drinking coffee with the fat landlady, Mary-Sue, in Berlin, Superman and Superwoman with her neighbors' little boy, Marlowe, Scrabble in Lichterfelde, limoncello with Sandra on the porch swing. Every day she remembers those things are a gift.

But the basement in Spandau is part of it as well, and Boenisch's voice, Runge's fingernails. She will always remember those. She is not granted the mercy of forgetting that.

And that one last day in Barcelona. It is like a painting that she's been sitting and staring at for five years, day and night. Aaron knows every detail. That a thin spider lives in the basin in the bathroom above which she cleans her pistol, a spider that  she leaves alive, that the scar on her collarbone is itchy, that the little boy in the lobby has dirty fingernails and when Jordi smiles he gets two dimples that she likes, that the seats of the Daimler smell of leather-oil and her heart on the journey south is a stormy sea.

The Sagrada Familia.

She could go back to the hotel and list them: the contents of the minibar; Niko's Colt, which is lying in the room-safe with the barrel facing strangely towards her, and she corrects that when she puts the Browning next to it, because if necessary, and that's always possible, you must be able to reach for the grip and not the barrel; in the lift, the restaurant menu, *merluza a la marinera*, twenty-one Euros and ten cents; a judder at each floor, because of an imbalance in the winch; a hint of a heavy aftershave that she finds unpleasant; a tiny patch of rust in the back inside corner on the left.

She could go back ten times and it still wouldn't be enough.

That the taxi they sit behind at the traffic light on Carrer de Mallorca has a scratch on the top of the boot and license number 343, that in Token-Eyes' face she can see all the people he has killed, who mean less to him than the dirt on his shoe.

That when her eyes and Holm's met in the tunnel she knows she should have said to Niko: "I love you."

Love at last sight.

But when she woke up in the clinic she didn't know what had happened in the warehouse. Until this evening. Until the flash in the firing range, when she was standing in this corridor again and shooting Token-Eyes in the neck.

It could be a beginning.

But the most important thing is missing.

Niko. The hall. Her flight.

The repellent stench of coffee is all that is left. That's why she forces herself to drink coffee again: perhaps it will help her to remember at last.

In the middle of the furious blaze Aaron clings to the fact that the missing minutes are of great importance, that she needs to understand why she acted as she did, because that knowledge can save her, because the pictures will go speeding backwards and it will be as if the fire had never raged. That everyone will be back in his place, once and for all. And Aaron will be standing high on a mountain-top, and will see her life below her like a broad landscape in which she knows every stone and everything that lies beneath.

"Go." She has fought so hard for that one word that her whole body is in pain.

Niko lets go of her. "So I never meant anything to you."

"No."

Between them there is always the truth, never a lie.

Alone. She turns out the light. Why? She hears the hiss of the air conditioning, the television next to it, feels the windowsill shaking beneath her feet that night in Wiesbaden, when the drunk in the street shouted at the top of his voice, "Come on, then, jump," and she wanted to let go, but the hope of getting back those minutes in Barcelona was stronger than the longing to be shattered into pieces.

She takes one of the other pills that she hates, so that she can finally forget.

Aaron is in a plane. She is wearing a pair of dark glasses, even though she isn't blind. All her dead sit in the rows in front of her and behind her; not one is missing, not even the ones whose deaths she was unable to prevent. Her schoolfriend Ben who fell through the ice and drowned, the woman in the Hotel Aralsk, the waitress in Delmenhorst, the barman in Brussels, the child in Cork, the shoe-shine man in Tangier, the taxi driver in Helsinki, Alina, Jordi, Ruben, Josue, Melanie Breuer, André.

The florist Eva Askamp.

And strangely, too, the school class from Zoo and two teachers, Aaron is trying to understand why.

It starts snowing. Fat flakes drift through the plane, soon so dense that the faces dissolve in a white swirl. Aaron's feet are bare. She touches the stilettos of the woman in the seat next to her. The woman atomizes into snow, which then becomes a ball and rolls down the central aisle.

Someone calls: "Pass it! Too dumb to wank!"

Aaron's father joins her. His face is blackened, as it was during the storming of the *Landshut*.

She grips his hand. "Where have you been?"

"With my own."

"How many are there?"

He says nothing.

"Can't you count them?" she asks anxiously.

His eyes bulge from his blackened face. "You never ask about mine and I'll never ask about yours."

She hears the voice of Captain Schumann: "Fasten your seat belts. We're making an unplanned stop in Tegel, you can expect some turbulence."

The plane rolls out of the prison sports ground. It has stopped snowing. Aaron presses a bag of hot chestnuts against her chest. She walks through the rows of her dead and her father's dead, which she sees as well, so many, all looking away. All but André.

He chucks her a comic, *Daredevil, Blind Justice.* Aaron's hand burns like fire, she drops the comic.

Her father is waiting at the foot of the gangway. He takes her dark glasses off and says: "You don't need those anymore."

He hands her a heavy suitcase.

She wishes her father could stay with her. But he is staring up at the entrance, where Souhaila Andrawes is making the victory sign.

The plane takes off. She walks with the suitcase through Block Six. Three doors open for her. At the last air-lock she sets the suitcase down and opens it. It contains Runge's souvenirs. She puts on the pearl necklace. She leaves the suitcase behind and walks on, and there is no one here apart from her and Ludger Holm and Boenisch, who are in the cell and don't notice her.

There is a white camellia on the bed. Holm's torso is naked and covered in tattoos. She closes her eyes, she doesn't want to see them.

The men's voices are a whisper in the night.

"Can I choose the woman?"

"Whichever you like."

"And then it will be Aaron's turn?"

"It will be her turn."

"And will you meet her?"

"Oh yes. She will see again, but she will wish she was blind."

Aaron feels Niko's breath, his hip against hers. He opens the door to the room where she sat facing Boenisch. It is enormous, infinite, without walls. There is a dance floor in the middle, and Niko gently rocks Aaron, while the music flows from him like a reassuring fire.

She sees his smile, his ginger hair with the stubborn cow-lick, his blade-sharp nose, his eyes, always sad and happy at the same time. He holds her tight. Aaron notices that her feet no longer touch the floor. She flies away with Niko, sees below her the prison, a fortress built of nothing but light, sees Boenisch and Holm looking up at her.

Reads Holm's thoughts: *an eye for an eye.*

She pulls the necklace from her neck, the pearls dissolve and turn into snowflakes.

Niko lets go of her and Aaron plummets. She falls into the light and screams and screams: "I want to be blind again!"

# 11

DEMIRCI ARRIVES home. Half-past three, it's hardly worth going to bed. And she had intended to stay at the party only as long as politeness required. She would have disappeared by ten at the latest, quietly and probably unnoticed.

After the shooting competition she changed her mind.

Something had altered.

She certainly couldn't boast about her performance. But afterwards the men treated her differently. It was as if they were in the same room with her for the first time.

Demirci knew what Aaron meant: that she might be able to issue orders to the men, but they themselves decided who would lead them.

Pavlik.

On the first day of the job her predecessor had wanted to introduce him to her. He said: "Your main man." But Pavlik walked past them in the corridor without so much as a glance. It was an affront that she doesn't understand even now. The next day he was friendly and professional, but didn't explain his early behavior.

"Why is he the main man?"

"You'll see," her predecessor said laconically.

He didn't feel the need to explain why he had kept on a lower-leg amputee who was approaching fifty. Demirci checked Pavlik's assessments. He had passed the endurance tests impeccably. Only average marks, but he couldn't have been expected to end up in the top three in athletics.

She met him at briefings.

Whatever decision Demirci makes, the men look to him. If he scratches his chin they get worried. If he nods slightly they relax. If a wrinkle runs from the bridge of his nose to his hairline, it's like an alarm signal.

Then Pavlik asks questions. And whether Demirci likes it or not, each one is justified.

*Wouldn't three cars be better? What if there's a fuse attached to the door? Are we really sure that our man's cover hasn't been blown? Why do we still need the hostages?*

They can't breathe freely until Pavlik is satisfied. Demirci finds that hard to accept.

Her career path has been steep, she has gained universal respect. Of course the Department represents a new height that she risks falling from. But she wouldn't have got the job if she hadn't been qualified for it.

Is Pavlik putting her in a bad light? No. He's just asking questions.

At first Demirci thought Pavlik's prestige was down to his age; some of his comrades could have been his sons. He is the most experienced, without a doubt. But that on its own wouldn't be enough. In a world in which a man's qualities are measured in fractions of a second, you constantly have to confirm that status with results.

She studied Pavlik's file. Basic studies in Maths at Army College; professional soldier, sniper with the paratroopers, training in one-to-one combat. Then police academy, SEK in Berlin.

In 1998 he was used as a precision sniper in the hostage-taking in the synagogue on Fasanenstrasse. Three heavily armed men from a Neo-Nazi group had taken the rabbi and five members of the congregation hostage and barricaded themselves in. They threatened to kill the hostages and themselves and demanded a live broadcast of a statement by the Chancellor on the evening news to the effect that Auschwitz had never existed and the Holocaust was only Zionist propaganda.

Pavlik's Special Enforcement Team, his SET, was on the roof of a house opposite. After six hours his replacement should have arrived;

no one can concentrate perfectly for as long as that. They could only see the outlines of their individual targets, they couldn't tell the hostages from the hostage-takers. They hadn't been given license to fire. They were listening in on the prayer room with a laser microphone. The first hostage was about to be liquidated. Pavlik killed the three Nazis with shots to the head. Not a single hostage was injured.

A week later the Department called.

He's been with them for eighteen years now. The synagogue and two other missions were recorded in the specialist literature. Last of all a life-saving shot from almost two thousand three hundred meters away. Demirci wouldn't have thought it possible.

After a few days Pavlik requested a meeting with her. It was important for him to say something about each of the men to her, at least to introduce them to her in a sense. He stressed the need to take their individual characteristics into account. They had different strengths, but also weaknesses that hadn't been listed in their evaluations, and which had to be compensated for. They were all fully trained, physical condition wasn't a factor.

He chose words that were strangely analytical and warm-hearted at the same time. He said that empathy was just as important as resolution, and as dangerous as arrogance. That a man with a strong sense of justice and a capacity for fellow-feeling should be matched with a partner whose qualities were obstinacy and impatience. That one should never be sent into action alone, because he couldn't bear the solitude, and another should always be in a team, because that was where he showed his best.

But it was also important for a married man always to cover an unmarried comrade rather than the other way around. She needed to know all of that.

*Empathy as a weakness and also a strength. A wise observation.*

Demirci asked Pavlik what his weakness was. He said: "Chocolate." She got up to shake his hand and say goodbye. She would never forget what happened next. As Pavlik was leaving she turned around and swept the pencil sharpener off her desk with her skirt. Pavlik couldn't possibly have seen it. But with his back to the desk he reached his hand behind him so quickly that Demirci's eye couldn't follow the movement, and caught the sharpener. He put it back in its place, nodded curtly and left.

And all questions were answered.

In her flat in Mitte, Demirci takes the pack of cigarettes from the locked drawer. She lights one, swears it's her last and knows that she's lying to herself. She steps out on to the balcony on the thirteenth floor. It smells of fresh snow. The sky is an arch of light above the glittering display of the city.

At two o'clock everyone apart from her and Pavlik had left the party. They sat in the shooting range among the leftovers from the buffet. He drank three or four glasses of schnapps without getting drunk, and asked if she had ever killed a person.

When she didn't reply he told her how he had once ridden his motorbike along a country road near Beelitz. He had driven into a patch of oil on a bend and come flying off. The bike had come after him like a shot from a cannon and torn off his lower leg before flying across the road at a female cyclist. Pavlik had almost lost consciousness. He had seen a man and a little girl kneeling beside the woman and shouting.

He knew how many people he had killed. It had always been unavoidable, and he could live with it. But even though the accident had been eight years ago, not a day had gone by when he hadn't thought of that woman. When he had been released from hospital he had gone to see her husband and tell him how terribly sorry he was.

The man had asked him in, but had then sat there in silence, rocking back and forth.

An hour had passed like that. Pavlik would never forget it.

Demirci looks at the block opposite. A television is reflected in a window. A Christmas garland flickers in another. A light comes on in the stairwell. Everyone has his own life, clings tightly to it, takes it for granted. Very few people know that you can't do that.

Demirci wasn't aware of it either. Until that day in spring when her mother visited her in Koblenz, where Demirci had her first job as an ambitious police inspector, until the evening in an uncle's restaurant where, cheeks blazing, she talked about her work and filled her mother with pride, until the discotheque that they walked past on the way home, arm in arm, for the first time as friends, until the shooting of the two drug dealers, until her mother collapsed beside her and her face was a bloody mask, until she shot the fleeing gunman in the back, until the scream that cut through her like an axe, until she called her father and that whimpering sound, still uncertain whether it emanated from him or from her, until the report certifying that she had acted properly.

That was the only time she had killed anyone. And it was enough.

She could never talk to her father about it. He lives alone in his house of pain. But she told Pavlik. He drank schnapps, asked the right questions: what was the visibility like? How far away was the man? How many times did she fire? Standing or kneeling? Two-handed?

She saw that Pavlik was reassured because she had revealed something that could not be read in any report, that she knows which words are important and how to say them.

Demirci cadged an unfiltered cigarette from him. They sat there for several minutes, confetti on the table, balloons above their heads quivering in the cigarette smoke. They were both watching the sixth lane.

Aaron. What a strange woman. She's everything that Demirci has heard and read about her. And yet she's quite different.

She looks for the word.

*Unhappy?*

No.

*Sad.*

But not because of her blindness. Demirci isn't sure that Aaron thinks of it as a handicap.

While they were sitting together at the table, she had concentrated completely on Demirci. But she was checking everything around her at the same time. Aaron always knew who was where, and Demirci hasn't the faintest idea how she does it. In some mysterious way, and without insulting anyone, she made it clear that she didn't want her conversation to be disturbed. If a third party was welcome, on the other hand, it only took the tiniest movement, a tilt of the head, the opening of her hand, a smile, and people came to her. Her warmth wasn't fake, everyone wanted to exchange words with her or touch her.

She guides every conversation, and you don't even notice it.

Then that shot. Blind, from eighty meters. Demirci studied Aaron. At the moment when she fired, something must have thrown her off balance, or else she would have fired a ten, she has no doubt.

What was it? Boenisch? Holm?

Demirci has learned a lot of Turkish proverbs from her father. Now that the icy air on the balcony of her apartment makes her wide awake, a thought suddenly enters her head: "Life is the school, pain is the teacher."

Sandra is sleeping peacefully. The baby lies beside her, with one foot in her hand, she smacks her lips, mutters, dreams with a peacefully crumpled face. Pavlik stands in the doorway and wonders how he can jeopardize this happiness.

The twins are big lads now, going through big changes. They've got another month at school in England, and their leaving exams aren't that far off. They don't call often, their voices sound almost adult, soon they won't need him anymore.

Until the evening a year and a half ago when Sandra put his hand on her belly and said, "Guess what's in there?" that was a comfort to Pavlik. That his sons had a father for as long as it really mattered. He keeps that from Sandra, even today. She would never forgive him.

What comfort is the baby to him? If he doesn't come home tomorrow, his daughter will know him only from her mother's stories, his photograph will show a stranger. As if her fist had never gripped his thumb, her smell never delighted him, her cries never woken him, as if she had never known him.

He goes into the kitchen where he finds the thermos flask with the strong black coffee that Sandra made for him because she knew he wouldn't go to bed. Just as she always knows what he wants and needs and what he has done and what he will do.

He steps out on to the snowy terrace, and drinks some coffee. He hears the faint sound of a car. It's approaching from almost precisely a thousand meters away. That's the maximum distance from which the faint sound of an engine is audible. South-south-west. Probably somewhere down by the branch canal. He could locate a car horn from two kilometers away; conversations: two hundred meters; cracking twigs: ninety; footsteps: thirty. A sniper has to be able to gauge these things. It's become so much a part of Pavlik that he doesn't have to think about it, he just knows.

Equally, he would know at full moon just before the summer solstice that the time in which there is enough light for a sure aim is very short, that with a waxing half-moon you can aim at a target without a telescope no later than midnight, and that a sloping position towards north or south deadens the moonlight. Even when he walks with Sandra through the park late at night, relaxed and unconcerned, he automatically checks that he has the moon behind him because it lights his path and would dazzle any enemy.

On a day off, when he's on the point of falling asleep in the hammock, he is aware that the powder in a cartridge burns faster in the summer, increasing muzzle velocity, and that he would have to aim very slightly lower than he would in cold weather.

He explained the stars to the twins. They saw the beauty of creation. Pavlik saw the conditions for a textbook shot.

He is ashamed of it.

The coffee cup warms his hand. But the cold doesn't matter to him, it's familiar. He could take all his clothes off and stand like that for hours without shivering and feel the snowflakes melting on his body.

Pavlik lights a cigarette, enjoys it, knows that it's unprofessional. Smoking reduces your night vision. And nicotine withdrawal can reduce concentration if he's lying for hours in position with his rifle.

He still has the eyes of a brain surgeon. But anyone who has tried to hit a trigger finger the size of a grain of dust knows that a thousandth is what counts.

How much longer?

When he advised Demirci always to send a married man to cover an unmarried one, rather than the other way around, he was thinking about himself. If a colleague suggested anything of the kind, he would say: "Oh shut up."

He hasn't been short of offers for a while now. Adviser, head of security, super-expert. Anyone who's been with the Department can take their pick. A quiet desk job, nine to five, nothing that wouldn't fit between the covers of a file. The money would be crazy. But they're doing OK. The mortgage is paid off, they've inherited a couple of things. Money isn't an issue.

Sandra isn't keeping on at him.

He could also become a trainer. The Department has a training center in Brandenburg, which takes its name from a derelict old windmill.

*And God knows, it really is a mill. You'd be a slave driver, and the men would hate you, like you and everyone else hated all your trainers and will go on hating them.*

Apart from her.

He remembers her joining them at a very young age. The first woman, the daughter of Jörg Aaron. She was so beautiful and so sad. And she stayed that way. All the boys fell in love with her immediately. Of course she must have been good, otherwise they wouldn't have taken her on. But everyone wondered *how* good she was.

He didn't. Her gait, her expression, her peace, the ease with which she did five things at once were all enough for him. She even poured coffee in silence. She wore her name as casually as she wore torn jeans to a reception.

The others could hardly wait for her to end up in the Mill. They weren't disappointed. It's hard to tell men like that apart. Pavlik can still remember her drinking red wine and Coke with the lads. One of them spat an incisor into his glass and asked: "Where did you learn to fight like that?"

She said: "When my mother was pregnant with me she watched Bruce Lee videos."

Everyone burst out laughing. But Pavlik saw the fear in her eyes.

At that time he didn't know anything about Boenisch's basement; she only told him about that much later, when they were friends. And then she became his little sister, the one he looked after. Always.

He recognized her.

Her hardness, her gentleness and her silence.

Sitting by her bed in Barcelona was like dying. The fact that she broke off contact with him shortly afterwards hit him harder than his father's death. Sandra feels exactly the same. Since then they have never spoken about Aaron. They both thought they couldn't bear it.

But Pavlik didn't stop taking care of her and secretly going with her along her path. He knows that Holm lives within her like a demon. That she won't rest until he is dead.

Two years ago he learned that she had been taken on by the BKA. He has a friend there who is an investigator, Jan Pieper. Pavlik asked him to check Aaron's computer every now and again. Pieper asked no questions. She had set up a program on the INPOL system to tell her every time the name Holm cropped up.

So far that hasn't happened.

But Pavlik knew, just as he knew about her karate training and the fifth Dan, which she reached last year.

Three weeks ago he had to go to Tegel for an interrogation and saw Sascha. He was hanging around with cold eyes, a cold grin on his lips, flicking away a dead cigarette butt. He had three or four prisoners around him, ordering them about with his little finger. He wore their fear like a warm coat.

Pavlik immediately began some investigations and got hold of the letters that Sascha and Eva Askamp had exchanged. It sounded genuine. He wasn't convinced. Until the psychologist's corpse was found in Boenisch's cell and Boenisch only wanted to talk to Aaron.

How can Demirci be so blind not to understand that all of this was about Aaron? If she knew what he was up to she wouldn't have spent this evening with him. They'd have thrown him out already.

*Maybe I want her to make the decision for me.*

When he woke up he was still determined not to say anything to Aaron. But after seeing her again, after that happy moment when she hugged him and whispered, "I love you," he couldn't do it anymore. She had a right to know.

But he has kept one thing to himself: that he knows the name Eva Askamp from somewhere else.

Only a man with an outstanding memory is suited to becoming a sniper or precision marksman. He needs to be constantly scanning the territory in front of him to discover the tiniest changes. Was that cigarette there an hour ago? The gravel, the paper tissue, the sheet of paper, the glass splinter? Pavlik trained himself in that just as hard as he trained his body.

He knows he's heard or read that woman's name somewhere before. He finds nothing on the INPOL database.

When and where? When and where? It's driving him crazy.

Almost as much as the certainty that on this day which is about to dawn, something awaits him that will test him more than anything ever has before.

He can't express it. But he knows.

Pavlik feels Sandra standing behind him even though he didn't hear her come out. She puts a blanket around his shoulders, just as he starts to get goosebumps.

"Did she get to the hotel all right?" she asks.

"Yes."

"Alone?"

"You know she doesn't take a single step alone."

"I don't mean that."

Niko's name is in Pavlik's silence, Sandra's fear in her whisper. "Whatever happens, you'll protect her."

# 12

AARON WAKES up. Light. Light. Light. The world is nothing but light. Her gaze flies through the white infinity, further and further, aimlessly, millions of kilometers in a flash. The light surrounds Aaron and is inside her at the same time, it fills her completely, streams through her like a mighty river. Aaron swims in that light, she is carried by the river.

She is light as a feather, she drifts along.

That's how it once was.

A month ago she came out of the cinema in Wiesbaden after the late show. On the pavement she was surrounded by shouting and laughter. Aaron sensed the energy of a lot of people, she was jostled, suddenly engulfed in a surge of people and pushed forwards, shoved around by party-goers. In the end she was able to break free. The group moved on, laughing.

Aaron no longer knew right from left, she turned round and bumped into a man. She asked, her voice quivering, if he knew the way to the bus stop.

The man didn't reply. He held her tightly for a moment. Or for hours, she doesn't know. Then he disappeared.

When Aaron opened her eyes the next morning, there was light everywhere. That gleam, the surging river. She was very excited and went to see an ophthalmologist, in the sudden hope that it might be an early sign of her eyesight returning. But he said she wasn't seeing white, just as before she wasn't seeing black. She wasn't seeing anything. Her brain was just producing colors. There are blind people whose worlds are gray, blue, even green or purple. With some it changes according to their mood, in others not. The cause is unknown. He was sorry. Ophthalmology wasn't an exact science.

In fact the light grew weaker after a few days. It had left her and turned into a washed-out curtain swelling in front of a window behind which there was nothing but endless night. One evening when she was going to bed there were flashes behind that curtain, and each one blackened a thread of the cloth. She watched until she fell asleep. When she woke up she was staring into the darkness as if the light had never existed.

Aaron called the BKA and reported in sick. She bought a ticket for the Neroberg funicular. During her time in the Department her official trips to Wiesbaden had always consisted of plane, taxi, meeting. Her colleagues from the BKA thought a trip on the old hydraulic railway was worthwhile; the view at the top was unrivaled.

She never found the free time. But since she's been in Wiesbaden the bench by the Greek temple has been her favorite place. She sits there and imagines a view which, on a clear day, extends all the way to Frankfurt.

That morning Aaron heard pigeons fluttering and children laughing. She felt cold. Her hands buried deep into her coat pockets; in her left was something small and hard.

She wondered.

But all of a sudden she knew what it was.

A coffee bean.

Suddenly she caught the smell of that man who had stopped her in the street outside the cinema. Camellia blossom. The realization that it had been Holm left Aaron as crumpled as a sheet of paper.

He had found her and could kill her at any moment.

She sat there shaking for a long time.

A month after going blind, she had visited a mobility trainer, but he told her he couldn't work with her yet. He only took on clients who had been blind for at least a year. He called it the "year of mourning." It was necessary, he said, to work through the shock of something incomprehensible and irrevocable happening. The loss of her eyesight had been as definitive as the death of a loved one.

Aaron was to take time to grieve. When she had done that she could call him again.

Two other trainers also refused, for similar reasons. Her father found the fourth. She doesn't know what he had said to the man. But he took her on. Normally the training takes eight weeks. She did it in four. In her free time she practiced her sense of balance, she did yoga and tai chi, she tortured herself with her body, which had become alien to her. Sometimes she touched it to check that it belonged to her and not to someone else.

In the fourth week her father died. She didn't take that year of mourning either. She started karate again. First on her own, because it was so ridiculous that she would have been ashamed if anyone had seen her clumsy movements, her reflexes, which weren't worthy of the name.

Later, when the fire flared up in the library of her memory, Aaron wondered desperately if it had been started by her impatience. Was the loss of her memories the price for her refusal to mourn?

"You have to go through four phases," the doctor had said in the clinic. *Shock. Denial. Depression. Acceptance.* She thought she had accepted her fate. But she had only pretended to do so. In the face of the fire she admitted to herself for the first time that she had never really tried to understand what had happened to her. She had never made peace with her old life. She still carried it around with her. Basically it had become an unbearable burden, and secretly she longed to cast that burden off at last.

Max Frisch says in his novel *Gantenbein* that everyone sooner or later invents a story which he sees as his own life.

Aaron too had to invent a completely new life so as not to be swept away.

The first step was the hardest: to admit to herself that she is blind, and that this means something other than not being able to see. That was the first time she buried her old life and wept for it and became the woman she is, and also wept for her father.

Since that morning on the Neroberg, where pigeons fluttered and children laughed and she found the coffee bean in her coat pocket, she has known why she didn't take her time.

But what does Holm want to take revenge for? For the fact that she put his brother in jail? After five years? Aaron racked her brains. In Barcelona she had killed Nina Deraux, Token-Eyes' girlfriend. She considered the possibility that Deraux was pregnant not by him but by Holm. But as part of the autopsy a DNA test had been carried out on the foetus, identifying Token-Eyes as the father. The hatred with which his brother had looked at her in the tunnel was etched on her retina forever. Why did Holm come after her on the freeway? The money? Certainly not. Money means nothing to Holm. The car somersaulted, she lay blind and helpless in the wreck. Holm could have stopped. It would have been easy for him to take the bag and disappear. He wasn't interested.

He became the master of her dreams.

Once he had a Mohican like Robert De Niro in *Taxi Driver* and said with a grin: "You're too slow."

Another time she saw herself as a seven-year-old girl with Ben, her best friend. The pond in the forest was frozen. Her mother had reminded her time and again not to walk on thin ice under any circumstances. But it drew her like an enormous bar of whole-nut chocolate that she needed to unwrap. And Ben was brave because she was brave. Hand in hand they flew across the white mirror; the blades of their skates drew cries of joy from the ice. Until Ben screamed and became so heavy that she had to let go of him. He sank into a black hole, reappeared and stretched his cold hand towards her. But she only touched his fingertips. He escaped her, and his tears were the last thing she saw.

In the dream she recognized that Ben was alive. He was Holm and wanted to bring her to justice because she hadn't saved him. She asked herself day and night: why did Holm hate her so much?

He was back, and for the last four weeks she had done nothing but wait for the moment when she would stand in front of him again.

*He alone will decide when.*

*How could I have been so naïve as to fly to Berlin?*
*But perhaps that's exactly what I wanted.*

Now, at six o'clock in the morning in the Hotel Jupiter, she is ready. If Pavlik had thrown the pack of cigarettes on the roof terrace, she would have caught it. And if she had been standing in the sixth lane…

*Don't be presumptuous. You're handicapped. You can't compete with Holm. And he won't give you a second chance. If you get a chance at all.*

She goes into the bathroom and looks in the mirror and imagines her face as she does every morning. She always sees herself in one particular photograph. She's posing, legs wide, on Sandra and Pavlik's terrace, wearing one of the twins' cowboy hats, drawing two toy revolvers from their holsters and laughing. That photograph is the only memory of her face. It will never age, and is frozen for all time in that moment on the terrace.

In every Shintō shrine there is a mirror. If you look into it, you're supposed to recognize yourself. Your own courage. Your own fear.

What you are.

Aaron has to pursue her own fate. The Department can't protect her, however many men they have. She will be alone when she faces Holm, with nothing but the light within her. But it draws the energy out of her body, lures her, tries to seduce her into falling into it. How Aaron wishes she could take some kind of pill that would give her a boost. Instead she stands under the shower, cold, hot, cold again. A thousand needle-points sharpen her thoughts. She will begin today by shaking off the two men who took over from Kleff and Rogge. Aaron is convinced that Pavlik has chosen the best, so it's good practice.

She knows her destination.

*The camellia has already been sold.*

When she steps out of the shower, she leaves the water turned on full. She brushes her teeth; she's known since yesterday where the buttons for the radio are, and turns on some music. Comes out of the bathroom, feels for the slit screw beneath the handle with which the door can be opened from the outside, and turns it shut with a coin.

She gets dressed. Clicks her tongue quietly. Receives the echo of the connecting door to the next room, which can be combined with hers to form a suite as required. Presumably it's free; Pavlik will have seen to that.

She opens the door with a hair-grip from her handbag. Listens. If she was wrong and woke someone up she'd look pretty ridiculous.

Silence. No breathing.

Good.

She puts her phone and a few banknotes into her jeans pocket, slips on her coat and takes the hotel Bible out of the bedside table drawer. She clicks again. When Aaron is extremely focused, she can locate objects with a thickness of at least two centimeters. She finds the standard lamp. Feels her way to it; there's a glass table beside it.

Aaron grips the lamp, takes a deep breath, smashes its metal foot against the table and drops the lamp on the floor.

Immediately there's a knock on the door. "Aaron? Yes, are you OK?"

She knows who it is: Peschel. He has a habit of starting most of his sentences with "yes." Peschel is constantly eating sweets, never puts on weight and has three children by three different women.

He's the best bodyguard in the Department.

*Thanks, Pavlik.*

"Yes, if you don't open up, we'll have to come in. Aaron."

She picks up her pumps, darts with the hotel Bible and the folded telescoping stick into the next room, quietly closes the connecting door and calculates fifteen seconds until they sense that something isn't right. Another five till they act.

The knocking gets louder. "Come on, say something!"

Aaron counts in silence. After twenty seconds the door crashes off its hinges. She has to assume that both men have stormed into her room, creeps outside into the corridor and turns to the left.

No one calls after her. Good.

She relaxes her shoulder, makes herself as light as possible, the thick carpet pile is her best ally. In one hand she holds the stick and her pumps, in the other the Bible.

*What could happen?*

*There's an obstacle in front of me. I stumble over it and make a noise. Unlikely. What could be in my way at this time of night?*

She knows the corridor branches off after eighty paces, approaches the spot unhurriedly, at a relaxed trot, two steps, one meter, silently. She hears very quiet knocking on her bathroom door, reads the men's thoughts: Aaron is in the shower, she's got the radio on—that's why she can't hear them. They see the shattered glass table, the lamp. But: fourteenth floor, the hotel façade is smooth, the window undamaged, no one could have entered the room unobserved.

In such situations they've been instructed to apply Ockham's Razor: if you have several possibilities, always go for the simplest one.

Peschel knows Aaron: he'll say, she's great, but when she goes crazy, stuff gets broken. She's under pressure, she needed some air, so she took it out on the table.

It would be very embarrassing to get into the bathroom, find yourself standing in front of a naked Aaron and have to stammer, "S-sorry."

*That won't put them off forever, of course. They stand still for another thirty seconds. Then one of them pushes down the handle and notices that the door is bolted. Why should I have done that, if I'm on my own? They'll break down the door.*

Aaron finds the turning precisely, sticks to the right and after twenty meters she finds the lift. Feels for the button and presses it. Puts on her pumps.

*What could happen?*

*First: the lift takes an eternity.*

*Second: it goes up, not down.*

Splintering wood. The two men have lost their patience sooner than she thought, and broken down her bedroom door. Now they know. She gives them ten seconds to get to the lift.

*Damn, where is he?*

There.

The door opens. She jumps into the lift. Which button is the ground floor? The bottom one? No. The hotel doesn't have an underground car park, it has a spa in the basement.

Running feet.

She pushes the button second from the bottom. The door closes so gently that Peschel's fists are still drumming against it when the lift finally goes down. "Yes, what is this crap?" Aaron hears his muffled roar.

One of them will call the lift, the other takes the stairs.

Eighty seconds, tops.

*Tight. Very tight.*

The lift is quick, thank God. Still it seems to her to take a painfully long time before it finally stops. What happens next is crucial. If she gets out and this isn't the lobby but a different floor, she can forget her plan.

She stands in front of the light sensor. Quiet classical music, a phone ringing, the click of a keyboard, suitcase wheels on marble. Relieved, she sets the Bible down in the doorway to stop the lift from going up. Aaron follows the sound of the suitcase, snaps the stick open, holds it like a pencil and swings it around as if in a training video for mobility instructors.

There's something in her way. Aaron reaches out her hand. Leather, a group of chairs. She reaches her hand along it and around the barrier, sends her stick dancing again; there's nothing in her way.

She taps against the metal edge of the revolving door.

Now comes the hardest bit.

Aaron has to vanish.

In less than fifty seconds.

# 13

SHE IS enveloped in damp and cold. Exhaust fumes mingle with snowy air. The city yawns, rolls over, doesn't want to wake up quite yet. She dozes amidst the whoosh-whoosh of a street-sweeping machine, the weary needles of diesel engines, the crunch of car tires, the rumble of the suitcase disappearing into the distance.

Everything is slow.

Only Aaron is quick.

She clicks her tongue, it takes her four steps to get to the curbside, almost slips, finds her balance and steps out of the sound shadows of the parked cars. Aaron likes streets with dense traffic. The stream of vehicles helps her find her bearings. When the first one stops and that continues from car to car until they're all at a standstill, she knows where the traffic light is.

That's better than having to cross a quiet street, with the risk of someone hurtling out of a turning or a side-road, while you stand helplessly in the middle of the carriageway and pray.

But here, on Leipziger Strasse, it's too far to the next lights. At this time of day the distances between the cars are variable. She has a window of between two and five seconds. That's impossible to calculate, and she has to get to the other side at a hell of a rate.

Aaron knows: on the four-lane street it takes her seven steps to get to the middle.

The second virtue: *Yu.* Courage.

She sprints off with her stick stretched out in front of her.

*See me! Please! Keep your eyes wide open!*

No beeping horns. Luckily she caught the perfect moment. Aaron stands on the dividing strip, her heart a punch press.

Aaron concentrates on the moment and runs again. This time cars have to break and skid: one brushes her stick, almost knocks it out of her hand. She runs into the light and imagines that the cars are made of light as well.

Only light, weightless. Light can't hurt her.

She is accompanied by a chorus of honking horns. But she makes it, she's on the other side.

*I've still got at least twenty seconds! It's enough!*

Euphorically she uses her stick to find the gap between two parked vehicles, where she will find refuge. In her mind's eye she sees the men charging out of the Jupiter, scouring the pavement and giving up, grinding their teeth.

Not bad for a blind woman! She's only sorry that Pavlik will miss her one triumphant escape.

Suddenly she comes to a halt. Her knee collides with an obstacle. She runs her hand over it. Just as Aaron works out what it is, chaos breaks out.

She has ended up between a truck and its trailer, and what she feels against her knee is the drawbar. The engine starts and the truck sets off.

Adrenalin floods her veins like a dam breaking. She jumps on the coupling piece, becomes a blind passenger. Everything happens at a crazy speed, but for Aaron time becomes infinitely slow. She has to let go of her stick. It falls under the wheels. Aaron hears of it being crushed, hears the dark roar of the engine, the metallic crunch under her feet, the flapping of the tarpaulin cover behind her, even the indicator of the truck, which is impossible.

As the vehicle slips among the traffic and accelerates, the balancing tips of her toes are her only contact with the coupling piece. Her hands seek something to cling on to and find a ventilation slit. She claws the fingertips of one hand into it like a free climber. She hammers with her other fist in the insane hope that the driver might be able to hear her. The truck speeds up. Right bend. They careen to the side. The drawbar bucks. Aaron has to stop hammering, she needs the fingertips of both hands.

And she slips off.

For a moment she stands freely on the drawbar like a surfer who has caught a monster wave and is riding with his keel on a single drop of water. Aaron knows that she will die if she does the wrong thing now. Everything gets even slower. The world almost comes to a standstill.

She falls backwards. At the same time her right leg shoots upwards. Aaron wedges one foot against the front wall while keeping the other fixed on the drawbar, presses her back against the plastic sheet of the trailer, spreads both arms to increase her body surface area. The stiffness of the tarpaulin is her salvation. She's going to be spending the next few seconds in that position as she reflects:

*I've got to stay on as far as a red light. I'll jump off then. But how will I know that it's a red light? If he just stops for a moment and then drives off again, I'm dead.*

The driver is also surfing, on a wave of green lights.

Another turning, to the left this time, sharp. Her right leg is stretched out as far as it will go, so far from her other leg that she's almost doing the splits and can't exert greater pressure.

Aaron sees the action in her mind's eye and guesses that she has a five per cent chance. She bends her right leg and stands on the drawbar like a flamingo. She puts all her strength on her left leg and catapults herself forwards. If she doesn't catch the ventilation slit at the first attempt, it will be the last movement she ever makes.

One hand reaches into the void, but the other finds the metal. Aaron pulls herself over with the tip of her middle finger. She reaches across with her other hand and somehow holds on. Suddenly she is thrown against the wall of the vehicle. Brakes screech.

The truck stops.

Feverishly she wonders whether she should jump off.

*Yes! Do it!*

But this thought and the jolt when the driver steps on the accelerator are simultaneous. He only paused for a pedestrian, a cyclist, a dog, for some random person. Having decided to jump, Aaron had reduced her body tension.

And is pulled apart by the drawbar.

She's only holding on by three fingertips. Her legs are dangling in the void. They look for the drawbar and can't find it.

*It's over.*

Just as she loses her hold and falls, the truck brakes again. Aaron plummets from the drawbar to the tarmac. Rolls up in a ball so as not to be hit by the trailer. Shifts her weight to the left. Is hurled under the chassis, can't do anything, is nothing but a pine cone, a faded leaf, a snowflake, a grain of dust thrown this way and that at the whim of a hurricane. Adrenalin explodes. Aaron screams and crashes against an obstacle.

She's out of breath. She sucks raging fear into her lungs.

Forces herself to touch the obstacle.

A wheel. Big. Static.

In her head there is the eye of a needle with a thousand thoughts trying to get through it all at once. They jostle and shove, they are in an incredible hurry, each one wants to be first.

Two questions make it into her consciousness:

*Right or left?*

*How many lanes?*

She opts for the most likely solution and creeps out from under the trailer on the right-hand side. Engines idling. She feels a warm, wet radiator, runs her hand along a bumper and stumbles over the edge of the curb.

The cars drive along behind her. The truck is so quiet it could be five streets away. She wants to snap her fingers, but they're stiff as a plank. Tries to click her tongue, but produces only a faint squelching sound. Tries again, until she feels her head will burst. It's like shouting into a storm. Somehow she emits a pitifully faint click.

But the echo comes back.

Her feet get moving. She bumps into the wall. The seven steps to the front door don't belong to her. She slumps down on the steps. The adrenalin is only an aftershock from the previous mighty flood.

Her hands trembling, Aaron taps her watch. The computerized voice blankly reports: "Seventh of January. Thursday. Six o'clock, seventeen minutes, eleven seconds."

She only left the hotel two minutes ago.

Her phone vibrates in her jeans. Pavlik.

A new wave rolls in. Tears this time. Aaron is sitting in front of a house in the middle of nowhere, weeping incessantly.

But not because of those two minutes.

The pain has many names. Boenisch, Barcelona, Holm, Niko, Sandra, Dad, all the others. She doesn't want to be strong anymore. Doesn't need to be strong anymore. Can't be strong anymore. She sits there until she is still crying but no tears come. Then she feels as if she's dead and can't even lift her head when she hears a friendly, concerned voice.

"Are you all right? Do you need help?" a man asks.

She doesn't even have the strength to answer.

"Do you speak German?"

Somehow she manages to stagger to her feet. "Can you tell me where I am?"

"Good heavens, look at the state of you!"

Only now does she reflect that falling under the truck, the mud she crawled through, must have left traces.

"You're injured."

"Where?"

"On your hands."

Blood. Her skin has been scraped off. No pain. Numb. She moves her fingers. They're in working order. "It's fine. Please, it's really important for you to tell me where I am."

"I assume you aren't from Berlin?"

"Why?"

"Because you're looking straight at the Holocaust Memorial."

"I'm blind."

"You don't look it."

"I know. Could you please call me a taxi?"

*

They drive along the Stadtring. The windscreen wipers are turned off, which means it isn't snowing anymore. In the back of the taxi she rests her temple against the icy glass of the window. Her hand finds the coffee bean that she always carries in her coat pocket. A single thought revolves on an endless loop:

*How can I stand up against Holm when crossing a street defeats me?*

Her phone vibrates again. Pavlik's third call. Then she listens to her mailbox. *"What are you thinking, have you gone completely crazy? Where are you? If you don't call right now I'm going to send out a search party."*

He has lowered his voice by a third. She has only known him so furious on one other occasion; she still remembers.

When the twins were eleven, one day they didn't come home from school and no one knew where they were. Aaron sat for hours with them while the search went on and Sandra and Pavlik were insane with worry. At ten o'clock at night the boys were standing at the door. They were both in love with a girl from the other class and had plundered their piggy banks to ask her out skating and show off a little bit.

Pavlik raised his hand to them. The twins ran to their room and locked themselves in. But when Aaron sat down outside their door and told them seriously how when she was eleven she fell in love with a boy who was as sweet as spring cherries, they let her in. She talked to them like adults, while Pavlik threw tools around in the garage and Sandra tried to calm him down.

Aaron told the twins that their father had slapped them not out of rage but out of relief. She asked what the girl was like, and the boys argued about whether the most awesome thing about her was her tousled hair or her freckles or her amazing ability to whistle through her fingers. She advised them to work out as quickly as possible which one of them the girl liked, otherwise it would all turn into the most dreadful muddle. Aaron ruffled their hair and said the smoke would have cleared by tomorrow. Perhaps over the next few days they should help their father clear up the garage. And it certainly wouldn't be a bad idea to get rid of the chaos in their room which was driving their mother to despair.

Pavlik had left and came back when Aaron was drinking another glass of wine with Sandra. He had been to see the girl's mother to apologize for his sons' behavior. The woman was drunk and hadn't even noticed that her daughter was out. Pavlik couldn't get over it. He fixed himself a drink. Even Sandra couldn't get through to him. After she'd yelled at him she left him alone with Aaron.

She wanted to talk to him, but he snapped at her angrily, saying that she couldn't possibly understand. She had no family. What did she know? Aaron got to her feet. She reached into her jacket and set down on the table the photograph in which she can still see her face, even today. A self-timed snap. Aaron, Sandra and Pavlik and the twins, all dressed up as cowboys and Indians. It was the five of them, and after that not much happened for a long time. Aaron always carried the photograph with her except when she was working under cover.

She left without a word of farewell.

The next morning she flew to Barcelona.

Pavlik showed her no sympathy at the hospital, it was his way of grieving. Before he left he put something in her hand. She knew straight away what it was. After he had gone she hugged the photograph, the picture in which from now on she would see herself on her own, as if the others had never been there.

The taxi driver brings her to the door. Aaron asks him to ring the bell marked Askamp. No, he doesn't need to wait. She assumes that the men observing the house are already on the phone to Pavlik. If no one opens, she will stand here until he comes and rages at her.

But the buzzer is activated.

She goes into the house. Doesn't know the floor. Cautious steps to the stairs. On the first landing she pauses.

"Miss Askamp?" she calls out quietly.

No reply.

Aaron goes up a floor. She clicks her tongue. The echo shows her the open door to a flat. "Miss Askamp?" Something darts past. A cat runs mewing down the stairs.

There is a rushing sound in Aaron's head that drowns out her heartbeat. She pulls off her pumps, takes off her coat and drops it on the floor. She goes into the flat. Smells camellia. Trips. She kneels down and feels a lifeless body. It is small. A child. She plunges down an endless shaft and crashes to the bottom, alone with the child. She tries to find the child's pulse. It's alive. High above her, music rattles from the speaker of a mobile phone. Roy Orbison's "Pretty Woman."

Icy cold flows into her body like a drip. The door falls shut. A hand grabs her, pulls her out of the shaft as if she is a doll and slings her against the hard floor.

She creeps through a tunnel of fear. A blazing flash pierces the light. It explodes and vaporizes in sudden darkness. Inside her chest the tunnel walls press together. She tries to get her breath back as she finds the handle of a drawer and drags herself up. Buttons. Stove. A kitchen.

Legs spread, she assumes the attack position. Bends her knee, turns her strong foot out. Her right fist is outstretched, her left arm along her body. Holm's voice comes from the realm of the dead. "Kind of you to accept my invitation."

He is standing right in front of her.

*Two meters.*

Aaron darts at him. Her left foot kicks at where she assumes Holm's kneecap will be. At the same time she turns on her own axis and aims her foot at his pubic bone, hoping to break it, destroy Holm's stasis.

She didn't even feel the draft when he jumped to the side. Aaron kicks into the void and is thrown against the door frame by the momentum of her movement. Roy Orbison continues to smarm.

Holm's voice is a breath of wind over a fresh grave. "Is that it?"

Aaron flies at him, her hands outstretched as if for an embrace. She claps them together, but misses Holm's head, and her empty palms strike against one another. He has silently switched position again, and is now standing beside her.

"A very effective move if it finds its target," he observes. "It takes only one bar of pressure to burst my eardrum. You can squash a fly with that. Do you think I'm a fly?"

Aaron tries to connect this voice with the man who said to her so charmingly in Barcelona: "I would even have waited two minutes for you." She can't do it. She knows Holm is talking to her. But he's someone else. No. He's only shed his skin and is revealing what he always was: her demon.

"Why me?" she asks querulously.

Words blow like ashes from his mouth: "My life belongs to duty; but in spite of death dancing on my grave, you will not have my good name to cover it with dark disgrace."

She feels him going outside. He hasn't made a single sound apart from the words he uttered. Aaron wants to take her phone from her jeans pocket, but can't do it straight away, she has no feeling in her fingers.

At last she succeeds.

But he's back. With a blow of his hand he casually flings the mobile phone across the kitchen. Something heavy crashes to the floor.

She hears a dull moan like an animal caught in a trap.

"This woman and I exist in completely different worlds," Holm says. "If she screams in her world, I don't even hear it in mine." He is hurting Eva Askamp, injuring her. She is trying to scream behind her gag. It sounds like glass being crushed in a mortar.

Aaron's thoughts run through her synapses at the speed of light. She is standing with her back to the stove. In just about every kitchen you'll find a knife block. If Eva Askamp is right-handed it'll be on the right of the stove.

She whirls round, wipes her hand across the work surface and pulls a big knife from the block. She feels the draft when Holm jumps. Her left leg jerks backwards into a standing split and strikes him on the temple. Aaron calculates that he's going to stagger to the right, and throws the knife over her shoulder. She knows she has hit him. Holm grunts with surprise. Aaron does a half back-handspring, brings her ankles together and catches his head in a vice. She brings Holm to the ground. Her crossed ankles throttle him while her right elbow bores into his kidneys, and with her left she grabs his crotch and twists her hand.

Holm's fist comes down on her cheekbone. A fast second blow catches her between chin and bottom lip. The pain makes her head explode. She has to relax her grip. He springs into a standing position, drags her up by her hair and throws her against the wall. She just lies there. Her body is finished.

Holm turns the music off. He chews ash and spits it out. "I will feel and touch this scar for as long as I live. Thanks for that."

He throws the knife on the floor. "I'm going to count to ten. Tell me why I followed you in Barcelona. If you lie I'll kill the woman."

Tears of despair shoot into Aaron's eyes.

"One."

"I shot your brother."

And knows it's not that.

"Two."

"I killed his lover."

And knows it's not that.

"Three."

"I had the money."

And knows it's not that.

"Four."

"Why me? Why me?"

"Five."

"I left Niko on his own."

"Six."

"I was a coward."

"Seven."

"I hate myself for it."

"Eight."

"Please don't hurt the woman anymore."

"Nine."

She begs: "Kill me. Not her."

"I'll give you one more chance," he says coldly and definitively. "Take time for your answer. For the woman, everything hangs on it." He savors the seconds.

"What was I thinking when we were looking at each other in the tunnel?"

"Eye for an eye," Aaron whispers.

"Ten."

Eva Askamp doesn't even groan. It's just silent. Terribly silent. Aaron plunges back into the shaft. She lies there with the boy and the woman and waits for death.

The ash floats down to her in the darkness. "Receive/when my life is over/my all-consuming love for you/from the smoke/that rises from my burning body."

She doesn't hear him leave. Just knows he's gone. She lies forever in the shaft until her heart starts beating again. She is so afraid of stretching out her hand. The woman is dead. The camellia flower lies in her lap. There is blood on Aaron's hand. She pulls Eva Askamp to her, takes the gag off her mouth, rocks her in her arms, dies a second, third, fourth time.

Footsteps in the corridor.

*He's coming back.*

She crawls across the floor. Looks for the knife.

Finds it. Throws the knife.

Hears it stick into the door frame and quiver.

"Aaron, it's me."

Pavlik.

She tries to creep out of the shaft. Slides back. Crawls her fingers into the stone and slides slides slides. At last she feels Pavlik gently lifting her up. He holds her tight, she lies against his chest. Memories fly past like snowflakes. She looks into a bag of newspaper cuttings. She opens the gift box with the Starfire. She rests her hand on Boenisch's television. She kisses Niko at the Djemaa El Fna. She drinks limoncello with Sandra. She lies on the ice and reaches for Ben's hand. She sees the Audi in the rearview mirror. She weeps for the woman in the Hotel Aralsk. She takes a bag of hot chestnuts from Niko. She sees Ben sinking into the depths. Nothing but snowflakes. They spray in all directions and are gone forever.

Pavlik strokes her hair. "I've got you."

She opens her eyes. Can hardly move her tongue. "How's the boy?"

"He's alive. Under anaesthetic."

"How did Holm get into the house?"

"Over the wall in the courtyard."

"Why were none of your men there?"

She feels Pavlik shivering. "Butz. Holm killed him."

*Butz.*

"Who called you?"

"No one. I knew you were here."

"Where are the men who were outside the house?"

He doesn't answer.

*Please don't say it.*

"Two point-blank shots to the head."

# 14

PAVLIK GUIDES her down the corridor of the Department. Not a sound. But Aaron knows that they're walking between two lines of silent men. Three dead comrades. Pavlik deployed her without telling Demirci. Only now does she realize what that means. Means for him. "Pavlik—" she whispers.

He goes with her to the toilet and closes the door. His voice is gone. "It wasn't your fault."

Aaron sinks down the wall. Pavlik crouches facing her. "How did Butz die?" she asks.

"Broken neck. No marks."

*One of the best. He didn't even see Holm coming.*

"He was on leave. But he volunteered for your sake. He didn't give a damn about Demirci."

She sees herself reaching towards her father's garden gate. Men walk by carrying some kind of load.

A familiar voice says: "It's me, Butz."

When he was still with the BKA, he saved the life of one of Jörg Aaron's men on an operation and put his own life on the line. Even though there was almost thirty years between them, they became friends. As far as Aaron knows, her father only had three. The two men recognized one another, whenever they were in danger they never let their feelings take over.

*Except in Antwerp.*

\*

140

That's one of the memories she wrote down before they were lost: Aaron flew to Antwerp with Butz for a "virginity test." There they handed two submachine guns with filed-off serial numbers to the men they wanted to buy fifty kilos of heroin from, to prove they were trustworthy. They assumed that their contacts were working for Eyck de Fries, the biggest drug dealer in Europe. He was the target, the one they wanted to trap.

The submachine guns were their tickets, the heroin deal was supposed to play out in an old army barracks. The evening before, Butz was nervous. Aaron didn't recognize him like that. He ordered jenever, even though he never normally drank. Butz thought their cover was blown. He couldn't explain it. "This one time I'm listening to my belly." They'd invested a lot in the case. Aaron talked away at Butz, and she managed to persuade him to go to the barracks as planned the next day.

When they parted in the hotel corridor she felt him watching after her. She turned around. "I'm gay," he said. "Your father knows. No one else. Now you do." He didn't expect her to answer and went to his room.

She stood there motionless for a long time. Butz, the beau, the great womanizer, as everyone thought, even though he didn't make a big deal about it. He had never been closer to her than he was in that corridor. She knew she could have told Butz he didn't need to pretend in the Department, but it would have been a lie. Aaron was ashamed about that. And she was ashamed on behalf of the others as well.

She had had a mute conversation with her father.

*I couldn't have imagined you being friends with a gay man.*

*Why not?*

*Because you're bursting with testosterone.*

*Engage your brain before you speak. But I'll tell you one other thing: when Stefan opens his mouth, you should listen.*

That night in Antwerp she fell into a sweaty sleep. She was dreaming that she wanted to put on a cheerful summer dress, but when she opened the cupboard all her dresses were black.

At dawn she suddenly knew why Butz had confided in her: because he thought he was going to die today. If Aaron ever got out of the barracks, he wanted her to remember the man he had been, and tell their comrades so that they would remember him that way as well.

She knocked at Butz's door and could see that he hadn't slept. She said: "We're not going." She contacted the Police Fédérale, who were in charge of the investigations into Eyck de Fries. There was a shoot-out with three dead, one of them a policeman. There was no heroin in the boot, but a load of Semtex that killed another two officers. De Fries had found out from a Belgian spy that there were two undercover agents on his back. Aaron owed Butz her life.

*It must have been exactly like that, because I wrote it down. But your face has gone. Your laugh. Your eyes, which I think were sad. And one day I will stand empty-handed in front of you.*

The toilet door opens. Pavlik says: "Not now." Door closed.

"Will you ask Butz's sister if he was with anyone?" Aaron asks.

"No, he was on his own. You know he did date a lot, but nothing serious."

"He was gay."

Pavlik snorts: "Nonsense."

"Butz was gay. He wanted you to know."

"OK," Pavlik says curtly.

"Who were the other two?"

"Blaschke and Clausen. You don't know them."

The door opens again. Peschel. "Yes, Demirci is there now."

Pavlik gets up. Slow, weary, heavy.

Aaron gets to her feet as well. "I'm sorry I dumped you in it at the hotel," she says to Peschel.

"Yes, but they were already dead by then. Pavlik, one thing is clear, we all stand by that. Just don't get it into your head to blame yourself for the whole damned thing."

Peschel leaves her alone.

"Wait." Pavlik runs some water, washes Aaron's face. The only person apart from her mother who's ever done that was a nurse in

Barcelona. She hated both of them doing it. But she feels Pavlik's touch as warm, careful, thoughtful. He dries her face. Takes her hands in his. "Never forget what you mean to me."

She says: "I'll come with you."

"No, you won't."

"Off you go. But you can be sure of one thing: I'll be sitting beside you a minute later." Aaron puts his hand to her cheek. "Never forget what you mean to me."

In Demirci's waiting room she is welcomed by a voice that she likes a lot. It belongs to Astrid Helm, the head secretary, who everyone calls Helmchen—"little Helm." Only Pavlik is allowed to address her informally. She's been here forever, and she's the soul of the Department. Her radar can always tell the right thing to do for someone, whether it's a smile or a bar of chocolate or a silence.

Ten things that Aaron misses:
Charlie Chaplin films
puppies playing
Sunday afternoons in the C/O photo gallery
being able to avoid dogshit
Al Pacino's smile
driving a '64 Ford Mustang
cherry blossom
de Chirico
looking at orangutans
Helmchen's concern

"Jenny—thank God." She strokes Aaron's arm. "I'm very glad nothing's happened to you."

"Thanks, Helmchen."

"I was in Bremerhaven at my brother's silver wedding anniversary yesterday, and didn't get back till late, otherwise we'd have seen each other at Ulf's birthday." Hesitantly she adds: "That's what you say, isn't it?"

"Yes, that's what you say, Helmchen."

Aaron hears the woman's deep sadness. The lads are her sons. She's been to a lot of funerals over twenty-five years.

"But heavens, you need to wear something else. I'll have your things fetched from the hotel. And I'll clean that coat quickly."

"Thanks." She takes off her coat.

"Show me your fingers."

"Just some scrapes."

"Nonsense. We'll clean them with iodine."

Helmchen turns to Pavlik. "I called Stefan Butz's sister and his father. And Matti Clausen's ex-wife. She'll have to tell the kids. Tom Blaschke's wife doesn't know yet. I thought you might want to go and see her."

"Yes."

"I've informed the youth welfare office about Miss Askamp's son."

Aaron's stomach feels hollow, and Helmchen says: "In a minute you'll get a croissant and a strong coffee. Black, no sugar, I know."

How has Aaron managed without Helmchen?

Demirci's door opens. "Mr. Pavlik—please come in."

"I'd like to be there for that conversation," Aaron says.

She expects Demirci to refuse, she wants to add a resolute "I insist," but Demirci says: "Of course."

They go into the office and sit down at the conference table.

"Do you need medical assistance?"

"No." Aaron straightens her legs. "The surveillance of Miss Askamp's house and my personal security were both authorized by me. I invented an instruction from the BKA and I take full responsibility for that."

"Forget it," Pavlik mutters. "Aaron knew nothing about it."

"What are you talking about?"

Pavlik is about to start speaking again, but Demirci says: "That's enough."

There's a knock at the door. Helmchen comes and sets down a tray. She guides Aaron's hand to the coffee cup. "The croissant is on the right." She goes and closes the door very quietly.

Aaron can't drink any coffee right now.

"Miss Aaron, I admire your strength of character. But the BKA don't have to issue us with instructions. Even though I haven't been here very long, I know how the Department works, believe me."

Aaron nods mutely. She tried.

"Mr. Pavlik, the day before yesterday we had a conversation in which you requested personal security for Miss Aaron. You explained that in great detail. Still, I doubted that it was necessary and refused."

"Yes."

"But you chose men to go behind my back."

"Yes."

"How many were involved in that operation?"

"Six."

"And how many were watching Eva Askamp?"

"Another six."

"Because you knew there was a chance of Holm contacting her."

"Yes. I couldn't rule out the possibility that she was in danger after Aaron and I went to her shop."

"Twelve. A third of all the available men. And I never even noticed."

A clasp snaps open beside Aaron.

Pavlik sets something heavy down on the table.

His gun.

He gets up. Demirci says: "The conversation isn't over."

Pavlik sits down again.

The sentences that follow are the most surprising thing that Aaron has experienced since she's been a policewoman.

"Three men down. That's bad, I don't know how I'll be able to justify that. But you, Mr. Pavlik, doubtless did the right thing. I would like to apologize for not listening to you. Otherwise I would have deployed more men and perhaps prevented the deaths of those three."

Aaron can't breathe.

Pavlik is a quiet man. But she's never known him so silent before.

"Bear in mind that those men were acting on my orders," Demirci goes on in a tone that tolerates no contradiction. "I will outline the reasons to my superior and am confident that he will understand my decision in view of the events."

For at least thirty seconds no one says a word.

After its creation immediately following the reunification of Germany, the Department was based on a single idea: it was to be a team of elite police officers who could, unlike the detectives of the BKA, operate without loss of energy through bureaucratic friction. The Wiesbaden office is a huge, sluggish tanker that's constantly being freighted with new responsibilities. The Department, on the other hand, is small, quick and accurate. It is ultimately run by the Conference of State Ministers and Senators of the Interior, operating in rotation. Demirci is answerable to whichever regional minister or senator is in charge of the committee at any given time.

As Aaron knows, this year he's the Senator of the Interior of Berlin.

*She is putting her career on the line. Three dead policemen. The Senator is put under considerable pressure by the media. He might choose someone to blame to save his own skin. Then she'll be finished. She's braver than anyone I've ever met.*

"So we've sorted that one out," Demirci says. "And the smoking ban in the building is lifted forthwith." She lights a cigarette and pushes the pack across the table.

They smoke like three people who really need it.

"I've studied the 'Chagall' file," says Demirci, coming straight to the point. "There's remarkably little about Holm in it."

"He grew up in Kaiserslautern," Pavlik says. "His father was a forestry worker, his mother a housewife. They had a terraced house. They had no contact with their neighbors. The shutters were usually down. The woman never exchanged a word with anyone in the street."

Demirci is as startled as Aaron. "How do you know that?"

"I called a former teacher of Holm's. He lived a few houses away at the time. He's an old man now, but he clearly remembers Holm and his brother."

*My Pavlik.*

"He says Holm was the most intelligent student he ever had. But he was held back twice, he took no interest in lessons. He wasn't particularly known for violence or cruelty, but no one ever picked a fight with him. When he was nineteen, his father disappeared without a trace. His car was found in the forest. Presumably he was murdered, but there was no corpse; investigations led nowhere. Holm took his eight-year-old brother off with him and was never seen again."

"He can hardly have been given custody?"

"No. And here comes the remarkable part: Sascha never went to another school, at least not under his real name, and Holm never showed up in the German social system. He paid no taxes, had no registered address, no driver's license or ID card. He simply disappeared with Sascha. To Barcelona."

"So what you're saying is: at the age of nineteen Holm became a professional criminal, since then he's been living a life outside of all social norms, while bringing up his brother at the same time?"

"Yes. After he was arrested on one occasion Sascha refused to give a statement. But when he went into hiding with Holm, an aunt placed a missing-person advertisement, in which she mentioned the port-wine stain on the back of his hand. That was still on the INPOL file. That's the only reason we know their real names."

Aaron picks up her coffee cup. Sets it back down again. "I wounded him with the knife. Did he wipe away the blood?"

"No," Pavlik says. "It's with Forensics."

"We may be able to link him with other crimes through prints or DNA, and establish some kind of movement profile for him."

A knock at the door. "Come in." The door opens. "Mr. Kvist—take a seat."

Niko sits on Pavlik's left.

*Thank you for not touching me. Not asking me how I am, or showing me in any other way that you're concerned about me. I couldn't bear it.*

"Mr. Kvist, you negotiated with Holm in Bruges. What sort of man is he?"

"Presumably he already knew that I was an undercover agent. But he still met me on his own. He was completely relaxed."

"Where would you put his intelligence on a scale from one to ten?"

"Eleven."

"And his physical condition?"

"It was perfect at the time."

Aaron says: "He's fifty, but his reflexes are still first-class. He aimed between my chin and my lower lip, which means that he has expert knowledge of the theory of acupuncture. He must be at least a third Dan in karate. He can lift a hundred and twenty kilos lying down. He looks after his body, but he doesn't worry about doing it harm. He can blank out pain, but if he wants it to, pain stimulates him. He's cultivated and speaks several languages. He's completely insensitive to the pain of others. In his world he's the one who makes all the rules. He likes beautiful things. But he doesn't own anything that he couldn't leave behind without a thought. He can never enjoy anything, apart from his own pain or the pain of others. He despises death and yearns for it."

A cigarette burns out. A watch ticks.

"You say he never does anything superfluous. Why did he kill the florist? What did he get out of that murder?"

A heart thumps.

"Miss Aaron?"

"How did he do it?" she asks Pavlik.

"She has cuts to her torso, but they wouldn't have been fatal. Presumably he suffocated her."

*It takes a long time for someone to suffocate. She was already dead when he started counting.*

Aaron's voice is strange and remote. "He wanted to show me that he's the master. That he's God. I'm supposed to acknowledge him. The three men he killed are a message to the Department: 'I don't negotiate with anyone.' Soon he'll make contact with us and tell us his plans."

"What do you think he's going to do?"

"Holm wants to get his brother out of prison."

"He needs accomplices for that," Demirci says.

Niko says: "No, he's a loner."

Aaron disagrees. "In Barcelona he used Sascha's lover. Holm knows how to exploit people. After that he throws them away."

Pavlik breathes from his belly. "I've seen Sascha. He was transferred to Tegel a month ago, but he's already in charge of Block Six. He's grinning like someone who's just passing through, and meanwhile picking other people's fear out of his teeth."

Aaron still hasn't eaten anything. She feels dizzy. "Sascha is scared of his brother, that was obvious in Barcelona," she says. "Holm has trained him like a dog. I assume that's also the answer to the question of why he waited five years."

"How do you mean?"

"Sascha shot the three Catalan policemen, but he made a mistake by letting one of them make an emergency call. Holm doesn't forgive mistakes. He was the one behind his brother's five-year sentence."

Ashes fall on the table. Someone exhales.

"But it's mostly about me."

"Why you?" Pavlik asks.

"I don't know."

"He could have killed you before."

"He wants to enjoy it. That was just the warm-up."

Niko has never smoked before. Now he lights a cigarette.

"Holm quoted something," Aaron says. "I think it's from a Shakespeare play. 'My life belongs to duty; but in spite of death dancing on my grave, you will not have my good name to cover it with dark disgrace.'"

"What does that mean?" Demirci asks.

"Holm is using the lines in the extended sense. Inazo Nitobe cites them in a very important passage in his standard work about Bushidō. It expresses the idea that we must not make our conscience the slave of a sovereign."

"*Your* sovereign."

"Holm means my official oath."

*He doesn't know my true sovereign.*

"He's challenging you to a duel," Pavlik says roughly. "Does he think you're a Samurai?"

"No. It's a reference."

Demirci again: "What to?"

Aaron doesn't reply.

After she killed for the first time, she wondered how she could justify it. The philosophy of karate led to Bushidō, the *way of the warrior*, the code of the Samurai. It contains the commandments of men she felt close to, because death was her brother. Whose highest good, however, was to sacrifice themselves for their sovereign. Aaron had to seek a substitute. The meaning of Bushidō lies in dying. What was worth giving their lives for?

She thought about that for a very long time, for years.

She found the answer in the underground car park of the Hotel Aralsk in Moscow. Today she can't remember the death of the young woman hit by the ricochet from her pistol. But she remembers one thing: that Nikulin's hitman was alive, and suffering from a shot to the belly, when she stood over him  and fired a bullet into his head.

She has never told anyone that, not even Pavlik. And certainly not her father. No one doubted that it was self-defense. What was she supposed to say? That she didn't want to save him? That she had been thinking about the incredibly expensive and incredibly brilliant lawyer to whom Ilya Nikulin would pay six hundred Euros an hour to get his hitman out of jail? That she wasn't exactly dying to meet the next hitman that Nikulin would send because he thought she was weak and naïve?

She had done it out of fear. And she admitted it to herself. It was right and wrong at the same time. She could tell the difference.

Aaron swore never to forget that. Facing up to fear made death a friend that she embraced every day and every night, with every breath she took.

Until it never lets her go.

That friend stayed with her even after she was blinded. She wakes up with it and goes to bed with it. For a long time she didn't understand it at all. Her old life was over. Why didn't death go on waiting for her the way it waited for everyone else? Since finding the coffee bean in her coat pocket, she has known the reason. Aaron hopes that her destiny will be completed with her death, otherwise it would be pointless.

"A reference to what?" Demirci repeats.

"To me."

Pavlik takes Aaron's hand under the table. She has talked to him about Bushidō. It isn't his way. He refuses to be embraced by death for the sake of Sandra and the children.

Demirci's practical tone conceals what she thinks. "Did you never see Holm before Barcelona?"

"Not wittingly."

Aaron hesitates.

*They wanted facts from me. And I have no facts. Holm communicates with me about my fears and my dreams. I can't prove any of it. But they need to know.*

"It was four weeks ago in Wiesbaden. I ran into him in the street. He didn't say a word. But it was him."

The air pressure in the room plummets.

"Did you tell any of your superiors?"

"No."

"Why not?"

"It was only a suspicion till now."

*What did I have? A coffee bean.*

Demirci's throat is tight. "If material things don't mean anything to him, the three million that he lost because of you are unimportant. What about the woman you killed in Barcelona?"

"She was his brother's lover. It's not about her."

Niko says: "Maybe he wants to take revenge for Sascha."

"Not after five years." Aaron touches the ashtray. "Holm played back a song on his phone. 'Pretty Woman' by Roy Orbison. Boenisch listened to it when I was in his basement. It's not in any file, and wasn't mentioned in the trial either."

"Boenisch told Sascha," Niko says.

"But how did Holm manage to get it to his brother?" Pavlik asks.

"Via Eva Askamp."

"There are worse possibilities."

Demirci goes to the door. "Miss Helm, tell the prison to send you the personal files of all the enforcement officers who have dealt with the prisoner Sascha Holm over the past few weeks. They've got an hour. The prisoner is to be put in solitary confinement straight away."

"How are we going to explain that without legal authority?"

"It's a defensive measure."

Niko has another cigarette. "Why did the Spaniards agree to him being transferred to Berlin in the first place? He murdered three Catalan policemen. And they just let him move?"

"I bet that was decided in Madrid," Pavlik said. "We know what they think about the Catalans. And presumably the whole joint was terrified of him in Barcelona. They'll have been glad to get rid of him."

Demirci goes back to the door. "And please call the Senate Justice Department. I want the correspondence about his transfer. Statements, documents, everything to and from Eva Askamp."

She discusses the next few steps with Niko and Pavlik.

Token-Eyes is to be interrogated, Niko will do that.

Aaron hears it as if there's a television on somewhere. Because her head is filled with a single thought: *Receive, when my life is over, my all-consuming love for you.*

# 15

IN FRONT of the Holocaust Memorial Magnus Sørensen watches his colleague Lena rounding up the schoolchildren and ordering them on to the bus.

*It's wrong.*

He said that to himself two weeks ago when he and Lena were the only people in the staff room and he only wanted to give her a book, but they were suddenly kissing and he walked away with his head in the air. He said it to himself again a day later in the store room after games, arranging medicine balls that didn't need arranging, and she came in and took his hand and put it under her skirt. Since then he's been saying it to himself every time he's lied to his wife about holiday replacements, teachers' meetings, group runs, and found himself thinking about the sweat on Lena's skin.

In his car by the edge of the forest, where he was just expecting a pupil's parents to knock on the misted window and ask him if he'd gone mad. In Lena's house when her husband was in Copenhagen.

Always, always, always.

In the café in Skanderborg, thirty kilometers from Aarhus, he tried to call it off. But as soon as she crossed her legs it was all over. He came home with lipstick on his collar and only noticed when he looked in the hall mirror and saw a coward. His wife hugged him. She whispered excitedly that their eldest daughter was in love for the first time, but for God's sake to keep it to himself. He held her tight, panicking that she might look at his collar.

And slept with her and thought of Lena.

And lay next to her and thought of Lena.

*It's wrong.*

He said it to himself when the colleague who was to go on the Berlin trip with Lena got flu, and the question hung in the air about who could go instead. Lena presented Sørensen with a fait accompli at the staff meeting, announcing that he would step in, they'd already discussed it. He was about to correct her, but saw himself nodding.

*It's wrong.*

He's been saying it to himself since yesterday at Schönefeld airport, where Lena, when they were loading the luggage on to the bus, touched his hand among the chatter of the children, and he already found himself calculating how many times they could be together.

*It's wrong.*

He said it to himself when he saw the beautiful woman and the man there, the man with the little suitcase, the woman on his arm and still a stranger. She was smoking a cigarette. The man looked at her constantly, but she gazed past him and he went off to fetch the car. Perhaps she had come to see her lover one last time in Berlin. And he had lied one last time to his wife, so that he could be unhappy this one last time.

When Sørensen, with Lena's knee pressed against his, waited for the bus to set off and became so sad that he knew he would burst into tears if anyone asked him a question, the man with the car came back.

She took two steps in the wrong direction. The man took her arm. He pointed out her mistake and protected her head with his hand as she got in.

It was then that Sørensen could tell that she was blind.

And a nameless fear crept over him. The fear remained there the whole day. In the Reichstag, by the Wall memorial, in the Zoo. They were near the monkeys, and afterwards Lena wanted to go to the nocturnal animal house, but only to grab him in a pitch-dark corner, to own him.

At six in the morning he peered out of her room at their little hotel and prayed that none of the pupils would see him. She kissed him.

She smelled of bed, of his desire to close the door again, for them to tumble into each other again, so that for the hour left till waking they would not be alone, they would gasp for air.

Sørensen teaches sport and physics. He believes that the world is held together by measurable quantities, and that that balance is unshakeable.

But he is still thinking about that blind woman.

The children are in the bus. Lena waves to him, he starts walking and barely feels like taking those ridiculous few steps. When he's about to get in, someone behind him says in English:

"Why don't we take a little tour of the city?"

Sørensen turns around.

She is standing on the roof terrace. The wind wails. She is shivering, because the suitcase that Helmchen brought from the hotel didn't contain a second pair of jeans, just the thin dress that she had brought for dinner in Paris and then worn at Pavlik's birthday party. Where she cried, laughed, danced. Before three men died because of her. Aaron's thoughts are icicles falling from the edge of the roof and shattering in the street far below her. No one had ordered her to sacrifice herself for them. Two of them she hadn't even known.

The lift door opens. Pavlik joins her. She feels his gaze. "Don't stare at me as if I owed you money."

"You just owe me the truth. What are you keeping quiet?"

Sirens wail.

"This isn't a day to keep things quiet," he says.

Tears come to her eyes. "Holm quoted something else. 'Receive/ When my life is over/my all-consuming love for you/from the smoke/that rises from my burning body.'"

"What's that?"

"The most famous Bushidō poem." She pauses. The sirens fall silent. "It was written centuries ago, and describes the highest form of love on the part of a Samurai. It is accomplished only when one reveals oneself in death."

The wind blows Pavlik's voice away from her. "How does he know about you and Kvist?"

"He saw us in Barcelona."

"Too long ago. And I'm sure you wouldn't have shown your feelings. You're too much of a professional for that."

"He could have watched us yesterday morning in Schönefeld. I smoked a cigarette in the car. Niko looked at me the whole time. I tried to ignore it and felt awkward. Holm is good at reading people."

The lift door opens.

"The name is familiar to me," Pavlik says.

"Which one?"

"Askamp. I can't get it out of my head."

"Have you heard it before somewhere?"

"As sure as I've got ten fingers."

"Pavlik?" Niko calls.

"What is it?"

"I need you."

Pavlik wants to go, but she holds on to him. "Today isn't the day to keep something to yourself."

He puts his arm around Aaron's shoulder and calls to Niko: "I'm here."

She thinks for a minute that Niko's going to leave them alone. But suddenly he's standing beside them.

"You put me and Jenny under surveillance yesterday. Did you think I didn't notice?"

"Demirci's orders, not mine."

"Don't lie to me."

"Ask her."

"I asked Peschel."

"Pavlik wanted to protect you," Aaron says.

"Stay out of it."

"No, I won't. Perhaps you should have a think about how long he's been your friend."

Pavlik puts his arm more tightly around her. "Leave it."

"Or did they have a watch on *me*?" Niko says. "Between ourselves, we're friends after all."

*What's he going on about?*

Pavlik says: "I wanted to go to Tegel with Aaron. You asked me to let you do it."

"And?"

"It had been decided a long time ago. Ask Peschel."

Pavlik is exchanging his thoughts with Aaron.

*He's got to find out.*

*I know.*

"Be careful," he murmurs. "It's possible that Holm has his eye on me too."

"Why do you say that?"

"He dropped a hint," Aaron says.

"What kind of hint?"

"A vague one. More of a feeling." Pavlik's phone vibrates. "Yes?" He just listens. Asks no questions.

A thousand icicles ring out below.

Pavlik's voice slips away. "We need to get down there."

At operation headquarters the hubbub of voices dies away. Demirci says: "The call came through six minutes ago. Mr. Krampe, please."

The tape starts. "We have thirty hostages."

"Who's speaking?"

"I'll pass you to someone."

A man shouts: "It's true. Thirty."

Headquarters again: "Who are you?"

A child cries loudly into the telephone.

"The little girl is afraid that they're all going to die. With reason. Put my next call straight through to the Department."

The conversation ends.

The space begins to rotate, centrifugal forces sling the other people's voices away from Aaron.

Her feet are bare.

She is wearing dark glasses.

Her father's face is blackened.

*A dream.*

The centrifuge stops abruptly. The men and women surround her again, talking across each other. Aaron catches the first question that fires back at her. "Was that all? Did Holm make any demands?"

"No," Demirci says.

"It's not him," Niko says. "I know his voice."

"That's wrong," Aaron insists. "It was him."

*Words like ashes.*

"Could he be bluffing?" Demirci asks.

"No. The man and the child were terrified."

"Holm says: 'We.' So he has at least one accomplice."

"Or else it's a smokescreen," Niko suggests.

"Wrong approach," Aaron says. "If we believe him and assume he's got thirty hostages, he needs one accomplice or several; it would be impossible to control that many people otherwise. If we don't believe him, we're starting with a lie and we can't work that way."

"Thirty," Demirci says firmly. "Let's stick to that."

"Claus, play it again," Aaron says to Krampe.

She listens with great concentration. "They're driving—slowly— it could be a lorry—no, a bus."

Pavlik says: "Holm will demand the release of his brother. He wants to make sure we don't know his location too soon, so that we don't attack. A moving bus is perfect."

"Can you tell whether it's a bus or a coach?" Demirci asks Aaron.

"No."

Pavlik again: "It's not a bus. If it didn't stop where it was supposed to, the people waiting would complain. The bus would soon be identified."

"Yes, on a normal day there are more than a thousand coaches in the city," Peschel says. "Who's going to check them all?"

"Miss Aaron, what about the man who confirmed Holm's information—a trace of dialect?"

"Claus," she says.

*"It's true. Thirty."*

"He doesn't come from Berlin," Aaron says. "Maybe the Ruhr. But I'm not sure."

Demirci says: "Have Sascha brought here straight away."

When ten people do a sharp intake of breath all at once, it can be very loud. Aaron reads their minds: *Holm hasn't issued any demands, and Demirci is giving in already.* But immediately clear to her what a clever move that is. Holm will call soon and demand his brother's release. He knows he'll have to give Demirci at least an hour. She is using every second until the call comes through, and she's already playing for time.

"Mr. Majowski, Mr. Büker, you take that one. Choose another four colleagues. Handcuffs and fetters, an armed transporter, two escort vehicles." Quick footsteps fade away. Demirci calls Helmchen. "Get me a phone appointment with the Federal Prosecutor's office. In the next fifteen minutes."

"Claus, again," Aaron says.

*"I'll give you someone."*

She hears a background noise. "Stop. Back five seconds."

*There.*

It's very quiet, but Aaron can identify it. "The bus was near an overground or regional train station. Two or three hundred meters away. A train just pulled in."

"Miss Grauder, call BVG and the regional railway: what main stations had trains stopping at 9:10?"

Aaron says: "We don't need to do that."

"Why not?"

"Because I know where the bus was."

Aaron stands by the prison workshop waiting for Bukowski. A welding machine goes thump thump thump. "Stand back from the platform edge," come the words over the wall.

"It was Holzhauser Strasse underground station. They were driving right past the prison. Two minutes later they were on the Stadtring and by now they're somewhere in the city."

*Where a bus is as conspicuous as a needle in a haystack.*

"Still, Miss Grauder," Demirci says, regaining her composure.

The hubbub of voices begins again.

A suitcase is opened.

A snowball rolls down an airplane.

Aaron's hand stings.

*It's not that.*

*Who else in the dream was still on the plane?*

Demirci says: "Mr. Pavlik, get two SETs ready for an attack. Inform our tactician and the logistics department. I want scenarios for the storming of the bus and a hostage rescue. Mr. Mertsch, get the Federal Police to send two helicopters and every available drone into the air and see if they can find a coach making unusual maneuvers."

"They'll be delighted to get instructions from us."

"I don't care. We have the right to intervene. Miss Aaron, I'd like you to question Sascha. Are you up for that?"

"I was going to suggest precisely that."

# 16

THE COACH drives along the Spree. Holm stands at the front with the driver. The children cower motionlessly in their seats. Some hold hands. A boy cries quietly, a girl shivers, another girl prays, another boy chews his nails to the quick. Holm watches disdainfully as Bosch counts the collected mobile phones again and puts them in a plastic bag. What is he supposed to think about a man who needs to count twice? But Bosch fulfils his purpose.

"Stop," Holm says to the driver. He brusquely tells Bosch to get on with his job. Bosch gets out with the heavy holdall of explosives and the plastic bag. Holm checks his watch.

Twenty minutes until the next call.

His eye falls on the teacher whose eyes are darting down the street even though he had told them all not to look outside. The man is waiting for a chance to give someone a sign. The woman sits next to him, gripping his arm.

He's a risk. Holm decides to put the brakes on him.

Back at the Holocaust Memorial he could tell they were lovers. He was looking among the dozen parked coaches for the right one, and saw the woman teacher using an unobserved moment in the labyrinth of concrete pillars to press herself against her colleague. If his brother had been there in his place, he would have chosen the bus for that very reason; Sascha would have had a lot of fun.

But not him. Holm chose the bus because of the mirrored windscreen. And of course because of the children. It was a sober calculation, they crank up the pressure.

"Switch places," he says.

She immediately gets up to swap with the man so that he's sitting by the aisle. Outside Bosch throws the bag into some bushes.

"Does your wife know?" Holm says to the teacher.

The man doesn't answer.

"I'm not going to ask twice."

The teacher's eye darts to the pistol in Holm's waistband. "No," he whispers.

"And your husband?" he asks the woman.

She shakes her head without looking at him.

"How long?"

Her voice breaks like a grass stem in a storm. "Eight weeks."

"Louder."

"Eight weeks."

"What's your name?"

"Lena Gaarskjaer."

"And you?"

"Magnus Sørensen." His knees knock together.

Holm brings his mouth close to his ear. "You feel guilty. But I can help you end it. I'll kill the woman and leave you looking like a hero. That would solve all your problems. You might even become famous."

Sørensen has to hold his knees still, they're shaking so much.

"Stand up."

Panic sweeps across his features. He stands up and totters.

"Say out loud: 'I, Magnus Sørensen, have been sleeping for eight weeks with your teacher Lena Gaarskjaer.'"

He can't get a word out. Holm presses the Remington to his head. "And I never issue orders twice."

"For eight weeks I, Magnus Sørensen, have been sleeping with your teacher Lena Gaarskjaer." He falls back down on the seat, buries his face in his hands.

Another child cries.

Two, three.

Lena tries to touch Sørensen but he turns away.

Holm puts the Remington back in his belt. Bosch gets back on the bus. He has stuffed the bag of explosives in the luggage space and turned on the detonator. They drive on, past Charlottenburg Palace. Tourists, souvenir sellers, traffic wardens around a breakdown lorry, a woman shouting at a dog.

"Sorry," Holm hears the driver say. "We'll soon be out of petrol."

Holm walks over to him, but checks that Bosch has his finger on the trigger of the short-barreled Uzi submachine gun. "You're lying."

"Look at the display."

A red blinking light.

"I took over from a colleague at the last minute, there wasn't time."

Bosch comes to the front and speaks to Holm under his breath. "We can't fill up. The risk is far too great."

He gives Bosch a glance as cold as all the graves he has left behind him. Sweat drips from Bosch's chin and seeps into his roll-neck pullover. Holm turns to the driver. "Where's the nearest petrol station?"

"On the North Loop."

"Go there."

Behind him Bosch bends down to a boy with a teary, exhausted face, and says quietly, "We're not going to hurt you."

Holm looks the child in the eyes. "Do you believe him?" While the eleven-year-old wets himself, Holm remembers that his childhood ended on a dirty blanket in the basement. He was nine, and he never cried again. He feels a draft behind him and turns around. He sees the driver reaching for the microphone. The man immediately pulls back his hand. "Before we started our tour of the city, we discussed a few things. You remember?"

The driver manages a nod.

"Repeat what I said to you."

His shirt drenched, the driver lists them: "If I try to flash the lights or give a sign in any other way, you'll kill one. If I ignore a traffic sign or jump a red light or cause an accident, you'll kill one. If I reach for the microphone, you'll kill one."

"That's correct. I'll give very careful thought to who it will be."

The driver grips the wheel. Holm sees the white of his knuckles. He picks up a thriller from the dashboard and reads the title. *The Highlander's Runaway Bride.* "You should read better things than this. Have you heard of Thomas Carlyle? No, thought not. 'The courage we desire and praise is not the courage to die decently but the courage to live manfully.' And what about you? Do you want to live?"

The man can't even nod.

The two-kilometer drive to the North Loop passes uneventfully. When the petrol station comes into view, Holm turns to the teacher and the children. "I will get out with the driver." He points his chin at Bosch. "At the slightest attempt to attract attention, he shoots. We'll do it like they do in school. All those who have understood raise your hands."

They all raise their hands.

The coach stops by a petrol pump. No one else is filling up. Lorries are parked in the big car park. The truckers are sitting in the service station fifty meters away or sleeping in their cabins.

"Do you know the pump attendant?" Holm asks as the driver introduces the nozzle.

"Yes."

"Will he want to chat to you?"

"Yes."

"All this time you may have been thinking about how you might give him a discreet sign. You mention that you had to take your dog to the vet, but you have no dog. He asks you about your wife and you give the wrong name. He asks if you had a good holiday, you rave about Italy, but he knows it was Turkey. There are a lot of possibilities. Each one means your death and the death of this man. You just need to blink."

Through the windscreen of the bus Bosch watches Holm going into the building with the driver. When he faced him for the first time a month ago he knew straight away that Holm was unlike anyone he had ever met. Holm had sought him out. He knew Bosch's innermost thoughts, and Bosch felt cold. Holm doesn't baulk, doesn't hesitate, doesn't doubt. He promised Bosch he would help assert his claim. Bosch knew he was telling the truth. But Bosch won't breathe out again until Holm has disappeared forever.

"Hello, Heinz," the pump attendant says.

"Hello, Lutz. Number three."

The driver sets down the company credit card.

Behind him, Holm is flicking through a car magazine. He sees the driver and the pump attendant in the security mirror in the corner.

"So, city tour?"

"School class."

"You're covered in sweat."

"I've got a cold. I've been dragging it around with me all week. It's a real pain."

"My tip: call in sick."

"Hmm."

"Have a schnapps tonight, that helps." The pump attendant gives the driver his card back and waves to him. "Or have your wife give you a rub."

"Good hot bath is what I fancy. Thanks, take care."

The other man glances outside. "Hey, your windscreen's completely filthy." He comes around the counter. "I'll clean it for you. There's nothing going on right now."

Holm spreads his shoulder blades.

The driver says quickly: "No, leave it, we should get going."

"OK. Well, get better." The man addresses Holm. "Can I help you too?"

"No, thanks. I just wanted to stretch my legs."

When he is already in the doorway with the driver, the pump attendant comes running after them. "Hey, you still have that tool-bag that I lent you in the bus. My boss has been asking for it. I'll come with you."

The driver, horrified, tries to tell him not to. But Holm has already pressed the edge of his hand against the pump attendant's throat just below his jaw and thumped it with his fist. It's all so quick that the driver doesn't understand what has happened, and watches in confusion as the man drops dead to the floor.

Holm points to the store room. "In there."

The driver doesn't move, and just slumps to the ground. Holm drags the corpse into the store room and shuts the door. He pulls the cable of the mini-recorder on which the video camera pictures are stored out of the socket behind the counter and puts the recorder under his jacket. He pulls the driver up and drives him back to the bus. Thirty seconds later they've gone. No one noticed them.

The tap drips. Five or seven times a minute, but never six times. Every now and again rain drums on the window, but not today. Every now and again a bird crashes against the bars, but not today. Every now and again a crow caws, and he knows that it is winter. The seasons have become meaningless. He knows that it is winter because a crow is cawing and snow lies around the entrance to the courtyard.

The thin Albanian in the cell next to him coughs.

Above him the Serb walks up and down.

Below him the Lebanese weeps.

Because of him.

At some point he beat him up and told him he was going to do that every day from now on. People like him, who were thrown in jail for a few hundred grams of grass, are blank sheets of paper. You can wipe your arse with them.

How pitiful an existence must be that consists solely of fear. He doesn't even notice these shadowy creatures when he causes one of them pain in order to numb his own with a few kicks and punches.

In Barcelona the Moroccans initially thought they could fuck him over. He washed out their leader's brain in the shower outlet. The Basques were next. After he had shown their two best men what their knives were good for, the others lived like dogs on the leftover scraps. Then came the Tunisians, the Algerians, the French. In the end they ran away every time he poked the wax out of his ears.

He knew it would be his brother who determined when his punishment was complete. Apart from his father, his brother is the only person in his world that he has ever feared, or will ever fear.

That was how it was, when he was eight years old and his brother dug the grave in the forest. That was how it was when their mother died shortly afterwards and his brother looked after him from then on.

That was how it was for all the beatings he took, every time he dared to glance at his brother.

The word love was never uttered between them, nor was their father's name, and not a single word about what had happened before the grave.

He learned to pay attention to his brother.

He learned to rule from his brother.

But if he could he would kill his brother.

His brother alone would determine the day.

He knew: four years was the minimum.

He would wait that long until the announcement in the prison newspaper.

*Now I understand my place. I want to find the person who knows what I'm like.*

Weeks passed with the question of whether his brother could see that he was kneeling in front of him. Perhaps that time had not yet come. But a month later the woman wrote to him.

*There is no such thing as fate, only destiny. I would like to know more about you.*

He had to write ten letters and got ten back from her. It was torture, inventing a life that was like the life of the shades, and each self-pitying sentence repelled him and made him feel soiled.

But that was part of his punishment.

Six months later she visited him in Barcelona. She was already shivering when he sat down next to her. Pretty. One of those women who usually turn their noses up at the world. But he had power over her because his brother had power over her. He saw that she was disgusted when he rested his hand on hers, and he was aroused.

He wanted to show her what you can do with a pretty nose like that.

She visited him a second time. He looked forward to seeing how agonizing it was for her to say the words she needed to say, to hear her voice breaking.

She passed him the message that contained everything he needed. He applied for a transfer to Berlin, sat down in front of the committee and crossed his legs. He marveled at the stupidity of the guys in suits, and knew that from now on every thought and every step and every day and every night would pass in a breath.

It was a pleasure sitting opposite the prison director in Tegel and knowing that this man who thought he was always a commander and never a follower was merely a dice that his brother was shaking in a cup.

He ordered him to get hold of the film.

Gave it to Boenisch.

When he saw the one Boenisch wanted, it was hard for him to keep his patience under control. The days leading up to the moment when he closed the door to the cell and the woman belonged to him were the best he had had in many years. But if he was asked what Boenisch looked like, what he talked about, what shadow he cast, he couldn't say. He means less than the shit on the sole of his shoes.

Just a shame that he wasn't allowed to have more fun with her.

He runs his finger over the scar on his neck, as he often does, and shuts his eyes, as he often does, and imagines Aaron's world. The dripping of the tap. The coughing of the Albanian. The weeping of the Lebanese. That's what she would get, that and nothing more. She was given the punishment that his brother thought appropriate. But it's only the first hell of many. He can list them all, and he likes every one of them.

The Serb walks back and forth above his head. Today he feels like breaking a couple of his toes for fun, just to hear him hobbling, but there won't be time for that.

The cell door opens.

Sascha smiles.

# 17

AT 9:40 a.m. the call is put through to operation headquarters. Holm's voice fills the room. "Are we all here?"

"Are the hostages unharmed?" Demirci asks.

"I'm only talking to Miss Aaron."

Aaron waits for ten seconds before she speaks. She has to prolong the phone call so that the phone can be located. "Are the hostages alive?"

"Yes."

"Prove it."

"You know I'm not going to bring thirty people to the phone. Don't let's waste time on nonsense. Put my brother in a car. A BMW 7-series automatic. There's a bag with five million Euros in used fifties and hundreds in the boot. If you do everything correctly, none of the hostages will be killed."

"To get your brother out of jail we would need to talk to the Senate Interior and Justice Departments. The decision isn't in our hands, there's no way I can give permission. The same applies to the ransom. It would take us hours to release such a sum. If we could do it at all."

*Has the phone been located?* Aaron looks inquiringly at Pavlik.

"Forget it," he whispers to her.

"Do you think I don't know my brother's already on his way to Budapester Strasse?"

Deadly silence.

"If he wasn't, I would have underestimated Miss Demirci. Miss Aaron, your negotiating skills are a real insult. There's fifty pounds of

C4 explosives on the bus, right beside the petrol tank. That's enough to turn Leipziger Platz into a crater. Or maybe Gendarmenmarkt? The detonator is primed. I'll give you two hours to get hold of the money."

He hangs up.

Aaron mimes that she wants some headphones. The recording is played back again.

Very quiet weeping. The sound of traffic. Indicators. The bus stops. Crying again. Whispering. The bus drives on. The whispering stops. Aaron takes the headphones off. "There are at least three children on the bus. That needn't necessarily mean anything, but it could be a school class."

Demirci says: "All the police in Berlin are to keep an eye out for buses full of children. If they're suspicious, they can observe them inconspicuously from unmarked cars. All bus companies in Berlin and Brandenburg are also to be contacted. Ask which of them have a bus booked out to a school group."

"We're talking about several hundred firms. That's going to take a while," Pavlik says. "Perhaps the Federal Police should do that one, they've got more people."

"Mr. Pavlik, I'm not going to talk right now. Miss Aaron, please come with me." Demirci puts Aaron's hand in the crook of her arm and hurries to the lift with her. "Normally I would bring in a case analyst from the State Office of Criminal Investigation, the LKA. But you know Holm better than anyone else. I'd love to take your condition into account, but I can't afford to. Sorry."

"No need."

"Miss Helm, I need to speak to the Senator of the Interior."

"Straight away. Enderlin, the director of the LKA in Berlin, has called twice. He says the State Office is responsible."

"That's what worries me." Demirci goes into the next room with Aaron and closes the door. "One moment." She makes a call. "Mr. Enderlin, I'll keep it short. The Department demands hostage release via the Federal Public Prosecutor, we're going alone. However, we do need a KT 6 from you." The bomb disposal unit. "Your team must be ready for duty in thirty minutes, our logistics expert will call you. If further support is required, I'll let you know." Her voice is assuming an irritable undertone. "I understand that. But the Interior Ministers' Conference has already been informed. Goodbye."

*No, they haven't yet. But they don't give a damn anyway. Wow.*

Aaron feels for the chair by the desk.

"Half a meter further to the right," Demirci says.

She sits down.

"Is there an alternative to the release of Sascha?"

"No."

"He could refuse a swap."

"Why should he?"

"In Spain he was sentenced to forty-eight years' imprisonment. When he was transferred to Berlin the sentence was made subject to German law. That means, given the seriousness of the case, that he could possibly be released in twelve years."

"That's your offer? At least another twelve years in jail and then a hope of clemency?"

"It's negotiable."

"We're not authorized to promise anything of the kind. Only a judge could do that. He has murdered at least eight people, including five policemen in France and Spain. What judge would get involved in that?"

"Sascha isn't a legal expert," Demirci says. "My chief goal is the release of the hostages. I'm concerned with gaining time until we've found the bus. Then we're in a different position. Holm won't kill thirty people and himself."

"Don't do it."

"What?"

"Underestimate him."

A pack of cigarettes rustles. Aaron imagines: the silent circling of the drones, hawks with no prey. Demirci says: "The armour you talked to me about belonged to a janissary. You know who the janissaries were?"

"No."

"The Sultan's lifeguard. They were trained to kill as boys."

"Are you referring to Sascha's upbringing by his brother?"

"Even though they had sworn loyalty to the Sultan, the janissaries rose up against him. Holm is sending Sascha into a hopeless situation, someone has to make that clear to him."

"Miss Demirci, for three hours you've been showing us why you're the head of the Department. So far you haven't lost your calm even once. But you're troubled by a bigger problem than Sascha. What is it?"

Demirci puts the cigarette back in the pack. "Even if we hand Holm's brother over to him, there's still the five million. I doubt that I'll get hold of a sum like that. Do you think it's negotiable?"

"No."

"You said money meant nothing to Holm."

"Money isn't what matters to him. It's power. I could also give you a practical argument. He knows the notes are registered, he has to wash them, and in the end he'll be left with half at most. But that's all irrelevant. Believe me: if you don't fulfil all his requirements, he will make his threat come true."

"And die himself?"

"He isn't worried about that."

Helmchen is on the intercom: "It's the Senator of the Interior, for you."

"Thank you, Miss Helm." Demirci turns to Aaron. "Would you please excuse me?"

"If you don't mind, I'd like to listen in."

"Fine." She switches to speaker phone. "Demirci."

"Svoboda."

"Senator, an hour ago we talked about Holm and the death of three of my men. The situation has escalated. Holm has got hold of a coach. He's threatening to murder thirty hostages. Possibly children."

Svoboda takes remarkably little time to process that information. "Where is the coach?"

"We don't know. Somewhere in Berlin. They're searching with all available forces."

"What are Holm's demands?"

"He wants his brother to be released." There's a whole world in Demirci's pause. "And five million Euros."

Svoboda snorts audibly.

"I'd like to take this case on."

"You've already done that. Enderlin complained about your tone. OK. Don't you think you should have talked to me first? Or has the line of duty changed overnight?"

*He's known about the abduction for ages. And he's making Demirci work. What a bastard. That's exactly how I remember him.*

Ten things that Aaron doesn't miss:
    postcards
    her face at seven in the morning.
    the films of Almodóvar
    girls putting on their make-up in pub toilets
    constantly checking the rearview mirror
    men gawping at her
    the eyes saying something different from the mouth
    menus with pictures
    looking into a cold tin of ravioli

"We specialize in hostage releases," Demirci says. "Holm has given us a two-hour ultimatum. I wanted to be sure the LKA wasn't treading on our toes."

Svoboda writes down each word separately in his file. "Three of your men are dead. I doubt the Department has the necessary strike capability today. Apart from that, I need to get you out of the inevitable media crossfire, not least because of my duty of care. You should know, however, that I have ordered an investigation. The press release is going out tomorrow morning. You have the chance to give a statement."

*Yes, of course. Care is your great speciality.*

Demirci stays calm. "Holm insists on negotiating exclusively with us. Or more precisely: with Jenny Aaron. That's a plus. She knows Holm very well."

"And I know Miss Aaron," Svoboda says. "When she was still with the Department she was lucky enough to be protected by your predecessor, otherwise she would have had to leave the service in the first year. She had certain abilities. But patience and skill weren't among them. Her character is completely unsuited to a negotiation like this. And—dear God—a blind woman."

Aaron suddenly sees him in front of her: his slack, gluey skin, his baggy cheeks, his manicured bony fingers. He would step over a dying beggar. She remembers this man as well as she remembers Boenisch and Runge.

The desire to speak constricts her chest. But it would compromise Demirci. A pack of cigarettes and a lighter are placed in her hand. She senses Demirci's self-control, lowers her pulse rate, takes the first drag.

"Miss Aaron enjoys my complete trust," Demirci replies. "She is advising me. Her analysis is extremely valuable. I couldn't imagine better."

Svoboda spreads his words as a peacock spreads its feathers. "Sometimes there's a lack of imagination. So: what's your strategy?"

"I've had Holm's brother fetched from prison. He will get here shortly. We will try to make him give up. I haven't raised my hopes. Everything depends on the demands being met."

"Five million Euros is completely out of the question."

"Senator, please: Holm will stop at nothing. If we try to get clever, he'll kill the hostages."

"Half a million and no more."

Aaron wishes she could knock Svoboda's complacency out of him, the shrug with which he sets the price for umpteen human lives. The door opens quietly. Helmchen whispers something in Demirci's ear. Aaron can only make out the words: "Two—before." Helmchen leaves them alone again.

Demirci's voice is thick. "I've just learned that the corpses of a couple have been found in a flat on Leipziger Strasse. Both victims had their necks broken. Directly opposite the flat is the hotel room where Jenny Aaron was staying. We have to assume that Holm killed the couple. Presumably last night."

The ceiling crashes down on to Aaron's shoulders. Demirci stands on the rubble making a phone call. "He has killed six people since yesterday. Thirty more will mean nothing to him. We need that money. Right now."

"I said no," Svoboda snaps. "It's a complex situation with a very particular dynamic. Are you overstretched?"

Aaron pushes against the enormous burden on her back. She gestures to Demirci that she needs to talk to Svoboda.

"One moment," Demirci says.

She opens the door, waits for a moment and closes it again.

"Senator, I asked Miss Aaron to do this." A dramatic pause. "Miss Aaron, do you think there's a chance that we might adapt Holm's conditions to our own possibilities?"

"The release of his brother and the five million Euros aren't negotiable," she says. "They're both a sine qua non."

"You're eloquent, I'll give you that," Svoboda says. "But your complacency throws up the question of why you of all people should negotiate with him."

"It was his choice."

"Maybe because he saw you as a pushover."

Aaron hesitates only very briefly. "We know each other. I'm sure you remember our last meeting."

"Should I?"

"Certainly you should. You were Secretary of State for the Interior at the time. A colleague and I were on an undercover mission in Naples. They insisted that we go to Berlin and give you a report in person before our crucial meeting with the head of the Mazzarella clan. You were told that it would endanger the operation, but you didn't care. When we got back to Naples an attempt was made on my life. It turned out later that the clan had been watching us, and our cover had been blown by our flight to Berlin. The Internal Affairs report confirmed in great detail your responsibility for what happened. But it was kept secret. The fact that the Federal Minister of the Interior was a fellow party member may have had something to do with it."

"How dare you, Miss Demirci, I would like to speak with you alone."

"Just as it never reached the public," Aaron continues unmoved, "that the German branch of the clan tapped your phone and were therefore extremely well informed."

"This conversation is closed."

"Not entirely. I took the liberty of copying the report. You decide whether I pass it on to the press or whether five million Euros will turn up at the Department in no more than an hour. In used fifties and hundreds. You just have to call the Finance Senator. You're eloquent, after all."

There's a click. Svoboda has hung up.

Demirci takes the pack of cigarettes out of Aaron's hand and lights one. Aaron smokes too. She taps her watch. The computer voice says: "Seventh of January. Thursday. Ten a.m., twenty minutes, three seconds."

Eighty minutes until Holm's ultimatum runs out.

"Now we have a common enemy," Demirci says.

"Would you rather have that bastard as your friend?"

Demirci's voice falters. "Do you really have a copy? I'm just asking because my career depends on it."

"No. But your predecessor does. I'm sure he'd be delighted to fax it to me from Sweden."

At that moment Aaron sees herself leaving the terminal in Schönefeld with Niko. Children are shouting by a bus, a Scandinavian language.

A snowball rolls down an airplane.

Aaron walks to the exit with a bag of hot chestnuts.

The children watch sadly after her.

"We're looking for a bus with a school class from Scandinavia. I don't know which country. The bus is probably from Berlin."

"What makes you think that?" Demirci asks, surprised.

"If I tell you, you won't take it seriously. Let's just leave it there."

Demirci presses the speech button and passes the phone to Helmchen. Again a helicopter flies over the house. "We can give Svoboda one more minute. If he hasn't called by then I'll clear my desk."

"He'll call. He knows I'm not bluffing."

"What makes you so sure?"

For the first time in her life she says: "I'm Jörg Aaron's daughter."

The phone in the waiting room rings.

"My predecessor gave me exactly the same advice."

"What was that?"

"Only ever to address the men by their surnames. But I can't bring myself to do it."

"That was yesterday. I like your style today."

"Are you still in touch with him?" Demirci asks.

"We speak on the phone from time to time."

"How are things going for him in Sweden?"

"He catches big fish."

"Say hello from me."

The door opens. Helmchen: "The money's on the way."

Two people sigh.

"And Sascha is here."

# 18

THEY TURNED up in a group of six and didn't say a word. He saw their rage and laughed at what they were thinking. They blindfolded him and cuffed his wrists and ankles, but he enjoyed it and didn't feel the cold of the metal. They drove quickly, and he knew why. They pushed him into a lift and dragged him down corridors in chains, and never had his feet felt so light. Many doors had closed behind him during those five years. He had hated them all. But this one was worth it.

Because *she* is sitting behind it.

He is pushed into a chair and his blindfold is removed.

Disappointment rises up in him like bile. He wants to jump over the table and kill Aaron straight away.

She looks him in the eyes.

A thousand times Sascha has imagined how it would be. She always stared past him. The urge to touch the scar on his neck is as powerful as if he'd been underwater for two minutes and suddenly needed to breathe. But he doesn't want to give the man leaning against the wall and the others standing behind him that pleasure. He concentrates on Aaron's swollen cheekbone. Sascha has no doubt that it was his brother who did that. He beat and humiliated Aaron, and Sascha wished he could have been there.

But the best thing, the best thing of all, is that she thinks he's in her power.

That she thinks she's safe.

He leans back, folds his arms casually behind his head and says: "I can see something you can't."

Aaron was waiting for Token-Eyes in the interrogation room, so that he couldn't laugh at her feeling for her chair. She knows Pavlik is there. Still, she will question him on her own, that's how they said they were going to go about it. But his very presence helps her. Token-Eyes' voice echoes inside her. It's scornful, scathing, angry. And yet it sounds like the voice of a child sulking under the Christmas tree because it didn't get the present it really wanted.

"I had you brought here because your brother is in Berlin. Do you know where he's staying?"

He laughs. "Blind, and stupid too."

"If you cooperate, we could talk about reducing your sentence."

"I'm never going back to jail."

"Mr. Holm, you seem to think we're going to let you go. That's ridiculous."

"Right, so you've just taken me for a little drive?"

"I've told you why you're here."

"I'm here because my brother fucks you over whenever and wherever he wants. What's that you have below your eye, you bitch? Did you take a tumble?"

"He's holed up with two hostages in a flat near the prison. But that needn't be a problem for us."

Token-Eyes giggles. "Wow. Has he killed all the others already? And how did he get the coach into the flat?"

*Shit.*

Aaron waits a moment to relax her vocal cords without showing her tension. "We assume that your brother has observed your transport. We want to lull him into a false sense of security. We just need some time. And you will be helpful to us in that."

"Blind, stupid, dishonest. Give me a cigarette, you piece of shit."

"We'll free the hostages and probably kill your brother. Do you want to die too?"

"Are you threatening to shoot me? And where my brother is concerned: he killed three of your men. As if he was scratching his balls."

Aaron sees herself shooting Token-Eyes in the neck. That helps calm her down. "You're not in a Spanish jail now. You've got another twelve years in Germany. Then you might be released."

"Blind, stupid, dishonest and desperate."

"That's still better than life meaning life."

"You're the one who's got life, not me. As far as I'm concerned you can add fifteen years for the ones I had fun with. And could somebody open the window? You stink of Boenisch's basement. Revolting."

*He's admitting to the murder of Melanie Breuer just like that.*

*Any second attempt is a waste of time.*

"I'm supposed to give you something from him. Maybe that bored cop standing against the wall over there would like to reach into my right trouser pocket. No rummaging, though."

Aaron nods to Pavlik. Token-Eyes gets to his feet. The rub of fabric. He sits down again. Pavlik puts something in her hand. She feels it and looks indifferently at Token-Eyes.

"Oops, almost forgot: I promised the sick fuck I would tell him how I killed you. And I always keep a promise."

She works out what she has in her hand.

Sixteen years go up in smoke. Aaron is a trainee working in Fourth Homicide, sitting in the tiny office that's been assigned to her. At this point no one knows about the basement in Spandau.

She reads the statement from the husband of one of the missing lawyers. *In the morning she gave me aftershave. It was our wedding anniversary. I'd completely forgotten.* Her eye goes to Boenisch, who has squashed himself onto a chair in the corner and is waiting for his third witness interrogation. He hasn't moved a finger for ten minutes. A drop of sweat hangs from his nose as if frozen there. Aaron goes on reading. *She's sad at work. Now I may never see her again.*

She notices that Boenisch is watching her and looks up.

"Sorry, I didn't mean to stare. But that dress really suits you."

He says it so nicely that she suddenly has a guilty conscience because she didn't ask him if he'd like anything to drink. "Are you thirsty?"

"Yes. Thank you."

She goes into the kitchen and comes back with a glass of water. Boenisch drains it in one. "Thanks." He is invited into the next room. She watches after him for a moment, a huge man with sandals and flesh-colored socks, who pauses in the doorway, looks back and says for the third time, "Thank you."

The next day Aaron searches in vain in the desk drawer for the locket that her mother gave her. She put it away because the clasp is broken. The locket means a lot to her. Even though she and her mother often have little to say to each other she knows it's a special present, because it belonged to her grandmother.

When she got it, the locket was empty. Perhaps her mother hoped Aaron would put a small picture of her in it. She could of course have given it to her with a picture already inside but preferred the thought of her daughter putting one in—that's how she is.

Recently Aaron has started to take an interest in Eastern philosophy. For her locket she chose the two Japanese signs for life and death.

A storm darkens the window, the first fat drops splash against it. Suddenly she's no longer certain that she put the locket in the drawer. She makes a note to check when she gets home.

But not today. In the late afternoon she reads Boenisch's third statement, compares it with the two previous statements and knocks on his door. But nothing is as it was before.

She clutches the locket in her fist. The memory was lost. For the third time since she came back from Berlin something is pulled from the fire. Aaron remembers what Pavlik looks like. She shot Token-Eyes in the neck. She holds in her hand the locket that Boenisch stole from her back then; a momento that he kept very carefully for all those years.

The flames have not destroyed the memories, she suddenly finds herself thinking. Perhaps the library has an infinite number of doors, each one heatproof, and the memories have hidden behind them, just waiting for the doors to be opened.

But that thought is immediately swept away by the realization that Boenisch is thinking about her at that very moment. He knows what she is holding in her hand. That amuses Token-Eyes. He wants to turn her into a rubber doll with which Boenisch can satisfy himself. She puts the locket in her pocket, lights a cigarette and blows the smoke in Token-Eyes' face.

Demirci and Niko stand in front of a two-way mirror in the next room, watching the interrogation. Büker comes in with Majowski. They were both responsible for Sascha's transfer.

"What's up?"

"Have you talked to the prisoner?" Demirci asks.

"No. Why?"

"He knows about the three dead cops," Niko says. "Did you blab about them? Did he listen in on you?"

"Do you think we're crazy?"

Demirci exchanges a glance with Niko. "I want to know if anyone was in his cell after he was put in solitary."

Niko leaves with Majowski and Büker.

The phone rings. She picks it up. "Yes? Stream the video from the interrogation room to my tablet." Demirci takes her iPad with her and puts a headphone in her ear. By the time she enters operational headquarters three doors further on, she can already see Aaron and Sascha on the screen.

"There's only one coach-load of Scandinavian children in the city," Giulia Delmonte tells her. "Some year sixes from Aarhus in Denmark. Twenty-seven pupils and two teachers. We've tried to call the driver but he didn't answer. His phone is switched off."

"Have the police in Berlin been informed?"

"A minute ago. We're trying to locate his mobile."

"Put the make, color and registration on all online media and Berlin radio stations, without mentioning the hostage-taking. We're looking for this bus, that's all they need to know. Do we know where he picked up the children?"

"The Holocaust Memorial. At a quarter to ten."

"It's patrolled by guards, have them questioned. And the people working at the snack bars and souvenir shops. Did anyone notice anything between eight and a quarter to ten? The American embassy opposite is watched by surveillance cameras. Contact them."

Demirci looks at the tablet. Aaron says: "I doubt that your prison career will be over today. I'd have thought you were smarter than that."

Sascha spreads his legs and smirks.

Demirci turns to Majowski. "Keep the two SETs ready for an attack."

"You mean we're to go in as soon as we've located the coach?"

"No. The getaway car with the money is being prepared. You take care of that."

Demirci hurries back to the room behind the mirror.

Pavlik sets a saucer down in front of Aaron. She stubs out her cigarette. Token-Eyes snorts his words back like snot. "How can a coward like you be so arrogant?"

"You're calling me a coward? A man who suffocates a defenseless woman with a plastic bag to give Boenisch a hard-on?"

"You know that wasn't the reason. You're here, and I'm here. That's what it's about, you whore."

She hears Demirci on her headphones. "We're taking a break."

Aaron says to Pavlik: "He wants to go to a cell."

"Cowardice can break you, or it can help you grow. Sometimes that decision is made on the first day of the tree in the month of affection," Token-Eyes continues.

Pavlik rises from his chair. "Right, show's over."

"No, wait," Aaron says.

*The month of affection.*

*That was the name for January in the age of the Samurai.*

*Today is Thursday. The day of the tree.*
*It's not Token-Eyes who's talking to me.*
*His brother.*
"Exactly six years ago today."
"What's he talking about?" Demirci asks.
*Six years. The first Thursday in January. What happened?*
"There's another name for the day of the tree," Token-Eyes says in his brother's words.
*The day of Jupiter.*
Now she knows: *the Ukrainian woman. Pi.*

For weeks she had put up two Ukrainian women in a supposedly safe house in Frankfurt an der Oder. They were the chief prosecution witnesses against the head of a people-smuggling ring. The women were protected by a complete Special Enforcement Team, five strong. Even though the curtains were closed, a sniper in position four hundred meters away from the house managed to locate one of the two women with a thermal sensor. He used armoured-glass-piercing ammunition and killed her with a single shot to the head. The surviving witness was brought to safety. They had only a night to get through because the trial was due to begin in two days' time. Aaron's colleagues chose the Hotel Jupiter. They arrived in the evening. Five men circled the Ukrainian woman as they left the limousine. Another shot was fired from the roof of a building opposite.

Ralf Paretzki, known to everyone as Pi, threw himself in front of the witness. Two bullets struck his torso, but bounced off his bulletproof jacket. The third caught him in the temple. Pi lost a lot of blood, but survived. Three cartridge cases were found on the roof. The gunman was never found.

Token-Eyes says: "I see you remember."
*Was he the killer? No, it was Holm.*
"He saved the woman's life and paid off his debt."
The hum of the fluorescent tube is the only sound.
Demirci holds her breath in the next room.
"I have no idea what you're talking about," Aaron says.

And knows very well. Pi had failed in Frankfurt an der Oder. He had been alone in the room with the Ukrainian woman and seen the red dot of the infrared sensor on the curtain. But he had thrown himself to safety and not dragged the woman to the floor as he should have done. It had been a reflex, none of his colleagues would have reproached him for it. But he couldn't forgive himself. They had all expected Pi to be removed from the unit. But their boss decided otherwise after a long conversation with him. In front of the Hotel Jupiter Pi confirmed that they had made the right choice.

*How does Holm know it was the same man? No, that's simple. Pi was just a meter seventy-five, the only terrier.*

"He was cowardly on the day of Mercury, but brave on the day of Jupiter. His sacrifice was not in vain."

*The day of Mercury. Wednesday.*

"Is the film playing out right now?" Token-Eyes asks.

An image flashes in front of her: Aaron is waiting for Niko outside a cinema, she can't remember which one. He kisses her on the cheek, so they aren't yet together. He buys two tickets for a film, but she doesn't know which one. She seeks and seeks.

Suddenly she stumbles into the memory.

She is leaving the cinema with Niko. They've just seen *Avatar* and still have their 3D glasses when they get to Alexanderplatz. They fool about. Niko buys her a bag of hot chestnuts. Stars sparkle in his eyes, and she kisses him for the first time. She takes him home and afterwards the windows are misted up. In the three hours that Niko is asleep she looks at him as if he is the most wonderful Christmas present she ever had. How could she have wasted those years? In fact she wanted Niko from the moment she saw him, and it was some kind of stupid pride that made her keep him dangling for so long.

She doesn't sleep a wink, makes breakfast at seven and is a bit worried about waking him. But he pulls her to him in bed again, and they enjoy each other like two people who have done the right thing.

They go separately to the Department. Serious faces. She learns what has happened in Frankfurt an der Oder during the night. The

Ukrainian woman is brought down the corridor. Aaron sees the fear on the woman's face, but it isn't her case, and all morning she feels butterflies in her stomach every time she thinks of Niko.

In the staff room she bumps into Pi. He avoids her eye. "I know what you're all thinking. And it's true."

He has to see the boss.

Niko has booked a table in an expensive restaurant on Kollwitzplatz that evening. She wears the black cashmere dress that he liked so much at their boss's birthday party. Aaron can hardly wait for him to take it off her.

Icy rain smears the windscreen, Peter Gabriel is on the car radio. She turns the music up as loud as it will go and taps out the stamping rhythm of "Solsbury Hill" on the steering wheel. There's a traffic jam on Potsdamer Strasse. No one dares to go faster than twenty. Her phone vibrates. Pavlik. Only one sentence. The Santas in her belly immediately sit down nicely. She plants the blue light on the roof and shoos the other cars aside. The car careens along the mirror-smooth thoroughfare, and she balances it out with her bottom. Aaron likes it when she can balance things out. But maybe not when ploughing past three  kilometers of stationary vehicles all the way to the Hotel Jupiter.

Pi is put in an ambulance outside. He takes her hand and whispers: "Now I don't have to be ashamed anymore."

She remembers all of that in a matter of seconds. Within that pain she looks for the number that represents what she has lost, and is afraid of that other number which she never allows to come near her.

The number three.

Knowing that something's pointless and doing it anyway.

The locket.

According to Zen, you must always have the signs of life and death in your mind's eye, and you should even draw the sign for death on your forehead. Only then do you have the energy to fight to the end.

*Holm knows what it means. The locket wasn't a present from Boenisch. It's from* him.

Pavlik hasn't said a word yet. But Aaron feels him looking steadily at her. He's too clever not to see what's happening to her.

"The Ukrainian woman refused to address the court, and she knew why. My client was acquitted, it was pure maths," Holm says to Aaron in Token-Eyes' voice. "But I don't like to leave things unfinished. For a while I considered punishing that officer. When he came out of the clinic I kept him under observation. I saw his little life with his wife and his baby. I gave him his second little life. But only because of his courage. If he had been cowardly again I would have killed him. Just as surely as you know the number of steps to the graves of your father and your mother."

Words like ashes. When Holm left her alone with Eva Askamp's corpse, it meant: *not yet*. She knows what she has to do. Basically she's known for five years, and everything that she has hoped for and suffered through and feared since Barcelona acquires a meaning at that moment.

"We're finished."

"See you," says Token-Eyes.

Pavlik brings him out. Aaron taps her watch: "Eleven o'clock, fifteen minutes, eight seconds." Demirci comes in and closes the door. "Have we got the coach?" Aaron asks.

"No. But you were right. A Danish school trip."

Aaron gets to her feet. "Put Sascha in the car with the money. His brother will call in twenty-five minutes and tell us where he is. Holm will cut it so fine that we can't make any preparations. If Sascha turns up a second too late, Holm will kill the first hostage."

"What was he just talking to you about?"

"That was just play-acting."

"Miss Aaron, back in your office when I said, 'Now we share an enemy,' we both thought the same thing."

"Yes."

"We thought, 'and we've gained a friend.'"

"Yes."

"Do you still think that?"

"Yes."

"Me too. Two hours ago I asked you why Holm let you get away in Eva Askamp's flat. You said: 'That was only the warm-up.'"

"I was mistaken."

"Do we have different understandings of the meaning of friendship?"

The door opens. Pavlik. "Leave me alone with Aaron."

"No," says Demirci.

"I must insist."

"No need," Aaron says. "She knows what Holm wants."

"How many steps is it to your parents' graves?"

"I don't count them."

"Show me the locket."

"Why?"

"Because I'm asking you to."

She gives Pavlik the locket.

He snaps it open. "What do the characters mean?"

"Truth and authenticity," she lies.

"You know where the coach is," says Demirci.

"You're mistaken."

Pavlik gives her back the locket. "No, you do."

"I wish that was the case."

Demirci's voice is frosty. "Under no circumstances am I going to let you be a hostage swap. Even if Holm starts killing children: You. Aren't. Going. Have I made myself clear?"

"Of course." Aaron takes her coat off the back of the chair and feels her way to the door. She leaves the room with Pavlik and Demirci and turns towards the lift.

"Where are you going?"

"To the roof. I need some fresh air."

"I'll come with you," Pavlik cuts in.

"No. The two SETs are in the underground car park. You're in charge of the unit," Demirci says.

"I'm not leaving Aaron alone for a second."

"She won't be on her own." Demirci shouts: "Mr. Kvist, take Miss Aaron to the roof terrace. You are personally responsible to me for her protection. I'll wait for you both at operation headquarters."

The minutes fly by. The coach driver's phone has been located. It was found on the banks of the Spree in a plastic bag along with the others. Novak turns up with a new piece of information. "The corpse of a filling-station attendant was found on the VUS-Nordschleife. The CCTV tape is gone."

"Cause of death?" Demirci asks.

"Still unclear. Haematoma on his neck."

*Seven.*

"When was he found?"

"At 9:39. The body was still warm."

A minute before Holm's second call.

"Did anyone notice the coach at the petrol station?"

"The Criminal Police are on to it."

Demirci drives into the underground car park. Thirteen men have taken up position by a black Ford Transit. Pavlik has already issued the two most important orders: the lives of the hostages have priority. He's the only one who can give the order to shoot.

Demirci says: "The man who's challenging us has killed three of your comrades. We will take time to mourn. But not yet. Anyone who has a problem with that will be replaced." Her eye runs over the balaclava-covered faces. Thirteen pairs of eyes gaze back. "Some of you were here when Jenny Aaron belonged to the Department. You may be friends with her, or at least hold her in high esteem. You know that Holm is responsible for her blindness. You must also get that out of your minds. One single error could lead to disaster. Whoever is responsible will wish he'd never met me. I will be standing behind everyone else like a wall, whatever happens. Off you go."

Sascha sits handcuffed in the getaway car, enjoying himself. Demirci opens the car door and speaks loudly enough for all the men to hear. "I'd like to give you something too. It's 11:37. Within twenty-four hours you will be either back in jail or dead."

She knows what it looks like.

Sascha's grin becomes a mask.

When she leaves the lift upstairs there's a minute left. Helmchen runs up to Demirci. "The Regional Interior Ministers, the president of the State Attorney's Office and the president of the Federal Police are holding a video conference and are asking you for a statement."

"Since when have they been asking?" she asks, as she strides down the corridor, and Helmchen has trouble keeping up with her.

"What shall I tell them?"

"To wait." Demirci opens the door of operation headquarters. She sees right away that the most important person is missing. "Where is Miss Aaron?"

Blank faces.

"Call her straight away. And Mr. Kvist."

Demirci shivers for a second: it's all she can do to keep from shouting. The door flies open. For a heartbeat she hopes it's Aaron, but it's Peschel. "Yes, we've located the coach. Outside the maths institute of the Technical University on 17 Junistrasse. A drone found it."

"Are there police on the spot?"

"No. But they're on their way. There will be patrol cars there in two minutes. Pavlik has already got going. The drone should be sending a picture at any moment."

Demirci looks at the second hand of the big clock.

Three, two, one. Holm's call is put through.

"I'm listening."

"We've got the money and your brother."

"Didn't I say I'd only talk to Miss Aaron?"

"She'll be there any minute."

"She's got thirty seconds."

Delmonte tells Demirci that she can't get through to either Aaron or Niko. The shaky picture from the drone appears on the video wall. It's circling at an altitude of about fifty meters, above the coach. A man jumps out. He looks up, his face covered with a balaclava. They see the flash as he fires with a short-barreled submachine gun. The picture dissolves.

"The thirty seconds are up."

"Miss Aaron isn't available."

"I've got one more condition," Holm's words hammer into the silence. "Miss Aaron gets into the car with my brother. As an additional hostage swap."

No one breathes. Everyone is looking at Demirci.

"Out of the question."

The speakers transmit the sound of a helicopter.

"You must know by now that there are twenty-seven schoolchildren and two teachers in the coach." Holm takes his mouth away from the microphone. "Say your name."

A whimper. "Magnus Sørensen."

"Either you confirm right now that Jenny Aaron is on her way, or I shoot this man and throw the corpse into the road. After that I will kill a hostage every minute until you change your mind."

They are the hardest words she has ever had to say. "I will never let you have Miss Aaron."

Sørensen kneels down in front of Holm. When he turned around by the Holocaust Memorial and looked into that man's eyes, he knew what was going to happen. But he didn't want to die without showing courage once in his life. In vain. Since Holm made him tell the whole class that he was sleeping with Lena, Sørensen has said farewell. To his wife. His daughter. Everything. He has so many regrets. Marrying too young. The fact that the years were whipped away as if by the wind and he didn't have the strength to resist. Not being a good father. But mostly kissing Lena in the staff room.

The shot rings out. Its echo is visible on the faces of Demirci and the others.

"It'll be a kid's turn next."

"You may get away with it today," Demirci says, and at that moment everyone in the room is terrified of her. "But I will hunt you down. However long it takes: I will find you."

"Excuse me for a moment, we have visitors."

They hear the coach door opening. Police sirens. The helicopter. The same hissing sound again.

"There's someone here for you." Holm passes her the phone.

Aaron's voice comes from the speaker. "When the plane landed in Aden, Captain Schumann was allowed to leave the *Landshut* to inspect the landing gear. He could have run away. Instead he went back to the plane. Why do you think he did that?"

Demirci closes her eyes.

"Well put," Holm says. "'True courage means living when it is right to live and dying when it is right to die.' For the Samurai mercy and courage belong together, perhaps that's what she's hoping. But she will have no mercy from me. I will give you ten minutes for my brother and the money."

He hangs up. Footsteps. Demirci opens her eyes. Niko is standing in front of her. His eyes are empty and gray. She takes his gun from its holster. "Mr. Kvist, you are suspended."

# 19

"YOU. AREN'T. Going." Demirci's words were lost in the infinity of footsteps it took Aaron to reach the lift with Niko. They hid their thoughts from one another. The door closed. The lift shook as they went up. Niko's hand bumped against hers. She wanted to reach for it, but he pulled it away.

Roof terrace. The door opened. She positioned herself inside it and blocked the sensor. "I've got to go."

"Where to?"

"You know where."

Snow blew into her face and melted away immediately.

Niko said nothing as time rushed by.

"Let me go."

"How can you think I would do that?"

"Otherwise he's going to kill them all."

"He only wants his brother and the money. He'll get it."

"He wants me."

"You're imagining that."

"Holm told Sascha what he was to say. He knows that Demirci will refuse to send me. Holm has put the fates of thirty people in my hands. And now yours too. If you don't let me go, the guilt for this will destroy us both."

"You want me to help you sacrifice yourself?"

"I want you to save thirty people."

"You want that for a different reason."

"Say I wasn't a coward in Barcelona."

The wind answers for Niko.

"I convinced myself that I might be able to live with it for so long that I ended up believing it myself. I tried to tell myself that time would help. That one day I would forget. But my father was right: I never will."

The lift shook slightly, even though it wasn't moving.

"There was nothing you could do for me. It was right."

"You gave me a bag of hot chestnuts. I kissed you. We made love. The next morning I asked you for something."

"Don't do this to me."

"I made you promise never to lie to me. I've never freed you from that promise. If you think only a single one of those children might get away, go down there with me now, and what we've just talked about will be our secret forever. If not, get out now."

The wind.

Her heart.

Police sirens.

She yearned to see Niko one last time.

She said: "It's *sisu*."

For thirty seconds Aaron didn't breathe. Then she reached for the buttons. She pressed for the ground floor. The door closed. She still wasn't sure that Niko had gone. She reached her hand out, searching. No one. She called the taxi number, said she was blind and the driver was to speak to her outside the building.

Aaron waited in the cold.

*Seventeen steps to my father's grave.*

*Six to my mother's.*

*Seventeen over six.*

"*Pure Maths,*" *Holm said.*

*The Mathematics building of the Technical University on 17 Junistrasse.*

*Two kilometers. So close.*

Aaron heard a helicopter. She didn't have much time. The taxi came. She asked the driver to hurry.

"I don't want to get a speeding ticket."

A hundred Euro note changed his opinion. He put his foot to the floor.

Every word she said to Niko had been completely honest. Just as the third reason for going was honest: Holm had the power over the fire that raged in her.

*And the power to extinguish it.*

He was in control of those minutes in the warehouse in Barcelona. He alone could give her that memory. Then she would understand. Why she ran away. Why Holm was tormenting her. Why he had waited five years, when in all that time he needed only to reach out a hand. He would redeem her. Perhaps it would involve her death. Even that admission was honest. But even if he understood her only at the very last second, at that moment she would be on the top of a high mountain, looking at her whole life spread below like a wide landscape in which she knew every stone and everything that lay underneath.

She heard a quiet staccato sound. *Uzi. Silencer.* The taxi driver probably wouldn't recognize the noise as gunfire.

*The drone being shot down.*

"Here it is."

"Can you see a coach anywhere?"

"I'll have to take a look."

Valuable seconds passed. Flap flap flap. The helicopter was above their heads. The police sirens could be heard even from far away.

"There's one. On the other side, in the car park."

"What does the coach look like?"

"Like a coach. The windows are covered over. With something light-colored."

"Drive over there and stop right in front of it."

"I can't get across there."

Aaron held out another fifty. Foot down. She was thrown against the door as he sped down the road. Metal crunched. Cars bunched together, they hobbled over a curb, the chassis scraped, the tires spun, the taxi skidded.

Hard brake. The driver grabbed the banknote. "Bit of cross-country riding for you there."

Aaron heard a single shot fired without a silencer.

*Too late, too late.*

She got out. The taxi roared away. The helicopter came lower. The sirens were so loud now that they drowned out the noise of the traffic. She stood there motionless and stared into the sky.

Bushidō requires you to travel the journey to the end, and says that death is a relief, salvation from shame. The sovereign's final favor was seppuku, honorable suicide.

Her sovereign, on the other hand, was truth. It alone could sentence Aaron to death. But only if she knew the truth. Until then she would fight for her life. If Aaron got the chance to flee, she would. If she was able to give the Department a clue about Holm's plans, she would. If she had the chance to kill Holm, she would.

The first virtue: *Gi.* Honesty.

*Here I am.*

*Heal me.*

*Take my body.*

*You won't have my soul.*

The sirens were only a hundred meters away. Something fell at her feet. Aaron knew it was a corpse. She was grabbed and dragged several meters, flew up a step. The coach door closed with a hiss.

Holm said: "At last."

# 20

CLOSE TO the Europa Center they end up in a traffic jam. Pavlik is at the wheel of the BMW, with Kleff next to him and in the back Rogge and Sascha. They are wedged behind the two black Fords whose sirens are no use at all. Cars are crammed in front of them, bumpers bashing against each other, unable to get out of the way because the bus lane is full of lorries. Sascha's grin appears in the rearview mirror. Pavlik's right earpiece is connected to the radio, through the right he's on the phone to Demirci.

A pedestrian squeezes past. He stops with a jolt when he sees the balaclava-masked faces of Kleff and Rogge. Pavlik gestures to him to keep going. The pedestrian flees as fast as his legs can carry him. The balaclavas serve to protect both of them. Sascha isn't supposed to know what they look like, so that he can't take his revenge on them. The men who transported him from Tegel airport to the Department wore balaclavas for the same reason.

Pavlik doesn't need all these precautions. Demirci tried to tell him to put on his balaclava before he went into the interrogation room. But he refused, and showed Sascha his face to tell him he wouldn't live to see another day. The message got through quite clearly. If Sandra knew she'd flip.

Demirci calls and drags him from his thoughts. "Holm has shot the first hostage."

He forces himself to ask: "A child?"

Kleff's glance.

Rogge's quick breathing.

"One of the teachers. But that's not all." The vain, unthinkable, definitive fact lies in her next sentence. "Kvist let Aaron go."

Pavlik has endured the silence of a man whose loved one was killed by his motorbike. He has spent three days waiting with Sandra for the result of a mammogram. He has had friends die, and sat by Aaron's bed. Nothing was as terrible as this.

"I should never have left her alone with him," Demirci says.

Pavlik looks in the rearview mirror.

Sascha smiles mischievously.

*You don't know me. And you don't know Aaron either. You'll find out who she is. But not in the way you expect.*

"Holm knows you're on your way."

They've been sitting there for a minute. He activates his throat mic and issues an order to the two Fords: "On to the pavement!"

The leading vehicle forces its way among the trucks being unloaded in the bus lane; the second Ford follows, then Pavlik. They hurry along the colonnades of the Bikinihaus. People jump out of their way, a little dog flies past on a lead. The front spoiler of the BMW hits a billboard and sends it flying through the shattered glass of a shop window. Pavlik sees the woman with the buggy at the last minute. He puts his foot down firmly on the brake and just touches the buggy, which seesaws for a second. The woman's eyes are the size of frisbees. She is pulled away by a grimacing, shouting, tooth-baring man, and hangs on to the buggy for dear life. The three-piece convoy thunders past the traffic jam, shoots back into the road at Hardenbergplatz and carries on unimpeded.

Pavlik wonders if he should tell the others that Aaron is in Holm's power. It will cause a shock. But if Holm comes out of the coach with her, the men need to be prepared or it's going to catch them off guard.

While he belts along at almost a hundred, through the gap in the traffic torn by the sirens of the Fords, he lends a matter-of-fact note to his voice. "We've got a new situation. A hostage has been killed. And one hostage is new. Aaron."

Rogge checks his Luger. Sascha grins.

"Roger SET 1."

"Roger SET 2."

They reach the monumental 17 Junistrasse, which crosses the Tiergarten park all the way to the Brandenburg Gate. The stretch they are driving along is the only part with buildings beside it: on either side the Technical University. Pavlik sees the bus in the car park on the left. The windows have been covered over with newspaper. Ten patrol cars keep their distance. The last passers-by have been taken to safety by the riot police. Pavlik starts the stopwatch on his wrist. "SET 1 to me. SET 2 in position," he mutters into the microphone.

The first Ford sheers off. He crosses the street and stops thirty meters from the coach. Pavlik overtakes the second car and turns, with the car in his wake, into the side-street that runs parallel with Prachtstrasse. "SET 2 to HQ."

"HQ here."

"Put me through to police headquarters." There is a click as the connection is established. "Get the girl out of there. And all the vehicles. Close off 17 Junistrasse from Ernst Reuter Strasse to Charlottenburger Tor right now. Have the university evacuated by the rear exits. If twenty kilos of C4 goes up, I don't want anyone apart from my people anywhere around."

*And not them either.*

Pavlik stops in a driveway beside the sixties building that houses the Faculty of Transport and Systems Planning. He jumps out of the car. At a glance he registers that the helicopter is moving away. The patrol cars swarm out to paralyze one of Berlin's main transport axes. The other SET takes up position in the car park. They use cars as cover. Pavlik knows that there's a hatch opening on the side of the Ford facing away from him, and Fricke is adjusting the precision rifle that he controls with a joystick inside the vehicle.

He takes time to look back into the BMW. Sascha looks out at him. It's only now that Pavlik puts on his balaclava, provocatively slowly.

He runs over to the men in his SET, ties a long plastic strip to the branch of a tree and sticks a sensor into the trunk. Reaches into his pocket. Each of them is carrying a hundredweight of kit as they hurry into the building.

A siren wails; through the loudspeakers people are told to make their way to the rear exits as quickly as possible. The men have to work their way through a throng of students and staff who are dashing down the steps past them.

Pavlik runs ahead and charges up to the second floor so quickly that the others can hardly keep up. It puts more of a strain on the fifty-year-old than they can imagine.

Every step he takes he's with Aaron. He's bringing her home for the first time and he knows, from the moment she and Sandra smile at each other, that they will be friends forever. He introduces her to the twins, and from then on they want her to come every evening. He has the Basque's garrotte around his neck in Paris, and she kills the man with the side of her sunglasses. He is sitting with her and Marlowe on the sofa, and they're playing at trying to outstare each other. He is in hospital in Barcelona, and he stays awake all night, afraid to close his eyes.

Pavlik pulls open the door to an empty lecture theater. Two men extend the telescopic stands and stretch out a black tarpaulin between them as a background to hide the five snipers from Holm; one man installs the video camera whose images will be transmitted to the operations center of the Department. A second camera is outside, on the roof of the Ford.

The routine that they're playing out with great concentration helps Pavlik to get his breath back. They cut circles with a forty-centimeter diameter in the window panes. He opens the gun-case and takes out the rifle. Pavlik likes to be mobile, so for targets up to three hundred meters he's got used to working with the Mauser, which is ancient but lighter. He likes the familiar feel of the antiquated wooden stock on his chin; he and the rifle are one. "I bet you've got a name for it," Aaron once teased him, "Jacqueline? Lucy? Mandy?"

The thing about the name is true. But he keeps it to himself.

When the telescopic sights have been set up, he puts on the lens cover so that the reflection doesn't give him away. Pavlik stretches the anti-mirage band over the barrel, to divert the heat when a shot is fired, and avoid the confusion of the wavy lines that appear with the alteration in air density. Last of all he screws on the silencer, which only removes the noise from the muzzle but not the sonic boom of the projectile. To eliminate that too, Pavlik ordered them to use the hated .308 caliber subsonic ammunition. They have to bear in mind that the bullets spin, that they're extremely sensitive to side winds and their trajectory has a lower velocity. But if the enemy doesn't hear the shot, it can be a great advantage.

He remembers his first training session at the Mill. "We don't say enemy, we say opponent," his trainer had yelled. "Remember that."

"Oh, like in sport?" he replied. "And what do we call the one who survives? The champion?" At the time he thought his career in the Department would be very short. Pavlik lay down to sleep, and when he woke up eighteen years had gone by.

He sees Wolter putting a .300 Magnum in the magazine of his rifle. Wolter is the only one who gets to Mach 1 with steel core ammunition. He's the one who will have to shoot at the getaway car. The bullet needs power if it's not going to be hampered by the cloud of glass dust it produces.

Pavlik, on the other hand, is already focused on the moment when Holm gets out of the coach with Aaron. He doesn't want to give him the chance to demonstrate his reflexes.

The plastic strip fluttering from the branch down below shows them the direction of the wind, north-east. The sensor in the tree trunk sends their phones information about air pressure, humidity and temperature. All of these factors need to be taken into account.

One below zero. So they'll have to aim very slightly higher.

The seventy-five meters isn't a problem. He's worked at thirty times that distance in the past.

The newspapers over the windows are a problem.

The gusts of wind are a problem.

The snow is a problem.

The thirty hostages are a problem.

The bomb is a problem.

Thirty hours without sleep is a problem.

Aaron is a problem.

A man like Holm is the sum of all these problems.

Fifteen seconds before the others Pavlik rests the rifle on its bipod, adjusts its height and flips open the sights. Last of all he glances at the stopwatch. Four minutes since he first saw the coach.

His right, dominant eye is the one that belongs to the sights. This is the killing eye. He keeps his other eye open too, checking the periphery so as not to be taken by surprise.

He can stay immobile like that for hours, without blinking. There's just him and the target. The distance separating them doesn't exist. His resting pulse is so low that he isn't aware of his heartbeat. During those four minutes Demirci hasn't given him any information inessential to his work, she hasn't addressed a single question to him.

He appreciates it.

On a stretch of road a kilometer long there isn't a single car, a single human being. The snow is falling so densely that the tire-tracks can't be seen. All outlines, even those of the trees, have vanished under a white covering.

The corpse lies two meters in front of the coach. It wouldn't be in their way. But they can't just let a corpse be covered up with snow. Pavlik doesn't need to issue the order, he already knows who will do what needs to be done. Hagen Kemper is a biker like him. Some Sundays they race each other on the Lausitzring; their last race cost Pavlik a bottle of expensive grappa. Kemper mightn't be the sharpest knife in the drawer, but he's always in the front row.

He sees Kemper leaving his cover and running bent-backed to the coach. He is wearing a bulletproof vest and a helmet. But that won't protect him against a shot in the face.

Because of the paper over the windows they can't use a laser mic to hear what's happening in the coach, so Pavlik expects Kemper to take the opportunity to do something else useful.

And in fact before attending to the corpse he presses himself against the bus just below the windows and swiftly attaches a bug to one of the panes, a transparent mic no bigger than a two-cent piece. Any noise, however quiet, will produce sound waves and make the windows vibrate. The bug turns those vibrations back into sounds.

Kemper picks up the dead teacher and runs back with him. Pavlik sees him laying the corpse gently behind a parked car.

"SET 2 to technical support," he murmurs.

"Technical support here."

"Activate the bug."

"It's activated."

The sound is transmitted to Pavlik's phone. He hears a man's voice. "What did he do?"

"Nothing important." Holm.

"He stuck something to the window." Holm's accomplice.

The man sounds uncertain and agitated.

"It's a microphone." Aaron. "You shouldn't trust him if he keeps something like that from you. There are only two of you, and you're putting yourself completely at his mercy."

The relief at hearing her carries Pavlik away like his Hayabusa when his knee brushes the tarmac on a hairpin bend.

"Two," he tells the SET down below. "Aaron is OK."

"Now you've instructed your colleagues, Miss Aaron," Holm says calmly. "Do that again and I'll kill the girl that you've been comforting so kindly. Please—is there anything else you'd like to add?"

He makes no attempt to communicate with them. They haven't got his phone number and have to let him call the tunes. He wants to break them down, demonstrate his power and show that he's setting the terms. But that vanity is stupid. Holm could have made better use of the first frantic minutes when the chain of command was unstable and the listening device wasn't stuck to the window.

His first mistake.

"Make your decisions within the space of seven breaths," Aaron always said.

They were clever, those Samurai. But that part of Aaron was always alien to Pavlik. He remembers the first time he came to her flat and could tell straight away that she could have left at any time without looking back. The only thing she might have missed was the old leather sofa. Just as Pavlik would have missed his.

At first she didn't talk about Bushidō, she kept that secret to herself. But one night out in the Mill, when they were both crouching in a muddy hole and Aaron's saliva was freezing in her mouth, she confessed to him that death was her friend, that she always felt its embrace.

He couldn't live like that. Pavlik took time for all his dead. With each one he thought carefully about why he had done it, and found a conclusive explanation. The dead don't keep him awake at night.

Apart from the one he never talks about.

But he knows that in his case there isn't a path that he has to follow. He doesn't believe in providence or fate. And if anyone is going to judge him, it will be himself.

Aaron's father didn't get it either. Once he tried to engage Pavlik in conversation. They weren't friends, but they respected one another. Jörg Aaron was worried. In Boenisch's basement something had awoken in his daughter, something that men like him and Pavlik kept at a distance. It was dangerous for her and for the others. It seemed to him that she was mocking death. And since she had chosen Bushidō he wondered if she even longed for it. Didn't the Samurai say that you must be firmly resolved to die at any moment? "She thinks about herself too much and yet at the same time too little."

Chinese whispers that Pavlik didn't pass on.

He remembers his answer: "If my chances are one in a thousand, there's only one person I'd like to have with me. And that's your daughter."

He asked her who her sovereign was. She refused to tell him.

Bushidō is a complicated world, Pavlik wished he knew more about it. Then he would have understood Holm's message as clearly as Aaron did. *The year of affection, the day of the tree,* the ideograms in the locket, all those hidden clues.

Then Pavlik would have been able to prevent it.

Niko.

What he did is unforgiveable. There may be a world in which the word is simply uttered in passing. Not in Pavlik's. He can't let it get to him, or he'll grab his gun, get in the car and drive to the Department.

He concentrates on the coach. "SET 1, give me your situation."

"The second window is open a crack. Five millimeters," Fricke reports. "Two movements in different directions twenty seconds apart. Someone's patrolling the aisle. Black clothes. Maybe a Johnny Cash fan."

"Should we give him a nudge?" Dobeck asks. Meaning that they could make contact via megaphone.

"Negative," Pavlik replies.

*Then Holm will think we're losing our nerve.*

The sky clears. The last snowflakes glitter in the harsh light that streams over the street and the car park. The coach immediately looks bigger in the sights. The light is coming from the left, and would deflect his aim. Pavlik increases the zoom to balance out this effect.

"He wants to talk to you," Demirci says.

He already hears Holm: "Are you in charge of the operation?"

"Yes."

"Where are you?"

"Close enough."

"You're here with two SETs. Five men in the car park. Six including the one operating the remote controlled gun in the Ford. The other five are the snipers. They immediately went to the second floor of the building opposite. They were in position within four minutes. You're one of them. That's unusual for the person coordinating the opposition. What gives you your special role?"

"It'll come to you if you think about it."

"How old are you?"

"I'm an adult."

"In a hostage situation the Department sends men between thirty and forty. If you were that age you could have told me straight away. Might we have had the pleasure yesterday? On the city freeway? You and Miss Aaron popped into a florist's shop and I had the opportunity to study your skills. It takes a lot of experience to control a car like that."

*The Phaeton.*

"Unfortunately you had mirrored windows so I couldn't see your face."

"Come over and I'll show you."

"Charming as that idea might be, maybe another time. What's been your best shot so far?"

"In the right-hand corner of the mouth from two thousand two hundred and eighty-four meters."

"Respect."

"I was aiming for the left-hand corner."

"So you've got a sense of humor as well. That's nice. A gift unfortunately withheld from me."

"What was your best shot?"

"Between the eyes from two meters."

"That's what I guessed."

"Now that we know each other a bit better: the car with my brother in it is parked right in front of the coach. The handcuffs will be taken off. Please confirm."

"Yes."

"Just for form's sake: the tank is full?"

"Yes."

"Give the order."

"SET 3 go into action. Front door," he says so that Holm can hear him.

"Roger SET 3."

Pavlik sees the BMW driving along the street.

"Is the bag with the money fitted with a transmitter?"

His first impulse is to lie. But a voice inside him says it would be a mistake.

"Correct."

"A good answer. I've got a bug detector, but I don't want to waste time scanning the bag. Lose the transmitter. Then the two men have to leave straight away."

The BMW stops in front of the coach.

"SET 3: get out, take the transmitter out of the bag and clear off." Pavlik's non-dominant eye is focused on Kleff and Rogge. Kleff opens the boot and reaches into the big sports bag. The five million weighs seventy-one kilos.

*Hope it breaks your back.*

Kleff shuts the boot and runs for cover with Rogge, joining the others.

"Now to the explosives," Holm says. "You know the quantity. I'll set off the bomb with my phone, the range is unlimited. We were talking about your best shot. Compared to two thousand two hundred and eighty-four meters it's insignificant. We know the likelihood of a lethal hit at that distance."

"A hundred per cent."

"Exactly. You're preparing to eliminate me with one fatal shot; you alone have that privilege. To do that you'll have to destroy my cerebellum, it's the only way you'll stop me moving my finger."

The possible coordinates at a similar height: frontally, the tip of Holm's nose, laterally the upper ear, from behind the transition to the base of the skull. Since Pavlik is on the second floor, he has to adapt the target window accordingly.

"Death occurs within one two-thousandth of a second. Too fast for a reaction. But there's a problem. I set off the bomb when I *let go* of the button. You know what that means."

"Yes, that you're a sick bastard."

"As soon as my muscles relax, the school trip is over. That's why I advise you not to consider that option."

*If you could register a patent for intelligence, this guy would be set up for life.*

"In spite of the schoolkids' handiwork you know that there are two of us. Before we leave the bus with Miss Aaron, I'm fastening a motion sensor to the door. I'll activate it as soon as we're out. If anyone in the bus moves after that, the bomb will be set off as well. The hostages have already been informed. Tell your men."

"SET 1: they're coming out now. Don't shoot. I repeat: don't shoot. We let them back away."

"If we're followed by a helicopter or even one single police car, our agreement is invalid," Holm says.

"I've got to pass that on to headquarters."

"Of course."

Pavlik makes the call. He's put through to the Berlin police. "Don't try and stop the getaway car. Your people are to let it get through."

"Roger."

"SET 2 to headquarters: keep a drone on it, but as high as possible and in the vehicle's blind spot. I want the picture on my tablet." He switches back to Holm. "I've authorized it."

"Fine. Then we're done."

"One more thing," Pavlik says. "I'm sure you've got a pair of binoculars. Look across to me." He stands up, pulls off the balaclava, walks to the window and opens it. The men beside him flinch. Pavlik doesn't waste a thought on the total silence from headquarters, his motionless colleagues down below, Demirci's quick breaths. He stands casually at the window, knows that Holm is watching him through a gap in the newspapers. "I've shown my face to your brother as well. Draw your conclusions from this." He takes up position behind the gun again and gets the coach in his sights.

Holm says: "Maybe we'll meet one day. It would be interesting."

"I don't think so."

"That it would be interesting?"

"That we will meet again. Aaron is blind. But she remains what she is, just as you do. You're a polite sociopath, your little brother is the trained monkey and this woman is your worst nightmare. She'll kill you both before daybreak. You have my word."

"I heard you." Dramatic pause. "Mr. Pavlik."

*Sandra.*

High-pressure fear fills Pavlik's heart and inflates it like a balloon.

"I'm curious about your driving skills. I took the liberty of following Miss Aaron to your birthday party yesterday evening. We must be more or less the same age. Men like you and me can't count on making it to our fiftieth, so belated happy birthday. You didn't get home till four in the morning. The taxi driver helped you carry all your presents to the house; you're clearly popular. He slipped on the pavement behind you. You did half a standing back split, holding heavy bags in both hands. He held on to your left foot, or else he might have broken something. You have the balance of a ballet dancer; I've seldom seen such artistry. The fact that you'd been drinking makes that movement even more astonishing. But the most surprising thing was that your trouser leg slipped up. You've got a prosthetic calf. I only noticed a very faint irregularity in your gait, a slight strain, nothing more, no real handicap. It's hard to impress me. Without a doubt the Department sent me their best man. But are you sure your wife is still alive? And your little child, with the pretty fairytale characters on her bedroom window?"

Holm hangs up.

Pavlik's gun is suddenly a block of ice. He can't feel the trigger. Demirci says: "We're calling."

In the quivering sights he sees a piece of newspaper being removed and a small box being fastened to the door of the coach.

The motion sensor.

While Aaron feels her way down the stairs, Demirci takes over. "They're fine."

Pavlik needs to bring his pulse rate down from its orbit around the earth. He breathes in and out several times, lets the air escape extremely slowly and concentrates on his diaphragm. He calms down eventually, and the gun snuggles against him once more. Behind Aaron, Holm appears with the second man. The coach door closes. Holm's Remington is in the belt of his trousers under his open jacket. He wears thin gloves and holds his phone in the air so that everyone can see it. The belt of a flat carry-case lies diagonally across his chest. Sixty by thirty, Pavlik guesses. He zooms in on Holm's left thumb until it fills the picture. The thumb rests on a button.

Pavlik turns to the accomplice. One eighty, bulky, carrying a small rucksack, Uzi with silencer, balaclava. He fixes his sights on Mr. Uzi's eyes. They wander over to him, scouring the street in both directions.

He aims the gun at Holm, who is opening the back door of the car. His brother gets out. Pavlik observes this meeting particularly carefully. They haven't seen each other for five years. But no hug, no handshake, not the slightest contact. All that Holm has for Sascha is a barely perceptible movement of his chin, which might with a certain amount of goodwill be interpreted as a greeting.

"Give me the order and I'll shoot off his thumb," Fricke murmurs.

"Don't even think about it," Pavlik replies.

"We've still got that bug in the BMW," Kemper says.

"That won't be any more use to us than the GPS."

Mr. Uzi opens the boot and inspects the bag of money. Holm isn't interested.

All of Pavlik's attention is focused on Aaron. With his right eye he sees her in extreme close-up, enlarged twenty-four times, while for his left eye she is small and a long way off. She stands there alone, quiet and collected, her face white as snow. She looks across at him, right into his sights, and his heart breaks.

But she shows no fear. Shares her thoughts with him.

*I know you don't understand.*

*And you never will.*

*We'll see each other.*

*In this life or another.*

*Tell Sandra I love her.*

Holm pushes Aaron into the back of the car. Sascha wants to get into the back seat again, but he freezes when his brother speaks to him. Pavlik sees Sascha's eyes stinging. There's a directional microphone on the aerial of the Ford. "What did he say?" he asks.

" 'You're not allowed to do that.' "

The brothers face each other, a meter apart, Sascha seems poised to jump, Holm is relaxed. He spreads his shoulder blades. Sascha lowers his gaze. When he walks around the car to the driver's seat, his gait is angular and stiff.

*Your muscles are seizing up because you're imagining yourself tearing out your brother's heart and eyes.*

Mr. Uzi sits down next to Aaron, Holm at the wheel. The BMW drives slowly out of the car park. It turns into 17 Junistrasse, speeds up towards the Victory Column and draws two slender white strips in the immaculate carpet of snow. Pavlik opens the window, hangs half out of it and stares after the car through the target sights. Mr. Uzi pulls off his balaclava. Pavlik has to settle for the back of his head. Ash-blond hair, drenched with sweat. His eye remains fixed on the car until it disappears from view by the Grosser Stern roundabout.

"SET 2 to technical support. Is the bug in the BMW transmitting?"

He isn't surprised by Krampe's answer. "Negative. He's using a scrambler, we're just getting white noise."

A transporter stops in the car park. The bomb disposal unit. The wind carries a rattling loudhailer voice across to Pavlik. "Stay where you are, don't move. If you follow our instructions nothing will happen to you." In German, then in English.

While Pavlik's tablet is coming on he calls Sandra.

"What's happened?" she asks immediately.

"Later. Bung the kid in the car and come to Budapester Strasse." He puts the call on hold. On the tablet he sees the picture transmitted by the drone. The BMW has joined the traffic, heading east via the Lützowufer.

Schöneberger Ufer.

Nationalgalerie.

Pavlik switches to Demirci's line. "He's taking the Tiergarten Tunnel. The drone is supposed to check the Invalidenstrasse exit. But I'm sure he plans to get to Central station. The Federal Police need to be informed. They're not to hound him, though. He could set off the explosives at any moment, we just need to know what train he's on. Send through their descriptions."

Demirci issues instructions. The echo disappears from the line. She has turned off the speaker so that no one else can listen in. "Have you ever met a man like this before?" she asks under her voice.

"No."

"He's thinking the same thing. He's never met a man like you before. And neither have I."

# 21

HOLM HAS driven along this stretch of road before. As soon as the traffic lights by the Nationalgalerie turn green it's twelve seconds to the tunnel. There he will accelerate to a hundred and sixty with one hand on the wheel, and if necessary use the hard shoulder for forty-four seconds to get to his destination. His left thumb doesn't move from his phone.

Sascha turns his head round to look at the back seat. "What's your name?"

"Bosch."

He looks at his brother. "What's the point of him?"

"To get us out of this," Bosch says, talking to himself.

"Put the phone down. Let's have some fun," Sascha says without paying any further attention to Bosch.

"Yeah, you'd have some fun," Holm murmurs. "Because you've never learned to distinguish important things from trivial ones. I sometimes wonder if you've ever learned anything at all."

He senses Sascha's hatred. It's always been like that.

At home there were no kind words, no laughter, no sleep without fear. There was the fist with the signet ring and the pliers and the belt with the spiky buckle. On good days it was the fist. There was their mother's empty eyes. Dinner at seven on the dot and the stairs to the basement. For six years he had to go down those stairs, counting the cracks in the basement ceiling, hearing his father's breathing.

Then Sascha turned four, and Holm's job was done. Upstairs he counted the cracks in his bedroom ceiling until he heard the basement door opening again.

Every evening his brother pleaded with him: "Kill him."

And every evening he said nothing.

His father was a woodsman with muscles like tree roots. Once a mastiff strayed through their garden in search of scraps. His father casually strangled the creature.

But Holm knew: *eventually.*

He started training in secret, lifting rocks at the abandoned quarry, fighting with the nastier boys, bigger and older boys, who inflicted pain on him.

Holm learned from them. He hid his growing muscles and avoided his father until he was strong enough.

*Sooner or later.*

For four years he heard the basement door being shut.

In the week before his nineteenth birthday he went to the area around the railway station and sought out a pimp the same size as his father. He threw him in an alleyway and drove the bridge of his nose into his brain and only eased off on him when he could no longer feel a single bone in the man's face. Then he knew that the time had come.

He told his father he would never touch his brother again. His father took off his belt with the spiky buckle, and Holm didn't defend himself. He enjoyed those minutes.

Every afternoon from then on he went to the forest where the woodsmen felled trees. For six days his father went out drinking with his mates after work. On the seventh he stayed on a little longer. It was just before Christmas, and he wanted to fell a Christmas tree. Holm could have split his skull in half with the axe, but he wanted his father to look at him. When Holm's fists were numb he picked up the chainsaw. He turned it on, looking his father in the eye as he did so. He saw him screaming but didn't hear it. He took the shovel out of the car and dug the grave in the deep wood and then washed in the stream. He went home, sat down at the dinner table and passed his brother the ketchup.

Their mother reported their father missing the next day. Policemen came and asked questions, came again and then stayed away. Their mother wept, but not out of grief. The way she looked at Holm told him that she knew. For two months she made him and his brother their favorite food. One morning she was dead. A stroke, they said. At the funeral some people Holm had never seen before said that he and Sascha would be living with them from now on.

While these strangers were eating cake, he ran away with Sascha. He looked after him for all those years. For a while he hoped his brother would eventually stop hating him. That day will never come. He dug the pit. But Sascha would never forgive him for those four previous years. Later it lost all meaning for Holm. He remembers the man he was many winters ago as little as he does some snow that he once shook from his coat.

He tried his best to be a good brother to Sascha. In his world that meant burning his fear like the jacket and trousers sprayed with his father's blood. While others stayed locked in their basement forever, whether that basement was in a house or in their head.

For a long time he was concerned that Sascha was doing badly at school. He gave him freedom, that was the last thing he would do for him. Perhaps one day his brother will understand that he must close that basement door once and for all.

Aaron tried to determine their position by their change of direction. The first right turn was simple, it could only be the Hofjägerallee by the big star in the middle of the Tiergarten. Shortly after that they turned left. Tiergartenstrasse or the Lützowufer.

Her hands aren't tied.

Aaron has done it in her mind.

She smashes Bosch's Adam's apple and grabs the Uzi that he's just put under his jacket. Before Holm or Token-Eyes can react, she has blown their brains out.

Two seconds.

She would probably survive the crash.

And twenty-nine people would die.

Another sharp left. Heading downhill, taking a long bend. The tires are no longer squelching in the muddy slush, and the sound of traffic makes way for a hollow rushing sound. She can tell that they're in the tunnel that runs beneath the government district.

Holm puts his foot down. Aaron is thrown into another tunnel. In the rearview mirror she sees an Audi and in it sits death wearing a made-to-measure Savile Row suit.

Suddenly she is kneeling next to Niko. His shirt is red, his mouth is red, his eyes are red, his voice is that of a dying man: "Get out of here."

Holm brakes hard. Aaron's forehead bangs against the headrest. The doors are pulled open. They are still in the tunnel. Cars speed past. Holm grabs her and presses her tightly to him, runs off with her. Behind them the boot is opened, the money. Aaron stumbles along beside him and clings to Barcelona, to Niko's last look.

Another door. "Keep your mouth shut," Holm snaps at her. The sound of a railway station surges towards them. "Attention passengers on platform six. The 15:12 Intercity to Hamburg, scheduled to depart at 12:58, will be delayed by twelve minutes." A train rumbles above her into the interchange station. A toddler shrieks, two throatily warbled sentences jitter by, Italian. Aaron is jostled, hears a muttered apology. Holm drags her onwards. Up the escalator. She slips, scrapes her ankle open. Holm whirls her back to his side. She tries to find the steps, keep pace, as he goes on dragging her after him.

Aaron lurches on to the platform. "Attention passengers on platform sixteen." The rattle of a suburban train, still quiet. He has calculated their movements precisely so that they get there with a second to spare. The idea shoots through her brain. She has lost all sense of time. When did they enter the building? Did the station police notice them? And what came next? A death sentence for her and for twenty-seven children?

Bosch stands on her left, lugging the money, pumping air, his lungs rattling. In the bus his voice sounded anxious but clear. But

when they got into the car and he said incredulously, "They're actually letting us go," she was numb. A moment later he pulled something off his head.

*A balaclava. He wasn't wearing it on the bus. But when they got out
he didn't want his face to be seen.*

At that moment she sees herself here with Niko, she's in love, she
tickles him, he tickles her back. Laughing, she looks into one of the
surveillance cameras and sticks out her tongue.

"Careful, take a look behind you," she says to Bosch.

She feels the movement as the man turns round. Holm's hand
clamps around her arm like a fully inflated blood-pressure sleeve.
"How stupid can you be?" he snaps at Bosch.

"Excuse me, could you take a picture of us?"

Aaron freezes.

But Holm says in impeccable Oxford English: "Sure. Say cheese,
ladies."

"Thank you very much."

"My pleasure."

The train is on the platform. "Step," Holm barks. They get in. They
are pushed from behind. The carriage is airless. Aaron pushes against
shoulders, gets an elbow in the ribs. Holm squeezes through with
her. Presses her on to a seat, pushes her to the window. Something
heavy is set down in the corridor, the bag of money. Some youths are
laughing and shouting behind them.

"Stand back from the platform edge!"

The doors close, they judder off.

Aaron is kneeling beside Niko in Barcelona. She sees his ribcage
twitching, sees his agony. "Clear off."

"Next stop: Bellevue," blares the speaker.

A phone plays a lilting little tune. A woman tells off a sulky little
girl. The youths noisily leave the train. "Hey, loser, out the way." Cold
air forces its way into the carriage, people press in. Fresh pear sham-
poo, wet dog, kebab. On the train from Wiesbaden to Frankfurt Aaron
has been addressed twice, because she was lost in thought and, without noticing, stared at men who thought she was flirting with them.

That mustn't happen now, it could be disastrous. Aaron turns her eyes towards the window. One more stop. After that they cross 17 Junistrasse. If she wasn't blind, she would see the coach.

"Next stop: Tiergarten."

Holm leans over to her. "You know the drill," he whispers. His voice is so quiet that even Aaron can barely hear it. "The bomb disposal guys will open the bag first. Of course that's a risk. There might be a sensor in the bag that will spark the explosives as soon as the zip fastener is opened. Alternatively, the robot might remove the bag from the luggage area to take it a certain distance away. But that would be an even greater risk; a pressure switch under the bag is a favorite trap set by bombers. So they go for the zip option. The robot cameras show that it's a relatively simple mechanism. I didn't need to go to any unnecessary trouble. They've decided to separate the blasting cap from the charge with a water-gun."

They pull into the station. The dog barks. Someone opposite her stands up. "Can I get through?" The seat is filled immediately. Bosch. Aaron hears him dragging the money bag over. Her heart thumps to a techno beat.

"Stay back!"

"The disposal guys have nineteen and a half minutes, that should be enough. Once we're on the bridge over 17 Junistrasse, I'll let go of the button. If I've miscalculated we'll know straight away."

Aaron stops breathing. The train gains speed. It's on the bridge. The dog whines. A newspaper rustles. A woman talks about four numbers she got in the lottery. Someone blows their nose.

"You're saving twenty-nine people," Holm whispers in her ear. "But you won't save yourself."

Pavlik calls Demirci. "Has the bomb been defused?"

"Three minutes ago. The kids are fine."

"Did anyone see Aaron at the station?"

"No. The Federal Police only have fifteen officers on duty at that time of day. And six of them were at a stabbing in the underpass."

"What about the cameras in the car park?"

"They were switched off. The getaway car is in the tunnel. They got into the building through a fire door. Where are they?"

"I'll be right there." Pavlik charges out of the lift on the fourth floor of the Department. He sees Nieser with Majowski and Delmonte. "Where is he?" Pavlik asks.

"Listen—"

"Where?"

"Interrogation room II."

The door practically crashes off its hinges and Pavlik comes flying in. He hammers his fists into Niko's kidneys. Niko goes down with a groan, Pavlik pulls him back up. Two in the ribs, one in the face. Niko's nose breaks. He doesn't resist the barrage of blows. Solar plexus, head, spleen, liver. The wall is all that is keeping him upright. Men come running, pull Pavlik off. Niko topples over. Pavlik breaks away and kicks him in the stomach. Four men can hardly hold him.

He roars: "What have you done?"

They try to drag him away but can't. He rages, flails his fists until he hears Sandra's voice. "I know, Ulf." Pavlik shivers. The men let go of him. Two of them help Niko to his feet. Blood streams from his nose as if from a tap. They put his arms around their shoulders and haul him to the door. Sandra gets in their way. Niko hangs limply in front of her. Her fist hits his nose-bone with all her might, breaks it again. Not a sound. There is more grief in his eyes than she has ever seen. She stands aside. The door closes quietly behind her. Pavlik falls to his knees. Sandra drops in front of him and pulls him to her. They both cry.

"It's my fault," Pavlik whispers.

She takes his head in both hands. "I give you five minutes to blub. Then you stand up and get them out of there."

Helmchen is holding the bawling baby in her arm. She uses a tin of paperclips as a rattle and calms the little one down with it. Jenny taps the new toy with her hand while Helmchen picks up the ringing phone off her with her free hand. "The Department, Helm speaking. Miss Demirci has been informed. Sorry, I don't know when she'll have time." She sees Pavlik and Sandra. "I'll call you back." Helmchen puts the phone down.

"I want Sandra and Jenny to be taken to the safe house in Cottbus. Who have we got?"

"Nobody. But Miss Demirci said the Five will look after both of them for as long as necessary. I'll call them in."

Inan Demirci enjoys personal protection, even though she might not put it that way. Even though the Department isn't actually part of the the BKA, its security division, known as "the Five," consists of men from that security squad.

Sandra takes the baby from Helmchen and puts her in the sling, where she laughs and waves her arms and legs about. Pavlik draws his wife to him. "I'm to tell you that she loves you."

New tears come.

His voice is firm. "Do you remember how we used to play cowboys and Indians with her and the twins in the garden?"

Sandra nods.

"Back then we used to play with toy pistols. She used to say, 'No one is faster than me, stranger.' It was the truth. There's no one faster. Tomorrow evening we'll play Scrabble with her and let her win."

Helmchen hangs up. "The Five will be there very soon."

Pavlik kisses Sandra. "I'll call you." He runs outside, turns around and lifts his daughter up to inhale her smell once more, because he doesn't know how long he'll have to do without it.

At operation headquarters upstairs, half the squad is standing around Demirci. She calls the police at the railway station on speakerphone. "They should have been in the building at ten to one. He calculated it precisely so that they would be on the platform just before the train pulled out. I want all trains that set off between 12:50 and 1:00 p.m. Long-distance and regional, underground and suburban."

"One moment."

Pavlik joins Demirci. Frantic activity in the room. For a moment the two of them are able to talk. "Thanks for the Five," he says quietly.

Demirci presses his hand for a moment, a surprising, warm touch that does him a huge amount of good. She turns to a colleague, asks precise questions in telegraphese, requiring similar replies. Pavlik gives her a furtive glance. All of a sudden, deep wrinkles have formed on her face. For the first time he notices how slender she is. Strong-willed rather than beautiful, her eyes two big blue splinters broken from a rough sapphire. The first silver threads in her fox-red hair, her nose curved like the beak of a bird of prey. Crows' feet reveal that she likes to laugh. But Pavlik has never seen her laugh.

"The U-Bahn towards Brandenburg Gate," the policemen tell them. "Three local trains: Westkreuz, Wartenberg, Potsdam. Four regional trains: Eisenhüttenstadt, Dessau, Rathenow, Nauen. The Hamburg InterCity. No, it was late. That's it."

Pavlik has a think. Regional trains don't make sense. Too few stops, too risky. The underground is out of the question as well. What would Holm want at the Brandenburg Gate?

Demirci and Pavlik say at the same time: "The local train."

The camera pictures from the station are fed into the video wall. They show the platforms from four perspectives. Not a trace of Aaron.

Fast forward.

"There they are!" cries Ines Grauder.

Potsdam. 12:55. The train is already pulling in. Holm has his arm around Aaron's hip, he holds his phone in his left hand. They run from the escalator to the platform.

Sascha and Mr. Uzi are right behind them. Pavlik turns his attention to Mr. Uzi. He is carrying the money. A gun bulges under his zipped-up jacket. He has a baseball cap pulled over his face, his head is lowered.

"Come on, let's have a look at you," Pavlik murmurs.

Aaron taps Mr. Uzi on the shoulder. He turns around and looks straight into the camera.

*Good girl.*

"Stop!" Demirci says. The man's face fills the screen. Mid-forties, fleshy, doughy skin, breathless. "Biometric match with INPOL," she tells Krampe.

They make a screenshot.

"What's Holm got there?" Büker means the box.

"A gun of some kind?" Demirci asks.

Pavlik shakes his head. "Too short for a rifle, too flat for a subma-chine gun, too big for a pistol."

The video runs on. Two Asian tourists speak to Holm. He removes his right glove with his teeth and takes a photograph of them with their mobile phone as the train comes to a standstill.

"Miss Grauder, put out a search for these two on the media, Holm's fingerprints are on the phone."

"They set off exactly twenty-five minutes ago," Pavlik says. "How long does the train take to get to Potsdam?"

"Forty minutes," is the answer from the Federal Police.

"If they're still on the train—where would they be now?"

"They'll be pulling in to Wannsee in a minute."

"Do you have any officers there?"

"Not right now."

"Could you send a drone?"

"No. They're all in the city and they've only got a range of fifteen kilometers."

"Do you have access to the cameras in Wannsee?"

"Yes."

"Then hurry up."

"Where else does the train stop?" Demirci asks.

"Griebnitzsee. Babelsberg. Potsdam Central."

"Get plain-clothes officers to the stations right now. If they spot them, they're just to observe."

Instructions are given out at the other end.

The pictures from Wannsee come in. The train is already by the platform, the doors open. A man with a dog. Three cyclists taking their bikes off the train. Two women with shopping bags.

Aaron.

Pressing her tightly to his left hip, Holm walks swiftly, but not too fast, to the exit. Sascha and Mr. Uzi follow.

"Next camera," says Pavlik.

They see the station concourse. The three men appear with Aaron. The display is being rearranged in front of a newspaper kiosk. A parcel of papers thumps to the ground.

Aaron stops and speaks to the newsagent.

In mission control the temperature suddenly drops ten degrees.

The newsagent shakes his head. Holm pulls Aaron on. They leave the building and are gone.

"Are there cameras in front of the station?" Demirci asks.

"No."

"Get some people over there. I want to know what she said to that man. Dig up some witnesses that you've seen leaving the station. They'll be getting away by car. I want the registration."

"There's a marina three hundred meters away," Pavlik adds. "Check it too. Just in case they've taken a boat."

Demirci looks at him. "Get some sleep."

"Don't need to."

"You do. I need you rested."

Niko sits motionless on a chair. His head dangles on his chest. Demirci comes in. She sits down opposite him. He looks up. His nose is swollen, his cheek burst. His mouth is covered with encrusted blood.

"I see Mr. Pavlik has already told you everything you need to know," Demirci says coldly.

"Get over it."

"I'm trying to understand what you've done. But however hard I try, I can't quite get there."

"That's between Jenny and me."

"The decision about your life."

"She begged me to let her go."

"It was your damned duty to stop her!" Demirci bellows.

"It's because of Barcelona."

Demirci lights a cigarette. She takes five deep drags before her voice calms down. "What does that mean?"

"She thinks she lost her honor there. That she was a coward. I couldn't persuade her otherwise."

"I know what you said back then. And what Jenny Aaron said too. There's just the two of us here, no one's recording the conversation. What was it really like?"

"That doesn't matter anymore."

"I'll decide what matters."

"Holm and Nina Deraux had hidden guns in the station concourse. His brother shot the three Catalans outside. I took two bullets from Holm. Jenny was able to get away. She killed Deraux and gave Sascha that scar on his neck. Jenny wanted to get me out of there. I was too heavy, I couldn't help her, I thought I was about to die. She was wounded. Holm was shooting at us. It was impossible. I sent Jenny away. There's no secret about it. She lives with a guilt that no one else can understand."

"No. I understand it. It would have been her duty to eliminate Holm and save you."

"You're talking as if you'd learned it from a handbook."

His nose is bleeding again. Demirci hands him a tissue. He doesn't take it. Blood drips down his chin and on to the table. "Did you see Gaudí's cathedral in Barcelona, the Sagrada Família?" she asks.

"What about it?"

"This is *our* cathedral. In our family there are laws that aren't written down anywhere. Some of them I had to learn. But one of them I knew already, because it's sacred: we don't abandon a comrade to a certain death."

"I've freed her from her duty."

"That's not within your authority."

"She was panicking."

"She never panics. If I'd been in Internal Affairs at the time I'd have brought a case against her. Maybe it never happened because of her achievements or because of her name."

"You heartless piece of shit."

"I'd have done it until yesterday morning," Demirci continues, unmoved. "But now I've met Jenny Aaron. Whatever led her to do what she did in Barcelona, it must have been highly significant. Something more significant than our code. What would it have been?"

"I don't know."

The sun is gone. The snow is coming back.

"There's something missing," she insists.

"She can't remember anything about the warehouse. She told me that yesterday."

Demirci stares at the blood drying on the Formica. Niko's jugular pulses. His voice breaks. "The only thing that isn't in the report is my fear and her fear and her face before she ran for her life."

The neon lights flicker. Footsteps patter by outside. Demirci's phone rings, she picks it up. "Yes? I'll look into it." She gets to her feet. "Tell me what I'm supposed to do with you."

Niko looks up. "If what I did was a crime, then it's one that isn't on the law books."

"You're suspended," says Demirci.

Pavlik has a sofa. Old and threadbare it stands in his office, occupying half of the small room. Ten years ago he found it by the side of the road and dragged it to the Department. It looks as if it has moths. Once he caught Aaron spraying it with disinfectant. But he does his best thinking on this dirty old settee. It's notorious in the Department. Anyone who's cocked up has to sit on it. And then when they're seen slouching disconsolately down the corridor, someone only has to say, "He's been on the sofa," for everyone to understand.

Pavlik can sleep anywhere and at any time, five minutes or five hours, and he's wide awake a second later. He slept in a hailstorm while his SET waited for the go-ahead. He slept standing up on the U-Bahn on the way to his colonoscopy. He slept when his daughter was getting her first teeth, and woke up immediately before her attack of croup, and calmed her by the open window. In the winter he slept under leaves in the forest, at a Rolling Stones concert and in a stream.

But now he's been lying on the sofa for twenty minutes staring at the ceiling. The door opens. Demirci. Pavlik immediately sits bolt upright.

"No witnesses in Wannsee. No one has seen anything."

He was prepared for that. Much more important is: "What did she say to the newsagent?"

"Verbatim: 'Excuse me, don't you live on Bübingweg?'"

He looks blank.

"Boenisch used to live there. It was in his file."

Pavlik thinks for a moment.

"She was trying to tell us something," Demirci says. "The information we need must be hidden somewhere in the record of yesterday's interrogation."

There's a quick knock at the door. Helmchen peers in. "Forensics have extracted Holm's DNA from the blood on the knife, but there's nothing in the database. And the prints have been wiped."

*We still have the two tourists whose picture he took*, says the look that Pavlik gives to Demirci.

"Sorry, I can't put the conference off any longer," Helmchen continues gloomily. "I need to at least give them a time for the video link."

"In fifteen minutes. Thank you, Miss Helm."

"From now on I'm Helmchen to you. If you like."

Demirci smiles for a second. "That'd be great."

"Helmchen, where is Boenisch's interrogation?" Pavlik asks.

"I don't know."

"On her phone," Demirci remembers. "She was going to copy the recording but didn't get round to it."

"It was on the coach, and now it's in my office. I'll bring it right down." Helmchen withdraws quietly.

Pavlik points to a spot on the sofa beside him. Demirci glances with disgust at a large stain. "Is that blood?"

"No idea."

"Right." She sits down, but keeps stiffly to the edge.

"He knows we're on Budapester Strasse," Pavlik says. "And he knows our tactics."

"Yes. That's concerned me too."

"How did he find out? We don't give anything away."

"A mole?"

"I've been through all our people. I can't imagine any of them doing such a thing. But I don't want to pretend it's never happened before. We need to look into them, one by one. But apart from the fact that we don't have enough time, I think Holm's source is someone at the top."

"The Conference of Interior Ministers…"

"It needn't be a minister; maybe a secretary of state," Pavlik says. "Holm banks on fear. He might have managed to blackmail somebody. There are other possibilities too. He's a Mafia contract killer. He buys political contacts. If I had to dine with big shots like you do, I'd be very careful who I raise a glass to."

Silence.

"Don't you want to know what Kvist said?"

"Why?"

"He calls her 'Jenny.' I've seen them dancing. How long were they together?"

"A year."

"Would he lie for her?"

"He'd do anything for her."

Demirci hesitates. There's a question she's itching to ask, but she lets the itch pass. "What have we got to work with?"

"Holm knew I was seventy-five meters away from him. He can determine distances very precisely."

"He studied the situation."

"Of course. But he didn't use a tape measure. 'Between the eyes from two meters away.' Remember? That was irony."

"You think he's a marksman?"

"We know of two attacks carried out with rifles. Once in Frankfurt an der Oder, when a Ukrainian woman was killed. And once outside the Hotel Jupiter. Sascha hinted at that one. He was speaking not on his own behalf, but on his brother's. We're not talking large distances. But I bet Holm can deal with different ones. It's a science, you have to learn it. Usually in the army, like I did. Where? He wasn't in the forces. If we can get prints from him, I'll compare them with the ones on the Pavlik list."

Demirci looks at him quizzically.

"My private archive. I've documented the shots from snipers who left clues at the scene of the crime. What about the third man? Did the biometric comparison throw anything up?"

"No. He's not a wanted man, no previous, no record on INPOL."

"He's bound to be on some system somewhere. And one more thing: Sascha wanted to get into the back with Aaron. But Holm said: 'You're not allowed to do that.'"

They exchanged a long glance. "He's not letting his brother take his revenge on her," Demirci murmurs. "Is that good or bad news?"

"Bad. It means he's got a punishment in mind for her that's worse than anything Sascha could do to her."

"You said something to Holm a little while ago."

"I've said a few things to him."

"That she's going to kill him and his brother. You gave your word. Did you mean it?"

"Yes."

There isn't a hint of doubt in the reply. As if Demirci had asked if there was a sofa in his office.

"What sort of physical condition do you think she's in?"

"I gave her a hug. Every muscle is toned. She's at her fighting weight."

"What good is that? She's blind."

"They were at the firing range. It was Aaron's lane. There's a notch in the gun rest, right in the middle, so that she was able to take her bearings. Still: a shot like that is a miracle. But that wasn't the real sensation. She *knew* it was a nine and not a ten. Do you have any idea what sense of space and physicality you need to have to be able to work out something like that if you're blind?"

"I can't even begin to." Demirci's thoughts are lost in the previous afternoon. *A metaphor? Personal experience.* "She saw the armour in my office."

"In what sense?"

"I don't know how she did it, but she knew there was something there that she didn't know from before."

He lights a cigarette. "Holm doesn't give his enemies a chance. But she still wounded him with the knife. I wouldn't worry about Aaron's physical condition."

"Does she want to live, or does she want to sacrifice herself?"

"She left us a message at Wannsee station. So she wants to live."

"She thinks she was a coward in Barcelona. Could she regain her honor by saving the children?"

"No. There was only one way the Samurai achieved that."

They both know. Only through death.

His breathing is calm but he isn't. "She once said: 'If there is still time at the end I don't want to ask myself why I must die,  I want to know why I have lived.'"

# 22

Fårösund, December 2013

HOW SHOULD I start this letter?

"Dear Aaron" sounds strange. We all call each other by our surnames, that's what we've done as long as we've known each other. Perhaps because it makes it easier when it comes to giving the ferryman his coin. It's never worked for me. And not for you either. There was only one that we called by his first name. And we don't talk about him anymore.

I still remember them giving me your file and saying, "You should take a look at this one." I'd never held an appraisal like yours in my hands before. But I want to be honest: in the meeting at the Ministry I asked you your name, more out of curiosity than anything else. I didn't want a woman on the squad. Big balls sit uneasily with short skirts. Forgive an old macho man, you know what I mean.

I'm sure you thought I was a snooty arsehole. I just had to see you coming through the door. The rest was idle chatter.

Apart from what I said to you right at the end. You'll remember.

You were with us for six years. You wore even shorter skirts than I had feared, and turned all heads. Even Pavlik's, of course. But everyone would have walked through fire for you. I don't need to tell you why.

A few times the fossils tried to stitch you up. You won't have known this, but the lads came to me one after another and said: "If Aaron goes I'm going too." Pavlik and Butz even put their guns on the table. The truth is: if I'd been forced to throw you out, I'd have gone ahead of you.

Because you were the best with a pistol? That too. Because of your intelligence? And that. Because you knew how to kill somebody with the frame of a pair of sunglasses? (Yes, Pavlik told me.) That as well. But basically just because the Department wouldn't have been the same without you. (And it isn't.)

When we have shooting competitions the sixth lane is left empty, the lads decided that without even bothering to talk about it. So you're always there with us.

In all the time I've known you, you've only disappointed me once. You thought I hadn't noticed about you and Kvist. I didn't say a thing. He wasn't right for you, but it was your business in the end. I'm not your father, even if I'd like to be.

He was probably the only person prouder of you than I was. Our paths often crossed professionally. I saw his eyes light up when I talked to him about you. But he was worried about you. Once he suggested that it would be better if I put you in shallower waters. I couldn't do him that favor.

He was a legend. But if I had had the choice between taking on him in his prime or you—I would have opted for you without hesitation.

I wasn't there in Barcelona. I have read a lot of reports in my life. (I'm weary of them all.) Some I approved, others not. But this one was less truthful than any other I have come across. It may all have been like that. With one exception: that you were a coward. Whoever wrote that never knew you. The only one who can assess a situation is the person in that situation. No report can explain why you acted one way and not another.

Maybe there's also something you're keeping to yourself. You'll have your reasons for that. If you feel like it, let's go fishing together and you can tell me all about it.

I'm retiring in two years. My successor has already been chosen. Inan Demirci. A woman, just think! (Well, you got the ball rolling.) She's pretty good, she just needs to loosen up a little. They're giving me a watch, and I'm sailing my boat to Sweden. The house is always open to you.

Right now I'm sitting here on the veranda. I'm enjoying a few free days with an old friend. He's sleeping in the hammock. You know him, he runs the terrorism section in the BKA. Last night I was delighted when he said you were working as a case analyst for them. (Before you come to the wrong conclusion: I didn't intervene.)

You impressed him. But that much was obvious.

How should I explain to you what I felt at that moment? When my son told me I was about to be a grandfather it was fantastic. Waking up after my heart operation. (Last year, but I'm fine.) And my thirtieth wedding anniversary. Because I can't get my head around the fact that I've survived all that and am still allowed to love this wonderful woman, even today. (I'm to send hugs!) This belongs in that category.

We can't change the direction of the wind, but we can set the sail differently. You did that. You are what you are. There is no situation so hopeless that you can't take control of it. You will always make the best of everything. That's who you are.

Now I also know how I should have started this letter. Welcome back, Aaron. That's what I should have said.

Your old friend, Lissek

For forty minutes she has been counting the seconds while thinking at the same time. They are on the freeway. Aaron can tell by the quiet vibration of the floor of the car, the low-noise asphalt, the lack of turns and traffic lights. Right after leaving Wannsee station she was thrown into the unheated cargo area. Holm told Bosch to bind her hands behind her back with a cable tie. He took the Uzi from him, he's taking no risks. "Don't be deceived by her blindness. If you give her the slightest chance she'll break your neck like a matchstick."

*Holm addresses him formally. Of course. He would never put anyone on the same level as himself.*

The cable tie cuts deep into her skin. As they drove off she clicked and worked out that she is in a transporter or a lorry. Bosch sits on the floor facing her. The bag of money is between them, she can poke it with her feet. The brothers are up front in the driver's cabin. She doesn't know if there's a window or not.

She worked out a long time ago that Holm doesn't want to leave her alone with Token-Eyes. She has his phrase in her ear:

*You're not allowed to do that.*

Aaron inconspicuously shifts her position for the third time. She has already explored the floor twenty centimeters to the right. She slips slightly to the left and tries to find something to rub through the tie that binds her wrists together. Nothing. Another ten centimeters.

Her fingers brush only grooved metal.

Bosch unscrews a water bottle. Drinks. Puts the top back on. Lights his sixth cigarette. She hears the click of the disposable lighter, smells the smoke.

"Can I have a drag?"

He doesn't respond, smokes hastily, ignores her. Aaron remembers his voice and tries to assign it a physique. She's not very good at that. Sometimes she thinks a voice is attractive and masculine and learns later that it belonged to someone fat, thin or bent-backed. A young voice can belong to an old person and vice versa. A life, the sum total of everything that shapes a voice, is not a matter of years.

Bosch's vocabulary is limited, he mumbles his words sloppily, treats them without love; the rhythm of the syllables is monotonous. His voice always goes up slightly at the ends of his sentences. As if he felt he had been treated unfairly, and always felt that he had to defend himself. There's a rage in him that he isn't allowed to express.

His fear of Holm is plain; he is completely subordinate to him. But there can't be anyone who isn't afraid of Holm, Aaron included. Bosch responds to instructions with a brusque "yes" or "good." She concludes from this that he has spent a long time in a system based on orders and obedience. He is used to the company of men who aren't repelled by it. The army, she suspects, but not an officer.

It's clear what Holm needs him for; Bosch gave it away in the BMW when Token-Eyes asked again: "So, what's the point of you?" Could be that he's good at stress situations, but today's events have been far too much for him. Bosch's nerves aren't under control, or he wouldn't have turned to face the camera on the station platform.

She needs to build up a relationship with the man. He's the only one who stands between her and the brothers. Could stand between them. "Just a drag," Aaron says again. She looks past him, pretends to be searching for his face, trying to arouse his pity. Again Bosch doesn't react. "They're my brand."

He leans forwards. She feels the cigarette between her lips and sucks greedily on it, Chesterfield. "What's your first name?" she asks. "Mine is Jenny. Actually Jennifer. But no one has ever called me that."

"I know what you're trying to do." He opens the zip of the bag. Counts money. Trying to distract himself.

"What's that?"

"Sweet-talk me."

He is speaking downwards, looking at the money. Aaron exploits the fact to slide over a few more centimeters. She grips something and carefully examines it. A hook for a lashing strap. "I just want us to get to know each other a bit better," she says, and starts rubbing the cable tie against the hook. "So that you listen to me when I tell you who Holm is. You don't seem to know."

"I don't care what's up between you two." He closes the bag.

"And even if you count the money ten times, you won't see a penny of it. Holm has never shared anything with anyone. Not even his brother. He can kill a human being in lots of different ways."

"He said you would try this."

"Did he also tell you we bumped into each other earlier today? Ask him."

"Be quiet."

"In the flat belonging to the florist. He mentioned it to my colleague. You remember?" She concentrates hard on the cable tie, holding her arms still, just moving her hands. Bosch lights another cigarette. She hears him trying to stick the lighter into the pack. He bungles it the first time, manages it the second. "Holm said: 'Tonight you will be dead, and my brother and I will be five million richer.' He didn't mention you."

"You must think I'm an absolute idiot."

"I think you're someone who doesn't want to die. Who should have a think about whether he has a place in Holm's plans. Do you know what he did with that florist? He flayed and gutted her like an animal. He threw her little child out of the fourth-floor window."

Bosch opens the zip again.

They are slowing down. They stop. Aaron's pulse is going at full speed. If Holm drags her from the truck with her hands tied in the middle of nowhere, she'll be defenseless.

*No, we haven't turned off. It's the freeway.*

Sirens are coming closer. Police and fire brigade, they wail right past her, getting quieter until they're a mere whisper. An accident far ahead.

Aaron checks her breath. "Why do you think his brother asked what the point of you was? If you help me you might stay alive."

She's working away on the steel hook. Her skin tears. Her wrists are burning.

*There is no situation that you can't master.*

Aaron hears Bosch taking off his jacket. The cigarette smoke comes closer. She feels Bosch's breath. Something touches her cheek. Moves along it, feels chapped, then sweaty. She recoils. He strokes Aaron's other cheek. She realizes that it's his forearm.

Scars. A landscape of pain.

"I've killed a lot of people," Bosch whispers. "I've been told my price. That would only be fair. It's a shitty business."

He sits back down facing Aaron and counts the money. His smell stays in her nostrils.

Aaron seeks protection in her inner room. The vibration of the vehicle. The smoke from the cigarette. The rustle of banknotes. The memory of Lissek's letter. Her bleeding wrists. This hook. Her fear.

That's all she has.

And the question: *Will Pavlik understand my message?*

*

Helmchen brings him Aaron's mobile. "It's turned off. Do you want me to get someone from technical support to sort out the PIN?"

"Not necessary. Where's the bus driver?"

"He's up at Keithstrasse being questioned by the Criminal Police."

"I'd like to talk to him."

"I've sorted that out already." Helmchen sets a little box decorated with a ribbon down on Pavlik's desk.

"You're not proposing to me, are you?" he says.

"Your birthday present. I wasn't here yesterday."

He picks up the box and turns it around.

"Eighteen years ago, when you turned up on your first day, and came and sat in the waiting room ahead of your interview with Lissek, I had some things on my mind," she says. "A good friend of mine was very ill. Usually I'm able to hide such things, and you didn't know me. But you smiled at me and said: 'For every rotten day there are ten good ones.' I was grateful to you for that."

Pavlik remembers.

"All the new recruits sat in my waiting room," she goes on. "They were all very preoccupied, they were wondering what to expect, whether or not they were about to be thrown into icy water, whether they would be up to the job. You weren't. You were quite calm and had time to address my worries. Even then it occurred to me that you might be the only one who would still be working in the Department when he was fifty."

Pavlik fiddles with the ribbon, can't open it with his fat fingers and finally pulls it apart in the time-honored male fashion.

The box contains a cartridge case.

"I asked the range attendant to give me the case from your first bullet. Congratulations, Ulf. And thanks for always being a friend, a brother, and even a father to the others."

Pavlik doesn't know what to say.

"I've only ever had that thought twice. You know who the other person was. That cartridge case is in my desk drawer. I couldn't bring myself to throw it away." She looks at him for a long time. He has never seen that expression on her face before. "You're all she has."

Pavlik merely nods. Helmchen leaves the room.

He studies the cartridge case, rolls it between his fingers. It looks like many thousands of others. And yet it's precious. Pavlik puts it gently back in the box.

Aaron still has a white phone. "A girly mobile," he used to tease her. He tries the last four digits of her old ID number. Invalid. When did Marlowe come into her life? He doesn't know. The date of her father's death? Invalid. He has one more go before the phone is locked.

1905. Sandra's birthday. Accepted.

Two folders of speech recordings. "Interrogations" and "Personal."

*"19 June. What happened in the bar in Paris?"*

*"20 June. Was I really with Butz in Antwerp?"*

*"21 June. What color are Pavlik's eyes?"*

*"22 June. What was the name of the hotel in Barcelona?"*

*"23 June. Did I have piano lessons as a child?"*

*"24 June. What does Sandra's laugh sound like?"*

*"25 June. Where did I learn Russian?"*

*"26 June. Which dress did Niko like me to wear?"*

He flinches.

*"2 December. Back to Barcelona. The most important questions: how long was I in the warehouse for? What happened during that time? What state was Niko in? Did he touch me? Did I touch him? Did we speak? What did we say? Why didn't I try to eliminate Holm? Why did I flee, leaving Niko behind? Why didn't I call the MEK, why didn't I call an ambulance?"*

He stands up and opens the window. The cold stings his face. Houses stand out against the low sky. Essentially, he knew the moment Aaron asked him what he looked like outside the Hotel Jupiter. But he hoped he was wrong. No, he was lying to himself.

That's why she handed herself over to Holm: because he knows the truth. She's prepared to die for that.

Outside, a discarded Christmas tree rolls around on the street. The phone rings. Pavlik gives a start.

"You wanted to know if anything was going on with Kvist. He's clearing his desk," he hears Fricke say when he picks up.

"Is the bug in his car?"

"Yes. Claus put it here. A mic under the headrest."

"We've got two men on him."

"Just like that. Why? Are they going to have a beer with him?"

"He was alone with her. He may know more than we do."

"He'll notice. Just as he did yesterday."

"Yesterday it wouldn't have mattered. Today it will. Peschel and Nieser are doing it in two cars. They can keep their distance, we've got the GPS. Call the BKA and send Kleff and Rogge. Tell them they need two cars from the Set of Eight." The vehicles from the BKA's Set of Eight have registration plates from the eight big German cities. "But not Berlin, Munich or the Ruhr. An old jalopy of some kind. Take over from Peschel and Nieser as quickly as you can."

"Just a second." A murmur. Then Fricke again: "We've got those two tourists. A guy selling city tour tickets at the zoo recognized them from the descriptions on the radio. The Federal Police are taking prints off the phone. If they haven't wiped it since the photograph was taken, we could be lucky."

"Compare with AFIS straight away." He shuts the window, sits down at the desk and starts to play the Boenisch recording.

*"I'm so sorry that you're blind. So sorry."*

*"… You work in the laundry. Do you get on with your colleagues?"*

A laundry van as a getaway car? No, they couldn't have known that at Wannsee station.

*"… One of the guards beat me up."*

Mr. Uzi: a warder from Tegel? Possible.

*"… Is the reception on your transistor radio good?"*

Electrical goods shop?

*"… I'm ashamed that I watched that film. I shouldn't have done."*

Video rental?

*"… I'm so glad you came that time. So glad. You saved my life."*

Pavlik shuts his eyes. He tries to imagine the young woman standing in the dark outside the house in Spandau. The young woman

Pavlik never knew. She was twenty, her future a big lucky dip. Certainly the trainers didn't give her an easy time because of her name. If anything it made them tougher on Aaron than they were on the others. Did she have friends among her colleagues? Maybe not. People like her attract people and unsettle them at the same time; you have to be able to tolerate their company.

Had she been in love with a nice boy, one of the tall, dark ones she likes so much? What were her dreams? Was she carefree? Arrogant? Happy?

When Aaron began her six months' probation with the Sixth Homicide Unit on Keithstrasse, Pavlik had been with the Department for two years. They were only five hundred meters apart. And yet a whole world. His work had nothing to do with the everyday running of the Criminal Police.

He went to the Sixth every now and again because they had the best canteen. Sometimes he wonders if he ever saw Aaron there. No, he'd have noticed. You can't help noticing her wherever she is. At first that was a problem for Lissek. He was unsure whether he should send her undercover. She could hardly make herself invisible. But he quickly realized that Aaron's appearance was a plus. No one would ever think a woman like that could be a policewoman.

Pavlik had heard of Boenisch sixteen years before, of course; the papers were full of him. There had been talk of a "brave police trainee" who had hunted down the serial killer all by herself. No picture of her. He wished he could have hugged and comforted her then, rather than only being able to do it so much later.

"… *My angel. Thanks for knocking at my door.*"

Pavlik looks over at the sofa. Aaron is sitting there.

They have known each other for two years now and have been friends for ages. She and Marlowe come to their house. They play Scrabble and Barricade, have barbecues on Saturdays. If she hadn't been in that bar in Clichy, his children wouldn't have a father right now.

She is as reliable as clockwork.

But yesterday she did something that startled him.

They'd gone training at the Mill. The LKA called. A man was holed up in a house with his wife and small son because his wife wanted to leave him. He was threatening to kill her and the child. Normally it would have been a case for the Brandenburg police. But the Mill was only two kilometers away, and the Department was asked for help.

A team of five arrived, forced their way into the house and found the woman and the child bound hand and foot but uninjured. The man had been hiding in the basement. None of them was aware that Aaron had already gone down there. The light in the basement was broken. Pavlik went down with the two others in the pitch dark. She was sitting on the floor. When he shone the torch at her, her pupils didn't dilate. The man was lying beside her, unconscious. Even though he was unarmed, she had broken three of his ribs, his jaw and one of his arms.

Pavlik saw that talking was pointless. He shouted at the squad to shut up, he sent Aaron home and wrote in his report that the man had attacked her. Lissek asked no questions.

In the evening Pavlik gave her a call, but she didn't answer.

Now she is sitting on a sofa, and hasn't said a word for ten minutes. He sits down beside her. More minutes pass. Then she tells him about Boenisch. Her voice slides along the groove of a record that she will hear forever. When she has finished with Boenisch she tells him about Runge and the waitress in Delmenhorst and the two others he killed. The ones she could have saved if she hadn't decided to save herself. Pavlik doesn't interrupt her. In the end she cries. He hugs her and says: "It's OK."

She says: "It will never be OK."


He can't bear the memory any longer. He resumes Boenisch's interrogation.

"*What do you like most about* Mr. Brooks?"

Boenisch's answer is drowned out by the sound of an airplane.

"*I didn't get that.*"

"*The main character.*"

"*Mr. Brooks…*"

"*Mr. Brooks isn't the main character... Mr. Brooks takes him to the cemetery so that Smith will shoot him. Smith pulls the trigger!*"

Cemetery? No.

"*... Why Melanie Breuer?*"

"*She reminded me of someone.*"

"*How did you feel when you went to her?*"

"*There was always the pressure in my head. She must have noticed. She was an expert.*"

Might her message be hidden in the psychologist's notes? Unlikely. Aaron didn't have time to study them.

"*... I silenced her. It's so lovely when they're quiet. Like being in a glider, when you can only hear the wind.*"

"*The plastic bag was opaque. But you love seeing fear in women's faces.*"

"*... I was so disgusted with myself.*"

End of the recording. That was it. Pavlik stares into the void.

*Aaron, what are you trying to tell us?*

She's never forgotten Lissek's last words at their first meeting: "We're taking you to the most dangerous place in the world. Your mind."

When the cable tie yields against the lashing strap hook and tears, Aaron has already played the attack through in her mind.

Since she doesn't know if Bosch has opened his jacket, his torso can't be a target. His solar plexus and ribcage are out too, as are his spleen, liver, gall bladder and kidneys. A three-finger jab to the hollow in his collarbone would paralyze Bosch's breathing. But only if his collarbone is exposed.

Too risky. Aaron has opted for the neck.

She needs to take his weight and condition into account. At the station she got a sense of his size. Eye-height, allowing for her two-and-a-half inch heels. Bosch was capable of carrying a bag weighing about seventy-five kilos up a flight of stairs. So he's about one meter eighty and at least ninety kilos, and he's fit. Aaron will have to use maximum force.

If she's mistaken and Bosch doesn't have the neck muscles of a bull, her fist will kill him.

She knows nothing about his reflexes. They can't possibly be as good as hers. Still, she advises herself to be prudent. She hears her father: *Never think about winning, think about not losing.*

They've been moving again for ten minutes.

Holm has left the freeway. Country road.

While she carefully stretches, extending her wrists behind her back to get the circulation going, Aaron is already breathing in such a way that her concentration shifts to her center of gravity in her lower abdomen.

Her greatest worry is that there might be a window between the driver's cabin and the cargo area. But she has made her decision. Her feet are unbound. "My legs have gone to sleep." She slips off her pumps, goes into a crouch and presses her back against the wall. Bosch isn't concerned. Aaron has had enough time to gauge his position, and is able to locate him precisely. He opens his water bottle and drinks. After that he always taps a new cigarette from the box. She will attack him when the first deep drag leaves his lungs. A person is at his most relaxed immediately after exhaling, so that is also the perfect moment to shoot him.

She presses the tip of her tongue to her palate so that she can avoid being knocked out in the event of a counter-attack.

Aaron bends her left little finger.

Bosch lights the cigarette. He puts the lighter back in the box, inhales the smoke and blows it out again. She pushes herself away and jumps, hitting his crotch with her knee. He groans with pain, something hot flies into her face; the ember of the cigarette that she knocked out of his hand before the middle joint of her little finger finds the Yang meridian on his artery. Through stimulation of the strain sensor in the aorta Bosch's circulation is fooled into thinking that his blood pressure is shooting like a rocket into the stratosphere. His heart sends an emergency signal to the sympathetic nervous system, which immediately brings activity down to zero thus causing a drastic drop in blood pressure. She has scored a perfect hit on Bosch. His body slumps before he can even blink.

Aaron feels his pulse. He's unconscious.

Her triumph lasts for two quick breaths. The vehicle lurches into a sharp right turn. She is slung away from Bosch and goes flying against the wall. They hurtle along a potholed path.

The window. Holm has seen everything.

She tries to get to the door. Again Holm swings the steering wheel round. She is flung against the other wall. Tries to hold on, finds nothing but smooth steel.

Holm brakes hard. She hears the driver's door and the passenger door flying open. Her shoulder is numb. She waits for Holm to open the cargo area. But it doesn't happen. She creeps over to Bosch, pats down his clothes and finds the pack of cigarettes with the lighter. Not a sound outside. The pack must be somewhere on the floor. She forces herself to stay calm, to explore every square centimeter around Bosch.

So. She picks up the cigarette pack and takes out the lighter. Her hands trembling, Aaron opens the bag and digs a hole in the middle.

*If I manage to destroy the money, they'll need me to make a new demand.*

She lights a bundle of notes, throws it in the hole, a second bundle, a third. She smells a pathetically thin thread of smoke. Not enough, not enough. She realizes desperately that she can't do it without a fire accelerant. It's so hopeless that Aaron wants to cry.

The door is unbolted. She assumes the attack position, breathes long and deeply to relax her muscles. Holm jumps on to the bed of the truck. He drops to the floor and slides towards her. She knows he wants to bring her down with a sweeping kick, and dodges him. She kicks out and catches him on the head with her ankle. She kneels down to knock him out with a one-two. But she doesn't put enough strength into it. He blocks her fist and jabs a finger at the base of her neck.

It's as if Aaron has a piece of meat stuck in her throat. A thin whistle escapes her lungs. For a minute she gasps for air, and convulses in such a way that her nose starts bleeding. Holm watches her. When he senses that she is losing consciousness, he grabs her and strikes her chest hard.

One breath. Two. Shallow. Hardly worth talking about. She lies on her back and has to struggle for every tiny scrap of air.

Holm drags Bosch from the cargo area and dumps him in the snow like a sack.

Three breaths. Four.

With each new breath Aaron is more exhausted.

Holm comes back and crouches down next to her. His voice thickens smugly. "I'd have been disappointed if you hadn't tried."

He holds something to his ear. She hears a very faint crackle.

"What... happened?" Bosch has come round.

"Do you know how you are able to hear him?" Holm asks. "Because I put a bug in his jacket. You said I'd flayed and gutted that woman. Bosch might believe something like that. But you know better: I'm not cruel. I act appropriately, you know the difference."

Aaron pushes herself against the wall. Her pain roars at her.

"It's a lie to say that I've never shared anything, not even with my brother. You can't understand just how deep that lie is. I have shared more with my brother than you can imagine. But looking at you I can tell. You don't know the first thing about me, and I know all about you."

Aaron tries to straighten up. Fails.

"You're speculating on your market value as a hostage? Do you actually think that your heroic courage on 17 Junistrasse was a blank check for your life?"

Plastic rubs against plastic, a screw top. Aaron smells petrol. Horrified, she wants to flee. She gets a little way on her knees, then Holm kicks her in the belly. She is overwhelmed with nausea. Again she is breathless.

Token-Eyes shouts: "What's going on? Are you crazy?" He jumps into the back of the truck. Groans with pain. Falls heavily on top of her. His clothes smell of cheap prison detergent. She tries to push his face away from hers, lacks the strength. Token-Eyes has stopped moving, he is unconscious or dead.

Holm pulls his brother off her. He drags him outside like Bosch and dumps him in the snow.

His silence as he comes back is a way of mocking her. He empties the petrol canister next to her. Aaron inhales the caustic fumes, unable to think clearly. She longs to give up and die.

"I'm giving you back your blank check."

A match-head scratches over the striking surface. Her heartbeat becomes the steady rattle of a machine gun.

Holm sets the bag alight. Aaron rolls away. The back of her neck is ablaze. She pulls off her coat and suffocates the flames in her hair.

Holm gets out.

He closes the door and leaves her alone in the inferno.

Aaron creeps across the floor, through hissing heat, trying to find Bosch's water bottle. She closes her stinging eyes. Her lungs fill with soot and ashes; she chokes, coughs bitter mucus. After an eternity she finds the bottle. She pours it over her dress and holds the fabric in front of her mouth and nose. In vain. She crawls to the door, hoping to find a crack that she can breathe through, sucks in nothing but searing, stinking smoke. She realizes that she is leaving the tormented, useless bundle that was once her body. The machine gun has fired its last, the bolt is striking an empty cartridge chamber, more and more slowly, more and more quietly.

Click... Click... Click... Click... Click... Click... Click... Click...

A thousand glowing sparks dance in front of her eyes and spray into the night sky above the remains of a pyre. Ben fidgets beside her, as excited as she is; the smell is earthyherbygreasy. There are five of them and they still don't know about the hole in the white pond. The farmer empties a big basket of potatoes into the embers. Aaron can hardly wait to grab for the first one, she already has that wonderfully soft, smoky, nutty pleasure on her tongue.

Her father, laughing, grabs her by the belt of her trousers, extends his arm and swings her back and forth as she shrieks and he pretends to throw her into the sky. The potatoes are fat and round and turn black and wrinkled. Aaron wishes she had huge hands to mash them all together into one single monster potato that belongs to her alone.

At last the potatoes are taken from the embers. Hot, hot, hot. Ben and Aaron throw them from one hand to the other and count: "One two, button my shoe, three, four, open the door, five, six, pick up sticks!" They scratch off the charred skin and paint their faces with their black fingers until they look like Indians on the warpath.

Aaron bites into the best potato of her life.

She is incredibly grateful to be able to die like this.

She wakes up with her face in the snow. Pain rages inside her like a hurricane. Aaron tries to claw her hands into the crunchy, icy crust, but her hands no longer belong to her. She can't even bite into the snow to get rid of the taste of burnt petrol. She has to wait for her body to absorb her once again.

"What have you done?" Token-Eyes stammers.

Holm says: "We're going to get another five million."

# 23

THE BUS driver folds his arms in front of his chest. "Could you please turn the heating up a bit?"

Pavlik goes to the window of the interrogation room and pretends to turn up the thermostat. He knows that Heinz Schwenkow isn't shivering because of the temperature of the room.

"Where am I?" Schwenkow asks for the third time.

Pavlik sits down again. "As I said, you're at the police station."

"I was driven to an underground car park in a closed vehicle, as if I was a criminal."

"That was just for your safety. So Holm didn't call his accomplice by name? Are you sure?"

The man sees that further complaints about his circumstances are pointless. "Yes. He barely talked to him. What he mostly did was jut his chin in various directions. The man would jump. Holm addressed him formally. Odd."

Pavlik isn't surprised. But Holm's manners are nothing but a mockery. If he were sitting on the electric chair he would be polite to the man who turned on the power.

"He quoted something from a book. No idea who the book was by. But I can't get the sentence out of my head, as if I'd learned it by heart. 'The courage we desire and praise is not the courage to die decently but the courage to live manfully.'"

"Think very hard, Mr. Schwenkow: wasn't there some kind of hidden reference to where the men wanted to go?"

Schwenkow shrugs helplessly and warms his hands on the coffee cup. "I'd love to help you. Not least because of Lutz." His cheeks twitch.

"The pump attendant?" Pavlik asks.

Schwenkow nods. "He was divorced. But he had two children. He was devoted to them. The older one's at university. He was so proud when she graduated from high school. He showed me a photograph. She's pretty."

Schwenkow tries to find words. Pavlik doesn't press him. He wants him to move calmly from one thought to the next, talk to himself, while Pavlik waits patiently for the man to think of something he could work with.

"All because of his tools." Schwenkow's eyes fill with tears. "I'd been meaning for ages to give him the tool-bag back, and I kept forgetting. I could have brought him the damned thing when Holm forced me to get out of the coach at the petrol station. It was under my seat. I didn't think about it. Just about me."

Schwenkow's fingers are yellow. Pavlik holds out a pack of cigarettes. He gratefully takes one. "I was actually supposed to have today off, but a colleague called in sick, the boss rang at six and got me out of bed, to my wife's great relief. On the phone a little while ago she just cried. I'll deal with it one way or another. But the children will never get over it. He just shot the teacher for no reason, he's not a human being, he's the devil. The other man was scared of him too, I can tell you that, he cowered away from that man Holm. He was in such a state that he counted the phones twice."

"Oh yes?" Pavlik cuts in.

"I saw him in the mirror. On the back seat."

"Did it seem to you at that point that he couldn't concentrate?"

"Yes, now you mention it. Holm wanted to know where the next petrol station was. And the other man was standing right next to him. But a few minutes later he asked Holm where we were going to fill up."

"Thank you, Mr. Schwenkow. Now go and see your wife. Tell her exactly what happened. And take some time off."

"I won't be home for long. The Criminal Police say I have to get back to Keithstrasse. They want to show me some pictures, from their file of known criminals. To see if the guy is one of them."

"I'll tell them that won't be necessary."

Ines Grauder runs into him in the corridor. "Email the photograph of Holm's man to all the Berlin hospitals with a memory clinic," Pavlik says. "Or rather: tell the Federal Police to send some people."

"Why?"

"There seems to be something wrong with his head. He may have been in treatment."

"And what if he isn't from Berlin?"

Pavlik studies her. "How long have you been with us now?"

"Two months."

"And you ask just like that." He walks away. "Once you've done it, come to the weights room," he calls over his shoulder.

Helmchen is waiting for him by the lift. She hands him a bowl of hot soup. "Eat this."

"I'm not hungry."

"Clear soup with dumplings, very fresh."

"Helmchen—"

"Or I'll call Sandra."

He sniffs the bowl. Where on earth did Helmchen get hold of fresh clear soup?

"The others are all upstairs," she says. "Apart from the emergency squad up at headquarters. Just as you said."

"Is Demirci still in her meeting?"

"For an hour and a half," Helmchen says, concerned.

"Did you listen in?"

"What do you take me for?" she asks, shocked.

He takes a spoonful of soup and blows: it's all part of her little game. "How much pressure is she under?"

"It's bad. Svoboda's Secretary of State is saying she should step down."

"Who's on her side?"

"North Rhine Westphalia. They suggested her for the position, and in fact she came to us from Dortmund."

"No one else?"

"It's chiefly Berlin and North Rhine Westphalia who are fighting. She's also under fire from the Federal Police. Because we're ordering them around. But Demirci lets them go on complaining. She's got the Federal Prosecutor on board, and no one messes with him, so that was a smart move. She's quite stubborn; like Lissek. I like that."

"And the investigation hasn't thrown up any results?"

"That's true—hang on—how do you know that?"

He eats his soup. It's delicious.

"Oh goodness," Helmchen says.

"Our secret," Pavlik replies. "Once Demirci knows you better, she can find something out about our little chats."

"Svoboda. I wouldn't put it past him."

Pavlik checks that there's no one nearby. "Do you remember those two Ukrainian women in Frankfurt an der Oder?" he murmurs, fishing out a dumpling.

"You mean Pi?" she asks.

"Yes. I want to know who was involved in the operation. Not just the guys in the squad. The logistics team, everybody."

Of course there had been an investigation back then. The sniper knew about the safe house and the Hotel Jupiter. When something like that happens in the Department, they act like the Maasai when a lion has killed a cattle-herd: they hunt it down until they kill it. Otherwise you can never be sure. Nights in the interrogation room, observations, phone-taps, house searches. Suspicion lay in their clothes like a bad smell. Pavlik had to calm down fights a number of times. It was bad. After a few weeks Internal Affairs closed the files without a conclusion. That was worse. For a long time there was no laughter in the building. But Pavlik still has the smell in his nostrils.

"It's in Internal Affairs' safe," Helmchen says. "Not even Demirci can get at that."

"These dumplings are great," he growls, and devours the last one. "It's just that they're not that easy to find."

"Give me two hours."

Pavlik plants a kiss on her forehead.

"Smarm your way in, why don't you?"

"Not me." He drinks the rest of the soup straight from the bowl and gives it back to Helmchen. "When we retire we could set up an old people's flatshare."

"And what will we do with Sandra and my husband?"

"We'll make it look like an accident." Pavlik gets into the lift. He thinks about Boenisch again. About Aaron's enigmatic message. He puts his foot in the door. "Helmchen?"

She turns around, already a few meters away from him.

"You used to live in Spandau, didn't you?"

"Yes. And?"

"Anywhere near Bübingweg?"

"Why do you ask?"

The door tries to close, bumps against his foot and bounces back. "Boenisch lived there. Do you know that area?"

"No, a completely different bit. Who'd want to live there, right in the Tegel flight path?"

Door closed. Door open.

"Like living on the runway," Helmchen says.

At that second he hears the plane that drowned out Boenisch's answer when he was being questioned. He hears him whispering at the end, "Like being in a glider."

*What did Aaron say? "Holm knows how to exploit people."*

It's like something out of the blue. "Ulf?" Helmchen asks.

"Could be that the third man is a pilot. Have the photograph sent to all airfields in a two hundred and fifty kilometer radius. And to the Federal Aviation Office."

The weights room on the fourth floor is the social center of the Department. It's where the latest gossip is exchanged. Where people resolve their differences, sweat, laugh, curse and say nothing.

For them, training is like eating and drinking. Their bodies are statues that they chisel away at every day. But none of them has a muscle too many. It would make them too slow, they'd get in the way when it came to storming buildings and fighting, and be too conspicuous on a lot of undercover operations.

"You need to work off a bit of weight, at least ten kilos." Pavlik doesn't know how often he's heard those words said to a new recruit.

If you saw him in the street, you might think: businessman? Taxi driver? Pub landlord? Artist? Doctor? Pavlik has the gift of letting people see him as he wants to be seen.

When he steps into the room and looks into the silence of twenty-seven men and one woman, he wants them to see their leader, the man whose calm reassurance they can depend on, whose doubts they know nothing about. He has to bear so many things in mind, always, and they must never be aware of it.

They worked well until a few minutes ago. The dynamic of events allowed him to ignore his thoughts about his dead comrades. His brain just got on with its job, undeterred by his anxiety.

Pavlik deliberately stopped the machine. He knows only too well that the adrenalin that is keeping it going will run out sooner or later. And it doesn't happen gradually, it happens all at once. The machine comes to a halt suddenly, and they will plummet into an abyss of grief. Pavlik is the mechanic who tends to the machine, oils it and looks after it and makes sure that it doesn't overheat. So they all have to pause now, even if it's only for ten minutes, and remember the dead.

He takes a non-alcoholic beer from the fridge, and sits down on a weight bench.

No one says anything.

There is boundless emptiness on every face, and behind it a door that no one dares open.

Pavlik takes a sip of his beer, puts his finger into the neck of the bottle and makes it pop. "Clausen was one of a kind," he mumbles. "I once went to his house. There was a wall in the sitting room with a full-sized photograph. The Arctic, complete with igloo and polar bear. It looked pretty crap. I said: 'You can't stand the cold, you even run about in a scarf in August.' He said: 'Exactly. I sit here nice and comfy in the warm and watch the polar bear freezing his arse off.'"

Someone giggles furtively, someone else grins.

"That's true," Fricke says, adding his bit. "He told me: 'I hope death gets me in the warm.'"

"And it did," Pavlik reflects. "I bet the car was so overheated that Blaschke was furious. There was nothing he hated more than heat. That's why I always liked to put him and Clausen on duty together, so they always had something to argue about."

Beer bottles circulate. Kemper plays with a barbell. "Clausen's ex had a little dog like a film star would have—"

"A chihuahua," Giulia Delmonte giggles. "A long-legged rat. She gave it a whore's rhinestone brooch."

Kemper nods. "Exactly. It was bigger than the pooch itself. Clausen refused to take it for walkies, he was mortified."

"Who wouldn't have been?" Nowak grins.

"But two years ago his ex was in hospital," Kemper says, picking up the thread. "Some sort of women's thing."

"With her looks, I'd have said it was her prostate!" Delmonte exclaims.

Everyone roars with laughter.

"At any rate, Clausen had to go out with that pooch morning and evening," Kemper resumed. "They lived on Kurfürstenstrasse, you know, where the hookers are. And when he was standing and waiting for the little shitbag to squat, a patrol car stops beside him. They get out and ask to see his papers. They thought he was a pimp. He filed for divorce the next day."

The squad whinnies.

"Do you know how come Blaschke got hold of his 1956 Porsche?" Pavlik asks.

"He never gave me a lift." Fricke grins. "He put a corpse in it and the stench never left it?"

"It was gorgeous. Beautifully looked after, full service history, not a scratch. It used to belong to an old grandpa in his nineties. He loved driving but he was blind as a bat. One Sunday, on a country road near Kyritz an der Knatter, he ignored Blaschke's right of way and rammed into him. Blaschke was about to call the police, but the grandpa begged him to go off the record. His grandson wanted to put him in a home, and he thought an accident would leave him vulnerable."

Majowski opens a beer bottle with his lighter. "Let me guess: he adopted Blaschke."

"He lent him the Porsche on the condition that Blaschke took him for a drive twice a week. He stuck to it rigidly. He even enjoyed it, they got on very well. The old guy died a year ago. He'd been an orthopaedic surgeon, left all his money to a foundation. But Blaschke got the Porsche. Every spare cent he had went on repairs, which is why he was always skint. It was worth it as far as he was concerned. He spent more time with the old car than he did with his wife." Pavlik sees Grauder coming in. She avoids his eye. He's sorry that he snapped at her before. His people should respect him, not fear him. "Grauder, you had a bet with Clausen recently," he says. "What was that about?"

"You," she says after a moment's hesitation.

"Look out!" Krupp mutters. "It's about to get exciting!"

"Let's have it," Pavlik says encouragingly.

"He said you cry at sad films."

"Is he right?" Pavlik asks.

"You were at the cinema with him one time. He showed me a video from his phone. You were bawling your eyes out. Cost me ten Euros."

Everyone grins.

"Did he ever tell you which film it was?"

"No."

"*Bambi!*" Fricke shouts.

"Not far off," Pavlik sighs. "*A Fish Called Wanda*. When that guy is forced to eat his goldfish, my floodgates open. Because I can't help remembering my own goldfish. My father flushed him down the toilet when I was three."

He has the laughers on his side. Even Grauder joins in. The door opens. Peschel and Nieser join them.

"I'll miss the piss-ups with Butz," Dobeck says. "That bastard just couldn't get drunk. An enzyme malfunction, he told me, happens to one in every ten thousand. I saw him empty a liter bottle of grappa as if it was water. But it had its useful side: he always drove me home, I saved tons of money on taxi fares."

"Yes, me too," Peschel agrees.

Nieser scratches his head. "And me."

"I once had to go on a trip to Latvia with him," Büker remembers. "On the last evening we went to a nightclub, planning to let our hair down. Two women joined us at the table, and well, you know. We had a bit of fun and I was totally pissed. One of them said we could visit another friend of theirs. Hallelujah, Butz is hot for it. Outside four guys turn up. One of them immediately knocks me over. When I come to, the four fuckers are lying in the street, and Butz is straightening his jacket. He looks at me and just says: 'Damn it, the chicks have gone.'"

Krupp winks at Delmonte. "I bet he tried to get into your knickers."

"No, he didn't, and I was really pissed off about it, as a matter of fact."

"His funeral will be fun," Mertsch says. "You'll get all these women turning up, who were told they were the only one."

"I guess it must be somewhere between twenty and thirty?" says Novak.

"Rounded down," Fricke grins.

Pavlik says: "I doubt that."

"Because none of them had his address?"

"No. Because he was gay."

Another roar of laughter. But when they see Pavlik's motionless face, the laughter dies away.

Fricke is the first one to pull himself together. "That's a joke, right?"

"How would you rather be remembered?" Pavlik replies. "As the joker of the unit or the man you really are?"

For a minute they all gaze into the distance. Butz is standing in the room, a big lanky creature with black curly hair, shoulders you could lean on, the dimples that he always allowed to have their full nonchalant effect.

Even though he somehow never was, Pavlik thinks. None of them knew Butz. Even he didn't know him.

"What does that tell us?" he asks. "That not everyone here in the room was glad to have Butz at his side, because they felt safer with him? That he didn't save three of your arses?" He looks at Dobeck, Büker and Wolter. "That you couldn't drag him out of bed in the middle of the night if you were having a rotten time?" Fricke lowers his eyes. "That he didn't go marching to Lissek when someone had been treated unfairly and was about to jack it all in?" Majowski blushes. "That he wasn't our comrade?"

"Well fuck me sideways," Fricke whispers.

"Squared," Krupp agrees.

"Have a think about what it must have cost him to keep it quiet for all those years. And what that says about us."

Shamed silence.

"We walk past that marble plaque every day, and we no longer even see it," Pavlik says. "But perhaps every now and again we should stop and read the names. There aren't many that have honored us as much as Butz did."

Some nod, some gulp, clutching their beers.

"Has anyone got a soppy toast they'd like to make?"

Krupp raises his bottle. "To Butz, the best of the bastards."

"To Butz, Blaschke, Clausen," they all reply and drink.

Pavlik wipes his mouth. "To business. Demirci is taking responsibility for the surveillance of Aaron and Askamp."

The ceilings are thick, but they can hear the phone ringing two floors up.

"If any of you insists on a different version, I'll have a disciplinary procedure on my back and Demirci will be signing on," Pavlik continues. "Have we understood each other?"

They all nod.

"You've got questions. Out with them."

"How did it happen?" Wolter asks.

"Butz was back by the wall. Holm broke his neck. He must have caught him by surprise, Butz couldn't even defend himself. Blaschke and Clausen were in the car, they were shot through the windscreen. Right through the forehead."

"Could have been luck," says Dobeck.

"No."

"What makes you so sure?"

"Believe me: Holm could start working for us straight away."

His words leave an impression.

"He injured Aaron in close combat," Pavlik adds.

That's enough for anyone who knows her. "So?" Büker says, speaking for the others. "She's blind. I know she had what it takes in the past, but that was then."

Beside him, Nowak raises a little finger. "She had as much as she needed. And if she can only do half of that now, it's still more than you or I could do."

Dobeck nods. "You weren't at the shooting range yesterday because you were on the night shift outside Askamp's house."

"She scraped a ten," Fricke says.

Büker and Majowski let that one sink in.

Nieser says: "The way she outsmarted Peschel and me in the Hotel Jupiter was pretty damned smart."

"My mad gran could outsmart you lot," Mertsch said.

Peschel growls: "Fuck you too."

"So what do they plan to do with her?" Kemper asks.

"Holm wants to take his revenge on her," Pavlik answers.

"In that case she's a goner," Giulia Delmonte says quietly. "She was cool. We had a brief chat. She was the first woman here. She gave me a few good tips. For example, that I should just scratch my nuts from time to time."

Three of them laugh. But Pavlik snaps at Delmonte: "Remember one thing: she isn't dead until her corpse is in front of me."

Delmonte blushes.

"Why did Kvist let her go?" Wolter asks. "I don't get it."

"Aaron asked him to," Pavlik says.

"I once asked a girlfriend to get her breasts enlarged, but she wouldn't do me the favor."

They've run out of steam. Pavlik stands up. "OK, back to work." Everyone leaves the room while he gestures to Peschel and Nieser to stay. He waits until the last one has closed the door behind them. "What's Kvist up to?"

"Yeah, he's driving around. Stadtring. He turned around in Frohnau and now he's back again. He doesn't seem to be headed anywhere in particular."

"He listens to loud music in the car," Nieser says. "Always the same song. 'Have a Little Faith in Me.' You can't get the damned thing out of your head."

"Yes, we heard that one at your party yesterday."

"It's Kleff and Rogge's turn now. I'm sure they can sing along by now," Nieser says.

Demirci comes in. Peschel immediately changes the subject. "Yes, we'll take care of the witness statements."

Pavlik nods. "Do that. Tell Büker and Delmonte to take over from Kvist in an hour's time."

They glumly register that Demirci has been informed. "What in?" Nieser asks.

"Two hired cars. Posh end, maybe an S-Class Mercedes, and a mid-range family saloon."

Their colleagues leave them alone.

Pavlik sees that Demirci is exhausted. "Had a nice chat?"

She takes the bottle out of his hand and drains it.

"Non-alcoholic," he says apologetically.

"I just needed to get something down my throat."

"Do you still have your job?"

"Yes. On probation. Any news from Kvist?"

Pavlik shakes his head. "He's gone off-grid."

"Maybe he's noticed he's being tailed?"

"Hardly." He looks at her. "Any news your end?"

"You see through me too quickly. I need to work on it."

"I'd be very sorry about that."

"An interesting trail has opened up, in fact. Thirteen years ago an Armenian got a life sentence for murder in Cologne. He ended up in Ossendorf Prison. A year later his father died. The Armenian was allowed to attend the funeral at a Cologne cemetery under guard. He was liquidated. The perpetrator was on a roof a thousand meters away, armed with a rifle. He escaped unnoticed, but he made two mistakes. First: he had parked the getaway car in a 'no parking' spot and got a ticket. That was why they were able to put out a search for the car and track it down. It had been cleaned with disinfectant inside and out."

"And the second mistake?"

"A clever officer in Cologne had the bright idea of looking at the cap of the petrol tank."

"Holm's fingerprints," Pavlik said straight away.

"Yes. The comparison with the thumb that he left on the tourist's phone gave us the match we needed. Just that, the only time he took his eye off the ball."

"The Armenian was inside for murder. Who did he kill?"

"A guy in charge of a chain of amusement arcades. The Cologne police assumed he'd been money laundering for the Mafia, but they couldn't prove it."

"I bet you've got a punchline coming up."

She smiles tightly. "The Armenian's father died a year to the day after his son killed the arcades boss. The death certificate said it was a heart attack, but there was no autopsy."

Pavlik reflects for a second. "Holm killed the Armenian's father first, without leaving any clues."

"That's it. The date was a message."

"But only so that his son could leave jail, and Holm was able to liquidate him at the cemetery."

"Correct."

"Do you know any details?"

"No, but I'm sure the cops in Cologne do."

"What was the prisoner's name?"

"Artur Bedrossian."

Pavlik calls Fricke and tells him to contact the Cologne police. "I want details on weather conditions, visibility, precise distance, number of shots fired, number of hits, angles, lab reports. I'll tell you later."

"I have another punchline for you," Demirci says. "Shortly before he died, Bedrossian had attacked and injured a prison warder. He was under arrest and wouldn't have been allowed out. But the director of the institution personally intervened to make sure that he was allowed to go to the funeral. Guess who that was."

"I'm not good at guessing."

"Hans-Peter Maske. He's been in charge of Tegel Prison for four years."

Pavlik is thunderstruck.

"What do we know about him?" Demirci asks.

"I've had dealings with him from time to time. He makes huge waves at the bows, but there's only a pedalo following behind. He knows the right people and farted his way easily to the top. Word is that he'll soon be taking over the Prisons Department in the Senate. Then he'll make himself even more important."

"Sounds as if I'd like him," Demirci smiles.

"Even his dog doesn't like him."

She turns serious again. "Eight hours ago I told him I wanted the personal files of all the prison warders that Sascha has dealt with over the last month. I said it was urgent. But he's ducking out of it. All I've had from him so far is an email from his secretary saying that Mr. Maske will prepare the documents with the, quote, necessary care, which unfortunately takes some time. Perhaps you'd like to motivate him a bit."

"Office organization is a secret vice of mine."

# 24

THEY'VE LEFT Oranienburg behind. Holm drives the car along the country road, heading north. The few vehicles coming towards them already have their lights on. Their pale beams flicker along dirty, frozen walls of snow and the bare trunks of the mountain pines that stand densely packed on either side of the road. Gusts of wind sweep the tree-tops. Crows flap about in the ditch and pick at a dead fox.

Sascha is sitting next to his brother. They haven't exchanged a word since he burned the money. Sascha is so furious that he could rip out the dashboard.

For five years he listed the things he wanted to have once he got out: two women in Lisbon every day. A red Corvette. A house with enormous windows. Ice cubes in whisky glasses. A Glock 33. Somebody pleading on a lonely road, an empty magazine, a white cloth to wipe the blood away. A black Corvette, a silver, yellow, gold one.

Five million as if it was scrap paper. His brother has always done things that Sascha didn't understand. He's more of a stranger to him than this other man, Bosch, whose blubbing at the sight of the charred money bag still nauseates him.

The secrets that his brother bears within him are countless. Sascha never knew why he took that road and not another one. Why they had stayed in one place and not another. Why his brother left, why he came back. Why he saw one person's death as important and allowed another one to live.

Even though his brother never said as much, Sascha knows what he expects from him: to burn down the house that he has never left.

But he can't do that. The worst thing his father did to him was to keep on forcing him down the basement steps day after day and making him lie down on the mattress.

There he dreams his way into his brother's head. He creeps inside as if into a rabbit hutch and looks along the infinite twists and turns for the path that led his brother to freedom but didn't do the same for him. But the search always ends up in the mirrored maze of his own head, and in every mirror Sascha sees himself lying on that mattress.

He wanted to shatter those mirrors. He wanted to smash them to pieces with his fists. He wanted to break splinters from them and poke his own eyes out. But the mirrors are indestructible.

His father made them that way.

And his brother let him do it.

Again and again Sascha planned to kill him in his sleep. His brother knows. And yet he often slept beside him. His hands now lie calmly on the wheel, even though the Glock Sascha's brother gave him is still in the belt of his trousers.

The Glock and a box of Lucky Strike. That was all he was given. He wants to light one but he lacks the courage, because his brother can't stand cigarette smoke.

He would bend the devil himself to his will.

Sascha has a thousand reasons for hating his brother. For head-butting him in front of Aaron and throwing him into the dirt like an animal. He could rip out the dashboard for that alone. He would spit on his brother's corpse.

Sascha has never doubted that his brother will allow him his revenge on Aaron. The first gift he would get from him. He has imagined unwrapping it countless times. But his brother took it away.

What does Aaron mean to his brother?

Sascha doesn't dare to ask. Whatever answer he got, if he got one at all, Sascha would reach for the Glock. And then he would be dead.

He needs to think of something else immediately.

That tart in Boenisch's cell. Her dress, with the buttons done up to the top. Her throat, which felt like an Aero bar beneath his fingers. Her suffocation and how long it took. The bag he had to use because he was running out of time, the plastic she sucked in as he imagined who might be doing it.

Her struggling, wriggling, groaning.

But minutes later he would have needed another one.

Five million.

Why did his brother do that? To torment him? Because money means something to Sascha and nothing to him? No. His brother never does anything for him.

Even though Sascha can't explain it, he remembers the note that an Italian gave him after a week in jail in Barcelona, his brother's note.

There was only one sentence on it: *It is the start of your journey.*

All of a sudden he knows.

The thought is so powerful that the electric signal which sends it through the contact points in his brain is too weak at first to enter his consciousness. But with a brief delay it finally gets there: his brother has decided that their paths should part. Barcelona was itself a farewell. His brother is liberating him, and he wants him to take with him only what he had when he was eight years old. The thing that is branded into his flesh. The thing he has never talked about. The thing that is clenched in his fist. That and the Glock and a pack of cigarettes.

That sudden awareness explodes like a grenade in his head and turns bone splinters into projectiles that shred his mind.

His brother is going away forever. For many nights he has lain awake and dreamed about it. For many nights he thought he knew exactly what he would feel, without any hope of it ever coming to pass.

But now it's true. A sob rises up in Sascha, a heartrending whimper. He feels his brother's eye on him and turns his head towards the window so that his brother can't see what is happening to him, can't see that he is shaking, gripped by terrible fear.

Everything blurs: the shadows of the trees in the last light, the dirty snow flying past like ashes, marker posts, pylons, road signs, crows.

He doesn't know where the salty taste on his tongue comes from. He doesn't know, because he has never cried before.

Suddenly he feels his brother's hand on his cheek.

Sascha wants to push it away, he wants to pull his arm from its socket. But all he can do is tremble, whimper, weep.

His brother strokes him gently, touching him like that for the first time ever, letting him know that he understands.

Something hits the transporter, which swings off and almost skids into the ditch. His brother grips the wheel with both hands and brings it back to the road. He takes his speed right down. The car is driving roughly, as if it's dragging something behind it. There's a farm road on the right. He turns into it and only stops when the road is out of range.

His brother gets out. Sascha stands where he is and fights back the tears as if struggling against a giant.

He reaches for the Glock to reassure himself.

He clutches the grip and can't feel it.

Holm has bound her hands and feet and thrown her coatless and shoeless into the stinking cargo area. She lies on the icy metal in her thin dress and knows that Bosch isn't going to let her catch him off guard again.

Aaron wishes there was a meditation that made you insensitive to the cold. Like many sharpshooters Pavlik never shivers, but he doesn't know why. She cursed the winter in the forest by the Mill. In hollows in the snow, rigid wooden lean-tos, among rocks that belonged to the north wind. Sometimes she was so cold that she threw up. When she couldn't bear it any longer she moved, even though it threatened her camouflage. It was a mercy to be able to do press-ups and sit-ups and short, quick steps on the spot. It worked for a few minutes, and then the beast leaped at her once again.

To distract her, Pavlik once reminded her of the motorcycle holiday they had gone on through Arizona and Nevada with Sandra and the twins. Three crazy weeks on Harleys, through the most searing heat she had ever experienced.

Quivering, abused, bound, she lies on the mattress in the transporter and sees flickering images as if in a cartoon.

One twin on the pillion of her big Electra Glide, the other behind Pavlik, the piled-up luggage reflected in the mirror. Dried-up riverbeds, scars cut in infinity, clotted yellow, green, red and purple boulders. Forests of cactus.

Aaron is amazed by yellow and green and purple as if she has never forgotten those colors. And the faded blue of the sky. And the powdery vapor trail of a jet fighter. And the creamy beige of her Harley.

It's so hot that they are sweating even in the airstream. They drink water from canisters. The powerful engine hammers beneath her backside, potato-potato-potato, her whole body vibrates, a boy's hands tightly grip her hips, constantly pinching her with excitement.

Sandra overtakes, riding freehand, laughing as she speeds by. She has a pirate bandana on her head, and is so tanned that Aaron is struck by the dazzlingly white strip on her shoulder where her top has slipped down.

She lies half-dead on the mattress and is grateful.

They are sitting outside a diner, pouring iced water over their heads, eating bloody steaks with chilli. The bike stands sink into the melting tarmac, the wind sings in the phone lines and plays on the highway with its silver thorn-bushes; their fries are seasoned with sand.

In Cayenne they visit Mary-Sue, who can't get her head around it. *"Are you fuckin' crazy—Arizona in July?"*

For days they carry on through this oven. They come up with words for it. Cannelloni heat, tar-barrel heat, fuel depot fire heat, supernova heat. They want to go to Las Vegas. The sun set ages ago, but it's still stuck like glue to Aaron. The sky is scattered with stars that look like grains of sand on skin after swimming. In the Bellagio she has a ten-minute ice-cold shower.

In the transporter, her teeth immediately start chattering again. She doesn't want to remember the air-conditioned casino where she feels freezing cold, or the fifty dollars she wins on a one-armed bandit while drinking beer from a pitcher swimming with ice cubes, or the banana splits with pink marshmallows that she buys for everyone.

She remembers the storm that night, and standing at the window of Sandra and Pavlik's hotel room watching a sea of lights drifting by. The five of them cuddle on the king-size bed zapping away before lingering on a film of the Hindenburg disaster, the mighty airship melting like cellophane; they imagine the screams as the silent pictures of the catastrophe disappear in a mirage.

The door flies open. Aaron is grabbed and pulled from the mattress by her feet. Her head crashes from the loading sill on to the bumper. The pain chisels her skull open.

Holm cuts through her shackles.

"We've got a flat."

Aaron kneels barefoot in the snow. Her body is numb. She hears a rushing sound. Very close. A river. Token-Eyes throws the big wheel-brace into her ribs. "Here you go, you sack of shit. Don't fuck it up or I'll use it to smash your head in."

Aaron picks up the wheel-brace. Can't hold it. Sticks her fingers under her armpits to warm them up.

"Let me do it," Bosch says, "it'll be quicker."

"You've made yourself look stupid enough already," Holm says.

As she waits for the blood to return to her hands, she tries to think. It's so hard. She has to struggle against a profound feeling of weariness, because her kidneys have been pumping out huge quantities of adrenalin today. And yet she knows that she's going to need a lot more of the precious substance—a whole ocean—if she's to escape death.

Aaron wonders why Holm allows Token-Eyes to torture her. He had made it unmistakably clear to his brother that he's not allowing him to take his revenge. And now he's granting Token-Eyes that satisfaction. Is it his way of apologizing to him for knocking him out a little while ago? For burning the money? No, Holm never apologizes, not even in such a perverse way.

*I'm not cruel for cruelty's sake.*

That's true. Everything he does follows a kind of logic. Something must have happened between the brothers. Aaron can hear it in Token-Eyes' voice. As hate-filled as it sounds, it has an undertow of grief, of loss. And it's not the loss of the five million that darkens his words.

The fact that Holm destroyed the money still takes Aaron's breath away. If he were another man she would think he was crazy. But from the very beginning she had no doubt that that wasn't the key issue for him. He despises people who think possessions have significance. Aaron's attempt to burn the money was merely helplessness. Holm showed her how ridiculous that was, how stupid. Certainly he has often owned a fortune and thrown one away. He was teaching Aaron and his brother a lesson.

Holm proved to them that only someone who can stand the smoke should light a fire.

But he said: "We'll get another five million."

*Why? Because he can.*

"I'll give you thirty seconds," Token-Eyes hisses. "If you don't get a move on, I'll break your nose."

She concentrates on the rushing sound, to her right. There's something new, too, a deep rumble, a stamping sound, getting louder. A ship. A barge.

During the nights in the Mill Pavlik and she had time to teach each other things. He never achieved real mastery in karate. Pavlik prefers the fighting style of the Israeli special units, which is just as effective but less philosophical. Aaron taught him the breathing exercises of the Gōjū-ryū, initiated him into the secrets of acupuncture and showed him meditation techniques.

In return Pavlik taught her sharpshooting skills.

He taught her to gauge distances. If it were summer, she would say: the ship is six hundred meters away. But in winter sound moves more slowly because of the low temperature.

*Four hundred meters.*

No, she has to take the wind into account. It blows her hair into her face, it's coming from the river.

*Five hundred.*

Just to be sure Aaron holds her breath for a moment. Her hearing is so sensitive that even her breathing puts the sound out of focus.

The ship is big, she can tell that by the loud noise of the engine, perhaps a convoy. That means the waterway is wide. The Havel or the Spree.

Token-Eyes says with gloating anticipation: "Time's up."

The cold separates her from her body. It moves without any intervention on her part. Her hands clumsily tap the wheel-brace against the wheel rim. Again, again.

"How pitiful, the blind whore," Token-Eyes says mockingly.

He isn't aware that Aaron is using the wheel-brace as an echo-sounding device. There are trees between her and the river, tall and slender. She suspects they are mountain pines, the palm trees of Brandenburg. They are no longer very deep and dense, Aaron can hear the great expanse opening up behind them. She assumes that the terrain is uneven, with humps and hollows covered thickly with snow, clumps of trees and shrubs.

Her plan is desperate. But perhaps it's her last chance to escape. And she has a trump card in the pocket of her dress that Holm knows nothing about. It's the little metal clicker with which she put Kleff and Rogge to the test in the hotel corridor.

*Was that really only yesterday?*

She fits the wrench over the first bolt, rests heavily on it and holds on to the roof of the vehicle to shift the jammed screw with her weight. After she has bobbed up and down a few times she succeeds. She undoes the others in the same way. The ship is slowly getting closer.

*Three hundred meters. But how far is it to the bank?*

"The blind man doesn't see the impossible."

Says Gantenbein in Frisch's book.

"Interesting," Holm observes. "Miss Aaron is going to a lot of trouble to convince us that she's reached her limit. But this silly business of changing the wheel is so undemanding that she's bored. Blind people as talented and ambitious as she is have abilities beyond anything we can imagine. Andy Holzer, for example, climbs the steepest rock faces in the Dolomites, and of course Aaron knows him. Or Zoltan Torey. He could dismantle a differential and put it back together gear-wheel by gear-wheel. I have no doubt that Miss Aaron could do that as well if the task was put in front of her."

*Yes, you smart-arse. Tomorrow I'll go down Nanga Parbat on skis, the day after tomorrow I'll fix your watch, and after that I'll build an atom bomb.*

Token-Eyes waves the jack in front of her. Her fingers run along the bottom of the transporter and find the notch. She cranks up the vehicle. The ground is frozen solid, the steel doesn't sink into it so much as a centimeter. She needs to make Token-Eyes so furious that he turns on her. "Listen hard when your brother gives you a private lecture. Even if you probably can't spell 'differential.'"

Token-Eyes' fist catches her on the temple. It's a hard blow, but she was prepared for it, her neck muscles were tense and her shoulders braced to cushion it.

"And how are you spelling that?" he roars at her.

"With a 'd' for dickbrain," she replies.

He kicks her in the crotch. "Just you open your mouth one more time."

Aaron falls in the snow, breathes to meet the pain, and imagines that her muscles are expanding to let it flow out of her. She pulls herself up again. Token-Eyes' breathing tells her that he's standing right in front of her. "I'd like to meet you without your dad. Just the two of us, nice and romantic. You dream of raping me, but how are you going to arrange that? I'm sure you were always the bride in jail."

His rage flies straight into her face. His fists rain down on her like hammer blows. Aaron curls up in the snow to present as small a surface as possible. Token-Eyes tries to pull her up, but she makes herself heavy. A kick catches her in the belly and brings acid spurting into her throat. She hopes against hope that she isn't mistaken, and that Holm sets boundaries for his brother.

"That's enough," she hears Holm saying calmly at last.

Token-Eyes refuses to let up. He grabs her by the hair. She waits for his fist again, afraid that he's going to beat her into a coma. But Holm pulls him off. "Enough."

"Let go of me!" Token-Eyes wails.

She hears him dragging Token-Eyes away and pushing him up against the vehicle.

The adrenalin factory opens its valves. Aaron's pulse soars into the snowy sky.

She leaps to her feet and sprints off, holding the clicker. Quick clicks. Two trees, five meters in front of her. She dashes between low pine branches that scratch her face, her open mouth. Runs in a zigzag through the invisible labyrinth, clicking every second. Locates the next obstacle. *Not compact: bushes.* She takes a big jump, almost gets entangled in a patch of thorns, but breaks through without losing her balance. No shots, Holm wants her alive. Breaking twigs behind her. He's coming after her. No. There are two of them, both brothers, one off to her right, the other on her left. Her saliva tastes resinous. A distorted echo flies back at her, she's unsure whether it's two trees close together or a single thick one. She runs straight into the confusion of frequencies. Her shoulder crashes against a tree trunk. She staggers and catches herself. Her tights are ragged. Her bare feet scrape over icy roots, branches, stones that rip her skin, even though she can't feel it. Just as she no longer feels the cold, her gastric acid, the wind. The ship is noisy, almost level with her, she must be very close to the bank. Shouting would be pointless. On board, all other sounds will be drowned out by the roar of the powerful diesel engine. But perhaps they'll see her. No, she's sure it's already dark.

Where are the brothers?

There. They're so close that she can already hear them panting. She has only seconds left. When she feels a glass-smooth surface under her feet, relief drags her across the ice like a sail. She skids towards the waterway. Water splashes her ankles. Her pulse races back to her and stops abruptly.

Aaron becomes perfectly calm.

She jumps.

"Breathing isn't necessary. Breathing isn't vital. Breathing is *everything*." Her father used to say this in the quarry, when she was still a child. Her teachers later found similar words. You can neglect your cover if there's no other option. You can disobey pointless orders. You can take a risk to survive. But you can never, ever forget your breathing.

She dives into the water. She doesn't feel the cold. She feels nothing at all. Her brain tells her she's swimming to the opposite shore in a moderate current and at a depth of one meter. Her brain tells her that her arms and legs are bringing her closer to her goal with each stroke and each push, even if she doesn't know where her arms and legs are.

She can't have been under water for more than fifteen seconds. But everything in her is already screaming out for oxygen. She forces herself to have a vision of inhaling air, she accompanies her breath through her throat into her bronchias, she sees it being attracted by her alveolae, impatiently awaits the gaseous exchange, follows the pure oxygen through the pulmonary veins into the cardiac chambers, where it is accelerated and catapulted through the aorta into the brain, which has already been ardently waiting for it.

It's no help. She doesn't think she can bear being under the water for a second longer. Still she counts to ten. Only then does she order her body to surface, prays that it will hear her.

Her head emerges. She opens her mouth wide, in the wake of the barge. Choking, she gasps for air. The next wave. A clump of ice seals her throat. Between breaths that sound like wailing she has her first clear thought.

*Holm is after me.*

He's somewhere behind her. Because he will never give up on his revenge. She inhales as deeply as possible, but the oxygen doesn't seem to shoot through her veins at high pressure; that was a hopeful dream. Her lung is a depleted bladder with a big hole in it, a laughable memory of the powerful engine that her body once was.

She dives again. The cold reaches her body after a brief delay, but it's so unbelievably intense that Aaron feels as if she's swimming against a wall. Her muscles quiver. Soon ice crystals will form in her cells; then she won't be able to move.

*I'm going to die in this filthy swill.*

*No, you aren't!*

She has a lead on him. He will have had to shed his jacket and boots, or he wouldn't have the smallest chance of catching up with her.

But what use will that lead be? She may get to the opposite bank before Holm does. But once there she would be at his mercy. There is only one way to survive: Aaron has to stop attempting to reach land as quickly as possible, and instead swim to the bows of the ship with all her might. If they both have to swim against the current and the swirl of the propeller, she can force Holm into a battle of attrition. She is fourteen years younger than him. He may have the advantage of having rested. But that makes them almost equal adversaries.

Aaron surfaces. The ship is on her left. She crawls towards it, and allows herself a breath with every third stroke. Jagged shards of ice collide with her arms. She beats them away, smashing them to pieces. When her head is in the water, the tail rotor roars like an avalanche; above the waves she thinks she can hear the thump of the pistons. The current becomes so strong that she feels she can't advance so much as a centimeter. Her muscles burn like fire, over-acidify, freeze.

But all of a sudden she feels herself becoming as light as a feather and moving quickly forwards. Relief shoots through her head now that her emergency motor has kicked in. Then she realizes that something else is happening: she is already so close to the propeller that it's sucking her in. She is dragged under water and flies towards the ruthlessly spinning blade that is on the brink of slicing her into a thousand pieces. She desperately tries to escape its pull.

Hopeless.

She can no longer defend herself.

*So this is how it ends.*

Her left leg is pulled back. Holm pulls her to him by her ankle, fights against the drag of the propeller without letting go of Aaron, fighting for two. She is too weak to help him. She knows that he wants to save her so that he can kill her in his own way. He battles stubbornly, endlessly. She feels his fear of losing her, his hatred, his will.

Suddenly the propeller releases her. Aaron squeezes air into the whistling bellows of her lungs. Holm seeks the kyusho point on the inside of her thigh, trying to paralyze her. A scrap of physical tension returns. With full force she kicks at Holm's head. Of course that doesn't disable him in the water, but it's enough to shake him. His grip loosens. Aaron rolls, finds his eyes and pushes her thumbs in as hard as she can. Holm cracks her elbows with his ankles. It's like an electric shock, her thumbs slacken. His legs wrap around Aaron's, both perform a ballet move, each trying to find the neuralgic vessels through which their energy flows.

When she feels two of his fingers on her hyoid, Aaron knows that she is only a second away from the unconsciousness that the pressure on that fragile bone would cause. She hurls the open back of her hand against Holm's lower lip, makes a fist just before impact and twists it. She is very familiar with the pain that penetrates every cell of his body.

*I have to drag him down so that he can't see anything.*

How Aaron longs to be able to take a sustained and controlled breath. But the little that she can scrape together wouldn't be enough blow out a candle. She manages to grip Holm's trouser leg and pulls him down with her. He barely resists, the pain is driving him mad. The river is deep, her ears are blocked, she doesn't have a free hand to balance the pressure. A powerful wave of nausea surges up within her. Her knee hits the muddy bottom. Holm is thrashing wildly around. Aaron knows that his lungs are collapsing. She lets go of him and puts both index fingers in his ears. His body slackens. Her eyes bulge. She wants to scream, she yearns so intensely for breath. She lacks the precision to hit one of the deadly spots that are barely a square millimeter in size. But she finds Holm's sixth rib, and jabs a finger in the space between the sixth and seventh.

She has just enough strength to push herself away.

That is the last movement she is able to make. There is as much air in Aaron's lungs as there is in the universe. She feels hot, incredibly hot; she wants to pull her dress from her body. Quivering somewhere in her brain is the idea that she has entered the final stage of exposure. She has been freezing because the vessels in her arms and legs contracted in order to transport as much blood as possible to her organs. But now they can see that it was hopeless. They are expanding, the blood is flowing back. That's why Aaron is sweating at a depth of five meters in zero-degree water.

*Ben must have felt the same thing.*

*I wanted to hold on to you, I'm so sorry.*

"That's easy to say," she hears him saying.

*Forgive me.*

Ben remains mute.

"There you are at last," she hears a second, tender voice. Her father. "Everything I've told you about breathing was nonsense. You don't need breath. It just gets in the way."

Many others agree with him, all the dead people that Aaron left behind as she was so busy trying to breathe. A mighty choir swells, but she can hear only a single voice. Niko's: "Are you just going to let me die?" When she kneels beside him in the warehouse and tries to rest his head in her lap, she becomes aware that it's André. He whispers: "The truth is in the sixth lane." She is already waking up in her Berlin flat because something has twitched her big toe. Marlowe bumps against her, purring, as if he had been lying against her forever and hadn't just jumped through the open window that night to stay for eleven wonderful years. She sniffs at him, he smells of stray females and morning dew. Suddenly Aaron is sitting on a stool in a bar in Clichy, drinking anisette, smoking an unfiltered Gitane, and the scar on her collarbone itches. She pulls open the door of the gentlemen's toilet, where Pavlik is staring at her from enormous eyes. She breaks off a leg of her sunglasses, and rams it to the hilt in the nose of the Basque who is trying to garrotte Pavlik. She tries to pick up Pavlik but is thrown into the arms of her mother, who is sobbing so hard that she can't get a word out. She has told her father she is leaving him, and Aaron knows that she is the reason, the daughter he took away from her the first time he went to the quarry for shooting practice. She wants to cry but can't, and is forced to her knees in an empty bedroom. She buries her face in the favorite shirt of her father, who died today. The smell of his cigars and his aftershave and something she couldn't name but which belonged only to him and told her that he would always protect her, allows her to find the strength, only deep in the night, to let go of his shirt.

"Stop resisting," her father's voice forces its way through to her out of eternity. "Look how lovely it is here."

Aaron opens her eyes. She sees Holm slipping motionlessly away from her. He rolls around in the current, she looks into his face. His mouth is slightly open, almost mockingly so. His black shirt and black trousers stick to his muscles. The three top buttons are torn off. Aaron recognizes part of his tattoo. It might be a Japanese character, but she isn't sure. The index and middle fingers of Holm's right hand are still as stiff as they were when he was trying to press them into her hyoid bone. Dumbfounded, Aaron watches a second body drifting down to join Holm's. It is her own. She has a scar on her hairline that is normally covered by her curls, the souvenir from a training session on the Neroberg a few weeks ago. Aaron is amazed at how tiny the scar is, she would have guessed it was bigger.

She taps at Holm, and he rolls around again. They look one another in the eyes. His are blue, with an iris of flames that look like swords. Aaron pushes him away, she sinks deeper and deeper, she isn't in a river now, she's in sea somewhere far away, it must be the Mariana Trench. A barbeled dragonfish skedaddles, a giant squid gives her a goggle-eyed stare, a bignose shark wearily circles her, a batfish winks at her as it darts by, welcoming her. Strange creatures, and she is the strangest one of all. She would like to stay here forever, because this is where she belongs.

But something takes hold of Aaron and raises her gently upwards. She doesn't want to go, she aches to be left in peace. Holm is below her again, drifting forlornly into the darkness.

High above her she sees a radiant white light, the headlights of a
diving robot. She clings to its gripper arm.

"Take your time, I'll wait," Ben whispers.

Aaron wakes up and pukes water. She doesn't know how long she's
been unconscious. She remembers André and Marlowe, the bar in
Clichy, her mother's tears, her father's shirt, her scar. But it's a mys-
tery to her how she managed to make it to the shore. Which shore?
How far did she drift?

A thought struggles in her head: it must be the opposite shore, or
Token-Eyes would have been here already.

The river rushes. A buzzard shrieks. Her heart is as quiet as the
ticking of a clock buried in the snow. Something hammers quite
close by. What is it? She listens and finally establishes that it's her
teeth chattering.

*I'm shivering. That's good.*

A car.

It gets louder, then moves away. There's a road somewhere, but
how far away? Aaron can't quite tell whether she's lying on her belly
or her back. She tells her left little finger to move. Strangely, it obeys.
Now the one on the right. It hesitates, then declines to twitch. She
cautiously approaches her arms. Incredibly slowly, they form a semicircle, as if making a snow angel.

*I'm lying on my belly.*

Her fingertips explore the ground beneath her. It's as if they were
sliding over polished aluminium, there is no feeling in them.

*What's that?*

*Soil? Snow? Wood?*

She has to get to her feet, even though she yearns to lie there and
sleep. Contorting grotesquely, she tries to stand up. Her muscles are
a gelatinous mass that yields and deforms at the slightest effort.

But she succeeds. She totters, clicks her tongue. No echo. Her feet
take one step, a second, a third. Arms outstretched, Aaron shuffles
across the icy ground like an old lady, falls, strikes her knee bloody

against a stone and uses the pain to distract her from her despair. When a twig brushes her shoulder and then springs against her face she knows that she is moving again.

Again she hears a car. It comes closer, then moves away.

*It isn't far.*

Her legs give. This time she can't get back to her feet. In slow motion she battles onwards on all fours. At last, at last she is crawling on snowy tarmac. Or a field. Or a pane of glass. Or a mountain.

The next car. She's on the road. With inexpressible relief she spreads her arms out. The driver brakes at the last moment. The car skids towards her and comes to a standstill so close in front of her that snow sprays in her face.

The door opens, footsteps come closer.

*I'm saved.*

The very thought exhausts her.

"Hi there, you sack of shit."

Aaron faints before Token-Eyes' fist strikes her.

# 25

THE PRISON warder who accompanies Pavlik to Block Six in Tegel is young, but her weary eyes, her deep wrinkles, her thin, chapped lips reveal that she puts up with insults, threats and humiliations for two thousand Euros a month before tax. Pavlik had asked her her name.

"Engelschall," she had murmured indistinctly. Since no one had noticed that Melanie Breuer hadn't been signed out and her corpse was found in Boenisch's cell the following day, the staff's nerves have been on edge. The investigations of the Homicide Unit didn't help.

As soon as Pavlik turned up unannounced in the security entrance and showed his ID, everyone there stuck their hands in their pockets. When the Department arrives, you have to be careful, best to say nothing, it only causes trouble.

An electric vehicle hums past, with two prisoners sitting on the box seat, with copper pipes on the load bed behind them. The driver has a thin self-rolled cigarette in the slack corner of his mouth, ash flying away with the snow.

"What was Sascha Holm's behavior like?" Pavlik asks the woman, whose quick, striding steps reveal that she wants to get all this out of the way.

"So so," she mumbles.

"No incidents?"

"Not that I know of."

"You work in Block Six, don't you?"

"So?"

"Do you want to be questioned by the Fourth Homicide Unit again?"

The twitch in her cheeks suggests that this isn't the most enticing prospect. After the moment's reflection that he allows her she mutters between her teeth: "The cock of the walk around here was a Lithuanian. He was a killer, no one dared go near him. Sascha broke his jaw on the very first day. That sorted that one out."

"Was he put in solitary?"

"Mhm."

He sees the room in front of him: a foam rubber mattress with no cover, barred lamps, glass bricks instead of windows, no heaters, nothing you could smash, video surveillance. When one prisoner seriously injures another, four weeks in this hole are the rule. "How long?"

"I'd need to check."

Pavlik stops and forces Miss Engelschall to do the same. "Say to your colleagues: 'I didn't tell him a thing. Smug bastard from the Department, met his match in me.' Anything we say is confidential."

Her gaze flickers. "He was in there for half an hour."

"Instructions from above?"

She nods.

"How often should he have been in solitary?"

"I stopped counting."

Pavlik goes on: "And how often was he?"

"He was never punished, not once, and no one knew why." Every word is furious. "For a while he had a fight with a Ukrainian who was a big drug dealer. Eventually he was found dead in the shower. We all knew it was Sascha. No one cared. He just grinned for a week."

"Did he hang around with Boenisch a lot?"

"Not that I saw." She notices his expression. "But I never paid much attention."

In the fenced-off area in front of Block Six, which looks like a big cage, Pavlik sees the prisoners who are desperate to get back into the warmth. But, red-faced, they have to keep on walking because he has ordered that the prisoners from the second floor must either be locked up again or wait outside until he has inspected Sascha's cell undisturbed. For most of them the cold is the lesser of two evils. When Pavlik walks past, one of them growls into the snowstorm: "Take your time, we're in no hurry."

He follows Miss Engelschall into the building. His phone rings. "Hello?"

It's Fricke. "I've got the details you wanted about the cemetery in Cologne. High summer, half-past midday, about thirty degrees, eighty-six per cent humidity, no wind. The roof Holm was lying on was one thousand one hundred and ninety-one meters away from the target, at a height of fifty-five meters. But I don't think he's as good as you think."

"Why not?"

"It took him three shots. The first one hit the guy's shoulder. He hit him in the temple with the second."

"Which shoulder? From the back or the front?"

"From the right, from behind."

"Caliber?"

".700 nitro express. Crazy, isn't it? Pretty well blew his head off."

Pavlik stops on the stairs. The hairs are standing up on the back of his neck.

"Are you still there?" Fricke asks.

"Yes. Thanks. See you."

He puts the phone away, brings his chin to his chest, hears the crunch of his top neck vertebra, so lost in thought that Engelschall has to call down to him twice, "Are you coming?"

She opens the door. Pavlik has seen a lot of cells in a lot of jails; no two are alike. He has had the opportunity to admire walls papered with nude photographs of the girlfriend, oriental lampshades, bed-covers made of football-club scarves, bottle-top curtains, toilet seats with pornographic pictures, sunsets over the Blue Grotto. Unsurpassed, however, is the plastic parrot that dangled from the ceiling in the Chinese guy's cell in Santa Fu, endlessly screeching "Fucking screw" at the top of its voice. There are more charming terms for prison warders.

But he had never seen a cell like Sascha's. Bare walls, no books, television, radio, not a single personal object. Not even food, a comb, a piece of soap. The bed is unmade, the woollen blanket lies gray and scratchy on the floor.

"Why has it been cleared?"

"It hasn't. It was like this already."

He opens the cupboard. A pair of trousers, a shirt, underwear. That's all. Pavlik searches through the clothes. "How did he pass the time?"

"Ask around. I can name you at least fifteen prisoners who haven't dared to go in the shower on their own for the last six months."

He kneels down and knocks against the skirting board. "Has the cell been inspected?"

"No one dared."

Pavlik unscrews the tap from the wash basin. Nothing. He straightens up and pats down the mattress. Turns the bed on its end and inspects the hollow legs with the torch from his phone. Sticks his finger into one of them and pulls out a little piece of paper.

On it is written: *It is the start of your journey.*

The paper is yellowed, folded countless times, the handwriting sharp and spiky, every letter an exclamation mark. Pavlik knows straight away that Holm wrote the words. It must have been a long time ago, perhaps even a message that he sent his brother in Barcelona. The text is beyond reproach, no warder could possibly have objected to it. And yet Sascha hid the piece of paper. What journey did Holm mean? Pavlik senses that it might be important.

"Pia, how much longer is this going to take?" a man's voice squawks from Engelschall's walkie-talkie.

"No idea," she says.

"When was he locked up today?" Pavlik asks.

"Just before eight."

"Our guys got him out of the cell two hours later. Did he have any visitors in between?"

She shrugs and looks past him.

"Have a think, Miss Engelschall. If you or your colleagues don't cooperate with us, we'll have a word with the prisoners who worked here. One of them is bound to have seen who you opened the door to."

She still doesn't reply. "Engelschall—the sound of angels. Such a pretty name. It would be a shame to land you with a disciplinary procedure."

"Maske was in there for five minutes," she says. "When he came out again he was drenched in sweat."

Things can get cramped in a boss's office six meters by six, if you've got four Federal Police officers in there apart from the boss himself, inspecting the PC, viewing files and correspondence. In the outer office, the secretary sits terrified in the corner while two other policemen turn everything upside down all around her.

Pavlik had met his colleagues outside the prison before asking to be shown Sascha's cell. To be sure that the director couldn't be warned by phone, one of them stayed by security until the others turned up at Hans-Peter Maske's door.

When he enters the outer office, Tom Döbler comes over to him. They've known each other forever, since police academy. At some point Döbler realized that searches were the thing he was good at. He could find a contact lens in a bottle bank.

"How's it looking?" Pavlik asks under his breath.

"There are only two files on Sascha Holm on the two computers," Döbler replies quietly. Six months ago an email confirming that he'd been admitted, and today a note about him being transferred to you. That's it. Otherwise you mightn't know he'd ever been here."

Pavlik isn't surprised.

"But I've got something else." Döbler hands him a scrap of paper. "Over the last month he called this number three times. No conversation lasted more than a minute."

Pavlik looks at the nine-digit number.

"A military satellite phone. You can forget the idea of locating it," Döbler says.

"How did you get Maske's phone data from the company?"

"I know someone who works there. We sorted it out unofficially."

"If anyone complains about the Federal Police, you can send them to me," Pavlik says. They exchange a grin. "Have you got any emails for me?"

"I've already printed them out." Döbler leans across the desk and hands him Sascha's transfer papers which have just been sent from the Senate's Justice Department because Helmchen insisted. Pavlik flicks through them and browses the most important passages.

In the next room Maske is yelling: "I demand to be allowed to make a phone call! You have no search warrant, this is unheard of!"

Pavlik walks to the door. "Hello, Mr. Maske, sit where you are. The Federal Prosecutor obtained a search warrant from the judge." Maske shrinks. "There is a temporary protocol, the formal decision will be coming in by fax at any moment. I'll come back to you." He closes the door before Maske can say anything, reaches for a chair and sits down straddling it opposite the secretary. "My name is Müller. Will you tell me yours?"

"Margot Burri."

Pavlik is good at spotting dialects. He locates the slight singsong of the Rhineland in the woman's voice. "How long have you worked for Mr. Maske?"

"Fifteen years."

"Ah—then you were his secretary in Cologne?"

She nods anxiously. But there is also a hint of a sense of power from being guard dog to a man in charge of seven hundred officers and six hundred and fifty prisoners.

"And if he becomes head of the Justice Department in the Senate, will he take you with him?"

"Yes."

"Where is the mistake in my last question?"

She looks at him, baffled. Mrs. Burri's face might appeal to a middle-aged man with a weakness for jerkily painted lips that are used to passing on instructions in an entirely humorless way. Her skin is heavily powdered, her hair-do a helmet, not a strand out of place.

"The mistake is this: Mr. Maske will never hold that position. He will be going to jail for a very long time, and not as a director. Is it worth putting your pension on the line for that?"

A drop of sweat digs a groove in the powder. "I haven't done anything!"

"Sascha Holm terrorized Block Six from day one. Why is there no correspondence about that, no memos, not the smallest piece of paper?"

"I don't know."

"Are you trying to tell me no warder ever called this office and asked Holm for a meeting with the director? Never sent an email? Never complained he hadn't been subjected to any penalties?"

"Mr. Maske dealt with such matters verbally."

"Is that normal? Did he do that with other prisoners too?"

"No," she whispers in a small voice and rubs her thumb over her fingernails, painted with colorless varnish.

A fax arrives. "Were you present at any of those conversations?" She shakes her head.

He looks at her ring. "You're married. Children?"

"Two."

"You have something to lose. The only thing I have to lose is my patience."

Her eyelids twitch. "Once," she admits.

Döbler comes in with the fax. "Here's the warrant."

"Mr. Maske will be delighted. Please be so kind."

Döbler goes into the next room.

Pavlik addresses the secretary again. "When was that, and what was it about?"

Every word is another farewell to her beautiful, freshly renovated office in the Justice Department. "A few months ago we had a dead Ukrainian in Block Six. Two warders said Sascha Holm had threatened the man. It was something to do with drug deals. Mr. Maske asked if they had any proof of Holm's involvement. They said no. He told them not to speculate about the Homicide Unit, it wasn't house policy."

"And they just stuck to that?"

The voice grows quieter. "They were given special leave and transferred to Access Control."

"This morning we requested the personal files of the officers in contact with Sascha. Where are they?"

"I'd need to check whether—" She breaks off when she sees Pavlik frowning. "Mr. Maske says I'm to stall you."

He stands up. "Tell that to my friends from the Federal Police. They'll do it in writing. That's *our* house policy."

He walks into the boss's office. The files fill three cardboard boxes, and the PC is packed away as well. Maske sits alone at the conference table, hands in his lap, eyes fixed on the wall as if he were seasick in a violently rocking pedalo on the open sea, staring at a point on the horizon to keep from throwing up.

"Are you OK so far?" Pavlik asks.

"Yes," Döbler says. "Do you still need us?"

"The secretary's statement needs to be written down, ideally by you. And have two men ready to arrest Mr. Maske here."

"Timo, Karsten, you take charge of that," Döbler says to his colleagues. Then to Pavlik: "I assume you'll want to have a little chat with him first."

"Yes." He taps a Lucky Strike against his lighter, waits till everyone is outside and the door is closed, lights it and looks around for something he can use as an ashtray. The vase of chrysanthemums that Maske got for his promotion will do the trick. He throws the flowers in the bin, puts the vase on the floor and makes himself comfortable at the head of the table.

*Eva Askamp—Eva Askamp—Eva Askamp.*

An announcement on the loudspeaker rattles against the window. "End of break." Maske's sallow skin stretches over angular cheekbones. "Do you think I'll allow myself to be intimidated? I'm not answering any questions without my lawyer."

Pavlik doesn't even look at him. He picks up Sascha's file and opens it. For the next ten minutes he is absorbed in his reading, underlining certain passages, making notes, tapping ash into the vase, while Maske gradually goes to pieces. At last Pavlik looks up. "I don't want to bore myself with your lies. Let's do it like this. I tell you what we know about your connection with Holm and his brother, and then I'll ask you a question. Just one."

Maske's pedalo is lifted by a mighty wave, flies over the crest and crashes down on the water again.

"Twelve years ago you were the governor of Ossendorf Prison in Cologne. You authorized the release of the prisoner Artur Bedrossian, even though he was under arrest. And—"

"His father had died," Maske interrupts. "Permitting him to attend the funeral was a matter of decorum."

"Don't use big words with me. Bedrossian was liquidated at the cemetery. We know it was Holm. I'm sure you were paid very well." Maske tries to cut in again, but Pavlik raises an eyebrow. "I've told you the procedure. If you prefer, we'll pass you over to the Federal Police, where you and your lawyer can have some fun going through the evidence."

Maske says nothing.

"You're wondering how we're going to prove that you received payment," Pavlik continues. "Very simply: while we're talking here now, there are officers in your house. If you have any foreign bank accounts, we will get access to them. We're interested in receipts from twelve years ago. If you were paid in cash, we will examine any large payments that you made over the next few years for the source of the money. I'm very confident about that."

Maske smiles faintly.

"I can't say exactly how many deals you did with Holm; we'll see. But one thing we do know: you played a part in his brother's transfer to Tegel. When he made the application in Barcelona, no one objected. They were all delighted to get shot of him. But the Justice Department in Berlin hesitated. As I can understand very well, because the documents that came in from Spain include a summary of Sascha's prison career. Even if we may assume that the Spanish left half of it out and played down the rest, we are still left with the picture of a man who would be flattered to be called a psychopathic killer. So what did the Justice Department do? It asked for your opinion. You worked tirelessly for the transfer. Hang on, where's that passage I like so much? Oh yes, here it is: 'Especially on the grounds of the prisoner's social prospects in terms of his girlfriend I consider the transfer to Berlin to be a very sensible course of action. I have already had a conversation with the young woman to assure myself in person of the genuineness of their relationship, and am persuaded that such is the case.' Well, fine, far be it from me to judge your prose style." He snaps the file shut. "This woman was murdered by Holm today. As were three of our men. But then you know that already. He called you at eight and told you to go to his brother and tell him right away. That phone call is documented."

Maske rests his hands on the table. They are shaking.

"Let's leave aside the question of whether you received a new payment for your services over the last six months, or whether you acted out of fear of Holm. What we do know is: you have covered up every crime that his brother has committed here. It's down to you that a whole prison cringed before him. We can prove that one. You've certainly abetted the murder of Melanie Breuer. I don't know what you pay in legal fees, but no lawyer in the world is going to get you out of this one."

Maske's face is white as ocean foam.

Pavlik's phone rings. "Yes?"

It's a Federal Police officer. "We've turned Maske's place upside down. We'll have to go through his financial papers in detail, but it doesn't look as if we're going to find anything. We're heading off."

As he thinks, *damn*, he flashes his broadest grin across the table, hangs up and says: "My oh my."

Maske's pedalo goes under.

"Now I'm going to ask you the question. Think carefully about how much the answer is worth to you. For me, it could be worth a conversation with the Federal Prosecutor's office. If I try really hard,

I might be able to get you seven or eight years rather than life. It's not a promise, just a vague possibility, you're so deep in it. And if you think your lawyer may get you a better deal, you're mistaken. He would advise you to kiss my feet." He looks at the man who has instilled fear in so many. "Do you know where Holm is headed?"

Pavlik sees that Maske has never wished so devoutly that he could give the right answer.

But he whispers: "No."

# 26

THE FIRST thing she hears is her heart. It is beating calmly and evenly, and brings to an end a dream that she will not remember. Her tongue moves slowly along her teeth, feels nothing. She wants to bite her lip, but can't open her mouth, something keeps it glued shut. Her eyes hurt. She doesn't feel cold. Her clothes aren't wet, they feel strange on her skin. When she moves her head, her neck scrapes against something rough. It smells burnt. The surface beneath her vibrates. They are moving.

She is back in the cargo area of the transporter.

There's someone else there. Probably Bosch. Aaron tries to speak. Her dry mouth opens. "Cigarette. Please." She sounds like a hundred-year-old woman on her death bed.

"I don't smoke."

She knows the voice. But it's impossible. It's the voice of a man who drowned in front of her eyes.

"We were both dead. What did you see?"

If she answers, it will mean admitting that he's alive. She can't do that.

"I saw myself dying," the voice says. "It was beautiful. At first I was disappointed when I came to and was drifting in the river. I was sweating. Were you?"

She wants to be unconscious again.

A knock, then a metallic scrape: the window of the driver's cabin. The voice says: "Give me a cigarette."

She can't feel her hands and feet. That means she's been tied up. She hears a match striking. The cigarette is put between her lips. She doesn't want to draw on it, it would be further proof of the existence of the man she saw dying. But she notices that the filter is being crushed, she's sucking so hard on it.

"I've studied you in detail, but I've underestimated you. I should have known better. You were able to escape from Boenisch's basement even though you were blind there too. In spite of your injuries, you felled a man weighing a hundred and thirty kilos with a rusty nail. And an hour ago you killed me."

Again he lets her take a drag on the Chesterfield.

"We have a lot of things in common. We were both in a basement."

"Did you have a nail too?" She can't believe she's really talking to him. She knows he can sense her craving, and is grateful to him for the next drag on the cigarette.

"Your nail was just a tool that fulfilled its purpose. But why did you stop halfway rather than going for retribution? Boenisch was lying defenseless in front of you. You could have let him bleed to death."

Aaron says nothing.

"I didn't stop halfway. That was why I was able to escape the basement forever and you weren't. I'll ask you again later. We'll explore the meaning of retribution in greater detail."

"Maybe I'd have become like you. That would be worse than my basement."

"I can bear that burden. It's a greater burden not having fulfilled my destiny. That unites us too. You know the nagging emptiness, the fear that everything since we were born, everything we did, hoped and suffered, was in vain if we died for no reason. But I will redeem you. Because you are my destiny, and I am yours."

The next drag tastes bitter. She turns her head away.

"You know what it's like when you crave something but you never satisfy that craving. Your nausea proves your weakness to you. But I can draw on this cigarette, which tastes of your lips. I could smoke a thousand or ten thousand and stop again straight away without remembering the taste. I gave my father what he deserved. Leaving after that was much easier than sticking a rusty nail in somebody's neck."

"Why did you take your brother with you when you went? He doesn't mean a thing to you."

"Really? You think so?"

"Can I have another drag?"

He allows her a lungful of smoke. She tries to ignore the fact that he was holding the cigarette between his lips.

"It was winter. We walked along snowy roads, slept in huts in the forest. No pain is greater than remembering happy times when you are in a state of misery. But what happy time did we have to remember? After a month the money ran out. Have you ever stolen anything?"

She doesn't reply, but she sees herself in Munich one cold February. The Department wants them to be able to move inconspicuously in any setting. Aaron was to learn how to survive in a strange city as a homeless person without a cent, and had to prove it for a whole week. Two days before she began she wasn't allowed to eat or wash. She was forbidden to ask for a bowl of soup at the station mission; they checked up on that. She tried to beg, but dirty and ragged as she was no one gave her anything. Eventually she was so hungry that she stole a loaf of bread from a shop. Aaron was beaten black and blue by the owner's son and couldn't defend herself because it would have blown her cover. But worse than that was the shame.

"Stealing is easy when you're hungry," Holm continues. "I just took what we needed. I left Sascha standing outside the shops, and always thought he would be gone by the time I came back. I didn't know if I'd have been relieved. I had to pay a debt, but he could have released me from it by running away. He didn't. He ate the bread I had stolen, and lay down beside me to sleep without a word. After a while I saw a woman coming out of a pub. I told her I wanted her little car, and that she was to give me her handbag. She screamed for help. I hit her with my fist and she was quiet. I had never sat at the wheel of a car before. But I drove as if I'd never done anything else. It was then that I realized that I can do something as easily as if I'm doing it for the thousandth time. When did you realize that?"

"The first time I fired a gun," she answers reluctantly, only because she hopes that he will ask Bosch for another cigarette if he talks to her.

"Yes, I can believe that. What was the model?"

"A 9 mm Starfire."

"Perfect pistol for a little girl. In my case it was a Tokarev TT, a Red Army service weapon, nickel-plated. The design was borrowed from the Browning Hi Power, as I'm sure you know. Isn't there a certain irony in the fact that you took that gun with you when you flew to Barcelona?"

Suddenly Aaron's ribcage feels as if it's made of concrete.

"Oh, that was easy. I followed you and Kvist to your training session with your Catalan colleagues. Kvist is a virtuoso gunman, he's very quick, a master. But he couldn't be compared with you. Anyone who hasn't seen you shooting doesn't know the meaning of perfection." He knocks on the window again. "Bosch, another cigarette."

He gives her a first, second, third drag.

"Sascha and I came to Hamburg. There were squatters living on a street near the harbor. They gave us a bed, shared their food with us, asked no questions. They hated the state. That was as strange to me in those days as it is today, even though I'm familiar enough with the feeling as such. I've hated three people in my life: my father, you and myself."

"Why me?"

"But those squatters also believed in something, a kind of justice. Night after night they talked of a world I knew nothing about. I read their books. I can pick up a fat book, flick through it page by page in two hours and remember every sentence forever. Of course you know that. We both enjoy listening to the constant chorus of knowledge in our heads, the beauty and clarity of sentences and thoughts, in the certainty that we will understand their meaning. I met Marx, Habermas, Marcuse, Adorno, Dussel and others. These were philosophies of liberation, but they wanted to liberate society, not themselves. That was why I set those books aside. I was more interested in the structuralists, even though they didn't answer the most important question: what gives structure to your world and mine?"

"Violence."

"We both discovered that early on. Have you read John Locke?"

"Yes."

"He's the philosopher I despise more than any other; he doubted that man could distinguish between good and evil. You and I are the proof to the contrary. Even though it's true that most people persist in ignorance."

"You claim to know the difference between good and evil? A man who has committed dozens of murders?"

The cigarette is right in front of her mouth. The smoke curls into her nose. But Holm pulls his hand away. "How many people have you killed?" he asks.

"I've always had a reason."

"And I haven't?"

"Why did you shoot the teacher? That murder was completely pointless."

"Was it?"

"You were well aware that Demirci wouldn't let me go even if you executed ten of them. You knew that his death was of no significance to the success of your plan. So why did you do it?"

For a long time all she can hear is the sound of the engine, the knocking of a cracked mudguard, the rattle of a hook.

"I killed him so that you could ask me that question. It was inevitable, that's dialectics," Holm replies at last. "The question deserves a more thorough answer. But not yet. Only at the right time."

Aaron hates herself for the gratitude with which she draws on the cigarette. She says: "I only killed to save my life or other people's. The ability to feel compassion distinguishes us from animals. I can do that, you can't."

"Did you ever have a pet, a dog, perhaps? No, you wouldn't want to be around an animal that was submissive to you. More like a cat. Did you have a cat?"

"Yes."

"After Boenisch's basement?"

"Yes."

"How many times that cat consoled you when it sensed that you were battling with your demons. Wasn't that compassion?"

She wants to scratch his eyes out because every word is true.

"As far as I'm concerned: I took off your wet things and put an overall on you. I put your coat over you and saved you from freezing."

"To kill me whenever you feel like it."

The fact that he has seen her naked drives her mad.

"Not when I feel like it. You'll learn that."

"There's nothing I could learn from you. What would it be? Letting your legs dangle in a stream of blood? Palming murder off as dialectics? Ignoring the pleas of a human being like chatter at a party? There's nothing."

"Oh there is, you'll see." He allows her a drag. "I also read the metaphysicians and the scholars. They believed that we are guilty from birth, I liked that. But they were slaves to their religion, which is why I refused to respect them. I cannot kneel before a God who has so little concern for me that he could throw me into a basement. How could I ask such a God to forgive my sins when he is himself sin? What do you believe in?"

"In what I see."

"I have never experienced friendship, but I've heard that a shared sense of humor is an important basis for it. Are you friends with Mr. Pavlik?"

She doesn't reply.

"As I thought. And with his wife too?"

*Bastard.*

"Then I'm surprised that you haven't asked whether my reference to his wife and child might not have been a little game."

"Because I know."

"How?"

"I can sense that they're alive."

"You can do that?"

"In case you think I could teach you, I can't. You would have to know what it means to be alive."

"And you're saying I don't?"

"Just as I'm saying you don't have either morality or the ability to feel compassion."

"Patience. Men with clubs came and cleared the house in the harbor. They had sworn the same oath as you, but they were strangers to compassion, or else they wouldn't have taken a girl I liked because she slept with me without asking about my sadness, and thrown her against the wall like a stone. They wouldn't have kicked in all the teeth of a boy who had read Sascha bedtime stories. The men would have claimed they were obeying orders. How many orders like that did they obey? How often were they cruel and heartless without wasting a thought on the matter?"

*Not once.*

*But I will never justify myself to you.*

"I wish I'd been able to help them both, but I had to escape with Sascha or they would have taken him away from me. At the back door a policeman blocked our path. He was little more than a child, you could see from his eyes that his heart was pounding. I took the club off him, used it as the others had taught me to, and thought about the girl and the boy. He fell dead at my feet, his unfinished face stared at me. I ran away with Sascha and hid in a shed for a long time and saw that cop going down. I was right to kill my father. This was different. I've forgotten most of them, but I remember the one in that house. Never tell me again that I don't know the difference between good and evil."

The transporter stops, the window opens. "Where do we go now?" Token-Eyes asks.

"Wait. Look for a suitable place off the road," Holm says. "Bosch, give me the box." He closes the window, lights a Chesterfield, puts it between her lips and leaves it there. "Who was your first?"

"A drug dealer."

"What did you know about him?"

"That he had rammed a knife in my belly."

"As little as that. But how long after that was it before you could sleep again, how often did you see his face? I'm sure it's in front of your eyes right now. 'It's like falling through the mirror, no one knows more than that when he wakes up again, like falling through all the mirrors in the universe, and afterwards, a little later, the world reassembles itself as if nothing had happened.' But we both know better, don't we?"

*That's from* Gantenbein.

Holm is talking again already. "The cleared house belonged to a wealthy man. Apparently he had plans. It occurred to me that the villas of people like that could be useful. It was as easy as pie. I sent Sascha to see them. He rang on the door, said he was lost and asked if he could call his big brother. If they let him in, he would check carefully to see if they were alone. He gave them the phone number of the café I was waiting in. The name he mentioned was the code and told me whether I could go into action. I came and took any money that was in the house. If I wanted a car, there was one in the garage. Sometimes I had to hit someone, but it meant nothing more than shooing away a wasp. Have you beaten and hurt other people to get answers? Just be quiet. Lenin said: 'The one thing worse than being blind is refusing to see.'"

Aaron explores Holm's voice. According to the theory of acupuncture there are twelve meridians in the human body, the streams of the life energy Qi. The index finger that she jabbed between his sixth and seventh ribs was aimed at a special kyusho point on the liver meridian.

*Dianxue.* The Touch of Death.

As to whether it worked, time will tell.

The symptoms were: labored breathing, visual and auditory disturbances, problems with balance and then a circulatory collapse.

But it's much too early for that.

You can expect it to take about five hours, you have to be patient. *If I'm still here.*

His voice is calm. "They were dead. And already they're checking your breath again. I've never seen anyone who breathes as perfectly as you do. The yogis believe that each human being is assigned only a predetermined number of breaths for a whole lifetime. They slow down their breathing to delay death. Do you think that's an option?"

"Do you want me to give you yoga lessons?"

He laughs a hard, bitter laugh that dissolves like a pebble swallowed up by a crevasse. "I never stayed for a long time in any place with Sascha, we moved around. It was a year since I washed our father's blood off me in a stream, but my brother still hadn't said a word. I broke into houses a few times. The owners of two of them were on holiday. We lived there for a while. There were expensive television sets and expensive brandy and books that had been put on the shelves unread. I indulged myself enormously. I let the days pass without counting them. I had become a petty criminal, like the ones you must have had to deal with when you were starting out in the police. Wasn't their despair at being locked up like background noise at a party you? If they'd arrested me back then, I'd have been a scribbled signature on an annoying police file. They would have known nothing about the void within me, so great that I thought my heartbeat felt like the dripping of a tap. I had a library in my head, but it was only a pile of letters. I didn't yet know my way."

The cigarette butt is wet and cold. He takes it from her lips and wipes spittle from the corner of her mouth as if she were a child.

"One night when we were sleeping in a car yet again, my head exploded. I was lying in the road, and four men who had decided to beat me senseless with baseball bats were standing around me and Sascha. They were considering whether to kill us or not. In fact all they really wanted was the expensive car. But there was an animal living within them that was eating its way through their intestines. That beast also rages in my brother. For a long time I thought he would defeat it. I had to admit that I don't have that power. Killing one, two, three or ten doesn't satisfy Sascha. The beast is insatiable. It is his nature."

"You say you can't bow down before a God. And yet it doesn't bother you in the slightest that your brother bows before you? Why? Because you see yourself as a God?"

"How do you define God? Can I change the course of the tides, the paths of the heavenly bodies, the wind? No. Can I send plagues, make miracles happen? No. But am I the master over life and death in my world? Yes. And in yours as well. It is true that my brother kneels before me. I could forgive him his sins. But he doesn't ask me to. He simply doesn't know what sin is."

"Have you ever knelt?"

"I have. That night, before the men with baseball bats. For my brother's sake. I begged. I pleaded with them so intensely not to kill him that I fainted from despair. When I came to they had left with the car and Sascha was sitting in the gutter. I crept over to him and pressed him to me and couldn't feel his heart. He said the first words he had uttered to me since we had left: 'Let me go back to the basement.'"

Minutes pass.

She could almost believe he had disappeared.

"The next day Sascha rang on the doorbell of a villa. When I grabbed the woman by the throat, her husband appeared behind me and stuck a knife in my back. I was lying in front of him. He looked down at me with ice in his eyes. Our fate, Sascha's and mine, was sealed. But that wasn't the worst thing. When I lay there waiting for death, my brother looked—" He breaks off and tries to find the words he needs.

"He looked at you and you realized he wanted to see you die," Aaron says.

"Yes," Holm summons the strength to say it.

Time passes.

Then his voice resumes. "But there was a knock on the door. Through a veil of fear I could see the guy with ice in his eyes going to a drawer, taking out a pistol and opening the door. A man came in. He was with his son, who wasn't much younger than me. Ice-Eyes closed the door and aimed the gun at the man. He ignored it. He said the man had stolen from him and he had come to get back what belonged to him. Ice-Eyes held the gun to the son's head. He said: 'I'm going to shoot your son now, then you will go away and never show your face here again.' But as if out of nowhere the other man was holding a gun as well." Holm lights a new cigarette and gives it to her. "What was the highest discipline for the Samurai?"

"Self-control."

"The man taught me that. I thought I knew what a sacrifice was, a loss. But he showed me that I was a child and he was a man. He shot his own son to demonstrate his final duty as a father, and to show Ice-Eyes the meaning of steely inflexibility. Ice-Eyes fired too. He hit the other man in the shoulder, and he fell over. Ice-Eyes aimed the gun at him and said: 'Now you're going to meet your son.' The man wasn't afraid. In fact he smiled. Suddenly I came back to life. I dragged Ice-Eyes to the floor, got hold of the gun and shot him between the eyes from a range of two meters. The man who had sacrificed his son stood up. He looked at me and said: 'What's your name, my son?' It was then that I said my name for the first time."

Holm kneels down. Aaron realizes that he is cutting through the cable tie, and knows that she doesn't have the strength to fight him.

"I have lots of memories of him. Some of them I carry on my skin." He takes her hand and runs it over his bare right shoulder. She feels the rubbery brand.

*A star.*

For a fraction of a second Aaron sees herself giggling with a young woman in the changing room of a boutique in the Hackesche Markt in Berlin.

*Alina.*

Aaron remembers: she was the lover of a man with an executive role in Nikulin's gang. The star-shaped scar was a distinguishing mark for those men, and their women were given the same brand, like cattle. Alina's lover had come with her to Berlin to undergo a complicated heart operation in the Charité Hospital. Since it involved a period of rehabilitation, he would be staying in Berlin for over a month.

That was eleven years ago.

Aaron was to find out for the LKA whether Alina, who was the same age as Aaron, knew anything about his business dealings.

She was very beautiful and very lonely. Aaron met her as if by chance in the shop, tried on the same dress and saw the brand on her shoulder. Laughing, shoes that she would never buy, a drink in Monbijoupark, a chat, an agreement to see each other again.

Alina befriended her. Aaron had to be careful, because the girl was followed at all times by two of her lover's bodyguards. They inspected the penthouse in the Hackesche Markt that the LKA had rented for Aaron, but they didn't spot the mini-cameras. They flicked through a fake family album, Aaron with a rich father who paid for her luxurious lifestyle, they saw her expensive jewelery, hired from KaDeWe, the Porsche in the garage. When she went to the toilet at the Michelin-starred restaurant, where she had been eating foie gras and drinking vintage champagne with Alina, they checked her phone and thought Aaron wouldn't notice.

A mistake would have been a death sentence.

She found out nothing about the business dealings of Nikulin's gang from Alina, just that her lover was a bastard. Aaron was glad when their time in Berlin came to an end and they went home again.

But her phone rang a month later.

That was when it all started.

Now, on the bed of the transporter, she suddenly knows the identity of the man that Holm is talking about.

Ilya Nikulin.

He had been living in Switzerland at the time, and already had a large kingdom under his sway. After the collapse of the Soviet Union he went back to his homeland and turned it into an empire.

*The man who showed Holm the meaning of true strength.*

*The man whose killer was waiting for me in Moscow.*

*The man whose empire I brought down.*

She is incapable of uttering a word.

Holm says: "'Life is nothing but an empty dream, and if you have understood a reason, many others will open up in front of your eyes.'"

He gets out of the transporter and leaves her alone.

# 27

PAVLIK IS standing at the window of Maske's office. The two police-men are leading the prison director out of the building in handcuffs. Prisoners lurk behind a fence, clapping and cheering. One of them shouts: "Hey, Maske, you old fucker, we'll see you in the shower!"

Pavlik's phone rings. "Yes?"

It's Helmchen. "You wanted to know who looked after the Ukrainians."

"Fire away."

"The squad was Peschel, Fricke, Butz, Ruff and Pi."

That's how Pavlik remembers it. Pi turned out to be a mole, Butz is dead and beyond criticism. Ruff was a tough cookie, who risked his neck time and again for the Department. Two years ago he died of leukaemia. And Pavlik would be willing to put his hand in the fire for Peschel and Fricke. "Who was following the operation?"

"Boll was in charge of logistics, Krampe took care of the technical side."

Boll is still with them, a calm, sensible man who lives on his own after two divorces. He inherited three apartment blocks in Berlin in his early thirties and doesn't need to work. His job is a passion. Pavlik doesn't know how he could be blackmailed. Which leaves Krampe. He studied computers and electro-technology and was with the BKA before he joined the Department eight years ago. He's always in the red because he has to pay support for two children. That could be a reason. Still, it can't have been him. He and Pi are best friends. When Pi left the Department years ago to make some money with a private company, he wanted to take Krampe with him. Krampe gave it serious thought, but stayed even though he could have earned a lot more by leaving. He is godfather to Pi's daughter Luise.

*Out of the question.*

"And a psychologist," Helmchen adds.

Pavlik's ears prick up.

"The two Ukrainian women were terrified about giving a statement at the trial. Lissek was worried that they would retract. So he brought in a psychologist from the LKA. He was in the safe house in Frankfurt an der Oder and he reassured the women."

"When exactly?"

"An hour before the attack."

"Could he have known about the Hotel Jupiter?"

"Yes."

"But Internal Affairs checked him over?"

"Very discreetly."

"What's the man's name?"

"Rolf Jörges. But he took care of himself."

"How do you mean?"

"He drowned in the Mediterranean."

"When?"

"A month after the trial against the prostitution ring collapsed because the surviving Ukrainian woman withdrew her statement."

"Any witnesses?"

"None. According to the records of the Majorcan police he overestimated his strength and swam too far out in a lonely bay."

Pavlik doesn't know which feeling is stronger: the rage at not being able to haul him over the coals or relief that it wasn't someone from the Department.

"How did you get into the records of the Spanish police?"

"*No me preguntes.*"

"I owe you."

"You say that, and then I only get a peck on the cheek."

"What did you have in mind?"

"One of Sandra's cakes. A really big one."

Pavlik laughs. "But we'll share it."

"Love you too."

She hangs up.

He sits down at Maske's desk, lights a cigarette and picks up the piece of paper with the phone number on it. He hasn't thought of anything else for an hour. When Döbler gave him the note, he was tempted to call immediately. But first he wanted to weigh up the pros and cons. It would let Holm know that they'd stumbled across Maske. What if Holm wants to use him again? No, that's unlikely. Maske has done his part.

Pavlik picks up the phone, keys in the number and starts recording the conversation. The phone is answered after the third ring. He says nothing. No one speaks at the other end either. Half a minute passes.

Then Holm says: "Mr. Pavlik, I assume."

"Yep. You think you're smarter than everyone else."

"You're making me curious."

"Your first mistake that I know about was leaving your getaway car in a 'no parking' space in Cologne before liquidating the Armenian. The second was cleaning out the car but forgetting about the fuel tank cap. We can pin the murder on you because you left fingerprints today; that was your third mistake. And fourthly: buying yourself a spineless arsehole like Hans-Peter Maske."

"You forgot to mention that I spent too long on the coach before starting to negotiate conditions. Wouldn't it have been cleverer to contact me as soon as you arrived, given that the chain of command hadn't yet been put in place?"

Pavlik is speechless for a moment.

"Let's start with that. I didn't want our conversation to take place during a phase before we'd got organized. You needed to collect your thoughts first so that you could listen to me with proper care and attention. During those initial frantic moments the danger of a reckless reaction would have been much greater."

*The bastard.*

"That was what I thought, because I didn't really know you. Now I know you never act recklessly."

"Am I supposed to feel flattered by that?"

"You're immune to flattery. So let's look at Cologne next. I actually made two mistakes there. I had my brother park the car and later told him to clean it thoroughly. He forgot about the fuel cap. I knew as soon as I talked to him about it; he's a bad liar. It was too late to correct that one, the car had already been found."

"You can't choose your family. But I'm sure you'll forgive him for his cockup in Cologne because that was many years before the *start of his journey*."

"So you found that note," Holm murmurs.

"It was a little thought experiment. In Barcelona you told your brother that your paths would part once and for all. Obtaining his release was a kind of farewell kiss. But Sascha can hardly have understood that, he lacks the brainpower. Have you already told him to clear off?"

"I don't need to. He will leave and never look back. He has learned to acknowledge his mistakes. And while we're about it: do you think I left my fingerprints on that woman's phone by mistake? I feel almost insulted. I wanted to help you establish the link between Cologne and Maske. That was why I didn't conceal my number when I called him. I completely agree with your judgement of him. He's the kind of person who would have given Jews away in the Second World War. I have as much respect for him as I do for an earthworm."

Pavlik can't help smiling bitterly.

"In Cologne he asked me eagerly if I wasn't interested in other prisoners in the institution," Holm goes on. "If I wrote him a list, some things could be organized."

"I'm sure he's *au fait* with lists."

"This phone call, which I'm sure you're tapping, wouldn't be admissible as evidence in a trial against him. Do you have enough evidence to send him down?"

*No, damn it. We could only pin Cologne on him if we managed to trace the flow of money. It looks like we're a long way off doing that.*

*And Sascha? It's not enough that Maske backed his transfer and saved him from punishment on a number of occasions. Which leaves the phone call with Holm today. But Holm will claim he didn't talk to him. Wrong number. He was only allowed into Sascha's cell because he was the director. Tonight he's sitting at home again, enjoying a glass of brandy.*

"I can tell from your silence that that could be difficult. Do you have a pen?"

"Yes."

Holm dictates a sequence of numbers. "That's the number of an account with the Anguilla National Bank in St. Kitts. I set it up for Maske under the amusing cover name of 'Joseph Clark.'"

Pavlik holds his breath.

"He wasn't rewarded for sorting out my brother's affairs: that became clear in a one-to-one discussion, you might have liked it. But the account still exists, I've checked. If he hasn't lived the high life, and I doubt that he has because people like him want to accumulate property rather than spend money, you'll find a large six-figure sum. Does the name Joseph Clark mean anything to you?"

"No," Pavlik says, collecting himself.

"I thought not. You're not a literary man, which in no way diminishes my respect for you. Joseph Clark was the name of the captain of the British steamer *Jeddah*, which set off from Singapore in 1880. On board were over nine hundred pilgrims on the Haj to Mecca. The ship sprung a leak on the high sea during a storm. Clark fled with his officers in a lifeboat and simply left the passengers to their fate. Joseph Conrad told the story in his novel *Lord Jim*. That captain is one of the most famous cowards in literary history."

"I won't thank you."

"I have no problem with that."

"Did you set up an account for Rolf Jörges as well?"

"Am I supposed to know him?"

"The psychologist who told you where our safe house in Frankfurt an der Oder was, and that we were using the Hotel Jupiter."

"Oh, him. That was amazing."

"Why did you wait a month to kill him?"

"He's dead?"

"Because you went swimming with him off the coast of Majorca."

"Sorry, but that's too much. I saw no reason to dry up that source. Sometimes a swimming accident is just a swimming accident."

*But he's confirmed it.*

"Since we're chatting, there was something I wanted to ask you this morning, but unfortunately the opportunity never arose. That shot from two thousand two hundred and eighty-four meters—that was last year in Norway, right?"

Pavlik doesn't answer.

"It's in the professional literature. It was a police operation the details of which were omitted for reasons of confidentiality."

"Tell me where you are and I'll come and tell you all you want to know. And a bit more besides."

"Shame, we'll have to put that one off. I know it was about a lonely farmhouse in the middle of a snowy wasteland, and you couldn't have got any closer without being spotted. You must have been able to hit a bent trigger finger that looked the size of a speck of dust through the sights. With a Barrett Light Fifty, a gun whose range is four hundred meters short of that, according to the manufacturer. The bullet was in the air for four seconds and descended towards the target from a height of five meters. That shot was a work of art. It saved the life of a Norwegian undercover agent. The fact that they asked you to do it says a lot for your reputation. I know you had to take everything into account, even the Coriolis force of the rotation of the earth. By the way, how did you lose your lower leg?"

"Playing poker."

"You always have to pay your debts."

"Why did you liquidate Bedrossian that time?"

"That was just a contract job. What he did with his free time wasn't directly relevant. But since you have a young child I won't conceal the fact that he had certain inclinations. You'd have been happy enough to kill him."

"What were conditions like at the cemetery?"

"I don't want to bore you."

"Professional interest."

"Unlike you, I had an excellent view, perfect thermal conditions. It was hot, thirty degrees. The deviation in the trajectory was twenty centimeters. It's so ridiculous that I'm almost ashamed to mention it."

"You fired two shots."

"I don't have your class."

"The caliber was unusual, a .700 Nitro Express. The bullets are used in big game hunting."

"I wasn't trying to win a prize for technical skill."

"But you did. You deliberately shot Bedrossian in the shoulder to blow his branded mark apart. A manifesto: 'This is what we do with traitors.' The second shot to the temple was a masterpiece, because you had to calculate to the fraction of a second how the man would fall if you were going to score a lethal hit."

Holm's silence is so complete that it leaves an echo.

"Ilya Nikulin hired you."

"You haven't disappointed me."

"What sort of a relationship did you have with him?"

"The answer would be too complex, we don't have time."

"I'm sure you could sum it up in two sentences."

"Brevity doesn't always do things justice."

"There's something you're itching to say. I promise I'll give you an honest answer."

"Fine. Why don't you beg for Aaron's life?" Holm asks after a brief hesitation.

Pavlik hears footsteps in the outside office. Demirci appears in the door. "Because this is how it is: you and that pile of shit that you call your brother are dead before dawn. Aaron will execute both of you. And she has my blessing."

He hangs up.

Demirci asks only: "Where did you get the number?"

"Maske." He unreels the phone-tap.

After that she exhales very slowly.

"There's something you need to know," Pavlik says.

"You're referring to Aaron. I took a look at her files and I'm up to date. She had Nikulin arrested at the age of twenty-five and after that she was recruited into the Department."

They exchange a long look. Could Holm's hatred for her have something to do with Nikulin? But why wait eleven years?

Demirci says: "In 2005 I was invited to the farewell party for the then BKA president Richard Wolf. At his request. I was very flattered. A remarkable man. He spent his childhood in Morocco, his father was ambassador there. Wolf's memoirs have a Maghrebi proverb as their epigram: 'Endurance pierces marble.'"

They both think of Ilya Nikulin. He was the head of a Russian Mafia organization with various business interests. His specialization was the criminal trade in raw materials. Nikulin bribed leading representatives of Siberian refineries, and with their help siphoned off huge quantities of oil and gas which he sold to countries in crisis, such as South Africa in the days of apartheid. He maintained a global network of bogus companies, which worked as intermediaries, not least in Germany. Later he cold-bloodedly exploited the UN aid program "Oil for Food" to get Iraqi oil past international sanctions, putting hundreds of millions of dollars in Saddam Hussein's coffers.

Nikulin had excellent contacts, particularly in the Caucasus. He tapped into the Baku–Novosibirsk pipeline, and had so many politicians in Russia, Georgia and Chechnya in his pocket that for a long time no one dared come near him. He was responsible for countless hit-jobs, but even that didn't do for him.

"He was as powerful as the Romanovs," Pavlik says. "It was only when he put dirty oil on the US market at dumping prices that it all got too much for the Americans. The FBI asked to collaborate with Wiesbaden."

Demirci nods. "But why did they send a fresh young officer from the Berlin LKA to Russia? She was in her mid-twenties. Capable, of course, she'd already distinguished herself. And yet it was a top-level mission by the BKA. Why her?"

"I asked her once, but she was evasive."

"Nikulin killed himself while awaiting trial, didn't he?"

"Yes. In Moscow. His friends all turned their backs on him. Presumably they'd just been waiting for a moment of weakness on his part. And Nikulin's empire collapsed, as big empires always do." Pavlik picks up his phone. "Just a moment." He taps on a stored number. "Hi, Richard, Ulf here." He laughs. "That would be great, maybe next week. Yes, I'd be delighted too. I need information, it would be worth a 1996 Barolo." He laughs again. "You rogue. Question: in 2005 the FBI hopped into your lap. It was to do with Ilya Nikulin. You paid for Jenny Aaron to go to Moscow. How did that come about?"

Demirci can't believe her ears.

"I see. Thank you," Pavlik murmurs. "We'll have that bottle of Barolo together. Say hi to Sophie." He puts his phone away.

Demirci struggles to control herself. "That was Richard Wolf?"

"I did him a favor once. He would say it was more than that. He's in his mid-seventies now, but he's still in great shape. We enjoy a glass of red wine and a Havana from time to time."

Her thoughts slide away, and Pavlik notices. "What is it?"

"It bothers me sometimes."

"What?"

"The men thing. Chatting over red wine, brandy, cigars. You won't understand that as a man, and it's not a dig at you either."

"I'm not allowed into ladies' circles either."

"That must be a terrible blow. What does Wolf say?"

"One of Nikulin's men had come to Berlin. He brought his girlfriend. The LKA put Aaron on to her. She won her trust, even her friendship. After she went back to Moscow, the woman invited Aaron to see her there. Wiesbaden got wind of it. Of course that was handed to them on a plate. According to Wolf, the Russian domestic secret service was involved as well as the BKA and the FBI. It's probably a bit much to say that Aaron caught Nikulin. But she must have played an important part in it, otherwise the Department wouldn't have taken an interest in her."

"If that was all there was to it, why didn't she talk about it?"

"Aaron is complicated."

"Now *you're* being evasive."

"I could call Wolf again. Or Lissek. Or a few other people. But what would be the point?"

"Do you think we're barking up the wrong tree?"

"It isn't about the Mafia, or oil or money or politics. It's just about Aaron and Holm. About something very personal. Forget Nikulin's business deals."

Demirci has run out of cigarettes. Pavlik holds a pack out to her. They smoke. Only now does he ask, "Why are you here?"

"The Federal Aviation Office reacted to the photograph of the third man. Armin Bosch, a former professional soldier. He has a helicopter license and one for single-engine planes, both from the Federal Defense Forces. I talked to his former commander; he's now in charge of the government air fleet in Tegel. I had to do something to keep from going mad."

"So?"

"Bosch was on combat duty in Afghanistan, he got a special bravery medal. Two years ago he was deployed in the Horn of Africa. His helicopter was stationed on a frigate. He was shot down over the sea by Somali pirates. Three of his comrades died. Bosch was the sole survivor, with severe burns all over his body. You were right about his short-term memory. He hasn't been able to concentrate since the crash."

Demirci follows her thoughts, and Pavlik follows his.

"Bosch couldn't get by on his small pension, and threatened his former superiors," she says. "He said he was going to come and get what was owed to him. His wife left him. She took their son with her and moved to her sister's."

Pavlik's neck muscles tense again.

"The Federal Police sent people to the house. They found the bodies of Bosch's sister-in-law, his wife and his child in the apartment. They'd been there for at least a week. A triple murder."

# 28

THE REMAINS of the covering still hang from the globes of the satellite antennas, flapping in the wind. Niko Kvist leaves the ruins of the US army base on the Teufelsberg behind him. Below him the city lies in a whirl of snow and light. The voices from Department headquarters are still ringing in his ears. They are carried by the bug that he stuck behind a monitor before Demirci took his service weapon away from him. They are searching, chatting, chucking theories back and forth. They know nothing. It drives him crazy.

He tried to cling on to an idea as he drove aimlessly around. In vain. He tried to control his breath while snow drifted above him. In vain. He tried to call her Aaron and not Jenny, as if that would help take him away from her. He yearned to stand on a mountain and be able to think clearly.

But now he is standing on that ridiculous pile of rubble and knows that it was all in vain.

On his fifth birthday his mother went away and left him alone with his father. His father took him to Finland, where he ran a video equipment store in a small town. His father was lonely, but none of the women that Niko saw coming out of the bathroom in the morning was up to much. His father started drinking, and when Niko was eleven there was a note in the kitchen and his father had left as well.

He came to Hamburg to live with an aunt. She told him that his mother had died a year before in Canada. She had been living there with a man that her sister had never met. He stayed with his aunt for seven years. When he packed his things at the age of eighteen, she was as much of a stranger to him as she had been on the first day. He never saw her again.

He joined the police because he wanted to belong to something. After five years he was asked if he wanted to join GSG 9, the counter-terrorism unit. Jenny's father didn't give him preferential treatment, but Niko knew that he expected more from him than he did from anyone else. He didn't take part in a single operation over the next five years because there were none. Just training.

One winter he and four comrades were sent to Kabul, where they were to protect the German embassy. It was a fortress, and outside it a life was worth less than a bag of millet. When they drove through the city in their armoured cars, they saw men who had been collecting leaves in the fields to sell as fuel. They saw women with no shoes in the snow, they saw three-legged donkeys.

Once they got a flat tire in some godforsaken part of the country. One of them changed the wheel, the others stood around him in a semicircle with their fingers on the triggers of their submachine guns. A dog trotted across the road with a human foot in its mouth.

Two of the comrades couldn't bear it and asked to be transferred. Others came. They asked no questions, just as Niko had asked no questions, because after a day in Kabul you knew everything. In the evening they played cards.

In the markets people were scared and flinched from them. But children begged for the chocolate that they always carried in their pockets because children's laughter was some consolation. One of the children in the marketplace in Yahya Khail didn't want any chocolate. The child exploded, taking three of Niko's comrades to their deaths. All that remained of the bomber was a red shadow on the wall. Niko only survived because he had stopped to watch a puppeteer telling a fairytale about a prince and a beautiful princess who was guarded by an ogre.

Niko barely knew two of the dead men, even though they had shared a room. The third had liked ice-hockey, which was why they called him Puck, and he had been his friend.

Niko had seen the child who wore the belt of explosives with a man hours before. He never told anyone. But from then on he went to the market alone every day. On the tenth day the man came. Niko followed him and stabbed him to death in an alley. He was spotted. It turned out that the Afghani was a CIA informer. He had had nothing to do with the suicide bombing, and had in fact warned the Americans about it.

Niko was sent back to Germany. Jenny's father was waiting at the airport. Niko was handed a plastic bag: they had cleared his locker. Jenny's father would say nothing about Yahya Khail. But Niko heard him say something that he would never forget. He knew that from now on he was dead to Jenny's father.

Niko fell ill. He stopped eating and sleeping and pulled the telephone cable out of the wall. One morning Pavlik was standing outside the door of his apartment in Bonn. They had known each other since a GSG 9 training course with the Department. That was years ago, but Pavlik had never lost contact with him. He had always been a wood-fire stove on which everyone warmed themselves.

Without knowing anything about what happened in Yahyahel, Pavlik had sensed that Niko needed him. He took some leave, looked after him and saved him. He never asked what had happened in Kabul.

After a week he no longer needed the sleeping tablets; he made breakfast and breathed. Pavlik said he had talked to his boss and there was an opening for him in the Department. They got drunk, and it was decided.

The Department became his family. They were like brothers, that was what he had missed at GSG 9. For the first time he felt at home.

He met André, and André became his brother as well.

The brother he would kill.

And then there was Jenny.

She had arrived a year before him. When she walked, the air vibrated for ten meters around her. When she fought, it was terrifying. When she breathed, he listened.

She was Jörg Aaron's daughter.

He wooed her, but she didn't let him get his hopes up. It was three years before they first went on duty together in Naples. Niko saved her life, and she thanked him by cooking him dinner. They met a few times after that although she never gave him anything more than her intelligence, her laughter, her charm.

A year later they came out of a cinema. He bought her a bag of hot chestnuts, and Jenny kissed him. She took him home to the apartment that she shared with a strange cat who gave him evil looks. That night and many others she thought Niko was sleeping, but he was wide awake.

They didn't tell anyone in the Department apart from Pavlik. He told Niko he would break every bone in his body if he ever hurt Jenny.

In Marrakech they made love from dawn till dusk. But Niko was unhappy. Everything about Jenny was perfect. And still it didn't work. She told him about Boenisch and Runge and the basement. He held her in his arms.

And still it didn't work.

Niko didn't know what was wrong. Perhaps her father, whom he had disappointed and who now stood between them.

*No. Of course I know. We couldn't be together. One of us would have stood by the grave of the other and hated themselves. That was why I decided not to love her.*

He wanted to call it a day in Barcelona, in the little restaurant on the Parc Güell, where he had booked the table. But that was before they drove to the harbor and he died in that warehouse while she sped down that tunnel where she died as well.

For five years he was afraid to see her again. For five years he told himself she had never meant anything to him. But yesterday morning he stood in the terminal and looked at her for an eternity as she waited for him. Then he knew that he loved her, and had loved her for all those years. It hurt so much that he needed a second eternity to find the strength to speak to her.

He hears Fricke calling Pavlik. "We've got the airfield."

"Where?"

"In Finow, up in Brandenburg. Bosch chartered a Cessna for 4:30 and paid in cash. Fake papers. But they recognized him from the photograph."

"Did the plane leave?"

"No. He called at a quarter to four. He said something had come up, and postponed the flight till tomorrow. The time is left open, the charter is valid for two days."

"Destination?"

"Supposedly Vilnius."

"How many people?"

Fricke lets a moment pass and then says: "Three."

Niko feels his shattered ribs. His face is numb. The snowflakes make way for crusted blood. He has the taste of copper on his tongue.

"Send two SETs straight away." Pavlik chooses the men. Fricke is one of them.

"Demirci wants me to stay at HQ."

"I'll talk to her. Have Mertsch tell the Federal Police to get moving. We need all available drones with infrared cameras up there. But no helicopters. Just a second—" Niko hears murmuring, Pavlik speaking to someone. "Tell the technical department that operation headquarters is moving to Finow. Get your arse in gear, we'll see you there. I want the Mauser and the Light Fifty."

"OK."

"Where's Kvist?"

"At the old American listening station. He's looking at the landscape. Maybe he wants to write a poem about it. He doesn't know anything, believe me."

"Don't lose him."

He is standing on the Teufelsberg. Snow falls on him and turns to blood on his tongue. She talked to him and he was amazed. She yelled at him and he was amazed. She danced with him and he was amazed. He has been dead for ages.

# 29

UNDER HER coat Demirci's blouse clings wetly to her back. It isn't because Pavlik is dashing northwards at full speed along the Berlin city freeway. Not because of the twenty centimeters between their car and the truck that he finally forces to the side. Not because he is tapping the number that Fricke just gave him into his phone as he does so.

"Three," they said.

Behind that number is the urge to chain-smoke and the certainty that there is no seat on the plane for Jenny Aaron.

A phone is picked up at the other end. "Germer speaking."

"One of my colleagues called you. Who's doing the paperwork for the flight to Vilnius tomorrow?"

"I am."

"Are you at the airfield?"

"Yes."

"When do you shut?"

"In half an hour, at eight."

"Is there anyone there apart from you?"

"Two colleagues who are staying a bit longer, till nine."

"Where do you live?"

The man gives him the address.

"Go home now, but don't hurry, take it easy. I'll see you there. Tell the other two to knock off now. Everything has to look perfectly normal."

"What's all this ab—"

"Later." Pavlik cuts him off and ends the call.

"Why would he have postponed the flight?" Demirci asks as they shoot past a slow car, touching its wing mirror and leaving an extended beep on the horn far behind them.

"There are a thousand possibilities."

"But you're banking on one."

"Aaron somehow scuppered his plans."

"Holm didn't sound concerned on the phone."

"If he was, we wouldn't notice."

"Why do you want to have Fricke there with you, of all people?"

"It's going to be a long night, the men are nervous. He always has a joke at the ready. Fricke does the others good, don't underestimate him. And when things get going, he's deadly serious."

They've reached the northern edge of the city. The passing lane is free now, and the dark freeway is up ahead of them. At two hundred and fifty kilometers an hour the central reservation looks like a burst of rapid-fire tracer bullets.

"I'm thinking about Kvist. Don't you think his behavior is curious?"

Pavlik says nothing.

"If you were in his place, what would you do?"

"Stick a .45 in my mouth and pull the trigger."

"I mean it."

"So do I."

"Please."

"What are you getting at?"

"You've got underworld contacts, you'd talk to informers, you'd ask about Holm or his accomplices, as our people are doing as well. You'd call one of your buddies at bomb disposal to find out what we know and so on."

"He may have done that already. We're only listening in on his car, we're not tapping his phone."

"Wrong."

Pavlik's head suddenly turns towards her. "Without authorization?"

"Since when have you been such a stickler?"

"What happened to the woman who used to sleep with legal clauses sewn into her bed sheets?"

"Every now and again the sheets need changing."

The car feels cold.

Change down, accelerate, change up.

"I've known Kvist for four weeks," she says. "When he went on that mission against the Romanians he charged straight into the flames. Looking at his files, you might think he'd done it deliberately. Quite honestly I even thought about having him transferred."

Pavlik brakes sharply because a dumper truck has pulled out in front of him without indicating. He hammers on the horn as if it might shut Demirci up.

"To call him a hot-head would be a euphemism," she goes on. "It seems to have started five years ago, after Barcelona."

" 'Would be,' 'seems,' 'you would think,' " Pavlik mutters.

"If she means so much to him, why isn't he trying to find something out? It's against his nature."

"You're beating around the bush. That's against *your* nature."

"Do you trust him?"

"He was my friend."

"That's not an answer."

Demirci has to hold on to the roof handle because Pavlik is swinging the car into the entrance to a car park. He skids into the parking space and gets out. She follows him into the icy wind. The full moon is riding over shreds of cloud. He lights a Lucky Strike with his jet lighter without holding the pack out to her. "You've known him for four weeks, I've known him for ten years. He has never shown fear, not even before Barcelona. Ask my wife. And she can't stand him."

"There was just him, Jenny Aaron and Holm. Come on, Pavlik, you don't think she was a coward as well, do you?"

"Our code doesn't require us to sacrifice ourselves."

"It does. And you know that." Her next answer plunges like a meteor from the sky and opens up a crater between them. "Did it never occur to you that Kvist might be in cahoots with Holm?"

"Hell would freeze over sooner," Pavlik spits.

But his cigarette tastes like a memory he'd locked away in a safe somewhere.

Three months after Barcelona, Aaron's father wanted to talk to Butz and Pavlik. Not on the phone. They flew to Sankt Augustin. Jörg Aaron poured them a drink and told them what Kvist had done in Afghanistan. His rage was like a bullet. He was capable of anything. Pavlik wanted to deny it. But what could he use in his defense? Friendship, loyalty, his understanding of people. Jörg Aaron didn't think in such categories. For him it was an equation with three unknowns: the supposed tip had come from Kvist's supposed informer. Kvist had made contact with Holm. Kvist had met him on his own in Bruges.

Butz wiped away the equation and suggested a new one: the informer existed; he had always been reliable. After that meeting in Bruges Kvist wasn't convinced that Holm had the Chagall, because there was no proof apart from a single photograph. Lissek slept on it and then gave the go-ahead.

"Jenny wanted to go in armed. Kvist talked her out of it," Jörg Aaron said.

"We make decisions. Some of them are right," Pavlik replied.

There was still a dreg in the whisky bottle. Aaron's father distributed it among the glasses. "The Minister of the Interior gave it to me for my farewell party. I've known a lot of brave men. None of them has been as brave as my daughter. I'm not going to leave it until I know the truth."

He was about to raise his glass. But it fell out of his hand and he was dead before it shattered on the ground. Pavlik will never forget the time he and Butz couldn't bring themselves to call Aaron. And how they looked out of the window and saw her feeling her way along the path with her stick. How they ran downstairs to be there before the paramedics arrived. How Butz took Aaron's hand and whispered: "I'm sorry." How Pavlik saw her tears and couldn't get a word out and couldn't bear her pain and Butz couldn't understand why he didn't want to show himself. How he stole away as if he had never been in this house, as if he had never grieved with her.

The wind eats away at Pavlik's cigarette. It is wedged wet and bitter between the two bloodless straight lines of his lips.

"Give me a single reason," Demirci says.

"He loves her. That's why."

"Holm had assured him that nothing would happen to her."

"Not Kvist."

"Just because he's her friend?"

The moon rides into a black abyss. More sleepless nights are reflected in Pavlik's eyes than she has ever had in her life. "I told her there was a notch in the gun rest in the sixth lane."

"Yes."

"It's from André. André and Kvist and me. The 'Three Dons,' that was what the others called us. André switched sides. Kvist tracked him down and killed him. Because I couldn't do it. No friend has ever done me a bigger favor."

When Demirci is able to speak again, she says: "You call him André, you don't call him by his last name."

The cigarette is whipped from Pavlik's mouth. "It's what he wanted. He said: 'If I step down I don't want anyone to pretend he barely knew me.' But that's exactly what happened. It's the first time in six years that I've uttered his name."

Bosch doesn't remember exactly when Holm scoured the valley with the night-view binoculars and chose the lonely farmhouse. But he remembers looking up at the sky outside his sister-in-law's house and hearing his mother say many years before, "Red sky at night, shepherd's delight." He doesn't remember if snow was falling when they left the transporter at the farmhouse and Holm told him and his brother to go inside with the woman who dropped her bucket outside the stable, to see if they were really alone. But he does remember that he had a terrible headache when he rang at his sister-in-law's door, that he was wearing his good suit, that he was holding a bouquet in one hand and in the other a toy fire engine for Elias. He doesn't remember what rooms he and Sascha looked at, what furniture was in it, what it smelled like. But he does remember a lamp flickering in his sister-in-law's stairwell, and hearing a watch ticking, even though it doesn't really tick. He doesn't remember if the woman said or did anything that made him furious. But he does remember that his sister-in-law wanted to close the door as quickly as possible, and a mighty noise enveloped him and swept his sister-in-law away like a cobweb. He doesn't remember how the woman ended up lying on the floor in the kitchen whimpering, how his fists clenched and stung, Sascha leaning against the sink with a cigarette and grinning. But he does remember he wanted to talk to Simone, tell her that everything would be fine, he knows that Elias didn't look at the toy fire engine and wept and flinched from him. He can't remember why the woman with the bucket is now lying in a different corner with blood spilling from her nose.

Suddenly Holm is standing in the room and throwing him in the air like a paper airplane. Before Bosch loses consciousness he sees Aaron feeling her way over to the woman, holding her, and he remembers looking down at Simone and Elias, who were silent, he remembers how his sister-in-law screamed and that made him mad and he remembers his watch stopping. But how it happened he can't remember.

Aaron runs her hand over the woman's soapy hair. "Don't worry, he won't do anything to you anymore." The woman very slowly calms down.

*Now she's my responsibility.*

Aaron's breath is halting. "Can you move?"

"I—think—so," she hears the woman sobbing. After every word a pause that in Aaron's first life would have been long enough for her to dismantle her Browning.

Bosch groans. Aaron helps the woman to her feet. Her hands aren't tied, but she barely has enough strength to stay standing on her own.

"Put the gun away," Holm orders his brother.

"What are we going to do with her?" Token-Eyes says.

Aaron looks at him. "If you touch her, I'm not going to lift a finger for any new negotiations."

"I wonder. I've got a few ideas."

At that moment the scent fills her nostrils.

"How lovely," Holm says. "You've got a camellia."

Aaron supports the woman. She is slender, not yet old.

"Where's your husband?" Holm asks.

"Hunting in Poland. With a friend." The syllables come so thick and fast now that she's almost babbling.

"When will he be back?"

"The day after tomorrow."

Aaron imagines Holm's expression, the certainty that the woman will not lie to him.

"Does he have guns in the house?"

"In the hunting room."

"She's just ballast," Token-Eyes says.

"Will he call you this evening?"

"No, he's having an evening with the lads."

"Anyone else?"

"No."

"Are you expecting visitors?"

"No."

Aaron hears a gas meter clicking. A tap drips. The flame in a boiler comes on. A train in the distance.

Holm says: "Stay here with Miss Aaron. If you touch her, you'll be digging your own grave behind the house." He pulls the woman away from her and takes her with him.

Something crashes to the floor. "Make some food, you piece of shit."

Aaron falls to her knees, collects pots, pans and ladles and knocks them together with a sharp clatter while Token-Eyes throws more and more utensils down on the tiles and gloats at what he sees as her helplessness. "Blind policewoman plays blind man's buff. Arsewipe!"

Holm comes back. "A cow in a byre, an earthworm in a dung-heap has more brains than you. You've just allowed her to take a look around."

The country road flies into the headlights. A gritter draws a sluggish line in front of them, is dragged into the rearview mirror and then magicked away by a sharp bend. Pavlik dashes over the black ice, through an arch of trees; the car holds the lane as if on rails. On a summer day he would enjoy the view across the far-off, flowing hills every time the forest opened up, he would have flipped up the visor of his helmet, the wind in his face, his body merging with the Hayabusa, the clouds mirrored in the windshield, he would speed along the snaking bends beyond the lift lock, would scrape the tarmac with his knee-guards, waste time.

Since the car park he and Demirci haven't exchanged a word. It isn't the kind of silence that's waiting for someone to break first and thus admit they were in the wrong; not a silence that could have been ended with a cliché, a remark about the weather, something trivial, because that would have meant something disappearing from the world without anyone making too much fuss about it. It's not that kind of silence. Kvist is the reason for it. What Demirci said cannot be taken back because she meant exactly what she said and any apology would be a lie. A phrase came out of the blue, and while it has not been proven right or wrong the crater it left will remain.

They reach the village. Christmas garlands still flicker in the windows of Manfred Germer's house; Santa Claus laughs from his neon-green sled, one reindeer has lost an antler. Germer opens the door as soon as they ring. They sit down with him in his old-fashioned German sitting room. He is an affable, fat man, the kind of person you would meet at a shooting-club party or a campsite, normally joviality personified, a cheerful chap, but right now a bundle of nerves. His wife, a dumpy little thing whose eyes dart from between rolls of fat, asks if they would like anything to drink. Or some Christmas cake, perhaps? No, thank you. She closes the door gently.

"What kind of men are they?"

"Dangerous men," Pavlik says. "That should be enough."

"Describe the pilot who chartered the Cessna," Demirci says.

"An experienced flyer, you can tell. He looked at the plane and noticed immediately that one of the valves had been leaking. He seemed a bit standoffish. I told a joke, but he just pretended to laugh."

"What name did he give you?"

"Martin Petzold."

"Did he show you IDs for his fellow passengers?"

"Copies of their passports. Hans Breuer and Uwe Askamp."

Demirci looks over at Pavlik.

*Breuer and Askamp. Holm's sense of humor.*

"And the charter is valid for two days?" Pavlik asks.

"Yes, a men's trip away, he said. We often get those, it struck me as perfectly normal."

"He must have given you a phone number."

"I've never seen a number like that before. Nineteen digits. He said he lived abroad."

"Did he seem agitated when he postponed the flight?"

"Hm. He was quite abrupt on his mobile."

"How do you know it was a mobile? Did the number come up?" Demirci asks.

"No, but a patrol car with a siren went past. But yes, I suppose he might just have had a window open."

Pavlik asked promptly: "When was that exactly?"

"At seventeen minutes to four. I checked specially after I rang my colleague."

Pavlik calls Majowski at Department headquarters. He wants to know where in Brandenburg an emergency police car was on the road at that time of day. He stays on the line.

"What's the procedure for tomorrow?" Demirci asks.

"He's going to call tomorrow morning and say when he's leaving. I'll check over the plane with him two hours before they set off."

"We'll swap you for one of our men."

Germer starts nodding, but his chin stops halfway down and doesn't make it all the way back up again. Demirci can see that his thoughts are slaloming in all directions. A man has chartered a plane from him under a false name, for himself and two others also with false names. Germer has probably listened to the radio, in the office in the afternoon or on the way home. There was something about a bus hijacking, a hostage-taking in Berlin. Three men escaped, they said, prepared for anything. He thinks about his wife. There are children's boots in the hall. If he says, "Out of the question," he will sleep tonight.

"But you don't want that, do you?" Demirci asks.

He wants to nod and shake his head at the same time, tries again and fails once more. "I said I'd be there tomorrow, he's expecting me." And he squints towards the door as if he knows his wife is listening behind it.

"Do you have a plan of the airfield?" Pavlik asks.

"Just a moment." Germer gets up and goes outside.

"Two hours," Demirci whispers. "Presumably Bosch will be coming alone, and the brothers will turn up just before the plane takes off."

"Yes. We need to get him on his own and make him tell us where the hiding place is. It's our only chance."

They are both thinking: *if Aaron is still alive.*

Majowski calls back. "At that time there was only one emergency unit on the road. In Freienhagen."

"They set off from Wannsee just after half-past one. It wouldn't have taken them more than an hour to get there."

"Checked that one. There was a serious accident on the freeway just past the edge of the city. A huge traffic jam that didn't disperse until three. Where are you planning on meeting the guys on the landing approach?"

"I'll tell them to wait." Pavlik hangs up. "They were just past Oranienburg, heading for Finow," he tells Demirci.

"We could send some men."

"They're not there anymore. In Holm's place I'd choose a hideout no more than ten kilometers from the airfield, to be there as quickly as possible tomorrow. No, they're somewhere very close by."

There's nothing exceptional about his words. But it's as if there hadn't been cigarettes cadged among the party balloons, as if there had been nothing between them when she talked about her mother, no gratitude on his part for the touch of her hand as it affectionately rested on his, and hers when he helped the men to mourn the death of their comrades because she hadn't time—no, she couldn't—not her concern and not her advice, which was to be so valuable to him. All of that suddenly seems to be lost, as if it had never happened, as if he were once again the man who walked unseeingly past her, not noticing her smile, and she was the woman who hid the fact that she was hurt. They both feel the loss and know that it could stay like this forever.

Germer comes back, spreads out a map and describes the last place in the world he wants to be the following morning, each touch of his finger a sleepless hour. "There are only two small buildings. This is the car park—this is the way in to my office, where the paper-work is done—then you go along this corridor to the ramp—the plane is parked over there."

"Does anyone work in the office apart from you?"

"No. There's just a desk. He knows that too, he's been there." Germer is so tense that his breathing is shallow, his words run away with him. His fingers move back to the car park as if they have a will of their own. "This would do, wouldn't it?"

*No. That would be the worst possible option. Bosch will be extremely nervous a moment before and a moment after getting out of the car; if he expects an attack, then that's where it will be. If there was an exchange of gunfire, the danger of killing him would be much too great. But if he's in there and everything seems perfectly normal, he'll be able to relax a little. That's the right moment.*

Pavlik stands up and goes to squat down by the sideboard where a model of a propeller plane with Japanese markings has the place of honor. "Brilliant. Did you make this?"

Germer's pride briefly outweighs his fear. "One hundred and ninety hours of work. Cut and painted each individual part myself. The landing gear is retractable."

"Really? How does that work?"

Germer shows him, while Pavlik asks in an astonished voice, "Can I have a go?" and Demirci watches them, big boys together. If she didn't know better, she might think that Pavlik has forgotten what they came for.

"What kind of plane is it?"

"A Yokosuka Ohka, it was just used for kamikaze flights."

"That must take a lot of patience."

"And a steady hand."

Pavlik smiles. "What do you think, Mr. Germer—would a person who is capable of making something like that not be relaxed enough to welcome our man, hand him some papers to sign and ask him to go on ahead to the runway because the phone has just rung at that very moment and he needs to sort something out?"

Germer thinks for a moment. His forced smile doesn't make it all the way to the corners of his lips. "Maybe."

When they turn off the main road into a country lane, Pavlik switches off the headlights. The wind has subsided, and the moon hangs between resting clouds like an inflated pig's bladder. Its light turns the snow pale blue and glitters in the branches of the hedge that brushes the car. The men arrived a few minutes before; the Fords are parked under the trees, camouflaged with nets, invisible from fifty meters away.

They mutely agree; Pavlik picks up a pair of night goggles and crawls over to Kemper who, similarly equipped, peers down from the top of the hill to the airfield. It lies below them, a pixellated green still life, surrounded by solar panels which hug the lower slopes like the terraces of a snowy rice field. A Soviet fighter regiment was stationed here during the Cold War, and its conning tower still stands. The stout sheds for the fighter planes were built to last forever, and planes stand in line in front of them; a museum that Pavlik once visited with the twins. They squeezed into an MiG and played dogfights, while he thought this was the real world, his world, but not the world of the other fathers whose children he could see.

The sport and business airfield is off to the north-east. Two low buildings. The closed hangar is big enough for a Gulfstream, but now it's empty, as Pavlik learned from Germer. There are three propeller planes on the ramp.

"Which one is it?"

"The Cessna."

"Fueled?"

"Yes."

"That must be tempting to Holm. Why wait till tomorrow? I'd make off with that plane tonight."

"The thought must have entered his head."

"The shelters would be a good place for him."

"Let's check them out."

They can only see part of the car park. "Less than ideal," Kemper murmurs. "We'd have a better view from the hill opposite."

"I know," Pavlik says, giving no further explanation of his decision.

Kemper leaves it there, he has known Pavlik for long enough. The light is turned off in the office building. A short time later two cars drive away. They take off their night goggles. Pavlik wants to get back to the others, but Kemper rests a hand on his arm.

"Why is Kvist under surveillance?"

"Routine."

"You never do anything just out of routine."

"You have a problem with that?"

"He got me out of a tight spot in Amsterdam. He's always ahead of the game. He's a great guy. And still you dropped him like a hot potato. It's not just me who thinks that."

"Since when have we been a democracy?"

"Since when have you shit on your comrades?"

Pavlik grabs Kemper's wrist. He knows that another word will turn him into a man that he never wanted to be, and has never been. He knows since he put his foot down on the accelerator on the freeway and noticed how thin the metal really is, and that it wasn't him speeding along the tarmac, it was the tarmac speeding under him. His eyes are black as onyx. "He will still be my friend when you have long forgotten him," he whispers. Kemper's blood pulses in his hand. Their breath hangs between them in a cloud; they can both still see the words when they have faded away.

Kemper nods. He has understood.

Pavlik's eyes change color very slowly; at first it's just a glimmer over an abyss, the hint of a distant light, then they assume the broken gray of the clouds. At last he lets go of Kemper.

The cloud of breath dissolves.

By one of the Fords Pavlik takes Demirci aside. "Do you really want to stay here?"

What he doesn't say: it would be better if we kept out of each other's way over the next few hours.

"My decision stands."

What she doesn't say: we will both have to live with that phrase.

They all put on dirty white overalls and smear their faces with camouflage paint. Pavlik divides up the teams: two men each to the tower, the ramp, the car park, the office building. Demirci goes to the hangar with technical support.

"Krupp, Nowak, come with me. We'll take a look around."

They put on helmets and night goggles and hang the equipment over their shoulders. They dart silently down the slope, cut a hole in the fence and blend with the trees. Pavlik, Krupp and Nowak break away from the others. They disappear among the solar panels, just as the wind revives and sweeps the sky clear.

The technicians assemble the equipment in the hangar. Krampe asks their positions. "SET 1 clear, SET 2 clear." Fricke barks in the bushes by the car park: "Clear and freezing my balls off."

"We're desperately sorry to learn of your discomfort," a voice says from the warm tower.

The video link is established with the Department; Grauder checks in: "Nothing new here." Automatic reactions. But they help Demirci through the first half hour. Pavlik's helmet camera sends wobbly images sprinkled with green. Check, secure, carry on. Demirci knows that he doesn't expect to find Holm. There are many possible hiding places in the surrounding area; remote houses, farms, dense woodland. Anything is better than the airfield. Pavlik is only searching the area because he is bearing in mind a probability of one per cent.

Demirci looks over at Krampe. He sits at his monitor with his eyes shut following the few whispered thoughts of the others. She has come to value his calm professionalism. Krampe is reliable, he finds a solution for every technical problem. The men treat him like a colleague, but call him by his first name. They wouldn't stand outside his door at night, pour their hearts out or get drunk with him after work. The foundation of their comradeship is the second that decides life and death. Krampe has often been a witness to that second, he has heard it as a quick breath into a throat microphone, a shouted command, the echo of a gunshot, a cry in the ether. But he knows nothing about it.

He laughs quietly to himself, perhaps because Fricke has told a joke. Demirci taps him on the shoulder. Krampe pushes up his right headphone. "How long have you been with us?"

"Eight years."

"Then you knew André."

You could peel Krampe's silence like an onion, and there would always be a new silence underneath.

"What was his surname?"

Krampe breathes the silence in and out again.

"Which bit of the question didn't you understand?"

"Neubauer."

"What kind of man was he?"

"Ask Pavlik."

"I'm asking you."

Krampe looks at his two colleagues. They are sitting at the end of the hangar, one of them dozing, one playing with his mobile phone, and they ignore both him and Demirci. He thinks about the answer as if it isn't as easy as it really is.

After a long pause he says in a quiet, throaty, sad voice: "He was a decent bastard, and everyone wanted to be friends with him. But only Pavlik, Kvist and he were the Three Dons. André had no family. Like Kvist, perhaps that was why. There was something about him that people liked. Like Pavlik—although he had other sides to him as well. And a laugh that made people feel good. Once he said to me: 'That's how I'd like you to remember me—as someone who liked to laugh.' We all went to his funeral. By his graveside we swore never to think of him again. He's the only one whose name isn't on the plaque."

"What happened?"

"He withdrew into himself. He stopped talking and laughing and lost his temper at the drop of a hat. He didn't even come to Lissek's barbecues. He blew his top with one of the lads in the shooting range. I don't know who, I got it third-hand." Krampe hesitates. "I'm not usually there when they need to clear things up. I just look after the technical side of things."

"That's as important as everything else," Demirci says encouragingly.

"Perhaps. It doesn't matter anyway."

"And then?"

"Even Pavlik couldn't get close to him. And neither could Aaron. André and Aaron liked each other, but there was nothing sexual. They both spat in the face of death, that was probably it." Again he fights for words. "André made some counterfeit money disappear. Kvist found out. Pavlik couldn't believe it. When André was in Prague on an undercover mission, they went to his apartment. They found a hundred thousand fake Euros under the floorboards. Lissek thought of ordering André back on some pretext or other. Except there was nothing that wouldn't have aroused his suspicion. So he sent Pavlik and Kvist to Prague to sort it out. But Pavlik got drunk. Kvist went on his own, without Lissek's knowledge. André wanted a grand finale. He got it. Kvist was suspended for three weeks."

"Were there witnesses in Prague?"

A shrug. "Internal Affairs wouldn't have closed the file if it hadn't been as clear as day."

"Maybe they just lacked evidence."

"What for?"

"Yes, what for?" Demirci hears someone say behind her.

She turns around. Pavlik has come back with Krupp and Nowak. A look from him is enough, and Claus Krampe quickly puts his headphones back on.

The three men stand there like a wall.

"Mr. Pavlik, he was your friend, I respect that. But we shouldn't let ourselves be guided by our emotions."

"I agree," he says coldly. "Aaron abandoned Kvist in Barcelona because he knew they would both die otherwise. Those are the facts, they're uncontested. It wasn't Kvist's decision to hand her over to Holm, it was her own. Maybe you're of the opinion that a blind woman can't make her own life decisions, just because she's dependent on the help of others. I don't see it that way. You talk about respect? Then let me do the same. Kvist respected her will. She was able to ask that of him."

"Then why did you beat him up? What about the .45 you wanted to stick in your mouth?"

"I had time to think."

"And André?"

"Not for you to judge. You didn't know him. You weren't at his graveside. You didn't grieve with Kvist."

If it was any quieter you would be able to hear it starting to snow outside.

Demirci whips out her mobile. "Helmchen, I need the Internal Affairs report on André Neubauer." She stares at Pavlik. "I'm aware of that. Get someone put back on duty."

Pavlik turns away. Exhaustion strays across his face like a shadow. The question he keeps asking himself, the question that wears him down, tortures him, as if someone had been tattooing it on his skin for weeks, day and night, the question of where he knows the name Eva Askamp from, has become so nagging, so agonizing, that it extinguishes all other thoughts like a migraine.

# 30

"WE LIKED each other as children. He was one of those wild boys with scabbed knees and a catapult and chocolate around his mouth. That was in Kleinhüderoda in Thuringia, a few randomly scattered houses, you'd need to look it up on the map. I come from the west, from Fürth, you can probably hear it, the Franconian accent sticks to you like chewing gum, my father always said. We had relatives in Thuringia, so we always went there for three weeks in the summer holidays. Klaus showed me how to whistle through my fingers and catch frogs, hunting was in his blood even then. He gave me my first kiss by the carp pool, we were eight at the time, but I still remember very clearly that he tasted of chocolate and vanilla."

Holm threw all the tools out of the tiny box-room before he pushed Aaron and the women inside and locked the door. Between the bare walls it is so cramped that they have just enough space to sit there pressed against one another, their legs drawn up, their bound hands in their laps. Aaron feels the woman shivering against her shoulder. She has only answered one of her questions: that her name is Vera. Aaron is familiar with two kinds of response when someone encounters death face to face. Some people can't say a word; their mouths are blocked by fear. Others talk uninterruptedly, they hurry through their lives, want to explain who they are, as long as there is someone who will listen, as long as they still have a voice. There is no point interrupting or consoling them. They need to talk until they are exhausted.

So there is nothing Aaron can do but wait, trapped in a single thought. The single realization. The single truth.

*Ilya Nikulin.*

*He was the father Holm had been looking for.*

*I was to blame for his suicide.*

Vera sobs. "At seventeen or eighteen I did my own thing in the holidays, camping with friends, Interrailing, Paris and Rome, I still like traveling. I didn't hear anything from Klaus, and never thought about him, we'd just been children. I always wanted to be an actress. I haven't got much confidence, my mother drummed it into me at an early age that I wasn't anything special. But I applied to the University of Dramatic Arts in Berlin. And they gave me a place. Perhaps by the skin of my teeth, but anyway! My parents were flummoxed. I stood in front of the mirror and said: 'You're going to be the new Meryl Streep, or at least the new Cher!'"

*How did Holm know about me and Nikulin? And for how long?*

*Did he know by the time we were in Barcelona? Yes, he knew by then.*

She sees him taking her hand again. "I would even have waited two minutes for you." That was the message in his eyes. The deep satisfaction at seeing her in front of him at last.

*He didn't sentence his brother to five years in jail because Ruben was able to make that emergency call. I was in a trap, and Sascha let me escape. That was why.*

*But why didn't Holm kill me in the tunnel?*

*Because I couldn't run away from him. He dazzled me, that was just the start of my punishment, the first circle.*

*What circle am I in now?*

*The circle of memory.*

In the car he quoted Dante: " 'There is no greater sorrow than to remember, in our present grief, past happiness.' " So true. One door after another opens up in Aaron's library. But she doesn't find the happiness she hoped for, because she used that up a long time ago. Sandra's nose wrinkling when she laughs; the little-boy face with which Pavlik scrapes the bowl; Marlowe's tongue; looking at Niko when he sleeps. "La Le Lu," she hears the tune of the toy clock that her father gave her. "Then comes the sandman, quietly up the stairs, to fill you up with lovely dreams, while you sleep unawares." With a slight scratch on "lovely dreams."

*How many circles of hell are there in the* Divine Comedy? *Eight, nine, ten? And after that Purgatory, where you atone for your sins.*

It's terribly difficult to join up her thoughts. One trainer said: "I'll take you to the edge. And when you've got there, I'll take you to the edge you didn't know about." Fricke and André were the best at dealing with sleep withdrawal.

They had their methods. For example, they thought about the extra equipment for dream cars they would buy when they were rich. Or the dumbest insults they could come up with: "I wish you scabies on your balls, and herpes on your fingers so that you can't scratch yourself." Or they listed places they wanted to avoid: Wank in Bavaria, Fucking in Austria, Bitsch in Switzerland, Hymendorf in Lower Saxony, Shitterton in Dorset, England. Boring in Oregon was probably the winner. Once André drew up a list of the ugliest men with beautiful wives. From A for Aristotle Onassis to Zadok, somebody in the bible; André swore that Zadok was covered with warts but had loads of women anyway. Sooner or later the laughter woke you up.

Vera talks and talks.

"Soon I noticed that other people were more talented, I'm not blind. Sorry. I found it hard to get bookings, perhaps partly because of my accent. But I still didn't give up, it was fine for the fringe. I made money as a cleaner, nothing was ever beneath me. One Sunday I crossed over to East Berlin with a friend, my first time even though I'd lived in the city for four years, crazy, isn't it? But now we're getting to it: on the Museum Island I turn around and Klaus is standing in front of me. We recognized each other straight away, and believe it or not the knees of his jeans were ripped."

The kitchen where Aaron "looked around" is, she guesses, about five meters by four. A gas stove, no modern appliances, she would be able to negotiate it without difficulty. The house is big. Thirty paces from the kitchen door and down a corridor. Twelve on the left to the box-room they're crouching in. Her legs have gone to sleep. At least part of her is sleeping. On the other hand Aaron's head is doing curious things. One half is as heavy as an anvil, the other as light as if it could fly.

"I know it sounds crazy, but we looked at one another and that was that," Vera says. "Sixteen years after the kiss by the carp pool. And he felt exactly the same."

She has probably told this story many times before, wittily, blithely, throwing the words into the air like balls and juggling with them. They are still the same words, except that now they sound as if they are all about to fall on the floor. Still, Vera has to stick to the script, every punchline, every turn of phrase, she mustn't change a thing so that she doesn't lose her balance.

"We talked like crazy, and I had to get back to the west by midnight at the latest. Klaus worked at VEB Robotron. 'Just think, we've developed the biggest microchip in the world!' he said and laughed. But he wasn't happy. Three exit applications refused. And he wanted to make one more. I'd never have dreamed of doing anything like that. Outside the 'Palace of Tears,' the name given to the border crossing where people tended to cry a lot when they said goodbye, we kissed. It was like a chocolate."

She stumbles after every second sentence because she senses that she should tell the story in a different voice, but she can't. She quickly sputters on, as if her heart would stop like a clock if she fell silent.

"It all happened in a moment. We applied to get married and we were granted permission, it was amazing, Klaus bought Crimean sparkling wine in the Exquisit shop. I commuted between east and west for six months, and then we got married in Alexanderplatz. Beneath a picture of Erich Honecker. You should have seen Klaus's suit! And I was all in white."

Aaron listens to what is happening in her own head. The left side is roaring, the right is in silence. Perhaps André, that mad bastard, was right. He was convinced that both halves of the brain could sleep and wake independently of one another, like albatross brains. And then he said such wonderful things as, "There's a hotel in Montevideo where only angels live."

*André, you and I were the sixth lane. How often have I heard you half-inhaling. But when you exhaled again, I wasn't with you. What did you mean that last time, with that kiss on my forehead that was supposed to be forever?*

"Klaus couldn't cope in the west. It was—how can I put it—like planting a palm tree at the North Pole. He was desperate to get to the west, but once he was there he wanted to go back, and by then it was impossible. We didn't know the Wall would come down two years later. I didn't have the strength to be strong for both of us. We got divorced and I was very sad for a long time. But life goes on, and I'm not the type just to break down and cry. I met a good man and married him. He wasn't the sweetest man in the world, but everybody has their foibles, I've always said. Having our daughter is the best thing I've ever done. She lives in Innsbruck and is six months gone. I'm about to be a grandmother, can you believe it? I gave up acting when I fell pregnant. After a few years I happened on the idea of looking for old chewing-gum dispensers; you wouldn't believe how many of those there still are, rotting away in attics and basements. And I sold them at the flea market on 17 Junistrasse. Not for the money, my husband had a very good job, he was an engineer, but it was a lot of fun. It could be that it was my father's fault because of what he said about the Franconian accent."

When did Holm give up sleeping? He can't have gone to bed last night. He followed Aaron to the party, and at four he came after Pavlik. He was in Eva Askamp's apartment early in the morning. But maybe he needs no sleep at all. An okapi only sleeps for five minutes a day. No, Holm isn't an okapi, he's a beast of prey. Lions sleep for twenty hours, the world is unjust. Maybe he's a shark. Sharks never sleep.

Vera is an okapi.

"One Sunday someone behind me asks how much I want for the chewing-gum dispenser that I'm particularly fond of. I dusted it down from the props department of Babelsberg film studio, it's decorated with little cosmonauts and rockets, and it takes East German 10-pfennig coins. I turn around and there stands Klaus, right in front of me. We were both lost for words at first. We had divorced nineteen years ago and never heard a word from each other in the meantime. He had lived in Berlin, in Friedrichshain, near the Märchenbrunnen, he had a small taxi company and was also married, but childless. He had just inherited the farm from an aunt. In fact he had always dreamed of living in the country, not least because of the hunting. We went for a coffee. When he told me he wanted to start an ostrich farm because that was the future, it seemed perfectly sensible to me. He could have been telling me he wanted to emigrate to Bongo-Bongo Land, and it wouldn't have mattered. Everything was somehow always good the way it was, I thought. But when we were about to say goodbye, we kissed rather than shaking hands, and he tasted like the best chocolate in the world. Then I knew that this time it was right. And he knew too. We both got divorced and moved here, and we've been breeding ostriches for eight years now. The chewing-gum dispenser hangs in the kitchen. You might think that cosmonauts and rockets aren't really appropriate for an ostrich farm, but I think they are. Those creatures are as thick as two short planks, they can't even tell the difference between food and your hand. You should see my hands, your eyes would pop out; they're covered with welts because I've been pecked so often. But one thing is certain: every day I've been happy. Not many people can say that."

The sudden silence wakes Aaron out of her slumber. She can tell by the twitching beside her that Vera is crying in silence.

"We aren't going to die," she whispers. "What's up with your mobile phone, did he take it from you?"

"Yes."

"Where's the landline?"

"In the hall. He cut through the cable."

"You showed him the weapons cabinet. Where did he put the ammunition?"

"He threw it in the pond behind the house," Vera struggles to say.

"Is there any ammunition anywhere else?"

"No. I don't know. Are you really a policewoman?"

"Yes."

"A blind one?" Vera asks dubiously.

"Yes."

"What do they want?"

"They want money, one of them wants to kill me. The one you took to the weapons cabinet."

"I'm not rich."

"They'll demand a ransom for me. I'm valuable, Vera, and I'm sure we're very remote here. Your husband is a hunter. An uncle of mine used to go hunting. Apart from the rifles he always kept a loaded revolver in the house, just in case."

"A revolver is no use to us. You're blind, and I don't know how to fire it."

"Where is the revolver?"

"I'm not crazy."

"We need to find a way of getting at the gun. You just need to give it to me, not fire it."

"I'm not doing that. I wouldn't have a chance against them."

"I can tell by your voice that you're a lot braver than you think."

Ten brave things that Aaron has done:
　　crossing the street for the first time as a blind woman
　　standing up to the brother of a Turkish classmate
　　going to the meeting in Tangier
　　eating in Cambodia
　　flying to Moscow
　　stepping on to the pond in the winter after Ben's death
　　riding with Pavlik on the Agusta
　　not opening the window in the clinic for three weeks
　　refusing to shake hands with a Minister of the Interior
　　waiting for Niko at Schönefeld

"You know absolutely nothing about me." Vera is crying again.

Aaron doesn't want to force her. She struggles to her feet to get her circulation going. Her feet are bare and icy cold.

*Holm wants me to stay awake. To concentrate.*

She puts her ear to the door and listens, hears quiet voices but can't make out a word.

Holm watches his brother attacking the ostrich steak, which he found in the fridge and fried for just long enough for it to turn gray, tearing it to pieces with his knife and fork, and then gulping them down without chewing them properly. Holm knows that for five years Sascha wolfed down institutional food in exactly the same way as he had eaten every one of his meals since he had known him. If he had asked his brother what he missed most in jail, decent food wouldn't have been high up the list. Just women, guns, some houses. But Sascha tortures women, empties magazines, lets houses go to rack and ruin. Just as he has let himself go to rack and ruin. Because he means nothing more to himself than a piece of meat that he gulps down.

Bosch eats his steak with patience and concentration. He cuts it into identically sized pieces. He chews every mouthful until the tap drips again. Before each bite he breaks off a bit of bread. As he does so he thinks. Holm said: "We're going to get hold of another five million." How? Bosch won't ask him; he barely dares to look at him. Holm just sits there. He experiences time in his own way. When Bosch raises his head, he looks into Sascha's eyes. He finds nothing there that he hasn't known for ages. Sascha will kill him at his first opportunity. The way he wipes his mouth with the back of his hand. Would Bosch be a match for him? Of course not: he wouldn't have a ghost of a chance. And yet he's not afraid of him. It's impossible to be in the same room as Holm and be afraid of someone else.

Sascha dips bread in the blood on his plate. "How much longer are we going to be sitting around in this place?" he asks his brother.

"That's entirely up to you."

"What does that mean?"

"That if I were you I'd start wondering about what the demands are going to be, what terms I'm negotiating, and where and when the money's going to be handed over."

"So you're not interested in that anymore?"

"No. The money's yours."

"And there speaks someone who sent five million up in smoke."

"Today Jenny Aaron saved a school class and sacrificed herself. The blind heroine. That's what the media will call her, something like that. She's the most valuable hostage in Germany. That's worth three or five or ten million. They'll pay up."

Sascha takes the Glock from the belt of his trousers and aims it at Bosch's forehead. "And I don't have to share."

Bosch puts down his knife and fork. There is one thing that won't leave him in peace. He shouldn't have brought Elias that toy fire engine. Maybe a scooter. Then everything might have been different.

"Bosch, ask our hostess which railway line we can hear."

The words are enough to keep Sascha from firing. Bosch goes outside. He's just as happy to stay alive as he would have been glad if Sascha had pulled the trigger.

"That wouldn't be a clever move," Holm says when he's alone with his brother. "You need him for your getaway. After that you can kill him whenever you like. Although how many million you have is irrelevant. You wouldn't know what to do with one million any more than you would with a hundred."

Sascha is holding the cocked gun. His finger is only a millimeter from the pressure point. No, less.

A thin film of sweat is all that lies in between.

A twitch would do it.

"Maybe you'd be happy for a second or two," his brother says, reading his mind. "And then? You wouldn't even be able to enjoy that."

"Why can't I have Aaron?"

"What do you want to take revenge on her for? For that woman you slept with? Who was pregnant by you? You'd have slit her belly open if you'd known. Because Aaron put you in jail? She didn't. I put you there. No, there's only one reason: because you lay in front of her bleeding. Because she saw you as you are, weak, and still the child pleading with me to kill our father. Who do you hate more? Her or yourself? The fact that she's blind has aroused you for five years. But today she even took that away from you. Because she isn't helpless. Because she's fighting for her life more than you could ever have done. That drives you so crazy that you would bite your fingers off if it was the price you had to pay to be able to kill her. But the same emptiness, the same hatred, the same pain would still be inside you. Because the one you really want to kill is yourself. It's the only way you can defeat the monster within. But you lack the courage. Nothing will ever free you, not a thousand screams or an ocean of money. On the other hand I have more of a right to my revenge than you could imagine. I can end something and you can't. I can forgive myself, and you can't. I can be redeemed. I won't explain it to you because you wouldn't understand. But be sure of one thing: my punishment for Aaron goes far beyond anything you could comprehend."

He stands up.

"Either you shoot me in the back right now, or you'll cry all the way to your grave."

Holm walks to the door.

Sascha aims the Glock at his brother, closes his eyes and hears the shot. He sees him collapse, sees that he wants to say something else, looks down at him, enjoys the blood pouring from his mouth, smiles and lets him slowly suffocate in his own blood.

No wish is as great as this, no quiver as great as his, when he opens his eyes again and stares at the door that his brother has closed behind him.


The icy west wind hisses in the juniper bushes and the rowan trees, beyond which the raging sea breaks against the cliffs. The man stands on the terrace of his house and huddles into his warm lamb-skin jacket, while in the bay the beam from the Svingrund lighthouse circles among the low clouds and the winter rain washes his face. He and his wife have just eaten the fish that he caught today, and then sat down in front of the television to watch the German news. Aaron's name wasn't mentioned, and neither were the names of the men who took a blind woman hostage. But none of that was necessary.

He set down the wine glass, picked up his jacket and went out on to the terrace without a word. His wife is sitting in the house, he knows she is crying. Two days ago, Pavlik called and told him about Sascha and the dead psychologist in Boenisch's cell. He said that Aaron wouldn't be coming to Berlin. That Demirci was bracing herself for the worst. Tacitly she hoped that he would call her.

But he didn't. When he took up the job all those years ago, he would have been grateful if his predecessor had initiated him into the tasks at hand. Of all the mistakes he has ever made, that is the one he regrets the most.

His mobile phone vibrates. In no great hurry, he takes it out of his pocket, never showing nerves or anxiety. Not even when he is alone.

"Hello, Lissek."

"Hello, Pavlik." His voice is calm and confident. The kind of voice to which men would entrust their lives.

Like Pavlik's own voice. "Have you heard?"

"Yes."

Pavlik is crouching under a solar panel. This time he went on his own; he didn't want to share the cold and wind with anyone. "She's still alive. Holm pressed for his brother's release."

"What have you got?"

"I'm in Finow. There's a Cessna here. Apparently they want to fly to Vilnius tomorrow. There's no seat in the plane for Aaron."

Lissek sees her coming through the door at the Interior Ministry. He thinks: she shines. And years later, when she has pulled him lightly from an abyss: she shines from within. He realizes that he's already starting to remember her. He mustn't do that. "I would gladly piss blood forever if I could just turn back time by two days."

"You couldn't have prevented it. You know Aaron. You'd have been throwing yourself in the way of a leaping tiger."

"Is she there of her own free will?"

"Yes."

"How did she manage that?"

"Kvist."

The terrace door opens. Lissek turns towards his wife. She sees that he is making a phone call and watches him, trembling. He gestures to her not to bother him. Controls his breathing. "Where is he?"

"Suspended. We're keeping him under surveillance."

On Fårösund the wind whips up the sea, in Finow it shakes the snow from the pines.

Pavlik sees a shadow sliding away under the clouds and reflecting the moonlight. "Stay on the line." He puts the conversation on hold and activates his throat mic.

"SET 6 to technical department."

"Technical support here," Krampe replies immediately.

"There's a drone buzzing around the place. If it flies any lower I can bring it down with a stone. Those idiots should take it higher."

"Got you. Over and out."

Pavlik switches back to Lissek. "I've got to ask you something, I wanted to ask you the day before yesterday."

"Yes?"

"That invented pen-pal's name was Eva Askamp. Does the name mean anything to you?"

Lissek thinks for a second. "No—*was?*"

"Holm killed her today." His eye follows the drone, which is gaining altitude and disappearing into the clouds. His voice plummets. "And three of our men."

"Who?"

"Blaschke, Clausen. And Butz."

Lissek gave up smoking thirteen years ago. But he knows he will have to go down into the village later and buy a pack of filterless Gitanes in the Värdshuset. He thinks of the eight o'clock plane from Visby via Stockholm to Berlin that he will board tomorrow, of Blaschke's wife, Clausen's children, Butz's sister. He thinks about the words he will have to find to tell them how he was connected with those men. Of course Pavlik and Demirci will already have paid their condolences. But it was Lissek who recruited them for the Department. That responsibility remains. That and a call he didn't make.

Pavlik knows all that. He waits patiently. At last Lissek clears his throat. "Why are you asking me about the woman?"

"Because her name is driving me mad."

"I've never heard it before." The rain trickles down his collar, reminding him of a different rain many winters ago and making him shiver. "How's Demirci coping?"

"Outstandingly, like you."

The undertone doesn't escape Lissek. "But?"

"She's asked to see the Internal Affairs report on André."

"I'd have done that in your place too."

"Bullshit," Pavlik growls.

"How long have we known each other?"

"A few days."

"And how many times have we been wrong?"

Pavlik doesn't need to answer.

"So don't say it's impossible."

"Enjoy your retirement, old man."

"Who are you raging at, Demirci or yourself?"

"The whole world."

"Rage isn't a useful counsellor."

"I've got to go."

"One more thing, my friend: we've always sorted things out in our own way. If it's true and you find yourself up against him, don't give him a single chance. He's too good for that."

# 31

HOLM OPENS a door. Even before she feels her way down the steps with her hands bound, even before she notices the musty smell, even before her bare feet touch the icy floor, Aaron knows they lead to the basement.

"A suitable place for the two of us, don't you think? Put your hands above your head."

She does it. Bumps into something dangling above her. Holds it tightly.

"You see: the lightbulb is cold. I'm as blind as you are. It will help us both to concentrate. You are longing for a cigarette. Those days are gone. You should be aware that you will never again have that taste on your tongue. It's time to talk about loss."

The cold gnaws its way through her body like an animal.

"I've taken your coat away. You are barefoot, you are freezing." He takes her hands and presses them against his naked chest. "Another thing we share. You have lots of questions. I want to answer them. The first is: what link was there between me and Ilya Nikulin?" Holm lets go of her hands but stays close in front of her. "And I need to see him with the eyes of the twenty-year-old boy. He lived in a big house on Lake Geneva, he had a lot of servants, a beautiful boat, elegant cars. I saw him issuing a check for a hundred million dollars. But all his possessions, the industrial subsidiaries he acquired, the politicians he bought, were not the result of greed. Nikulin didn't accumulate these things to fill a void. Do you know why he did it?"

"Out of boredom?"

"You're still joking. How stupid."

The back of his hand comes so quickly, landing on the base of Aaron's nose, that she doesn't feel the draft until it's too late. The pain knocks her legs from under her. She falls to her knees. Her brain chafes against the inside of her skull.

"Let's try again: what was the spur?"

"Power?" she pants.

"To a certain extent. But not the way you think. What drove him lay deep in his childhood. His father was taken from him when Nikulin was eight years old, the same age as Sascha when I dug the grave. He was a surgeon in a hospital in Novgorod, and he fell victim to one of Stalin's big purges. The pretext they gave was the so-called doctors' conspiracy, a supposed plot by doctors accused of having contacts with western secret services. In fact the arrests were aimed at the Jewish intelligentsia, and the crime laid at Nikulin's father's door was that of having Jewish friends. He disappeared into a gulag, and Nikulin never saw him again. Or his mother, who was buried somewhere or other. He was put in a state orphanage. The little boy swore that no one would ever have power over him again, and recognized that the only way to reach that state was to achieve power himself. So he became the man he was. The man I called Father."

Aaron creeps backwards over the floor until she bumps into the wall. She opens her eyes. Closes them again immediately, because it hurts too much.

"Do you have any idea what it must have been like to grow up in an orphanage in the Soviet Union in the 1950s? He only spoke about it once. He said: 'We had lice even in our noses.' What was done to him and his parents would have left anyone embittered for the rest of their lives. Not him. When he met me, I was a twenty-year-old nobody. The basement experience was reflected in my brother's eyes. But he took us with him, and he left behind the corpse of his physical son. In the house by the lake he led me to his huge library of first editions and said: 'Spend as many hours here as you like. But know that none of these books will teach you how to close the eyes of a loved one.' I never encountered those words in the works of any philosopher. Nor have I ever heard anything so true."

Aaron feels her way around her surroundings with her bound hands, seeking something with which she could defend herself. There is nothing. Only dust and stones.

"What did your father teach you?" Holm asks.

"To shoot, to laugh and to be tender. And that evil exists."

"What a wise man. My first father taught me to rely on my fists. He taught me how many cracks there were in the basement ceiling. He taught me how to use a chainsaw. But he didn't have the strength to teach me pain. My second father taught me everything else. I could list the useful things: how to use a rifle; he was a master, he had learned with the Spetsnaz. How to speak Russian, French, English, Italian. How to make yourself amenable to people, read a balance sheet, negotiate. How a suit should fit, and that you can tell everything about a man by looking at his shoes. How to appreciate a good meal and not eat like a pig. Many other things besides. But the most important things were: that the will must be greater than fear. That you can take everything from me, but not that. How to stand by a grave without despairing at the question of why you're not lying in it yourself. How many people have you seen go? I don't mean killing. I mean *dying*. Looking other people in the eye, hearing words that are too quiet to understand, holding a hand or only waiting with revulsion for someone to be silent at last. How often?"

"Six times."

"Who were those six?"

"A shoe-shine boy in Tangier, a taxi driver in Helsinki, a woman in an underground car park, a schoolfriend, my mother." She hesitates, before whispering, "And Niko."

"He survived."

"For me it was as if he had died."

Holm's breathing becomes a shade more labored. Is the Touch of Death of Aaron's index finger between his sixth and seventh rib, beginning to take effect?

She summons the courage to ask the question: "Have you ever watched the death of someone who was close to me?"

"Who do you mean?"

"The man who was guarding Eva Askamp's flat."

"He was good. He sensed that I was after him, even though I didn't make a sound. It was a matter of centimeters. I broke his neck with a jump kick. He was still alive. There was no grief in his eyes. He had had his time. I gave him the coup de grace with a *nukite* to the heart."

Aaron feels herself being led to the courtyard by Pavlik, kneeling down beside Butz, reaching for his cold, snow-covered cheek and saying goodbye to him.

"What was his name?"

"Butz. Nice name. My father witnessed his young wife dying in a car accident. Later he saw his son and their oldest daughter die. I was there both times. He kissed his son's forehead and called him by his pet name. His daughter suffered from a rare disease, no doctor could help her. In her last weeks he only left her room to go and wash. But when he had closed her eyes and I tried to comfort him, he looked at me with such indifference that I pulled my hand away. I'm sure you know what I mean."

"That it's unworthy of a Samurai to show emotions."

"Yes. You refuse to obey that commandment. As I do. My father wanted to teach me, but that one time I was a disobedient student. Eventually his second daughter died as well. Natalya, his Natashenka, the apple of his eye. He couldn't be with her to hold her hand. But the man who brought him the news told me that my father banged his head against all the mirrors. So in the end the student was right, and not the teacher. No pain can be so great as to be worth hiding."

"You became Nikulin's right-hand man," Aaron says.

"Much more than that. I visited a lot of countries, he initiated me into his business secrets, and showed everyone else that I had assumed the position of his son. When my apprenticeship was over, he called me in and put a photograph on his desk. It showed a good-looking man, perhaps in his early fifties. My father gave me the task of killing him. He didn't tell me why. The man lived in London.

I observed him there for days at a time. He led an unremarkable life in the suburbs, he didn't seem to be particularly wealthy, he had a pretty young wife, children. I could see him reading stories to them through the window. He played with them in the garden, he was affectionate towards them. I struggled with myself. I couldn't see why I should take the children's father away, the wife's husband. While I was thinking about that, day after day and night after night, someone forced his way into my hotel room. He thought I was asleep and tried to press the silencer of a Beretta against my forehead. After I had smashed his face in, I watched him dying and learned my lesson." He is breathing heavily again, it takes him a long time to utter the next sentence.

"Who sent the man?" Aaron asks.

"The same one that Nikulin had told me to kill. His unremarkable life was just a façade."

*Footsteps upstairs. Token-Eyes. For how long will he manage to contain himself?*

"Yes. He was a rival. I shot him in his garden, right in front of his children. My father had taught me that mercy and the readiness to die for it are one and the same."

"And what did your father teach your brother? How to spit on graves?"

"He sent him to expensive boarding schools. First in Lausanne. When the Soviet Union fell and we went back to Russia with him, it was one near Lake Baikal. But bad news started coming in. Sascha was torturing other children. He had to change school five times. The last one was in Kaliningrad. He was told to get something from a basement store room. When he didn't come back, another pupil was sent down to get him. The boy was found dead in the basement. Sascha had rammed a broken wine bottle into his jugular. It was then that I understood that I would never be able to pay my debt." Holm says nothing. When he resumes talking, his tone is leaden and dull. "My father made sure that my brother wasn't locked up. You can do a lot of things with money, it even eases some parents' grief. He put Sascha in the care of a man who was indebted to him.

The man wasn't afraid of my brother. But today you can see what he taught him. In later years my father gave Sascha jobs for which he was ideally suited. I didn't think it was a good thing; my father was skilled in cruelties that I didn't share. But he was doing all this not for my brother, but for me. What did your father do for you?"

"Nothing you need concern yourself with."

"I challenged my father. You never challenged yours. I saw the way you talked to him at the graveside. Your devotion is unconditional, you showed him obedience even in death. He was a man of iron principles, I studied every sentence of his that was ever written down. When I asked why you didn't let Boenisch bleed to death, you were evasive. Wasn't it the case that you talked to your father in the house in Spandau? Hadn't you already decided to set yourself up as Boenisch's judge? Did your father forbid it?"

She is mute and rigid.

"I don't want to have to hurt you again to get an answer."

"Yes, it's true."

"Have you regretted it?"

"No."

"You're lying."

Yes. She has been regretting it constantly since the day before. When she ran her hand over the sticky trickle in Boenisch's cell. When she remembered Runge and the waitress. When she rocked Eva Askamp's corpse in her arms. When Pavlik said "Butz." When the shot was fired on 17 Junistrasse. Each time Aaron wished she hadn't listened to her father's voice that day.

And she wished the same thing now.

She goes into her inner room. She needs to think.

*How is it possible that he knows my thoughts, my whole life, all my secrets? My friendship with Sandra and Pavlik. What my father represents to me. Gantenbein. Marlowe. That I had a rusty nail in Boenisch's basement. That I've stolen. That I love Niko. That I follow Bushidō.*

"You've been in my flat." Aaron practically vomits the words, she feels so ill.

"That took you a long time."

It's a shock. Like a rape.

"There's a painting by Eşref Armağan in your bedroom. You probably don't want to know what it shows. I'll leave you with your illusions. You have a lot of books. I thought that was strange at first, but then I understood. It's enough for you to know that the books are there. Like the lamps, the plants, the painting. I was struck by two books in particular: *Hagakure—The Way of the Samurai* and, of course, *Gantenbein* by Max Frisch. Your favorite sentence from that one might be: 'Every human being sooner or later invents a story that he sees as his life.' Another passage strikes me as more apt. 'I'm blind. I'm not always aware of it, but sometimes I am. Then again I doubt whether the stories I can imagine are not really my life.' You read it. But you didn't understand it. If you had faced that truth, just once, you would know that your life has been a lie for eleven years."

"You want to avenge your father. Say it."

"I'll leave the simplistic answers to you."

He's swallowing his consonants. Aaron is sure now that the Touch of Death is responsible. The first symptoms. To be able to fight him she needs to wait until his circulation breaks down. But she will only have a brief window to do that, and then Holm will recover.

"I sat on your bed," he goes on. "Even in sleep you control your breathing, did you know that?"

"I bet we both do that."

"Are you trying to pay me a compliment? If I were an illusionist in a music hall and you jumped up after each of my tricks and cheered, do you think it would mean anything to me? The applause of a blind woman?" He snorts. "For you, I learned Braille. I read your notes and felt your despair on my skin. You're losing your memory, that perfect machine is running out of fuel. For me that would be worse than blindness. The fear of having been cowardly in Barcelona is growing in your head like a tumor. You are yearning for the truth. But which truth? You hoped that I would grant you absolution, that you were acting correctly. That's why you're kneeling in front of me right now. But what if everything was like a nightmare that you have never been able to escape? That you betrayed the Department's code, and broke the seven commandments of Bushidō, and your only way out was *seppuku*. But not even that concession was made. I wouldn't allow you that honorable death."

"Tell me what happened in Barcelona. Please."

"'Did Niko touch me? Did I touch him? Did we speak? What did we say? Why did I flee, leaving Niko behind?' That's the only reason why you came to 17 Junistrasse. Because I'm the only one who can tell you the truth."

"That's not true," she whispers. "I was concerned about those thirty people."

"For the Samurai lying is not a sin. It is much worse than that, more deplorable even than weakness. I will now give you my gun. It's loaded, you'll be able to tell that from the weight. I'm offering you the chance to kill me. It's very easy. But then you will never know the truth. You won't have another day of happiness, and you will die aware of having been cowardly. It's entirely up to you."

He puts the Remington in her bound hands. Her heart rushes full pelt into the tunnel and performs a somersault. She hears steel eating its way into concrete. She has the stench of coffee in her nose.

Hears herself screaming.

He grips her hands and brings the barrel of the pistol to his forehead. "What do you want more: to kill me, or to have a moment of recognition?"

She orders her index finger to pull the trigger.

Orders it, orders it, orders it.

But it won't obey.

Holm takes the gun from her feeble hand. Aaron weeps and curls up on the cold, dirty floor, just as Niko curled up in the warehouse.

Holm gives her time. But not out of consideration. He wants her to feel the pain for as long as possible, the pain of knowing that he is forever telling the truth and she is forever lying to herself.

Only when she is silent does he say: "Alina invited you to Moscow. How did you react? Were you tempted to refuse and tell your superiors nothing about the call?"

Not for a second.

All night Aaron sat facing BKA chief Wolf, a colonel from the Russian secret service, the FSB, and some FBI agents. Suddenly the success of one of the biggest international operations depended on her. She had reached the goal of all her dreams.

"No." She has to fight for every word. "It was the chance I'd been waiting for."

"Even though you knew it could mean your death."

She remembers: at the end of the conversation Richard Wolf asked her to stay while the others left the room. He thoughtfully lit a cigar. "Miss Aaron, you are very young, and you've embarked on a remarkable career. But those men you met a little while ago are already putting bets on your head. I assume the rate won't be very flattering to you. In Moscow there will be so many people from the FBI, the FSB and our own organization in the background that it's going to feel like a works outing. Except that it isn't one, it's a suicide mission. Forget the organization. You'll be on your own. Is that clear?"

"Yes."

Wolf looked at her quizzically, then reached out his hand.

"You've left out something important," Holm says.

She remembers: Wolf didn't release her hand straight away. "A name like yours can break you. My daughter has her own opinion on the matter. Your name can't be the reason why you're going. Are you sure that isn't the case?"

"My name has nothing to do with it," Aaron replied. And she knew that Wolf didn't believe her.

"I'm waiting," Holm says.

"I wanted to demonstrate whose daughter I was."

"That's the first true sentence that I've heard from you in this basement. You see, yesterday all that was missing. But now I'm giving you back your memories. They won't be the last." He leaves the words hanging in the air like a death sentence. "I didn't care about Alina. She was the property of a man from the middle ranks of the Nikulinskaya. A silly flibbertigibbet. But I knew her brother very well. And so did you."

*Fyodor. A Maths genius.*

*He was the most handsome and the most lonely person I've ever seen.*

He had developed an algorithm for calculating the maximum profit on trade in raw materials. Fyodor was indispensable to Nikulin. He knew a lot about his business deals. Most of it repelled him. Alina introduced him to Aaron. He liked her sad eyes. And she liked his. When she told the Moscow FBI resident about Fyodor, he gasped with excitement. "Whatever it takes, make him cooperate with us."

"My father ruled over his empire like a Tsar. He was unassailable. Until you came to Moscow and prostituted yourself to take everything away from him."

"You see me as a whore? Like your brother does? Yes, I slept with Fyodor. When he was very unhappy. And I was too. Because the man who saw Alina as his possession slit her open from belly to throat the night before. Because he'd taken some kind of drug. Or because she'd spoken out of turn. Or maybe just because he felt like it. That was why Fyodor clung to me and confided in me. But she was just a silly little girl."

She hears him breathing for a minute. It sounds like gravel sliding from a tipper truck. Then he asks: "Did you see my father back then?"

*I remember that too.*

"Once. The man who owned Alina was invited to a birthday party in the Petrovsky Palace. She took me along too, her German friend with the platinum credit card, and no one was suspicious of me. Women were part of the backdrop at the Nikulinskaya; they were displayed like a gleaming car or a gem-studded watch, but you know that. Nikulin held court in another room. His sidekicks sat around him, boring him with their eagerness. You can judge the status of a man by the number of his lackeys. I went with my father to state receptions where presidents attracted less attention. When I'd freshened up, Nikulin approached me in the corridor. His shoes shone like mirrors, his expression was quizzical. If the FBI agent had been there he would have drooled. But in Nikulin's eyes I saw the cruelties that are supposedly alien to you. I would never have got into that cold bed. Alina was butchered that night. Fyodor was transferred to an FSB safe house. He only agreed to be questioned by me. I had to stay there for two days. The longest of my life."

"You knew my father had put a price on your head."

"Yes. Where were you? I'd taken Fyodor away from him. Didn't I deserve to be killed by his son?"

"I was in St. Petersburg."

"I'm sure you've often regretted that."

"You wouldn't believe how often."

"The guy in the underground car park was enough for me. I haven't missed a thing."

"You knew he'd be waiting there."

"Yes."

"And you still went."

"I don't like standing people up."

"Still as arrogant as ever. You fired a bullet into his brain even though he was kneeling defenselessly in front of you after taking a shot to the belly. Don't deny it, it's in your notes. Who was the hitman? Him or you?"

"Did you know him? Was he your friend?"

"What did you say?"

"I asked if he was your friend."

*Auditory disturbances. The next symptom.*

Holm laughs. Again a rock comes away above a chasm. "He wanted to ingratiate himself with my father, and lay your corpse at his feet like a mouse. Do you think I would respect someone like that? He died like a mouse, quite rightly. But in the Hotel Aralsk you didn't prove that you were your father's daughter. Just that you were a coward."

Ten cowardly things that Aaron has done:
Barcelona

"You asked why I shot the teacher. For just one reason: because it was completely pointless. Like what you did in the underground car park."

"You sadistic bastard! It isn't that I think I'm superior to you, it's that you think you're superior to the whole world! If someone jostled you in the street, you'd cut their heart out and say they deserved it! You haven't understood a single one of the books that you've read! You haven't even understood that there isn't the slightest difference between you and your brother!"

She feels it coming and throws herself sideways, but the butt of his gun catches her on the ear. A mechanism starts up in her head and catapults her at hyperspeed through a worm-hole of myriads of colors. She sees galaxies that are the bat of an eyelash, suns emerging from the dust of dying stars and fading away again; she plunges into the storm of spiral nebulas, into the intensity of a pain that makes her eyes explode.

At first she thinks it's her own whimpering. Then she realizes that it's coming from someone else. Vera. Holm has clubbed her, just as he clubbed Eva Askamp. Vera lies at his feet, choking on her terror.

"I chose the same way as you. The way of honor. Who was my prince?"

"Nikulin."

"I'll count to ten. If you don't give me the right answer I'll kill the woman. One."

"Your father!" she shrieks.

"Two."

"Other people's fear!"

"Three."

"The hatred of all possessions!"

"Four."

"Please! I want to answer all the questions honestly!"

"Five."

"Fyodor!"

"Six."

"Your brother!"

"Seven."

"If you do this, I'll have been completely correct!"

"Eight."

"Violence is your prince!"

"Nine."

A storm rages in Aaron's head, blowing Holm's words ahead of it like leaves: *Time for us to talk about loss—how to close the eyes of a loved one—being able to stand by a grave without despairing of the question as to why you aren't lying there yourself—no pain could be so great that it would be worth hiding.*

"I'm waiting."

"Your prince was a woman."

For a very long time her heartbeat and Holm's breathing and Vera's whimpering are the only sounds.

"Right," he whispers at last. "Let's take a break."

Sascha hears the basement door opening. In the hallway he sees his brother with Aaron and the other woman. Sascha barely recognizes him. He seems to have aged ten years. Gray sweat lies on his brother's ravaged features. His eyes cower dully in their sockets. Even the tattoos on his bare torso have lost their color.

His brother totters, supports himself on the wall and tries to look at him, but his eyes slide away.

"I need Aaron," Sascha says.

Holm waits until his brother has pushed the two women into the kitchen, then follows them. When he crept half-dead from the Havel, fell into the snow and didn't know how to get back on his feet, it was easier than it is now.

# 32

"Put me through to the Department," Token-Eyes says.

Vera is sitting beside Aaron at the kitchen table. She isn't making a sound, she isn't even shivering. That unsettles Aaron more than tears, pleading, a scream. She needs this woman. Somewhere in the house there is a weapon that no one else knows about. A weapon that everything might depend upon. A weapon that Aaron can't get to. As long as she doesn't know the truth about Barcelona, Holm can feel safe. He's proved that to her. After that, Vera is her only hope of survival. But if she stays like this Aaron won't be able to get through to her.

Bosch stands by her side. His sweat smells like sour milk. Holm is sitting opposite her. That thing that sounds like faint snoring is his breath. His circulation is going haywire. Presumably he is already suffering from balance disorders.

Token-Eyes has turned on his speakerphone.

Because *he* is in the room.

Holm leaves the negotiating up to him. Token-Eyes could have the discussion without him, but he doesn't dare. He sees the state his brother is in, even though he can't explain it. Never has it been easier to kill him, to savor that thing he has dreamed of since he was eight years old, when Holm lay bleeding in front of him. But Aaron knows that Token-Eyes' fear of his brother will end only with his brother's last breath. No, not even then.

"Demirci."

"What's the whore worth to you?"

"Who are you talking about?" Demirci's voice rings out.

*That's not operation headquarters.*

It could be a bunker, a hall, a warehouse with a concrete or stone floor, a high ceiling, bare walls.

*A hangar. They got my message.*

Relief carries Aaron over the abyss of her despair like a glider.

"Who indeed," says Token-Eyes.

"You've had five million."

"So?"

Demirci's voice is as relaxed as if she were ordering a pizza. Aaron knows how much strength of will it must take. "I want to talk to your brother."

"You're talking to me. If that doesn't suit you I'll hang up and shoot the blind bat in the head. No, I've got a better idea. I'll blow her brains out first, then I'll hang up."

"Prove she's alive."

"One word out of place from the bitch and I'll poke the other woman's eyes out. That'll give them something to talk about."

"I'm fine," Aaron says. "There's a second hostage."

Demirci has startled her several times today. But nothing like this. "I'm sorry, I've got a meeting. Talk to Mr. Pavlik."

Even Holm holds his breath.

"Here I am," Pavlik says. "What do you want?"

Just the sound of his voice! Aaron's glider finds the updraft, rises high into an endless sky, above the clouds, leaves the abyss far below.

"Has she lost her mind?" Token-Eyes says, regaining the power of speech.

"You'll have to make do with me. So?"

"Five million. Used. Small denominations."

"Have you spent the money already? I hope you spent it on something sensible. Brain surgery?" Pavlik asks.

"Either you pay up or tomorrow you'll have big headlines: '*Department Sacrifices Blind Heroine.*' Is that what you want?"

"You know we're not going to give you another five million. So get thinking. And chin up: you can make a lot out of not very much. Suggestion: call me if anything happens."

Pavlik hangs up.

She imagines Token-Eyes' face. Again she thinks about the furious boy sitting under the Christmas tree. She knows what Demirci and Pavlik are doing. They want Token-Eyes to believe that her life is much less valuable than he thought, that those five million were paid for the schoolchildren and not for Aaron. She was making it clear to him that he isn't negotiating from a position of strength, thus raising his inhibition threshold for doing something to her. It's only absurd at first glance. She's all Token-Eyes has. If you were rich once and you're suddenly reduced to poverty, you learn to value the little you have left. During her time in the Department the tactic was often used successfully in ransom demands. The "Lissek maneuver."

*And once we failed.*

It's risky. She feels cold. If her life is seen as being of so little value, how insignificant is Vera's?

She imagines Token-Eyes looking at his brother.

Holm struggles through the words. "You have never taken an interest in economics. Otherwise you would know that the burned money doesn't represent a loss for the Berlin Senate." His lung rattles. He pauses, then starts again. "As if they had never paid it. It was just paper. They just need proof." Again he breaks off and collects himself. "On the other hand you have Miss Aaron. It's up to you whether you want to let them go on treating you like a… like a schoolboy and…"

He lacks the strength to carry on.

Bosch still hasn't said a word. But it smells as if the sour milk has been heated up.

Token-Eyes paces up and down, and stops behind Aaron.

"Then we can get rid of this one too," he barks.

Aaron knows he doesn't mean her, he means Vera, that he has drawn the Glock and wants to kill Vera, that he needs this the way other people need headache tablets. She pushes her knee against the edge of the table and topples over on her chair. At the same time she shoots her leg up vertically and strikes Token-Eyes on the head. She feels a stinging pain in her ankle. Aaron tries to straighten up, but can't do it quickly enough to dodge the kick that Token-Eyes has aimed at her chin. He grabs her by the throat and begins to strangle her. Her bound hands wrap around his neck. She jerks her arms down and feels him somersaulting. Aaron throttles him with the cable tie and presses her knee against his throat.

And stops abruptly. The muzzle of the Glock 33 presses against a spot between her collarbones. "Not what I expected," Token-Eyes chokes from under her knee. "But the hell with it."

The gun goes off.

Holm has fired. Aaron hears the Glock clattering to the floor. She tries to reach for it, touches it with her fingertips, but the gun skitters over the tiles when Bosch kicks it away.

Token-Eyes wails like an animal.

There is a slight strain in his brother's voice. "You have three possibilities: complain about your little scratch. Pick up the Glock and try to kill me. Or call the Department. I'm fine with any of those."

Aaron pulls one of Token-Eyes' teeth out of her foot. She straightens and places herself in front of Vera to protect her, going into the attack position opposite Token-Eyes. Her legs are about to give. A gate bangs in the wind behind the house. Once, twice, three times. Nothing else.

Token-Eyes rises to his feet. Groans. Takes the phone. "Put me through to the Department."

The sound of the gate again. Aaron thinks about Pavlik and knows how hard it must be for him to leave Token-Eyes floundering. At last he speaks: "I'm all ears."

"The five million has been burned."

"Were you cold?"

"I can prove it."

"Have you got it on video?"

Aaron gets a shove. "Tell him, you piece of shit."

"It's true. I was there."

"They're holding a gun to your head. That's not proof."

"I'll throw her body out of the car somewhere. You'll find the ashes of the money during the autopsy. I'll force the whore to eat them. Then you'll have your proof."

"Let's just do some calculations for a second. This morning your brother had thirty hostages, and we paid five million for those. Now you've got two. Mathematically speaking that makes, just a second, three hundred and thirty-three thousand. I don't want to cheat anybody, so I'll round it up, seeing as we're all friends."

"You've got ten seconds and then I'm putting the phone down."

"I'm a good person," Pavlik murmurs. "A million. Non-negotiable. Take it or leave it."

Vera sobs. Aaron finds that strangely reassuring.

Token-Eyes lets the gate bang four times.

"You have two hours to get us the money."

"And then?"

"We'll dump them somewhere."

"Sure. And I'm Father Christmas."

"Two hours." Token-Eyes ends the call.

It's only then that Aaron notices that she's bitten her lip till it bleeds.

In the hangar Demirci feels the men's eyes on her. She shivers in her lined coat. She knows: everyone is waiting for Senator Svoboda to call. Instead she turns to the screen showing Berlin HQ. "Mr. Majowski, how much counterfeit money do we have in the evidence locker?"

"About two million Euros."

"Have a million put in a bag with a tracking device. Prepare Delmonte and Büker for the handover."

Majowski is speechless.

"Have we had reception problems?"

"No," he says, composing himself.

Demirci avoids making eye contact with the others and walks quickly to the end of the hall. She opens the door to a narrow corridor. Closes it. Sits down on the floor, leans her head against the wall. Minutes pass. Pavlik comes. He sits down beside Demirci and holds out his pack of cigarettes. They smoke in silence, down to the filter.

Then Demirci says: "Jenny Aaron and Svoboda have a score to settle. She reminded him of that today. He won't authorize any more money. When she's dead he'll sigh with relief."

"Don't worry about it. Her life doesn't depend on a million or a billion. Sascha doesn't make the decisions, and his brother didn't care about the money from the get-go. I could have told him to fuck off as well."

"They burned the money. How come?"

"It was either Aaron or Holm. That would be his style. To demonstrate that he's finished with everything."

"Do you think he wants to die?" Demirci says, sitting up.

"For thirty years he's invisible. But all of a sudden he sends us his fingerprints. Why?"

"And the chartered plane for three?"

"To reassure Bosch. Holm never intended to get on that plane."

"Or else Finow was just a distraction. They might have left the country long ago."

"No. They were in Freienhagen. That's just off the freeway, on the way here. The airfield remains an option for Sascha and Bosch. Holm will let them get on with it. He's only interested in Jenny Aaron. Once he's taken his revenge, he will kill himself."

"Why should he do that?"

"His references to Bushidō. At first I thought he was only talking about her. Not anymore. He lives by its rules just as she does. At any rate that's what he imagines, however insane it might be." Pavlik fumbles a cigarette from the pack and rolls it between his fingers before putting it back. "I think I know what's in the bag that he carries with him."

Demirci gives him a questioning look.

"A *seppuku* dagger."

Her hands are so cold that she has to stick them in her coat pockets. "What reasons did the Samurai have for doing such a thing? Do you know about it?"

"Only what Aaron has told me. Infringement of the code, loss of face, to honor the prince. I'm sure there are others."

"And she follows those laws?"

"I've never really tried to understand."

"So then in her eyes André deserved to die."

Pavlik nods vaguely.

"And in yours?"

"No, it was just money."

"Kvist clearly saw things differently."

"He shot him in self-defense."

"I've read the Internal Affairs report. They were very dubious. It was a second-class acquittal."

"André died for one reason alone," he shouts at her. "Because I was a coward and Kvist wasn't!"

"I knew your twin brother," Demirci sad. "At first glance it's barely possible to tell you apart. We didn't get off to a good start, but then he became a big support to me and my most important adviser. He was a stranger to self-pity. If you ever see him again, tell him I miss him."

"He can fuck off."

They gauge each other for a moment.

Nowak opens the door. "You need to listen to this."

They follow him to the hangar. The picture and sound of the video display are out of sync. Majowski's voice follows his lips after a short delay. In the pauses between the sentences it looks as if he's repeating the last words he said, and can't quite believe them. "Mertsch and Stemmler took over the surveillance of Kvist thirty minutes ago. He caught up with the train at the Buckower Chaussee crossing. He accelerated to the other side, right in front of it. They couldn't keep up with him. They've just found his car on the Fritz-Erler-Allee. His phone was in it."

"You've lost Kvist?"

"Yes."

Demirci looks at Pavlik. Something falls from his face, like a stone that has just been hit with a hammer.

Vera has been crying until just now. All Aaron could do in that cramped box-room was to rest her head against Vera's, to feel her fighting for each breath, stiffly swallowing her tears. Now Vera is so drained that she's choking on mucus.

"Where's the revolver?" Aaron whispers.

No answer.

"In the bedroom?"

Vera tries to weep again, but all that emerges is a lengthy wail.

"I'd like to get an idea of the house. Will you help me?"

Silence.

"Give me a guided tour. You can do that."

"Maybe." Vera's breathing is short.

"How many rooms are there on the ground floor?"

Vera thinks. "Kitchen—guest toilet—dining room—front room—this box-room—office—hunting room." The biblical Aaron could have cast the Golden Calf in the time it took her to deliver the list.

"Now I'd like you to imagine the paces you would need to take. A completely normal, unhurried walk through the house, no hurry." Every pace takes half a meter. "We'll start in the kitchen, because I know it. Where do I go next?"

"The corridor."

"And then?"

"The guest toilet—I think it's nine paces. Yes, nine."

"Go on."

"From there you go into the dining room. It's a long corridor. Wait—I can't say exactly, it's hard if you just imagine it. But if I had to give a figure I'd say twenty paces." Vera's voice becomes firmer, picks up speed. The task that Aaron has given her helps her to think of something other than her parting from her husband this morning, not a good one, no kiss, just because of his moth-eaten favorite pair of trousers which she secretly threw away. "The corridor bends on the left. The box-room is there. Twelve. Another little way and you reach the front room on the right. Nine—no, more like eight. But you can also go through the dining room."

"You're doing a great job. Let's go into the dining room from the corridor. How many paces to the front room?"

"Just a moment—ten, I'd say. On the left."

"Is there anything in the way?"

"No. That is, there's a bearskin with the head on." Vera's account is becoming increasingly lively. "Klaus is very proud of that, he shot it in Canada. I tripped over it and, snap, there went its jaw. I fixed it with superglue, and Klaus never noticed. You're best off sticking to the wall."

"A grizzly?"

"No, a brown bear."

"Where's the revolver?"

Aaron senses Vera stiffening, and goes on talking. "We're in the front room now. How is it furnished?"

Silence next to her.

"I'm sure you've got lovely furniture."

Vera battles to give her an answer. "Biedermeier."

"Three-piece suite?"

"A sofa and two chairs. A television. Dresser on the left. From the dining room you get straight for the French windows on to the terrace."

"How big is the room? In paces?"

Vera walks across it in her mind. "Quite big. Twelve to the French windows, fourteen in the other direction."

"Where's the office?"

"Behind the hunting room. Oh yes, the door also leads on to the corridor, I forgot, sorry." Vera's voice wanders along an empty channel of tears. "And that one leads to the basement."

"How many paces from the kitchen to the office?"

"Just a moment, I'll have to start again from the beginning, I'm getting very confused."

Aaron doesn't press her.

"Twelve. On the right. Straight ahead is the corridor with the front door. And the stairs. Seven, I would guess."

Aaron knows the way into the house through the hall into the kitchen, just as she knows the way to the box-room and the basement. Vera only ever miscalculated by a single pace. But for Aaron a pace could mean the difference between life and death. "I want to go back into the front room. There's a dresser, you say. And the other furniture?"

"A sideboard and a chest of drawers."

"On which wall?"

"On the right. So not where the chest of drawers is. The other one on the right."

"Carpets?"

"Velvet."

"Where is the revolver?"

"They'll get their money. They'll let us go. You heard."

"He's lying."

"How do you know? If you go on asking about the revolver I'm not saying another word."

"Let's go into the office. What's in there?"

Vera reflects that her husband didn't beep his horn when he drove away as he usually did. And he didn't wave.

"But there must be a desk?"

"On the right by the window," she answers mechanically. "A shelf of files. Lino. All the way through the hunting room. Eight. That's where the antlers are. All in green, not to everyone's taste. In the middle there's a big table for the hunters. And a fine rug. There's a beer pump and the weapons cabinet."

"Where's the revolver?"

# 33

A SMALL animal flies into the thicket, a wildcat or a raccoon. It leaves an excited zigzag in the snow that glimmers green in the display of the infrared goggles. Crystals spray from the trees. The wind is coming from the east with the moonlight, just under fifty kilometers an hour. The cry of an owl is followed by the sound of a jaybird's imitation; it sounds as if it is returning the call, when in fact it is mocking it.

As he creeps through the undergrowth he listens to the duel, which the owl will lose. He is wearing a ghillie suit, and the hood of the shaggy camouflage fatigues is pulled down so far over his head that he can only see his surroundings through slits. His footsteps are slow but fluid. He sets down the outside of his feet first, and then rolls them inwards to avoid making a sound by breaking twigs. He has covered a kilometer like this over the last hour, he has left the solar panels behind and finally climbed the hill where the Fords are waiting under their snow-covered nets.

He creeps the last few meters, hugging the ground, pushing himself along with one leg. His head leans to one side, his cheek touches the snow. Before each movement his hands feel their way through the undergrowth and gently move aside anything that could make a sound, however faint. He advances inch by inch, taking four minutes to cover the short distance to the hilltop. He drags his rifle with him, holding the strap between thumb and index finger. There is a condom over the muzzle of the Barrett Light Fifty to keep out the snow.

Pavlik removes the infrared goggles. He takes the white roll mat out from under his ghillie suit and wriggles on to it. When he was here with Kemper a few hours ago he saw the boulder he would use as a rest for the Light Fifty. He mounts the silencer and covers it with the condom to keep condensation from collecting inside it. He wraps the barrel loosely with a bandage. He focuses through the night sights on the hill on the other side of the runway, the clearing there. It's a popular picnic spot in the summer because of the panoramic view over the airfield. A sign exhorts visitors to keep their dogs on a lead. He can read the text very clearly, from what must be eleven hundred meters. The rangefinder shows one thousand and ninety-nine.

The questions were simple: what would he do if he had chartered a plane and didn't want the Department to find out about it? Someone will have to scout out the airfield. Who? Certainly not Holm. Sascha would be unlikely. Bosch. He is the most dispensable, and he knows his way around airfields. When? Not before one o'clock in the morning. Where? From the point with the best view.

Pavlik had considered lying in wait on the other side. But an exchange of fire would have been too great a risk. He needs Bosch alive, it's the only way he can force him to give away his hiding place. That's why he comes up with another plan; for that he needs the Light Fifty with the silencer, the distance is too great for the Mauser.

His eyes had become accustomed to the infrared goggles, and now they have to get used to the darkness once again. He knows it will be thirty minutes before they have fully adapted. Pavlik deliberately looks at the target window using only his peripheral vision; in that way he stimulates the photo-receptors on the edge of the retina, the ones responsible for night vision.

"Fear dusk, not night." The old sharpshooter proverb has entered his blood.

While he was climbing the hill, it stopped snowing. But blustery clouds are still drifting in the sky, and could break at any moment. The snow he is lying on, the snow that covers everything, is his friend, because it illuminates the night. Pavlik takes this fine snow into his mouth to cool his breath, so that it won't give him away. But the other snow, the snow coming from the clouds, is his enemy, it obstructs his vision, it plays temperamentally with gunfire. He is also concerned about the wind. It can determine speed and direction for fifty meters at the most, and he doesn't have precise knowledge about the conditions on the other side of the slope. The tree-tops that bend gently at the edge of the glade don't tell him much; even a deviation of five kilometers an hour alters the ballistics of a bullet.

Without his noticing, under his ghillie suit his left hand plays with the cartridge case that Helmchen gave him. Eighteen years. Every hour of those years lies deep in his bones. He knows he somehow has to stay awake.

Before he set off, he called Sandra. So many times he was grateful to her during those calls for never showing him how worried she was, and for not wanting to give him further cause for anxiety. Rather than firing questions at him, she talked about their daughter, about how she had drunk her fill and was now fast asleep, how sweet she looked with her favorite toy in her hand. *Her* name was never mentioned. And why would it have been? Sandra knows he would give his life for Aaron. She doesn't need to waste another word on the subject. If it happened, she would only scream at night. But then she would wrap Aaron in her arms and grieve with her.

There was another name that his wife did utter. She said something that made him think for several minutes, crouching on the concrete floor, eyes closed, smoking.

"When he came back from Barcelona, you invited him to our house. You were in the cellar fetching beer, I was alone with him for a few moments. He couldn't look at me for a second."

Pavlik remembers that evening. Sandra went to bed early. She took a tablet so that she could get to sleep, as she had done for six months. He was sitting with Kvist on the porch swing in the snowy garden. They emptied a case of Beck's and only opened their mouths to drink. Eventually Kvist got up to go to the toilet, or so Pavlik thought. But when he checked ten minutes later he had disappeared.

They had always said goodbye the same way.

*See you, Don Pavlik.*

*See you, Don Kvist.*

Not this time.

He wraps his fist around the cartridge. How many nights pass in eighteen years? One of those, the last one, will decide whether everything else was right or in vain. Whether he has to give his life or take the life of the man who was his best friend.

The black spot that is starting to dance in front of his right eye tells him to close it for several seconds because it is overtaxed. So quickly. Ringing Sandra again would be pointless. Pavlik's attention would wane; he would become sad, because at such times he wonders whether he might be hearing her voice for the last time. Without planning to do so, he always ends those phone calls with a word that sounds like a farewell, a sentence in which Sandra might later be able to find consolation. It used to be: "Give Jenny a kiss from me and whisper to her that she makes her father very happy."

She knows that. But they've never talked about it.

He ties on the mouthguard of the ghillie suit, puts in the earpiece of his phone and calls Demirci.

She picks up immediately. "Yes?"

"Tell me something," he whispers. "Ask a question that will make me think. Or else let's just chat." He is careful to bring his voice down an octave, keep the vowels short, lisp the sibilants.

*Let'th jutht chat.*

"Just a moment."

A door opens, and closes. He knows she's in the corridor now, undisturbed. "What did you think when you heard you were getting a female boss?"

He laughs silently. "I said to Lissek: 'He was good. Have you another one like that?'"

"Not enough testosterone?"

"What nonsense. Aaron was with us. And she has the biggest balls outside a bowling alley. Without wanting to tread on your toes."

"So what was it?"

"Half of your job is politics. Our arses depend on it. Those guys in their pinstripes have more swagger than any of us. Well, maybe not more, but different. I wasn't sure whether you would be taken seriously and whether you'd be able to watch our backs. But today I know the answer to that one."

"But you didn't think that much of me."

"I know you think that, but you're mistaken. Before you came, I did some digging. A mate of mine, Jan Pieper, a head honcho at the BKA, knew something about your time in Dortmund. Abdul Öymen."

"What did he tell you?"

"Öymen collected protection money right across the Ruhr. You investigated him in relation to thirteen murder cases; the victims included women and children, but you couldn't hang anything on him. One evening you strolled into his local, where he was sitting at a table with eight men, and told him in front of all the guests, probably in excellent Turkish, that he was a total coward and his cock would fit in a matchbox. Öymen followed you into the street. He wanted to hit you. The special unit that you brought with you temporarily held him for attempted bodily harm. They didn't even question him. But that same night you had your informers spread the word that he had squealed on his own people. The next day his lawyer got him out of jail. Six hours later Öymen's corpse was drifting in the Ruhr with a bullet to the back of the neck. Dortmund's supposed to be a quiet little spot these days."

"You were fed complete lies."

"Ah."

"Yes. I told him his cock would fit in a thimble, and there would still be enough room for his brain."

"I thought you were a lady."

"I thought you wouldn't remind me."

"Do you do parties?"

This time it's Demirci who laughs quietly.

"I like that," Pavlik murmurs.

"What?"

"When you laugh. Do it more often."

"I like it when you lisp."

"And I had elocution lethonth and everything."

Her tone changes. "I'm sorry about what I said about your twin brother."

"That's OK. I can't stand the old whiner."

"The fact that Kvist has disappeared doesn't prove anything."

"Now you're being sentimental."

He hears a voice in the background. Nowak.

"Just a second," Demirci says. She holds her hand over the phone. The snow in Pavlik's mouth melts. Then she's back on the line. "Sascha has told us the handover terms. Regional Express Berlin–Angermünde. Leaves in fifty-seven minutes. He'll let us know when and where the bag is to be thrown from the train."

"Does that line go past Finow?"

"I don't know yet. I'll call you."

By now they've walked through the house four times in their heads. All the paces on the ground floor and the first floor, thirteen steps, stone, a bend to the right after eight. They lead to the bedroom and the guest room, to Vera's room, her refuge where she likes to sit and read actors' biographies, then to an ironing room. There's no loft extension. Aaron knows where each lamp stands or hangs, she knows the furniture, the floorings, the rugs, the color of the curtains. If the door to the box-room was open, they could run off and probably reach every room, every item of furniture, without bumping into things more than once or twice.

But Vera still hasn't told her where the revolver is.

There's a second room, too, Aaron's inner room. In there, she was thinking. She would hide the gun somewhere where she could get hold of it straight away if she had to. A burglar, at night. So she decided on the bedroom a long time ago. The only issue was the side Vera's husband was on. Just on the left of the door. But: under the bed or in the bedside table? There's a huge difference; Aaron will have only a fraction of a second to decide where she's going to reach.

A car drives out of the courtyard. A powerful engine, in a low gear.

"How many cars have you got?" she whispers.

"Three. My runabout, a Mazda—I like nippy little cars—our van and Klaus's jeep."

*The transporter we came in.*

*Or the van.*

"But Klaus is away in the jeep." Vera finds a few tears she had forgotten. "If you'd seen his old trousers, I'm sorry. All the things he'd done in those. Chopping up deer, clearing the stable, driving to the bait shop. And you could tell. He even wore them at the dinner table. And the stench of them. You'd have thrown them away just as I did, wouldn't you?"

"Did he wear them when he cleaned the revolver? The one he kept in his bedside table drawer."

She can tell by Vera's twitching, her vain attempt to shift away from Aaron in that cramped space, her suddenly quick breathing, that she's hit the bull's eye.

"It's fine. Don't worry."

"Please don't do that," Vera begs.

Aaron wants to calm her down, reassure her that she won't make her go and get the weapon, but the door to the room opens quietly. Token-Eyes' smell hits her nostrils. She senses a rapid movement. Vera sighs. The door is closed and locked again, just as quietly as before.

"Vera?"

Not a sound.

Aaron's voice fades away. "Vera? Vera, please say something."

Trembling, her bound hands search the lifeless body beside her. Vera's ribcage is soaking.

Aaron smells the blood. She screams and screams and screams.

He dreamed that Sascha was four, and wanted a toy bulldozer for Christmas, but got only shoes and coloring pencils and a sketch pad. He dreamed that the man who had once called himself father first pushed Sascha down the steps two days after Christmas. But when the man who had once called himself father opened the door, standing behind it was the one the man had called son, the one the man had taught how to use a chainsaw. He cut the man who had once called himself father in two down the middle. The two parts fell to the ground to the right and left, and there was a stream on the ground that washed them away. He hugged his brother and heard him say: "I wasn't scared, because I knew you would protect me." He dreamed that they drove into town with their mother and she bought Sascha three scoops of ice-cream and him a new shirt. That they ate something with ketchup when they got home and a crow pecked at the window.

He dreamed that his brother watched him as he slept.

That Aaron jabbed a finger between his ribs in the river and he had to rest on the floor beside the little room until the Touch of Death let go of him.

*Now.*

That Aaron was screaming.

He wakes up, but doesn't yet open his eyes. He sits up, hears Aaron sobbing behind the door to the room, and knows what his brother has done.

Holm flexes his muscles, feels them obeying him, flowing, filling his tattoos.

He goes into the kitchen. Sascha is sitting at the table smoking. Holm sees his brother enjoying every drag. He'll hold out for five minutes, maybe ten. Sascha doesn't look up. He's with him in three paces that might just as well be one. He bangs Sascha's head so hard against the tabletop that smears of blood are left when he pulls his brother up by the hair and throws him in the corner. Before Sascha can reach for his Glock, Holm is kneeling beside him with the Remington in his hand, forcing him to open his mouth. He pokes in the barrel of the gun until Sascha chokes.

"It would have been better if our father had killed you so that you could never remind me of my guilt. I'm paying off that debt now by letting you leave this house alive. Get your money. If you come back, I will choose for you one of the deaths that I dreamed up and rejected for Aaron."

He pulls the Remington very slowly out of his brother's mouth. His eyes are two bottomless pits.

Sascha somehow drags himself up. He dodges his brother's eyes like a dog dodging a stick. The front door closes. Holm stands still, in a different time, until he hears Sascha driving away in the Mazda.

He goes to the door and opens it.

Aaron flies at him.

He effortlessly stabilizes her double knife hand, crashes his fists into her kidneys, grabs her and throws her back into the room. She lies next to the dead woman. Holm can see her tears.

He sits down in the corridor. His thoughts are as clear and calm as the sea after a storm. So he speaks: "I am following the seventh virtue by being loyal beyond death. I respect the sixth virtue by acting honorably to the last. The fifth virtue commands that the truth be told. I have always done that too. In line with the fourth virtue I call you 'Miss Aaron' and not by the name that I want to give you. The third I showed with the coat that I wrapped you in when you were cold. I have just discovered how heavy the second weighs. Freeing myself from my brother took more courage than anything else. But the first is the most important. Righteousness. That virtue led you to stand by the bus open-armed. It forced me to acknowledge that I loved Ilya Nikulin's daughter. His little Natashenka, his everything. Even though I knew he would never allow me to spend a happy minute with her. He had sacrificed his son and seen his eldest daughter die. His greatest fear was that he would have to close Natalya's eyes as well; so he concealed the fact that she was his daughter. Like the man I liquidated for him in London, she led an inconspicuous life under another name. Nikulin gave her a legal business that had nothing to do with his own dealings. He also insisted that she was only employed there for show; that was how scared he was. Righteousness also includes justice. You knew Natalya. Because she was the woman you killed in the underground car park of the Hotel Aralsk."

# 34

"The railway is just five kilometers from the airfield," Demirci tells him. "It leads through the Barnimer Heide, a huge area of woodland. Seven villages in a radius of fifteen kilometers, lots of remote farmhouses. The Federal Police are on a state of alert, but I've told them to keep a low profile. It would take days to comb those woods, apart from the fact that we'd just startle Holm."

Pavlik would have done exactly the same. He knows that everything will be decided here in Finow, between the hill that he is lying on and the one on the other side, the clearing that he is endlessly staring at. His pupils contract painfully. Demirci's voice is the only reason not to give in to the temptation of closing his eyes for several minutes. She told him how she grew up, a Turkish girl in a small town in Hessen in the seventies; about the mockery of the other children—"garlic eater," "wog"—about the teachers who immediately put her in the back row, her first proper friend at twelve, the daughter of an Italian guest-worker, the parents who taught her to be proud of her origins, police academy—"what's someone like that doing here?"—her colleagues at her first posting in Koblenz whose idea of a joke was to hang a headscarf in her locker, her obsessive desire to be the best.

Pavlik thinks of Aaron, and how similar the two women are.

"My superior officer's name was Himmler," she says. "He never considered changing it, he was above all that. Once when I had a fit of the blues, he said: 'Who knows anything about you? A handful of people. No one else cares.' And I had to—"

"Psst," he interrupts her. Blackbirds are chattering in the glade. Blackbirds are reliable warning signs. Pavlik turns into the path that leads to the viewpoint. No headlights, no engine noises. When he aims his sights into the glade again, a fox jumps out from under a picnic bench. It looks straight into Pavlik's goggles; he can see how disappointed the fox is to have revealed itself.

*We both know that feeling, my friend. But you aren't going to give up and neither am I.*

"False alarm."

"There's something else I've been wanting to ask you for ages," Demirci says. "Why were you so cold with me when I took up the job? I held out my hand, but you walked right past me without a word. Was it something personal, or did you suddenly feel wrong-footed?"

Pavlik says nothing.

"Stupid joke, sorry."

"No, I tell the best one-legged joke myself." She hears him breathing gently.

After a long time he says: "In November MI5 came to us. They suspected a 'Real IRA' cell of financing their war on the British presence in Ulster by arms-dealing, and created the story that a German was interested in doing a deal with them. Lissek sent me to Belfast. Have you ever been there?"

"No."

"Wouldn't bother. It says in the papers that the war is over. Not true. The cell was small, intelligent and suspicious. But my prosthesis was the perfect disguise, as it so often is. I managed to win their trust. They only talked to me about politics. I didn't have to make too much of an effort to share many of their views, although maybe not all of them. Don't these men have the right to fight for their homeland? What do you think?"

"I'm a Kurd."

"Then we agree. The days turned into weeks. Patrick O'Byrne was their leader, eight years older than me. He wouldn't have got through a doorway, had a chest like a Guinness barrel, a bird could have nested in his curls. I spent long evenings in pubs with him.

Pat wanted to get to know me before he did any deals with me, he wanted to be sure the weapons would be used in a good cause. They weren't the Mafia, they were patriots. He told me what had made him the man he was. Have you heard of Long Kesh?"

"No. What is it?"

"A jail that the British built specially for IRA prisoners. Pat spent five years in there. The warders took away his mattress, his blanket, clothes and shoes, they tied his hands behind his back. They hung a bucket of water in front of the cell window and scattered broken glass on the floor. He was forced to walk barefoot over it so as not to die of thirst. I don't know what it's like for Kurds in Turkish jails, but it can't be much worse."

"You can't build a global empire without a touch of cruelty. And where the Kurds are concerned—a nephew of mine would contradict you."

A snowflake dances into Pavlik's sights. Soon it isn't alone, and loses itself among others. Now what he had feared is happening.

"What is it?" Demirci asks.

"Enemy from above."

She knows immediately what he means. "A lot?"

"Not yet, but soon." His picture distorts, and he corrects his sights. "I told Pat about myself as well. But nothing about Sandra, the twins, the baby. I told him about an empty villa in Düsseldorf, a failed marriage, a son I wasn't allowed to see anymore. When we staggered drunkenly out of the pub and went our separate ways I walked through the Catholic part of the city, screened from the Protestant east by an eight-meter fence. Dogs fought over rubbish. Armoured cars, patrols. I kept thinking I heard footsteps behind me. In the hotel I kept my Walther under my pillow with the safety catch off."

"I know about that operation."

"No, you don't know a thing. Pat hugged me. He wanted to go ahead with the deal. I whispered the truth in his ear. When I saw his face I thought I would shatter into pieces. He left. I flew back to Berlin and told Lissek that MI5 had fallen for some fake information. Sandra asked the right questions: how many brothers and sisters does Pat have? How long has he been married? What sort of music does he like?"

"Has he got any children?"

"John, Seamus and Maria. She's fifteen, she was with her first boy-friend." His mouth is dry and furry. "The next week it was Lissek's farewell party. We got wasted in the Irish Pub, we dragged out all the old stories and swore never to change or forget one another. The last toast was mine: 'May the dead wait for us.' At the same time an SAS team launched an attack in Belfast. Pat was killed in the exchange of fire. I heard about it the next morning. It was the day you took up your post. I drove home and chopped wood. I wanted a new cup-board in the sitting room anyway."

For a minute he stares into the dazzling snow, while Demirci is unable to speak. Then she whispers: "Don't do that to me."

"Chopping wood on police time?"

"You're thinking of stopping. But that's impossible. I can't get by without you."

"When I saw you standing beside Lissek like that with the bouquet in your hand, I thought, if I stop now, then—" He breaks off. "The bouquet that you—bouquet—"

"I hear you."

A moment later he remembers Aaron coming to their house with Kvist for the first time. They sat in the garden. Pavlik went into the kitchen to fetch some ice. On the table was the crumpled paper from the bouquet that Kvist had brought for Sandra. He threw the paper in the bin.

He glanced at the sticker.

*Eva Askamp—World of Flowers.*

"Pavlik?" Demirci asks.

Suddenly the dazzling snow has gone. The moon winks from between ragged clouds. He hears an engine, pivots towards the path across the field and sees the transporter approaching the picnic area with its headlights turned off. The clouds part and the moon grins over the hill. "Contact," Pavlik whispers. He hangs up, takes the con-dom off the muzzle and puts fresh snow in his mouth.

\*

Bosch first stopped to think a few kilometers behind the farmhouse. Holm was ill. Bosch didn't know what had happened to him over the previous few hours, but he doubted that he would survive the night. Then Bosch would be at Sascha's mercy. He wouldn't see any of that million, and he would just have to wait for a bullet.

If he went back to the farm.

What did he cling to in life? The question sounded so simple and was so hard to answer. He couldn't even put on his Sunday suit and buy flowers for Simone and a present for Elias, tell them everything would be fine. What was the point?

He drove on, through snowy woods that looked like the forest in one of the fairytales that he had read to Elias, and stopped for the second time. Perhaps there was still something in life that he clung to, he reflected. Because otherwise he would never have gone with Holm, he would never have taken so many risks. Yes, that seemed to have a logic to it.

He drove along the only road again, and passed through a village where people were leaving a pub. Probably a family party: someone was pulling drunken faces. A car was parked crookedly in the road and Bosch had to wait. A man was having a snowball fight with his son, who was as old as Elias would have been in ten years' time. Bosch saw the father being caught off guard and raising his hand in mock defeat.

On the way out of the village he stopped for the third time. Suddenly he knew that he only wanted the money because he hadn't been treated like someone who had clung to the tail of a helicopter that had been shot down, until he was rescued from the sea; whose friend and colleague Matthias had drowned beside him because his arm had been ripped off and he no longer had the strength to cling on; who had to look his wife in the face when the bandages came off, and could tell by her eyes that she was now repelled by him.

That was why he wanted the money: because it was his due.

And if he had got it, it would have been fine. Once that was clear to him, all his fear evaporated. He knew what he would do. He would collect the Cessna, rise high above the clouds, see the stars and then close his eyes and think of something beautiful. Perhaps that time on the coach when he touched the hand of the little girl with the grip in her hair and smiled at her and she stopped crying.

He stumbles along the path that he knows already because he's been here before; at eight o'clock, he scoured tower, hangar and surrounding buildings through his binoculars and saw no sign that anyone was waiting down there.

Or were they?

He isn't really sure anymore. Has he really been here before?

The transporter is hidden by bushes. Pavlik sees Bosch darting through the moonlight, lying down on a bench and putting on night vision goggles. Pavlik has him in his sights. A minute passes like that. Then Bosch switches position. He searches Pavlik's hill. Pavlik isn't worried in the slightest: the boulder that his gun is resting on protects him from giving off a heat signal. The snow in his mouth stings his teeth but makes his breath invisible. His finger rests on the trigger, his resting pulse is twenty-eight. A doctor would be tempted to declare him dead.

Still crouching, Bosch sits up. Pavlik's finger doesn't move a muscle, he has merged with the gun's hammer.

A shadow leaps at Bosch, apparently hardly touching him. The shadow kneels on him. For a long time. Its face is averted from Pavlik. But he doesn't need to see it. Even if the ginger hair were hidden by a hood he would know who it is. Kvist kills Bosch with a swift punch. When he sprints to the transporter, gets in and turns around, Pavlik swings the barrel of the Light Fifty towards him.

He has known what his target is for hours. A tire. Even before Kvist accelerates, the lights still turned off, Pavlik holds his breath. He can do that for ten seconds until the lack of oxygen creates a barely perceptible quiver. The bumpy path across the field is shielded by hedges, leaving him only a single spot to fire at. A forest cutting, no more than two meters wide. After nine seconds the transporter reaches the spot at high speed. Pavlik's concentration is focused entirely on that moment. Nevertheless, he is surprised by the gunshot, which he unconsciously fired a fraction of a second earlier than planned, so that it was perfect. The bullet strikes the rear tire of the transporter. Most sharpshooters, capable men, would swear that such a hit was impossible. Kvist didn't notice a thing; since it was a full metal jacket, it will take several minutes before the transporter has a flat tire. It leaves the field of vision. Pavlik runs with his rifle to the Fords and with two quick jerks pulls the camouflage netting from one of them. He pulls off his ghillie, jumps behind the wheel and reverses hard.

Aaron's world is small. It consists of the room she is sitting in. Vera's cold body beside her. The endless silence that Holm has bestowed upon her, the silence in response to her unchanging whispered questions: what kind of person was Natalya? For how long had he known that it was Aaron who shot her? What happened in Barcelona?

She has come to believe that she will never hear his voice again, that he will kill her without having told her the truth, casually, as if she were a nuisance, as if she merely got in the way of his grief.

Then Holm breaks the silence: "Her great beauty wasn't the reason I loved her. She had green eyes, like you. But it wasn't that. She revered the Russian poets as I do. But it wasn't that. She could walk into a room, and suddenly you would notice that it had been dark a moment before. But that wasn't it either. It was her twin brother, Anatoly, whom her father had left alone with Ice-Eyes. She could have hated me for what happened. But on the day she found out how he had died I was standing by the shore of the lake in the grounds of the big house, and she came and rested her hand on my cheek and said: 'Now you have a family.'"

Aaron sees his words skipping across the water like stones, and each time they kiss the surface it is a source of pain.

His and hers.

"At that moment I knew what I felt for her. I hid it. Because I had never experienced love my fear of it was as great as my fear of that basement. But once I let my guard down, and my father saw the way I watched Natalya as she put a camellia, her favorite flower, in her hair. His hand weighed heavily on my shoulder. He said: 'You're not allowed to do that.'" Time passes, then the stones start skipping again. "Natalya and I were very young at the time, but my father had already set out my life for me. He didn't ask me if I had understood him. He didn't need to tell me the price for disobedience. In later years Natalya and I saw each other only rarely, at family parties. She always stroked my cheek and smiled. Nothing more than that. But I thought she felt the same thing."

She hears that he wants to sob and can't.

"What was it that killed her? I don't mean your bullet, I'm not blaming you for the ricochet. What really killed her?"

"My ambition," she whispers.

Bright orange muzzle flashes. Aaron flies into the underground car park at the Hotel Aralsk.

The hitman is chasing her through the rows of parked cars. He is fast, an intelligent predator. If she lifts her head for a second he fires. She has a graze wound on her temple, blood is running down her face. There are only four cartridges in her spare magazine, twelve in the magazine of his Glock, even though he has inundated her with a hail of bullets. She dives over a car bonnet, shooting at him as she does so. A bullet catches her mid-leap. Aaron is hurled to the ground. Doesn't feel a thing. She sees him leaving his cover. No rush. He thinks she is dead or unable to move. When she brings up the Browning she takes him by surprise. Her shot is pure recklessness: she aimed at his gun hand. The Glock clatters to the floor. Aaron hears a shout, but not his, she is too dazed to identify it. In a reflex action she fires again, this time aiming at the belly. The man looks startled and falls to his knees. Aaron forces herself to her feet and touches the entry wound in her waist, then the one in her back, and ascertains that the bullet has passed smoothly through. She walks over to the man, bends down and crawls. Stands up again, in excruciating pain, and kicks the Glock away. Only then does she see the woman. She is lying by the entrance to the hotel, motionless, a hole on the side where her heart is, a fountain bubbles.

The man kneels in front of Aaron, presses both hands to his belly, breathes as Niko will breathe in Barcelona. There is a pleading expression on the man's face. She looks down at him, more ruthless than ever before or after, and fires her last bullet between his eyes.

The memory is like a birthmark.

Holm says: "Every time I heard Natalya's voice I also heard my father's. *You're not allowed to do that.* I don't know if she reciprocated my feelings, I don't know what I was more afraid of: her doing so, or me only imagining that she did. Our most tender contact was a kiss on the cheek. I've never been so intimately connected with a woman. Many years passed. I didn't think about her constantly, not for every second of every day, as people do in trashy novels, but sometimes I would be standing in a lift, sitting in a car, lying in bed, and the knowledge that I wasn't allowed to desire her stopped the world and made me furious. Eleven years ago, in the winter, I had a routine matter to sort out. I shot a man who got in our way, in a florist's shop. When he fell, he pulled a pot to the ground with him. It was a white camellia. It lay next to the man, blood flowed from his mouth on to a petal. I stood there for a long time. The owner ran away, I didn't care that he was about to call the police. I suddenly knew I had to make a decision. Wait until I was led away, or confess my love to Natalya. There was no third way." He keeps finding new pebbles. "Have you ever told a man what you feel for him?"

*Too late. In the tunnel it was too late.*

"No."

"Why?"

She can't reply.

"You refused to recognize the man's capacity to love you. You're ashamed now because you knew he was prepared to die to show you his feelings. And yet I was cowardly. The Samurai said that lovers are the boldest people. *Bushi no nasake.* You know what that means."

"The tenderness of the warrior."

"I loved, sincerely, but I lacked the courage to reveal myself only in death. You, meanwhile, were perfectly willing to do just that. And I respect that. I couldn't muster that supreme self-control. Just as I lacked the courage to face Natalya." In the silence a pebble skips ten times before sinking. "I wrote her the only letter I have ever written in my life. It's hard to put words on paper that you have never been able to utter in real life. You know them all, and yet each one is a stranger to you. If I wasn't hoping in vain, she would come to St. Petersburg, run away with me and leave everything behind her. I crept away from my father like a thief. I didn't say goodbye to my brother either. I had given him everything I could. I took nothing with me but clothes. I waited in St. Petersburg for three days and nights. I stood on the bank of the Neva, I saw a big bridge opening for a ship decked with Chinese lanterns, and I waited. I ran down alleyways where strangers were hugging, and I waited. I whispered her name in the darkness of my hotel room and I waited. By the end of the third night I knew she wasn't coming. Again I stood by the Neva. Everything within me was extinguished, and I no longer had a home. Was it like that when you woke up in Barcelona and looked in vain for the world?"

"Yes."

"Four men appeared on the riverbank. They wanted to kill me. When I saw their corpses drifting in the river I came to my senses. Who had sent those men?"

"Nikulin."

"My father. He had intercepted my letter to Natalya, she had never received it. He had been suspicious of me for all those years. I had never been free and I didn't know it. That night you shot Natalya. My phone rang, and I shattered all the mirrors with my gun while my father was doing the same. I flew to Moscow to show him what cruelties I was capable of. But sad-eyed Fyodor had signed his statement, and the arrest warrant against my father had been issued.

There was a technical problem with the plane, so I turned up half an hour late. But I saw him being led to the street in handcuffs. Our eyes met. He could read the message in mine. How did he die?"

"He took his own life in custody. He unscrewed the overflow pipe from his sink, broke a splinter from it and slashed his wrists."

"Didn't that strike you as strange? He had half the judiciary in his pocket, he could easily have got himself acquitted. Suicide? Is that the type of thing he would have done, even if we take into account the death of his Natashenka? No, nothing could ever have swayed that man. After you returned from Russia you were given a medal and a post in the Department. What for? Shooting a woman more loved than you have ever been. For breaking my heart. Otherwise you have achieved nothing. It wasn't you who brought down Ilya Nikulin's empire. I did. I paid two warders in the Butyrka prison to kill him. They let him bleed to death and watched, and I had them tell me what it was like. You should have done that with Boenisch. Believe me, it would have been more satisfying than a shot to the head in the underground car park. It was the last time I touched any of my father's money. I know about all his accounts that no one ever found. There's two billion dollars in Riyadh alone. I would sooner chop one of my hands off than lay a hand on a single cent. Hold out your hands."

She is frozen, trapped in a cocoon of fear.

"Do you really think that's going to be your punishment?"

Quivering, she holds them out to him.

Holm cuts through her bonds. She hears him unbuttoning his shirt. Pausing. "I wanted to show you something. Let your fingers stroke the white camellia on my heart. The camellia I planted on Natalya's grave. But now I don't want your hand to touch my chest again, I couldn't bear it."

Neither could she. But not out of revulsion.

"I've been tormented for so long by the question of whether Natalya would have followed me if she had read the letter. Whether she would still be alive if I had held her in my arms in St. Petersburg that night when you went to the Hotel Aralsk. Whether I was right to kill my father too, or whether he bore no responsibility." Pebbles skip in an endless chain. "Did you hold Natalya in your arms? Did she say anything else? Did she say my name?"

Then Aaron understood. Holm's need for her to remember after all this time is just as great as hers. That's why he told her his story and didn't kill her long ago. So that she will get her memory back. So that she will redeem him. Because he clings desperately to the hope that the woman he loved was thinking of him as she died.

But she doesn't know if that was so. The last image she has from the underground car park is the shot she fired between the hitman's eyes.

"I don't remember," she whispers.

"Let me help you, I know what's blocking you!" Words like ashes. "I have thought ceaselessly about the punishment to inflict on you. I could fire my gun close to your ears so that your eardrums would burst, leaving you deaf and blind, locked forever in a body that would be your lonely prison cell. I considered cutting out your tongue as well. But wouldn't that still be too little? What if I killed everyone who meant anything to you? Even all those you had a good word for, the woman who cleans your flat, the usher in your favorite cinema? Even now I'm still not sure. Whatever seems appropriate."

If Aaron had the strength to scream, she would.

"But your worst punishment has been decided. Recently when I planted a white camellia on the grave in Moscow, I promised Natalya: during the time I grant you, you are to live with the fact that the only man you have ever loved is responsible for your blinding."

He isn't the one skipping stones across the water, she is. She stands by the shore, near a huge pile of stones. Each one she picks up is so heavy that it couldn't possibly skip over the waves. And yet it does.

"What do you mean by that?" she whispers.

"Think very hard."

Suddenly Aaron is no longer standing on the shore, but on the mountain she dreamed about because once and for all she would be free up there. But a chasm gapes below her. The stones start sliding, her memory drags her with it like an avalanche. In one great whirl she plunges into the void and screams.

She is holding Niko in her arms. He is choking on his blood, coughing it up, pulling her towards him with the last of his strength.

"We were going to share. He promised he wouldn't do anything to you. Let me go. You have to."

As she speeds along the freeway, it never occurs to her to summon help for him.

"You fled because you wanted me to kill him," Holm says.

She plunges into the neon light under the Plaça de les Drassanes. Holm effortlessly brings his Audi up alongside Aaron's car. They look at one another. A moment that has lasted longer than the whole of time. Now that the shockwave is breaking against her heart she knows that in the second before the flash that sent her world up in smoke she didn't regret never telling Niko that she loved him.

Her last thought was: *I let Boenisch live. But not you.*

# 35

THE SNOWY road disappears into the forest. He is standing by the open tailgate of the transporter, with the flat spare tire in front of him. He knows his only chance is to stop a passing car, and he also knows that there is no one on the road in this godforsaken place at this time of night. He looks at his watch. Four precious minutes have passed already. He left his phone in Berlin, because they could have located him with it. The stolen SUV is in the place in the forest where he crawled through the undergrowth and ran to the clearing. Too far, half an hour on foot. That was how he ran out of options. It isn't the wind that's making him shiver, or the cold. It's his despair, and also the knowledge that he made a bad decision when he took the transporter to avoid attracting attention when they arrived at the farm.

Headlights.

They shimmer over the hilltop, quickly drilling two holes in the blackness. How relieved he is. He goes and stands in the road and raises one hand. The other one is ready to draw his Makarov if the car doesn't stop.

That won't be necessary.

Before the driver stops and gets out, Kvist knows who he is.

Nothing distracts Pavlik. No grief, no fury, no memory. His right hand also hovers over his gun, the Walther. The silent forest curves towards him, absorbs him, lets him feel its calm.

"You should never have sent flowers to my wife."

"I knew you would work that one out sooner or later."

"Anything else you want to say?"

"You can run away from something forever. But you take with you the one mistake that you have made." Kvist holds his head lowered, his voice barely louder than the wind.

Pavlik is not deceived.

"In Kabul I killed an innocent man. Jörg Aaron called me a criminal."

"Accurate enough."

"I forgot it. But that Pashtun had a son. He was an interpreter for the American embassy in Kabul. During an attack he saved the life of the CIA station chief. That put him in danger, so he got a visa to the USA. The American paid off his debt by telling him who killed his father, and where to find me. He wanted to take his blood vengeance. I shouldn't have stuck my knife in his throat. But in his eyes I saw that other man, the one in Kabul. His son, still breathing, would have been a permanent accusation against me. I got rid of his body."

Pavlik doesn't need a measuring tape to know that he is standing exactly a meter away from the Ford on the left, with the door closed, a body's length behind the front axle. He thinks about how he whacked—broke?—Kvist's ribs. The wind is behind him, whirling the snow over the road, blowing grainy sleet against Kvist's trouser-legs.

"Why didn't I confess to you, or to André? What would you have thought? That Jörg Aaron was right. I could have claimed self-defense. But even then I would have had to admit my guilt. To myself. I stopped sleeping after that, I lost my bearings completely. I wasn't even sure that I was still alive."

He speaks slowly, as if every word is an incredible effort. But Pavlik knows that Kvist is trying to gain time to play out the battle in his mind. Pavlik does the same.

*Not pistols, please. I wouldn't stand a chance.*

"A Romanian introduced me to betting on sports. Second Chinese football league, kickboxing championships in Malaysia and Indonesia, that kind of thing. The adrenalin helped for a while. But then I lost. Eventually I was so far in the red that I couldn't see a way out. I started paying in counterfeit money."

"And André found out," Pavlik says.

"I was supposed to hand myself in. Before he came back from Prague. You can't imagine how glad I was that you got drunk, otherwise I would have had to kill you as well. I laid André's head in my lap and closed his eyes. But I didn't stop gambling. As if someone else had died in Prague along with André. That one died when you asked my forgiveness for not being with me. He died later in Barcelona and then again this morning in a lift; you wouldn't believe how many times you can die."

"I give you my word: today will be the last time."

"I started losing more and more. The guys made it clear to me what it meant to have debts with them. But they knew of a solution. They put me in touch with Holm, who came up with the idea of the Chagall. He gave me his word that nothing would happen to Jenny."

Pavlik can hardly bear to hear her name on Kvist's lips. He sees him relaxing his muscles. A tiny stretch of the shoulders, the neck. His left hand hangs down, seemingly slack, but his fingers are splayed. So casually that most people would have ignored it.

But how long have Holm and Kvist known each other?

"In Barcelona I inhaled my own blood. I told Jenny who I was. That's why she abandoned me. When I woke up in hospital I was sure it was over. It was a liberation. But nothing happened. I didn't understand it. I went to her room, and her father was there. No one spoke. I thought she was covering for me. I was so overwhelmed that I fell to my knees in the corridor. I have lived in fear of you and Holm for five years. I have lived in shame."

Pavlik will never forgive himself for not having realized.

"Eventually I pretended to myself we were quits. He hadn't got any money in Barcelona, and I'd taken two bullets. But last winter he was suddenly standing in front of me, and said he wanted to transfer his brother to Tegel. He needed a pen-pal for him, nothing more than that. It sounded fair. I had known Eva Askamp's husband; another gambler. I remembered his wife, and the fact that she couldn't cope after he died. She agreed to do it for a ridiculously small sum of money."

"Weren't you surprised at someone like Holm contacting you about a pen-pal? He could have asked hundreds of other people," Pavlik says mockingly.

"Yes. I preferred not to think about it. It was only when Boenisch got involved that I understood. That was Holm's punishment for me: putting the woman I loved at his mercy. Last night I discovered the truth: that she's lost her memory, that since then she's been torturing herself about abandoning me like that. When I left the hotel a man asked me the time and I knocked him down."

Kvist's voice is getting quieter and quieter, the words a faint drip. Pavlik knows why. He is supposed to have to concentrate, understand, be distracted.

"I let her go to the coach not because she pleaded with me, but because I hoped she would remember."

"You've got a tongue in your head."

"I wanted to say something. But when her eyes looked for me and she felt for my hand I saw what I had done to her, and my voice died in my throat." His fingers vibrate above the Makarov. "Bosch told me about the hiding place. Take me there. Let's rescue her, that's all I ask."

"I'm never turning my back on you again. You'll pay for both her and André here and now, in this snow."

"I want to explain. I want to see her one last time."

"She says hi."

"Without my help you won't know where she is."

"I can't believe I just called you my friend. You're nobody, you've never had honor, you've never existed."

"You never beat me in training."

"Correct: that was just training."

"See you, Don Pavlik."

"See you, coward."

By the time the Makarov has leaped into Kvist's hand, Pavlik has rolled under the Ford and drawn his Walther. He fires three times in quick succession, but Kvist has already dived out of the headlights into the darkness. Pavlik's eyes dart around the road. No. He must have chosen the shortest trajectory and disappeared into the undergrowth on the right. There's nothing he can do with the Ford. Pavlik has the immobilizer and Kvist knows that theft-proof electronics means the vehicle can't be hot-wired.

He turns himself around so that he can see the edge of the forest. Three meters away, with a ditch in between. If he crawls out from under the car he'll be serving himself up on a plate. Pavlik rolls out on the other side and, crouching, sprints up the road. One of the bullets that come after him penetrates the left sleeve of his overall, but only nicks his upper arm. Pavlik throws himself into the ditch and listens.

Breaking twigs. On the left. Kvist withdraws into the forest and waits for him to come after. Pavlik wriggles into the bushes, snakes along the icy ground and calculates his chances. Kvist is eleven years younger than he is, and in better condition. With the pistol he's in a better position than Pavlik. On the plus side he puts: his eyes, his knowledge as a sharpshooter, which helps him read clues and find his bearings, his experience, Kvist's ribs.

In close combat they're a match for each other. They both prefer the visceral krav maga, and remain suspicious of karate.

Pavlik reaches a slope. He reads the snow, the fresh, shallow shoeprints. A frozen stream loses itself among pine trees, a thirty-degree slope. Further below, the trees stand like a black wall. Pavlik lowers his breathing and is only aware of his heartbeat. The crunch of the snow is as quiet as the creak of his neck vertebra. Twenty meters downhill.

He slides into the stream, barely needing to use his legs, and slips silently down. He pauses. Kvist has taken off his jacket, it's on the ground to his left. His footprints show that he has left the stream.

But one of the footprints in the snow is too deep. He immediately grasps that Kvist has jumped from there to the other side to put him on the wrong track. Pavlik pulls up his right elbow, parries Kvist's blow and spins. His legs grip Kvist's torso and catapult him into the stream with such force that they start sliding. They go skidding down the slope as if on a bobsled, headfirst, Pavlik on his back, Kvist on top of him. They both drop their guns, and pummel each other with quickfire blows. Pavlik's fists drum on Kvist's ribs. Kvist presses three fingers together into a spear point to drive them into Pavlik's eye, but he blocks him with his left hand and brings the ball of his right hand crashing under Kvist's chin. He feels the jaw breaking. When he is about to bring a hammerfist crashing after it, his heel gets stuck in a tree root. His prosthesis loses its suction and comes off. He loosens his vice-like grip on Kvist. He wants to keep him from grabbing him by the calf, he knows what's there. But they plunge three meters off the quarry edge.

Pavlik falls hard on his back. Pain sears like acid through his neural pathways. He loses consciousness for several seconds. When he comes to, he vaguely sees Kvist standing over him, clutching the knife that he jammed into Pavlik's belly in mid-air.

"You should have listened to me."

Pavlik's voice battles against the thunder of the blood in his head. "There's one more thing I've got to say to you."

Kvist bends down to hear him more clearly. Pavlik sticks five stiff fingers into his side, so deep that they disappear to the last joint before he twists them. Kvist's eyeballs bulge.

He drops to his knees in slow motion. He wants to scream.

But this time his voice has definitely gone.

"I taught my little sister a lot," Pavlik whispers. "And she taught me too. That's called 'Mute Hand.' I know you understand me, but you can't move or speak or breathe. Now show me the meaning of *sisu*."

He watches as Kvist suffocates very slowly. When his face falls silently into the snow, Pavlik wants to go on lying there as well. He reaches clumsily for his phone, but can't find it. Each thought is a star that fades in an instant. It takes him some time to realize that he must have lost his phone in the fight, somewhere up there. His throat mic is no use to him here, he's out of range.

Pavlik crawls towards the rocky wall; he doesn't know how, but he manages to get there on his one leg. A branch of the root that tore off his prosthesis dangles above him, long enough for him to grab it with both hands, in his belly a fire that rages all the way to the tips of his hair. He pulls himself up, thinks he hasn't a chance of getting there, but he manages to grab the edge of the quarry wall, and feels around for a rocky overhang. With one last desperate effort he manages to roll himself over the edge. It's as if the knife were plunging into him a second time. He hears his breath, which feels like someone else's. He wants to sleep.

His eyes are already half-closed, when he spots his prosthesis, only half a meter away.

*Move!*

*Too far.*

*Come on!*

He stretches out as dozily as a sloth, manages to grab the false leg, puts it in place, releases the valve that produces the suction. Feels the shaft hugging the stump.

*Keep going!*

He rummages in the snow and struggles on. He soon abandons the hope of finding his phone or one of the guns. He doesn't know how long it will take until he sees the road at last, the headlights of the Ford. His belly is now made of ice, and everything else is on fire. He just needs to make it through the ditch.

*I can! I can! I can!*

Pavlik drags himself up on to the transporter that Bosch arrived on and squeezes himself behind the wheel, groaning with pain. Now he'll discover whether he was right, and whether Bosch entered the address of the hiding place in the satnav because of the damage to his short-term memory. If he is wrong, he won't have the strength to creep to the Ford and drive off. Then he'll just sit here and die.

# 36

AARON KNOWS that Holm has been watching her for an eternity, reading all her thoughts, while she plunged deeper and deeper into the abyss, feeling each of her deaths, sure now that she hasn't omitted a single one.

"I tried to find out who it was who had done this to me. The BKA shielded you and I couldn't get to the truth. But I never gave up hope. When I talked to Kvist about the Chagall, I demanded detailed information about the policewoman who was going to set herself up as an art expert. I usually prepared just as meticulously as you do, and insisted on a copy of your files. I can't describe what it meant to me to read your name and Ilya Nikulin's, to know my search was over. I'd have to be a writer."

Aaron waits for him to finish.

"Originally I had wanted to use a different art theft for my purposes, a still life by Cézanne, which someone unknown had stolen from the Musée d'Orsay a year previously. I had to change my plans because the painting turned up again, and I had opted for the Chagall because of Natalya. *The Dream Dancers*, that was us, but only as a fantasy, we were never able to embrace, even though we were standing on the high wire. I observed you in Barcelona, I saw the way you pressed up against Kvist and kissed him. I knew straight away that I had made the perfect choice."

*It's true. I too was standing alone on the rope. Then I fell, and I'm falling still.*

"I stopped in the tunnel. Within me raged a fury that I could barely tame. The fury of having given in to my rage and shot you in the head. From the depths of my soul I hoped you were alive so that I could ask you a question. The car was lying on its roof. I looked inside. You screamed: 'My eyes! Where are my eyes?' At that second I decided to be patient and open up the door to your first hell."

"And I stepped through it," she whispers.

"And yet you were loved and you knew it. That's more than I was ever granted."

"No, he never felt anything for me, or he wouldn't have done that to me."

"No, you're wrong. Kvist was a gambler, he was desperate, that's why he got involved in the deal. You were with him in a restaurant in Barcelona. When you got up to go to the bathroom, I saw his eye gliding over the back of your neck. He did the same thing yesterday at the airport when you were smoking and he desired you. I must refuse you that mercy as well."

For a moment Aaron thinks she feels a new abyss opening up below her. But however strange, however alien the thought might be that Niko might have loved her, that he has always loved her, it's reassuring rather than frightening.

It would mean that he has known of his guilt for five years, and that he was sent to a hell of his own.

*What's it like there?*

*Do you see me every night and scream?*

"I have one consolation for you: I'm sure that Pavlik already knows the truth. He is too intelligent not to have found it out. Kvist may have impressive skills, but he isn't an adversary on Pavlik's level. Pavlik is a man to whom the oath he swore on the laws of his country means less than the love he feels for you, because it is a kind of love. He will kill Kvist, I have no doubt about that."

*Yes, then he will do it.*

"You have so many certainties, and I have so few. All I have is Natalya's hand on my cheek and her smile, and how tenderly she uttered the pet name for Vanya, because that was what I was called in Russia, because of my father's father."

It's as if the oxygen has abruptly been sucked from the flame. She runs through her library as if in a dream, sees that everything is in its place, opens six doors, then the seventh, the last, and finds herself in the underground car park. She rests the woman's head in her lap, knows that the ricochet from the Browning is responsible for the gushing red fountain. The woman's eyes are as dull as cracked varnish on an old painting. Aaron takes her hand. It's hot. The woman is trying to say something.

After a few minutes, during which she only grips her hand, the woman manages just a single word.

"I will ask you the question once again," Holm says. "If you refuse me the answer, I will complete your punishment. Bear in mind that I will be able to tell by your voice if you are lying to me." She inhales the ashes exhaled by him. "Did Natalya say anything else before she died? I'll count to ten."

"You don't need to," she whispers. "I held her hand until it was as cold as mine. She said 'Vanyushka.'"

*Now!*

She leaps to her feet, ready to fight Holm, but her fists meet empty air. She runs twelve paces to the left, then down the corridor to the right. She clicks and clicks. Twenty-three to the hallway. Aaron doesn't know if Holm is following her, her bare feet drum on the floor, her breathing is so loud that it sounds like a long cry. Stairs. Eight to the landing, sharp bend; Vera miscalculated by a step, Aaron falls, thinks she hears a noise behind her, clicks her tongue, pulls herself up, charges on, dragging her fear with her like a heavy weight. Another five steps, correct this time. Three to the right, click, avoid the standard lamp, open bedroom door. Two flying steps to the bedside table. She pulls it open and gets her hands on the revolver, feels that it's loaded, cocks it. Legs spread wide, she aims the gun at the door. Never has she yearned more to bring her pulse down.

She sees herself standing there, shaking, she needs someone else for her fear: the Aaron who only watches.

The woman with the gun calms down because the other one has freed her from her trembling.

Not a sound.

She dives over the bed, kneels and aims the gun.

Nothing.

Again she sprints to the door, flies through the door-frame, rolls away, bumps against the wall, aims at the stairs, clicks.

Not a trace of Holm.

Suddenly she knows where he is.

She gets to her feet like a sleepwalker, goes down the stairs to the corridor, to the little box-room. He is still sitting where he was.

He is talking away from Aaron, his back towards her. "Just like you, I tried to find my way for a long time. When Ilya Nikulin asked me my name I thought I had found it. I was lying to myself." A hinge snaps open. "Isn't it strange that we began the same journey on the same night? Since executing the man sent by my father, you have followed the Bushidō. As have I, since all those mirrors shattered. My journey is over. I am fulfilling my destiny, I have no grief. Wouldn't you too like to sleep at last? You may be granted that wish quite soon. A while ago I said something to my brother that he can't forget. He opened a bag full of paper, and at any minute he will be here to do something that he has been afraid to do all his life. By then I will be dead, and unable to protect you." Steel slips from a sheath. "You know what you owe me."

"Yes." She puts the revolver to the back of his head.

Aaron knows that he is plunging the blade of the seppuku knife six centimeters beneath his navel, pulling it to the left, bringing it up beneath his breastbone and severing his aorta. Holm doesn't make a sound. She feels him trembling. Aaron pulls the trigger and hears his body slumping sideways.

A car pulls up.

# 37

IT WAS only ten kilometers, but Pavlik couldn't have driven another meter. He just manages to bring the Ford to a standstill. So much blood. His blenched hands slip from the steering wheel. He wants to get out, he wants to do that so much, but his body lies in the forest and refuses to take orders. His eyes close. Gunshots. Three bullets shatter the windscreen. They don't hit him. He struggles confusedly to understand. Holm wouldn't miss, not at that distance.

It is harder to open his eyes than it is to crawl up the slope. It's impossible. But he sees Aaron standing in the headlights. She grips a revolver two-handed and fires again. He feels the draft above his head. Pavlik tries to reach for the door handle but misses it, again and again. A bullet pierces the radiator. At last he finds the handle. He lets himself fall against the door so that it swings open.

"Aaron—it's—me."

His voice is so ridiculously quiet that he thinks she couldn't possibly hear him. But he sees her running away, stopping in front of the car, looking for it, feeling her way along it.

Then she is with him.

He weeps, and even that hurts.

Aaron takes Pavlik's hand. She knows that cold sweat. She is gripped by terrible fear.

The voice isn't his. "We have to get out of here."

"What is it?"

"Stomach. Knife. You've got to drive."

She freezes.

He tries to slide across. Fails.

"Wait." Aaron feels her way to the passenger side and tries not to think about what Pavlik is asking of her. She opens the door and wraps her arms around his upper body. He groans. She tries to pull him to her, can't do it, he's too heavy.

There. The faint noise of an engine. It can't be more than a kilometer away, quickly coming closer.

"Apparently you were once with the Department," Pavlik murmurs, light years away. "I don't believe it. You were shooting like a blind woman."

"Don't blub on me, you great pussy!" With one last desperate jerk she pulls him to her side. Who was screaming, was it him or her? She lowers the window and prays that the icy wind will somehow keep Pavlik from falling asleep. It takes her a shockingly long time before she's back on the driver's side, sitting behind the wheel. She puts the gun in Pavlik's hand.

"Sharp right," he whispers. "Not too fast, narrow path, a hundred meters."

She changes into first and rests her foot on the accelerator. "It took you bloody ages. Great friend you are. Keeping me waiting like that." And then she cries too.

"I had—to say—hi to Kvist—from you."

The meaning of his words reaches her after a brief delay, like the pain of an injury.

"Slow down—stop. Left, country road, no cars." He is getting quieter and quieter, Pavlik's voice is lost in the throb of the engine as she imagines it's just idling and she isn't accelerating to over a hundred kilometers an hour and speeding into a tunnel made of adrenalin.

"Straight on—two—lanes."

Wind rushes in on the passenger side, blowing Aaron's hair into her face. She hears the Colt clatter to the floor, he can't hold on to it any longer. "Can you see him?"

"Behind—us," he gasps.

Shots are fired. The wing mirror on the left shatters.

"He—wants—to—pull—up—beside us—get—into—the middle."

*

*I'm paying my debt by allowing you to leave this house alive.* When he got into the car, his brother's words hammered in his head like a compressor. At the railway embankment, where he waited for the train, they prized open his veins and his blood poured into him while the compressor hammered, hammered, hammered. That was how little value his brother placed on his debts. After being forced to go into the basement for four years, all he got in return was the permission to stay alive? He had endured all kinds of humiliation, all kinds of shame. But only because he knew that his brother was in his debt. When he was eight years old and didn't run away while his brother stole bread. When he saw him die in that man's house, and coming back to life. When his brother sentenced him to five years in jail. But the hammering was telling him what he would do as soon as he had the money. Then his brother would pay the *real* price. Sascha would look at his brother's corpse as if it were a piece of wood or a stone, a bit of roadkill, rotten seaweed on the beach. He would step into the labyrinth, and this time it will be childishly simple to find his way out. He would wonder why he didn't do it a long time ago. It was just a door that he kept closed. He would go to the box-room and open it.

Imagining how he would show *her* that there are worse things than being blind filled him with such satisfaction that he almost missed hearing the train in time. He made the call and the bag flew from the door. He opened it and saw the money. He knew what he had to check. When Sascha held the banknote against the light in the car the denomination on one side was almost a perfect match for its counterpart on the other. But only almost.

At that moment the hammering stopped. Because the pictures he saw in his head, the pictures of all the things that would happen in the house were so violent, so terrifying and so wonderful, that all other wishes, even the wish for money, paled in comparison. He drove to the farm.

And he saw the Ford weaving along the road.

*

Aaron rams the Mazda. The car lurches, she tries to straighten up, but how do you do that when you're blind?

"What's he doing?"

No answer.

"Pavlik!"

"Fall—back—he'll try—on the right."

She pulls over, metal crunches again. The windscreen with the bullet holes can no longer withstand the pressure and bursts. Splinters whir inside the vehicle hitting her face like shrapnel. Aaron yells at Pavlik: "What does the road look like? A bend? Oncoming traffic?" Not a sound. "Please say something or I'll have to stop! It's impossible!" Her desperation drags the vowels out of her words, shredding them.

"A bus—a hundred meters—overtake—now."

Aaron switches to the left-hand lane, hears herself touching the Mazda and the Mazda falling back. Shots. She puts her foot to the floor and speeds past a bus that she can't see.

Pavlik has two words left: "Truck—oncoming."

The panicked honking from the lorry driver roars in Aaron's ears. He can't avoid her, can't brake, she can't go back.

*So this is what it's like right at the end. I've got my life back, but now I'm giving it up on this road. Pavlik is with me. I'm not dying alone. But please, please, God, if you exist, let him get back to Sandra, to his children, tell the ferryman only to take one.*

Remembering in those nanoseconds how she played cowboys and Indians with the twins is an indescribable joy. Remembering how Pavlik barely nodded to her at the end of the second week. "You've got pretty legs. But the rest isn't bad either." Planning the surprise party for Sandra's hated fortieth, seeing him grin. "Let's just put a ribbon on your head, that would be her best present." Being seventeen and secretly baking star-shaped cinnamon biscuits to cheer up her mother. And how rock-hard they are. Holding her father's gun for the first time and feeling that this is what she's meant to do.

Sitting with her father in the headmaster's office after kicking her friend Hatice's brother—a good head taller than she was—between the legs when he wanted to beat up his sister. Noticing the way her father puts his arm around her. "He should thank her: when this kind of thing happens I've taught my daughter to kick first between the legs, and only then in the head."

Suddenly she hears Holm.

*The most important thing my father taught me was that the will must be greater than the fear.*

She is aware of the wind again, she can tell by the drop in engine noise and the gust of air blowing into the cabin from the side that she has overtaken the bus. Aaron eases off on the accelerator and shoots into such a tight gap that the wing mirror is completely torn off. Behind her, steel bores into steel, like scrap metal being crushed. She knows that the Mazda has crashed against the lorry, which pushes it screeching off the road. She slows down, can't calibrate her braking on the icy road surface, becomes aware that the car is spinning, faster and faster, the pirouettes of a giant with her perched, a tiny figure, on his shoulder.

Then the giant stands up.

"Pavlik," she whispers and reaches out her hand to him. His jugular vein sends faint Morse code signals beneath her quivering finger.

# Echolocation

THE MEN are waiting in the corridor of the intensive care ward, so quietly that they can hear the hand of the big wall-clock jumping to six. The door opens.

Demirci comes out. "He's pulling through."

No one says a word. She turns to go back in.

"Good job," Fricke says behind her.

She turns around. "You too. All of you." Demirci hesitates for a moment. "I could tell you now that with immediate effect we're all going to call each other by our surnames, while still calling each other *du*, like my predecessor did. If I don't do it myself, it's not out of a lack of respect. My grandparents observed the old traditions. I always addressed them formally, and yet we were very close, and they meant a lot to me. Should the time come, I will mourn each of you as if you were family members."

It's only at that moment that Lissek says goodbye.

Aaron and Sandra are sitting by Pavlik's bed. He is too weak to talk. Aaron's eyes are closed. She is in her inner room. She is still listening to the echo of the gunshots. Was she given the punishment that Holm intended for her? He blinded her. For him that was only the first circle of hell. But what could be worse? Niko? If, opening her eyes in Barcelona, she had remembered the warehouse, that's how it would have been, plunging through a hall of mirrors. But she thought she had abandoned the man she loved to certain death. That was another kind of hell, and part of her was consumed by it. Now she feels no shame, no longing, only hatred. Which will eventually fade away.

Perhaps.

Hatred can be a punishment too. Was that what Holm had in mind? Many days and nights will pass before she has an answer.

Demirci comes in. Sandra gives her husband a kiss. She pulls Aaron's head to her and strokes her hair so tenderly, so naturally that Aaron knows that if Pavlik hadn't made it her friend wouldn't have blamed her, either out loud or in secret.

"Yes," Sandra says simply. She goes outside and leaves them alone.

Demirci sits down beside her, and asks at last: "How did you survive all that?"

She doesn't open her eyes. "I had some help."

Demirci puts Pavlik's hand in Aaron's.

"I didn't know you knew the 'Lissek maneuver.'"

"What's that?" she asks.

"You put Pavlik in charge of negotiations with Sascha, and in that way you diminished my value."

"I only did that so that you would hear his voice. I hoped it might comfort you."

Aaron feels a gratitude that cannot be expressed in words, because no word would be big enough. Pavlik wants to talk, but his tongue feels too big for his mouth.

"Tomorrow. Have a rest."

Another echo resounds inside Aaron.

*Wouldn't you too like to sleep at last?*

Yes, a leaden weariness had filled her like concrete, and was trying to drag her down to the bottom of a black sea above which a desolate sky stood guard. That weariness has gone; it disappeared when the giant stood still and Aaron jumped from his shoulder. Perhaps also because at that moment something happened which she doesn't want to be aware of now, something she doesn't want to take into consideration for fear of deceiving herself.

That's why her eyes are closed.

Aaron leaves her inner room.

"What is your earliest memory?" she asks.

Startled, Demirci thinks. "I was two years old and I crawled over the back of a chair. I still have the scar on my head. I don't remember the pain, just the sensation of falling."

"I remember my parents talking to me and me not understanding a word," Aaron says. "It was very strange."

Pavlik joins in with a croak. "My father flushing my goldfish down the toilet. You can still see the after-effects of that today."

They laugh.

There's a quick knock at the door. Aaron hears Helmchen's voice. "Excuse me."

Demirci says: "No, stay."

Helmchen joins Aaron. She takes her hand and puts something on the palm. Aaron feels it with her fingers. A cartridge case. As she wonders what it might signify, Demirci says: "Miss Aaron, there's a request I'd like to ask of you."

"Yes?"

"Come back to the Department."

Aaron says nothing.

"Of course I'll give you some time to think about it."

Minutes pass without an answer, and Aaron's eyes stay closed.

"A blind woman and a one-legged man. Dream team," Pavlik groans.

"At least think about it. All the men have pleaded with me. But they didn't need to. I made up my mind yesterday morning."

Aaron opens her eyes.

"Could you turn out the light?"

She senses Demirci's perplexity.

"Please."

Demirci gets to her feet.

"And on again."

Her heart asks her breath to dance.

"I can tell light from darkness."

# AFTERWORD

I DID as much research as I could. You can read up on a lot of things, but personal conversation, the individual view, is irreplaceable. I would like to thank the mobility trainer Dr. Roman Schmeissner, whose commitment to his blind patients is exemplary. And also Christa Maria Rupp from the Saarland Association of the Blind and Partially Sighted.

I met four hugely impressive blind women during my research. Kerstin Müller-Klein is as much in control of her life as my Jenny Aaron. Ugne Metzer showed me that high heels can be used as a sonar device. Susanne Emmermann holds her own in the accounts department of BVG, the Berlin transport company, and Pamela Papst is a successful defense lawyer who tells her story in the fabulous autobiography *Ich sehe das, was ihr nicht seht* (I See What You Can't).

Professor Jürgen Kiwit, the senior physician in the Neurosurgery Department at Buch Clinic, was a great help to me, as was the neurologist and psychiatrist Dr. Norbert Helbig, who was extremely enlightening on the subject of memory and amnesia.

Dr. Peter Kleinert always had time for me. I've fired so many medical questions at him that anyone else would have lost patience long ago.

Professor Peter Höflich of the Viadrina European University enlightened me on the subject of the European Convention on the Transfer of Convicted Persons.

My most important specialist adviser is Professor Bernhard A. Sabel, Director of the Institute of Medical Psychology at the University of Magdeburg. He has worked for many years in practical research with blind people. Patients from all over the world come to him for help. His specialist skills and critical notes have been incredibly valuable to me. I was very lucky to be able to read the manuscript of his new book in advance. He is a real inspiration to the visually impaired.

Professor Sabel provided notes and ideas for the novel, and will continue to advise me in future—Jenny Aaron's story isn't over yet. His support means a lot to me.

Anyone who wants to find out more about FlashSonar, the astonishing form of echolocation used by blind people, can approach the association World Access for the Blind. Daniel Kish has made himself a master of the technique, and his videos on YouTube speak for themselves.

To anyone who wants to know about the extreme achievements that blind people are capable of, I would recommend three autobiographies. They show that Aaron's abilities are not fictional.

*Balancing Act: How a Blind Man Climbs the World's Highest Mountains* by Andy Holzer.

*My Path Leads to Tibet* by Sabriye Tenberken.

*And There Was Light: The Extraordinary Memoir of a Blind Hero of the French Resistance in World War II* by Jacques Lusseyran.

I couldn't resist using a sentence from Lusseyran's book: "Wait till the blind man has seen him."

I was also enriched by *Touching the Rock: An Experience of Blindness* by John M. Hull, and Oliver Sacks' *A Neurologist's Notebook*.

There are four quotes from the *Hagakure*.

I have, of course, taken some liberties. You will search in vain for a twenty-storey building on Budapester Strasse in Berlin, as you will for Hotel Jupiter on Leipziger Strasse or the Hotel Aralsk in Moscow. The same applies to the two hills near the airfield Flugplatz Finow. But they are my high-rise building, my hotels, my airfield. I hope the men who risked their lives during the storming of the *Landshut* and the liberation of the hostages would forgive me for giving Jörg Aaron their courage and resolution.

"The Department" exists only in Aaron's world, not in reality, however much some politicians might wish it was real. But the working methods of this special unit are based on years of research that began with my first novel, *Operation Rubikon*.

Any factual mistakes are mine alone and have nothing to do with my sources.

There are four close friends that I would like to thank: Murmel Clausen and Hans-Joachim Neubauer for their talent, their critical reading and their advice, and Jürgen Haase for being the first to be able to imagine a blind policewoman as a main character. Hans-Ludwig Zachert, the former head of the Bundeskriminalamt (BKA), is, as ever, my *consigliere*.

Many thanks to Katrin Kroll from the Eggers Agency, who immediately believed in the novel and gave me a great deal of encouragement. And to Thomas Halupczok, my editor, whose motto could be: "The good is the enemy of the better"; a great man. It's reassuring to know you have a team like Suhrkamp's behind you. If the company didn't exist, we'd have to found it. The same applies to Jonathan Landgrebe, whose words helped me at a difficult time.

The dedication reveals my wife's contribution to the success of this book. She always supports me in everything and is my first reader. Her keen eye improved a lot of things. I would never part with anything that she doesn't think is good. May that day never come.